P9-CEV-855

Disaster Status

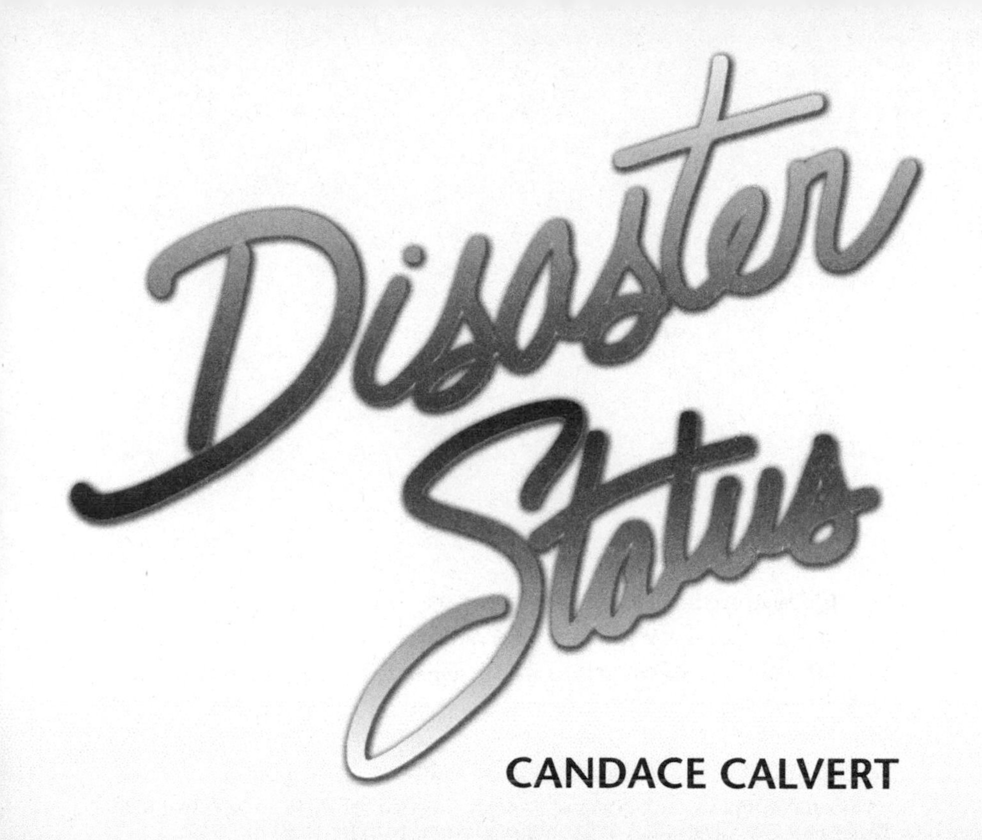

CANDACE CALVERT

TYNDALE HOUSE PUBLISHERS, INC.
CAROL STREAM, ILLINOIS

Visit Tyndale's exciting Web site at www.tyndale.com.

Visit Candace Calvert's Web site at www.candacecalvert.com.

TYNDALE and Tyndale's quill logo are registered trademarks of Tyndale House Publishers, Inc.

Disaster Status

Designed by Mark Anthony Lane II

Edited by Lorie Popp

Published in association with the literary agency of Natasha Kern Literary Agency, Inc., P.O. Box 1069, White Salmon, WA 98672.

Printed in the United States of America

ISBN: 978-1-61664-305-8

For my amazing daughter, Brooklynn,
who hikes to mountaintops, listens in pristine stillness . . .
and knows her strength.

ACKNOWLEDGMENTS

Heartfelt appreciation to:

Agent Natasha Kern—for all that you do and especially for your strong belief in and support of this story.

The incredible Tyndale House team—editors Jan Stob and Lorie Popp, who graciously loaned my characters her family name.

Critique partner Nancy Herriman—you are a true blessing.

Lowell J. Berry, lieutenant colonel, U.S. Army (retired)—for generously sharing insights regarding the Gulf War.

The U.S. military and their families—for dedication and sacrifice in service to our country.

Tim Sturgill, MD—for kindly acting as a medical resource. Any inaccuracies are mine.

Fellow nurses and medical professionals—as always, this story means to honor you.

Santa Cruz Beach Boardwalk—for sand in my shoes and memories in my heart.

St. Helena's Church, Community of Hope, and Bible study sisters—you're great!

My family, children, and grandchildren—your love and encouragement mean the world.

My amazing husband, Andy Calvert—for insisting I take that first online writing class and for your patience and support in the roller-coaster years since.

The Lord is my strength and my shield;
my heart trusts in him, and I am helped.

—PSALM 28:7

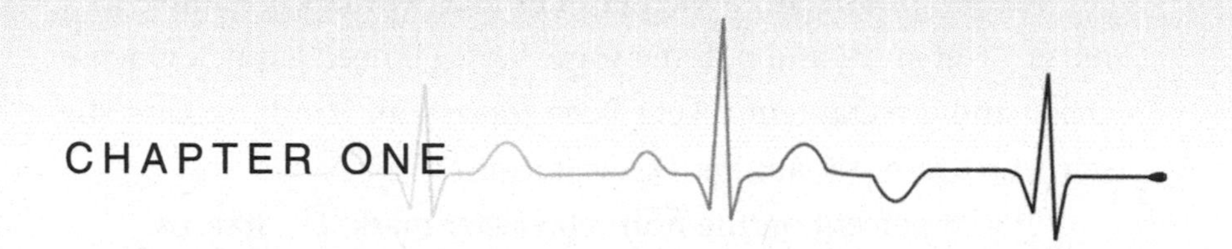

CHAPTER ONE

Fire captain Scott McKenna bolted through the doors of Pacific Mercy ER, his boots thudding and heart pounding as the unconscious child began to stiffen and jerk in his arms. He cradled her close as her small spine arched and her head thumped over and over against his chest. "Need help here. Seizure!"

"This way." A staff person beckoned. "The code room. Someone page respiratory therapy stat!"

Scott jogged behind a trio of staff in green scrubs to a glassed-in room, laid the child on a gurney, and stepped back, his breath escaping in a rush of relief. He swiped a trickle of sweat from his forehead and tried to catch a glimpse of the girl's face. He'd swept her up too fast to get a good look at her. Now, with merciful distance, Scott's heart tugged. Six or seven years old with long black braids, frilly clusters of hair ribbons, little hoop earrings, she looked disturbingly pale despite her olive skin. Her dark eyes rolled upward, unfocused, as the ER team closed in to suction her airway, start oxygen, and cut away her flowered top and pants.

The alarms of the cardiac monitor beeped as a technician attached gelled electrodes to her tiny chest. Thankfully, the seizure ended, although saliva—foamy as a salted garden snail—still bubbled from her parted lips.

Scott inhaled slowly, the air a sour mix of illness, germicidal soap, and anxious perspiration. He thought of his nephew, Cody, lying in a pediatrics bed two floors above.

The ER physician, a vaguely familiar woman, gestured to a nurse. "Get an IV and pull me some labs. I'll need a quick glucose check and a rectal temp. Let's keep lorazepam handy in case she starts up again. What's her O_2 saturation?"

"It's 98 percent on the non-rebreather mask, Dr. Stathos."

Leigh Stathos. Golden Gate Mercy Hospital. Scott nodded, recognizing her—and the irony. *She left San Francisco. I've applied for a job there . . . and everywhere else.*

"Good. Now let's see if I can get a medic report." Dr. Stathos whirled to face Scott, her expression indicating she was trying to place him as well. Her gaze flickered to his badge. "Oh yes. McKenna. Didn't recognize you for a second there. So what's the history? And where's the rest of your crew? Are they sending you guys out solo now?"

"No. But no crew. And no report. I was here as a visitor, until some guy waved me down in the parking lot. I took one look at this girl and decided to scoop and run." Scott nodded toward a woman crying near the doorway. "That could be family. They were in the truck with her."

"Seizure history?"

"Don't know. My Spanish isn't the best. I think they said 'sick' and 'vomiting,' but—"

One of the nurses called out for the doctor. "She's starting to twitch again. IV's in, and the blood glucose is good at 84. No fever. How much lorazepam are you going to want? She weighs about 20 kilos."

Dr. Stathos moved back to the gurney. "We'll start with one

milligram slowly. But let me get a look at her first, listen to her lungs, and check her eyes." She looked up as a blonde nurse appeared in the doorway. "Yes, Sandy?"

"Sorry, Doctor. I couldn't get much, but her name's Ana Galvez. Six years old. No meds, no allergies, and no prior seizure history. I think. There's a language barrier, and I don't have an official interpreter yet. But thought you should know I've got a dozen more people signing in for triage, all with gastric complaints and headaches. The parking lot's full of farm trucks, and—" She stopped as the child began a second full-blown seizure.

Two respiratory therapists rushed through the doorway.

Scott tensed. A dozen more patients? Then his Spanish was good enough to have understood one last thing the terrified family had said before he took off running with their child: *"Hay muchos más enfermos"*—There are many more sick people.

He glanced back at the child convulsing on the gurney. What was going on?

+++

Muscle it. Punch through it. Control it. Be bigger than the bag.

Erin Quinn's fist connected in one last spectacular, round-winning right hook, slamming the vinyl speed bag against the adjacent wall. And causing a tsunami in her grandmother's goldfish tank. Water sluiced over the side.

"Whoa! Hang on, buddy. I've got you." She dropped to her knees, steadying the tank with her red leather gloves. Everything she'd done in the last six months was focused on keeping Iris Quinn safe, secure, and happy, and now she'd nearly KO'd the woman's only pet.

Erin watched the bug-eyed goldfish's attempts to ride out the wave action. She knew exactly how he felt. Her own situation was equally unsettling: thirty-one and living with her grandmother and a geriatric goldfish named Elmer Fudd in a five-hundred-square-foot beach house. With two mortgages and a stubborn case of shower mold. She caught a whiff of her latest futile bout with bleach and grimaced.

But moving back to Pacific Point was the best option for her widowed grandmother, emotionally as well as financially. Erin was convinced of that, even if her grandmother was still skeptical . . . and the rest of the family dead set against it. Regardless, Erin was determined to put the feisty spark back in Nana's eyes, and she had found the change surprisingly good for herself as well. After last year's frustrating heartaches, being back in a house filled with warm memories felt a lot like coming home. She needed that more than she'd known.

Erin tugged at a long strand of her coppery hair and smiled. The fact that her grandmother was down at the chamber of commerce to inquire about volunteer work was proof they were finally on the right track. Meanwhile, she had the entire day off from the hospital. March sunshine; capris instead of nursing scrubs; time to catch up with her online course work, jog on the beach, and dawdle at the fish market with her grandmother.

She turned at the sound of her cell phone's *Rocky* theme ring tone, then struggled, teeth against laces, to remove a glove in time to answer.

She grabbed the phone and immediately wished she hadn't. The caller display read *Pacific Mercy ER*. "Yes?"

"Ah, great. We caught you."

"Not really," Erin said, recognizing the relief charge nurse's voice and glancing hopefully toward the door. "In fact, I was just heading out."

"Dr. Stathos said she's sorry, but she needs you here. Stat. We've got kind of a mess."

Mess? Erin's breath escaped like a punctured balloon. In the ER, a mess could mean anything. All of it bad. She'd heard the TV news reports of a single-engine plane crash early this morning, but the pilot had been pronounced dead on the scene, and there were no other victims. The hospital shouldn't be affected. Then . . . "What's going on?"

"Eighteen sick farm workers," the nurse explained, raising her voice over a cacophony of background noise. "Maybe a few more now; they keep coming in. We're running out of gurneys, even in the hallway."

"Sick with what?" Erin asked. The sheer number of patients qualified as a multicasualty disaster, but only if it were a motor vehicle accident, an explosion, or a similar tragedy.

"Dr. Stathos isn't sure. But she's thinking maybe food poisoning. They're all from the same ranch. Everyone's vomiting, and—"

"It's a real mess," Erin finished, sighing. "I got that part. But how come the ambulances are bringing them all to us? Dispatch should be sending some to Monterey."

"They're not in ambulances. They're arriving in work vehicles. A couple of guys were even sprawled out on a flatbed truck. They're lucky no one rolled onto the highway. The police are at the ranch investigating, but meanwhile we're overwhelmed. And of course the media got wind of it, so now we have reporters showing up. You know how aggressive they get. I'm sorry, but I feel like I'm in over my head with this whole thing."

The nurse was new at taking charge, and Erin remembered how scary that felt when things went south in the ER. Monday shifts were usually fairly tame, but this sounded like . . . "Tell the nursing supervisor I'm on my way in and that we'll probably need to go on disaster status and . . . Hold on a second, would you?" She yanked off her other glove and strode, phone to her ear, toward the miniscule closet she shared with her grandmother. "Close the clinic and use that for overflow. Get security down there to help control things, the chaplain too. And see if the fire department can spare us some manpower."

Erin pulled a set of camouflage-print scrubs from a hanger, then began peeling off her bike shorts with one hand. "I'll get there as soon as I can. Just need to take a quick shower and leave my grandmother a note." *And kiss my free day good-bye?*

No, she wasn't going to think that way. As a full-time charge nurse, the welfare of the ER staff was a huge priority. Besides, Leigh Stathos wouldn't haul her in on her day off if it weren't important. Erin had dealt with far worse things. Like that explosion at the day care center near Sierra Mercy Hospital last year. In comparison, food poisoning wasn't such a big deal, even two dozen cases. Messy, yes. Life-altering, no. Central service would find more basins, she'd help start a few IVs, they'd give nausea meds and plenty of TLC, and they'd get it all under control.

"No problemo," she murmured as she hung up, then realized the inarticulate phrase was pretty much the extent of her Spanish. She made a mental note to be sure they had enough interpreters. Interpreters, basins, more manpower, and a full measure of TLC to patients—and her staff. That should do it.

Ten minutes later she snagged an apple for the road, wrote Nana a note, and stowed her boxing gloves on the rack beneath the TV. She wouldn't need battle gear for this extra stint in the ER. And then she'd be back home. In a couple of hours, tops.

+++

When Erin turned in to the hospital parking lot, she realized she'd forgotten her name badge. Good thing security knew her. Her eyes widened as she approached the ambulance entrance. She braked to a stop, her mouth dropping open as she surveyed the scene at the emergency department's back doors: four dusty and battered trucks—one indeed a flatbed—at least three news vans, a fire truck, an ambulance, and several police cars. She quickly put the Subaru in park, then opened her door and squinted up at the sky. Oh, c'mon, was that a helicopter? A plane crash wasn't big enough news today?

Several nurses stood outside the doors holding clipboards and dispensing yellow plastic emesis basins to a restless line of a least a dozen patients in long sleeves, heavy trousers, and work boots. Including one elderly man who seemed unsteady on his feet as he mopped his forehead with a faded bandanna. A young uniformed firefighter paramedic, the husband of their ER triage nurse, was also helping out. Good, Erin's request for extra manpower had been accepted.

Reporters in crisp khakis and well-cut jackets leaned across what appeared to be a hastily erected rope-and-sawhorse barricade. It was manned by a firefighter in a smoke-stained turnout jacket with the broadest shoulders she'd ever seen. And an expression as stony as Rushmore.

Erin locked the car, grabbed her tote bag, and jogged into the wind toward the barricade, trying to place the daunting firefighter. Tall, with close-cropped blond hair, a sturdy jaw, and a rugged profile. He turned, arms crossed, to talk with someone across the barricade, so she couldn't see all of his face. But he wasn't a full-time medic; she knew them all. An engine company volunteer? Maybe, but she hadn't met him. She was sure of that. Because, even from what little she'd seen, this man would have been memorable. Her face warmed ridiculously as she slowed to a walk.

But her growing curiosity about his identity was a moot point. There wasn't time for that now. She needed to slip between those sawhorses, hustle into the ER, touch base with the relief charge nurse, brainstorm with Leigh Stathos, and see what she could do to help straighten out this mess.

Erin stopped short as the big firefighter turned abruptly, blocking her way. "Excuse me," she said, sweeping wind-tossed hair from her face as she peered up at him. *Gray.* His eyes were granite gray. "I need to get past you. Thanks. Appreciate it." She attempted to squeeze by him, catching a faint whiff of citrusy cologne . . . mixed with smoke.

"Don't thank me. And stop right where you are." He stepped in front of her, halting her in her tracks. There was the slightest twitch at the corner of his mouth. Not a smile. He crossed his arms again. "No one can come through here. Those are the rules. And I go by the book. Sorry."

By the book? As if she didn't have policies to follow? Erin forced herself to take a deep breath. *Lord, show me the humor in this*. Called to work on her day off and then denied access. It was funny if you thought about it. She tried to smile and managed a pinched grimace. This was about as funny as the mold in her shower. She met his gaze, noticing that he had a small scar just below his lower lip. Probably from somebody's fist.

"I work here, Captain . . . McKenna," Erin explained, reading the name stenciled on his jacket. "In fact—" she patted the left breast pocket of her scrubs, then remembered her missing name badge—"I'm the day-shift charge nurse. But I forgot my badge."

"I see," he said, uncrossing his arms. He pointed toward the trio of reporters leaning over the barricade. "See that reporter over there—the tall woman with the microphone and bag of Doritos? Ten minutes ago she pulled a white coat out of one of those news vans and tried to tell me she was a doctor on her way to an emergency delivery. Premature twins."

"But that's unbelievable. That's—"

"Exactly why I'm standing here," the captain interrupted. "So without hospital ID or someone to corroborate, I can't let you in."

Her jaw tightened, and she glanced toward the ER doors. "One of your paramedics is back there somewhere; Chuck knows me. He's married to my triage nurse. Find him and ask him."

McKenna shook his head. "Can't leave this spot."

"Then call." Erin pointed to the cell phone on his belt. "Better yet, ask for Dr. Leigh Stathos. Tell her I'm here. She'll verify my identity. The number is—"

"I've got it," he said, lifting his phone and watching her intently as he made an inquiry. He gave a short laugh. "Yes. A redhead in what looks like Army fatigues . . . Ah, let's see . . . green eyes. And about—" his gaze moved discreetly over her—"maybe five foot nine?"

Erin narrowed her eyes. What was this, a lineup?

The captain lowered the phone. "Your name?"

"Erin Quinn," she said, feeling like she should extend her hand or something. She resisted the impulse.

"Hmm. Yes," he said into the phone. "I see. Okay, then." He cleared his throat and disconnected the call.

She looked at him. "Did you get what you needed?"

"Well," he said, reaching down to detach the rope from a sawhorse, "it seems you're who you say you are. And that I shouldn't expect a commendation for detaining you. Apparently it's because of your request that I'm here. Not that I wanted to be. I still have men out on the plane crash, but . . ." He hesitated and then flashed the barest of smiles. Though fleeting, it transformed his face from Rushmore cold to almost human. "Go on inside, Erin Quinn. You're late." His expression returned to chiseled stone. "And for what it's worth, I'm sorry. But that's the way this has to work."

"No problemo." Erin hitched her tote bag over her shoulder and stepped through the barricade. Then she turned back. "What's your first name, McKenna?"

"Scott."

She extended her hand and was surprised by the warmth of his. "Well, then. Good job, Scott. But going by the book isn't always the bottom line. Try to develop a little trust, will you? We're all on the same team."

Twenty minutes later, Erin finished checking on her staff and rejoined Leigh Stathos in the code room. They both looked up as the housekeeping tech arrived at the doorway.

"You wanted these?" Sarge asked.

"Yes. Great. Thank you." Erin nodded at the tall, fortysomething man wearing tan scrubs, his brown hair pulled back into a short ponytail and arms full of plastic emesis basins. "Put those in the utility room, would you? And I think we could use some extra sheets and gowns too. If you don't mind."

His intense eyes met hers for an instant before glancing down. "Yes, ma'am, double time."

Erin smiled at Sarge's familiar and somber half salute, then watched him march away, his powerful frame moving in an awkward hitch to accommodate his artificial leg. She returned her attention to Leigh and the dark-eyed child on the gurney beside them. The ventilator, overriding her natural breathing, whooshed at regular intervals, filling the girl's lungs. "She had two seizures but none before today?"

"Looks that way." The ER physician, her long mahogany hair swept back loosely into a clip, reached down and lifted the sheet covering the child. "But see how her muscles are still twitchy? And her pupils are constricted. I'll be honest: I don't like this. The only thing I know for sure is that the X-ray shows an aspiration pneumonia. Probably choked while vomiting on the truck ride in. I've started antibiotics. Art's coming in," she added, referring to the on-call pediatrician. "And I paged the public health officer."

"Good." Erin's brows scrunched. It was puzzling; an hour after arrival, Ana Galvez remained unresponsive, her skin glistening with perspiration. Though Leigh had inserted an endotracheal tube and the child was suctioned frequently, she was still producing large amounts of saliva. Her heart rate, barely 70, was surprisingly slow for her age. She'd had several episodes of diarrhea. *Poor kid. What happened to you?*

Erin glanced toward the main room of the ER, grateful things appeared to be settling down out there. "I still don't get this, though. Ana came from home? Not the ranch where everybody got sick?"

"Yes, but—" Leigh fiddled with the stethoscope draped across the shoulders of her steel gray scrub top—"she'd been there earlier. Felt sick after lunch and her father took her home."

"So that goes right back to the food. But salmonella takes time. Still, the symptoms fit. Triage says most of the patients are complaining of headache, nausea, cramps, and diarrhea." Erin checked the monitor: heart rate 58. *Why so slow?* "What did they eat?"

Leigh sighed. "Sack lunches. Every one different. That doesn't fit at all. I wanted it to be huge tubs of chicken stew that everyone shared. That would make sense. But Sandy's seen twenty-six patients in triage now, and the story from everybody sounds the same: picking strawberries since 6 a.m., lunch together around eleven, and—"

"I'm sorry to interrupt, but something's . . . wrong." Erin and Leigh turned at the sound of the triage nurse's voice at the doorway.

Erin's eyes widened. The triage nurse looked awful—pale, sweaty, teary-eyed. Sandy was holding her hand to her head, trembling. *What happened?*

Before she could ask, Sandy's eyelids fluttered and her knees gave way.

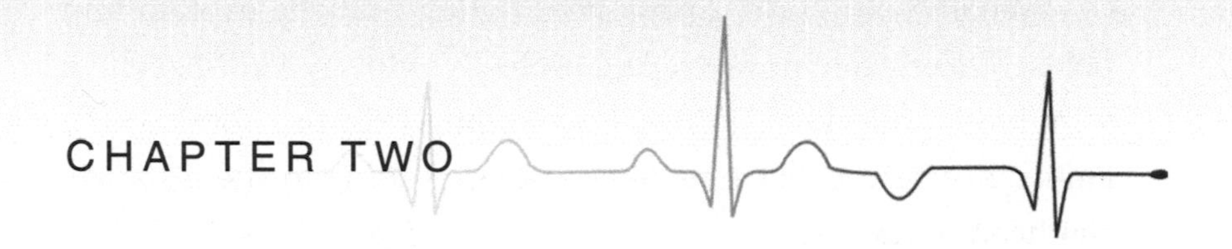

CHAPTER TWO

Erin and Leigh each slid an arm around Sandy and eased her down into a chair.

"What's wrong? Did something happen out—?" Erin lunged for an emesis basin as Sandy began to gag. Then noticed, with rising anxiety, the young woman's constricted pupils. She slumped lower in the chair. Erin supported her weight, relieved to see that her breathing remained steady. "Hang in there; we're going to get you lying down. Don't worry." She stared at Leigh, her mind whirling. Sandy and her husband had been trying to start a family, but this seemed far worse than early pregnancy symptoms.

"Let's get some help." Leigh turned and shouted through the doorway. She caught Sarge's attention and waved. "Tell the staff we've got an employee down in here. Have someone bring a gurney!" She knelt beside Sandy's chair, grasping her wrist. "Strong pulse but slow."

In an instant, the doorway was filled with staff, one of the nurses taking over the care of the sick child, while Sarge and the relief charge nurse lifted Sandy onto a gurney and wheeled her away. Sandy's paramedic husband, Chuck, dashed to her side and grabbed her hand.

Erin and Leigh followed—the doctor shouting orders for an IV and oxygen—but they were cut short by the arrival of two police officers. And Scott McKenna, holding a squawking emergency radio to his ear.

"What's going on?" Erin asked, noting that the captain and police officers were now wearing protective gloves. And that there were more uniformed firefighters standing near the doors to the ambulance bay. A lot more. Sirens began wailing in the distance. Her heart quickened.

"Pesticides, they think." Scott lowered his radio. "We just got the word a few minutes ago from the incident commander on scene. There's a lot of confusion, but witnesses saw an ag plane spraying artichokes on the adjacent property earlier this morning. Some of the workers on-site remember a 'fog' that made their eyes burn. There's enough wind to account for significant drift. The plane that crashed a few miles away was set up for aerial spraying—most likely this is all related. We're trying to get hold of the artichoke rancher to confirm. We'll know soon. "

Erin's stomach lurched. They were dealing with a toxic exposure? She ticked off the symptom acronym for pesticide poisoning, SLUD: Salivation, Lacrimation—excessive tears—Urination, Defecation. All bodily excretions increased in response to nervous system excitement from pesticides exposure via breathing, ingestion. *Or even through the skin.* Like Sandy, handling multiple patients' saturated clothing. It fit.

Erin's gaze darted toward where Sandy was receiving an IV. Her husband, obviously worried, stroked her hair. Erin saw, too, that the ward clerk and a few of the registration staff had gathered near the nurses' desk, their expressions anxious. In the distance Sarge emptied trash bins. Trash, patient clothing—all toxic sources now. *Everyone's at risk.* "What poison?"

"Organophosphates." Scott nodded. "At least that's what the rancher at the crash site contracted for. There was a related structure fire, so they're still sorting things out. And now with what's going on here . . . Trust me, there's going to be plenty of agencies investigating this incident."

Leigh lifted her stethoscope from her neck, frowning. "I'm sure. But my biggest concern is getting these patients turned around as fast as I can. At least I have something to work with now." She turned to Erin. "Have the ward clerk get poison control involved. Tell the pharmacy we're going to need all of the atropine they have. And make sure we've got pralidoxime—2-PAM—in case we need it. And do whatever you need to do to get all those patients undressed and decontaminated."

Within seconds, Erin alerted the operator and an overhead page blared throughout the hospital, announcing a hazardous material incident: "Code Orange ER. All departments be advised: we are now instituting Code Orange."

Her mind raced to formulate a plan. She'd ask the relief charge nurse to cover triage; per policy, the supervisor would already be designating house staff to assist in the ER, and the hospital chief of staff would need to be apprised of the situation. She strode back to where Scott stood. "Is there an estimate on how many more victims there are?"

"Maybe ten so far. The strawberry rancher employs casual workers, mostly migrant, so there aren't addresses. But the deputies are going house to house." He lifted his radio. "County dispatch is handling things now, and any new victims should be transported to Monterey hospitals. They've been told to give you a break."

"Good." Erin thought aloud. "I'll have engineering set up a

temporary shower to get people washed down, and Sarge can put biohazard bins outside for clothing and waste, and—"

"Taken care of. All of it." Scott interjected. "My hazmat team is two minutes out, and they'll be setting up the county's decontamination tent. I have six EMTs already outside, and city PD will stand by in case there's any security breach. One of my volunteers is hosing the pavement right now." He seemed to take in the confusion on Erin's face. "Oh, maybe I should have explained. The chief has appointed me the incident commander on-site."

"Which means?"

"You're handling it in here; I've got it covered out there." The smallest suggestion of a smile teased his lips. "Just like you reminded me, we're on the same team."

It was four hours before Erin came up for breath, and by then all of the ER staff wore scrubs borrowed from the OR, and most had snagged at least one bagel donated by the manager of Surf & Snack across the street. The connection between the downed plane and the accidental spraying of the strawberry ranch workers had been confirmed. Same plane, same pesticide.

They'd dealt with hordes of reporters and representatives of every conceivable agency—local, state, and even the federal government. Police, sheriff, fire department, the district attorney's office, EPA, public health, FAA—an activist group expressing concern over the filming of possibly undocumented workers—and at least a dozen members of the Safe Sky Environmental Protection Group. At one point, the various agency representatives by far outnumbered the patients being treated.

But despite the red tape, every farm worker and family member—plus a few flustered interpreters and even the hospital chaplain—had filed behind privacy screens set up outside in the ambulance bay, shed their clothes, and showered in the county's huge plastic decontamination tent. A contraption that looked strangely like one of those kids' party bounce houses, but no one was having fun. And everyone seemed to be confused. Except for Captain Scott McKenna, who had calmly—stubbornly, if you asked Erin—taken charge of her ER by his book of rules. Which set her teeth on edge.

Though the department was still staffed to disaster response level, things were considerably calmer. Two additional farm workers, suffering intractable vomiting, awaited admission, but they were improving after IV fluids. Sandy stabilized after reversal of her symptoms with atropine sulfate. Both she and the still-unconscious Ana Galvez were being monitored in the intensive care unit.

The news reporters were dividing themselves among the disaster sites, but in Erin's opinion, there were still far too many camped outside. She was holding on to a sliver of hope that things would wind down, and she'd be able to claim at least a few hours of her day off. Leigh had retreated to her office twenty minutes ago to work on medical records, and at present Erin had no patient responsibilities. She walked to the automatic doors of the ambulance bay, peered into the distance, and spotted the fire captain. He would likely know when the disaster response would officially end.

She'd gotten as far as the orange plastic cones and began to stoop under one of the yellow plastic Do Not Cross tapes when a familiar throaty voice called her name. She turned. "Nana?"

Her grandmother, tall and willowy and dressed in classic gabardine slacks and a shirt the same shade of blue as her eyes, smiled warmly from behind a sawhorse barricade. She brushed a wavy tendril of rust-colored hair back into her tidy upsweep, before waving heartily. "Apparently I'm not to be allowed in." She raised her fist. "And I'm thinking of marching in protest!"

Seventy-seven-year-old Iris Mallory Quinn had done that more than once in her youth. And had a scrapbook of clippings to prove it. Erin walked over to her grandmother and hugged her over an awkward expanse of sawhorses. "No more agitators, please," she teased, nodding toward the remaining pair of environmental protestors hoisting blue umbrellas and No Poison Rain signs. "We've had enough to deal with. Seriously, why are you here? You found my note?"

"Note? No, I haven't been home yet. Actually, I saw you on TV," Nana explained. She smiled at the confusion on Erin's face. "The chamber of commerce said the community's biggest need for volunteers is right here at the hospital. So I came to apply. Can you imagine, volunteering at the same hospital I worked for way back when?"

Volunteer . . . here?

Her grandmother continued. "When I saw the newscast, I hurried down to be sure you were okay."

Erin saw the concern in her eyes, the same shadow of anxiety she'd bravely tried to hide all the long months her husband was dying. Erin made a mental note to do whatever she could to discourage her grandmother from accepting a volunteer position. She didn't need to be around any more sickness and tragedy.

Nana sighed. "Anyway, I just wanted to say hello and give you a kiss, darling." She looked past the barricades to where Scott McKenna stood guard. "Except I'm not allowed in. That man does everything by the book, believe me."

"Hmm," Erin said, hoping the terse firefighter had at least been polite with her grandmother. If he hadn't, well . . . Erin patted her grandmother's hand and nodded. "I'll call you before I leave for home. It shouldn't be long. But right now I need to talk with Captain McKenna."

She watched until her grandmother made it safely back to her car, then walked toward Scott.

But before she could get to him, a reporter shoved a microphone in her face. "Amy Carson, Action News, here with . . ." The heavily made-up and rail-thin blonde squinted to read Erin's makeshift name badge, a strip of adhesive tape scrawled with a magic marker. "Yes, we're talking with Pacific Mercy Hospital employee Eric Quinn, RN. Will you answer a question for us, Eric?"

Eric? Erin frowned, hoping it was her hasty penmanship and the shapeless OR scrubs that accounted for the gender mistake. "It's Erin. And I don't have anything to say."

"Can you at least confirm that one of your staff, the wife of a local paramedic, was successfully treated for symptoms of this very toxic exposure?"

"No." Erin took a step back from what appeared to be a camera lens the size of her head. Where on earth was the hospital's public information officer?

"No? You're saying the treatment wasn't successful?" Amy Carson raised a well-sculpted brow and pressed eagerly forward. "There's been a fatality?"

"Fatality . . . fatality?" A hungry roar erupted from the gathered news crew, and several reporters surged forward as if someone had thrown raw meat. A second and then third microphone were thrust at Erin's face.

"Channel 7 news, Eric. What exactly is the hospital doing to ease panic among the patients? Is it true an OB patient called an ambulance to transport her newborn out of harm's way?"

What? "Please, I can't comment." Erin stepped backward again, stumbled over a traffic cone, and struggled to regain her balance. She caught a familiar scent of citrus mixed with smoke, seconds before a strong hand gripped her arm from behind.

+++

After Scott steadied the teetering charge nurse, he addressed the crowd, making certain his tone left no room for argument. "Everyone needs to get behind this barricade. Right. Now. Or be prepared to strip down and shower in that tent."

"Shower?" The blonde reporter hugged her pink linen jacket protectively around herself and retreated behind the barricade. The others followed.

Good. He was tired, and his already-thin tolerance for the media was shot.

"That's better," he told them, nodding. "These rules are made for safety. And now, if you'll be patient, I'm sure the hospital spokesperson will provide an update very soon." He waited as they walked to the vans before glancing at Erin, more aware than he wanted to be of the warmth of her arm under his fingers. He let go. "You're okay?"

"Yes, of course," she answered. "Nice tactic, by the way, teasing them about having to shower in the decon tent."

"Not teasing. True. They could have to shower. That's policy. If they violate the barricade, there's a risk of contamination. It's a matter of public safety." Scott stopped himself from offering her a copy of the Monterey County hazardous material protocols. He was sure she'd have a problem with that. "Anyway, I've given the same warning to everyone all day."

"Including my grandmother?" Erin pointed back toward the

parking lot. "She was here a few minutes ago, looking for me. Late seventies, fairly tall, wearing—"

"Blue. I remember her." How could he forget?

"And you told her she'd have to strip down?" She crossed her arms, color rising on her cheeks.

Scott shook his head slowly, barely resisting a smile. He had no doubt she'd slug him if he smirked. "No. I told your grandmother I was here to protect her safety. That she should call you instead. I even offered her my phone. But I got the distinct impression she wasn't satisfied with that. What's that old saying about apples not falling far from the tree?"

She narrowed her eyes. "Meaning?"

"Only that I would've known you two were related even if she hadn't told me. Twice."

"Oh." Erin reached up to tug at her ponytail. "The red hair. Dead giveaway, I guess."

"Hair? Oh, sure. But I was thinking more in terms of your—" he hesitated before choosing the words this time—"self-assurance."

"Self—?" The short siren yelp from an incoming ambulance cut her off. "Haven't we received the last of the patients from the ranch?"

Scott lifted his radio. "Yes. But this could be the ambulance the OB patient called. It was supposed to be canceled. At any rate, I can't have it at the back doors right now."

"OB patient? You mean it was true? I thought the reporters were making that up."

He asked a couple of questions, gave a quick order, and then lowered his radio. "It's okay," he said to Erin. "This ambulance is here for a routine transfer. They'll move to the front entrance. But that reporter was right. Plenty of your in-house patients saw the news coverage. Which, as you can imagine, is painting a grim picture. It doesn't help that the Safe Sky group is stirring things up again. Their spokesperson has been on every TV channel since the news broke." He frowned, knowing this incident was far from over.

He glanced at the ER doors. "That's where your public information officer is now—helping administration calm things down. Assuring folks the entire hospital isn't contaminated." He lifted his gaze toward the upper stories of the hospital, his thoughts on Cody. "I need to get up there myself."

"Up there? But aren't you stationed out here?"

Scott gritted his teeth, deciding not to remind this charge nurse that as incident commander he made the assignments. She clearly had issues with territory. "I'm doing my job," he told her, his tone more defensive than he'd intended. "No need to worry about that." He nodded toward the hospital doors, thinking of the little girl he'd carried in there several hours earlier. Cody must have heard about her. "You just be sure you keep things safe inside."

"Hey, wait. I didn't mean—" Erin stopped short. "Never mind." She jogged away.

Scott had the distinct impression that if she'd stayed a few seconds longer she'd have taken a swing at him. He probably deserved it. He shrugged, a vague sense of regret replaced by irritation. He didn't need any of this. Where were those bagels?

+++

Erin handed Leigh her coffee cup, a mug with a fading photo of the Golden Gate Bridge, and took a seat opposite her at a pebble-topped visitors' table adjacent to the ambulance entrance. "Just the way you like it, less than twelve hours old."

Leigh sniffed the coffee. "Is it?"

"Probably not. But since the EPA wasn't taking samples from the pot, I'm thinking that at least it's not toxic." Erin grinned weakly and watched as Leigh took a sip. She noticed that the ER physician, despite the brightness of her dark-lashed eyes and a faint, girlish sprinkle of freckles over her nose, seemed suddenly older than her thirty-five years . . . and bone weary. Erin was glad she had convinced Leigh to come outside for a few minutes' break. Sea breezes and shafts of sunshine—finally breaking through the thick coastal fog—had to be good medicine. And a reward, since it appeared they'd survived the worst of the pesticide disaster.

Erin glanced back at the ER doors and noticed Sarge Gunther leaning his bulky frame against the stucco wall as he took a long drag from a cigarette. His usual spot. He was finally getting a break too. Thank heaven he'd been working the day shift today. He wasn't much on conversation, but she could always count on Sarge to pitch in when the going got tough.

Erin turned back to Leigh. "So how're you doing, Doc?"

"Oh, boy." Leigh sifted her fingers through her hair. She looked out across the hospital parking lot, frowning as her gaze swept past the decontamination tent and settled on the remaining news van. And a pair of hoisted blue umbrellas. "Long day. Twenty-seven exposures—twenty-eight, counting Sandy. But we finally got things under control, including heading off that inpatient stampede. And Sandy's stable." She reached for her coffee. "Maybe you should ask God to keep our staff safe, in addition to helping us care for our patients."

Erin nodded, knowing the doctor was referring to Faith QD—named after medical jargon for "faith every day"—a Christian fellowship Erin initiated a few months ago. So far she'd welcomed a dozen or so staff members from several departments. Not Leigh yet, though she hadn't given up on her. The group gathered a few minutes before the start of their shifts; someone had dubbed it, "Asking God to be our team leader." Or maybe even their—Erin glanced toward the fire captain still standing watch—*incident commander*? Which reminded her that she was dying to know what, if anything, Leigh Stathos knew about him.

Leigh continued. "And I want you to know how much I appreciate your coming in today. I hated calling you on your day off. I hope you didn't have a date."

Erin snorted. "The only date I had was a steamy tryst with a scrub brush and my moldy shower grout. I didn't mind your calling. Except for the trouble getting past the fire department's newest gladiator."

"You mean Scott?"

Erin nodded. "I don't think I've ever seen him before."

"I had a tough time placing him myself. But then I remembered him from the ER in San Francisco."

"He works there too?"

"Off and on, I think. Or did, anyway. Commuted to pick up a few paramedic shifts. And he dated one of our nurses for a while. But I think his family's here. Speaking of family, how's Iris doing?"

"Better," Erin answered, feeling a twinge of regret that the subject had changed. But she smiled as she remembered her grandmother's warm hug earlier. "Getting feisty again, puttering around with her baking, even looking for a volunteer job. But now she's applied here at the hospital, so I've got to jump in and stop that."

"Why? I think it would be great if she came back here. I still can't get over her old photo in the lobby, with that button-front nurse's uniform and the white stockings. She looks just like you."

"So I've heard," Erin said, tempted to glare in Scott McKenna's direction. She picked up her coffee. "But as for Nana's volunteering here, I'm afraid it would be too hard on her. Fighting my grandfather's cancer took so much out of her. Physically, emotionally—" she felt the familiar snarl of anger twist in her stomach—"and financially. I still can't close my eyes without seeing that bank-owned sign pounded into her lawn. Those heartless vultures. But then we all kept thinking the expense of the experimental drugs and all those alternative therapies would be more than worth the cost."

Leigh reached across the table and touched Erin's hand. "Of course you did. And I know Iris appreciates your moving here with her. Uprooting yourself, putting your life on hold to live here for two years. You're amazing."

"I'd do anything for her," Erin said, uncomfortable with the praise . . . and the reminder that her family wasn't happy with her plan. "And if Nana occupies that house, she'll get the tax break when she sells. But I also think living here could help her recover, you know? That's my real goal. And letting her volunteer goes completely counter to that. This place is full of everything she's trying to forget—tragedy, sickness, and death. There's no protective gear against that kind of exposure.

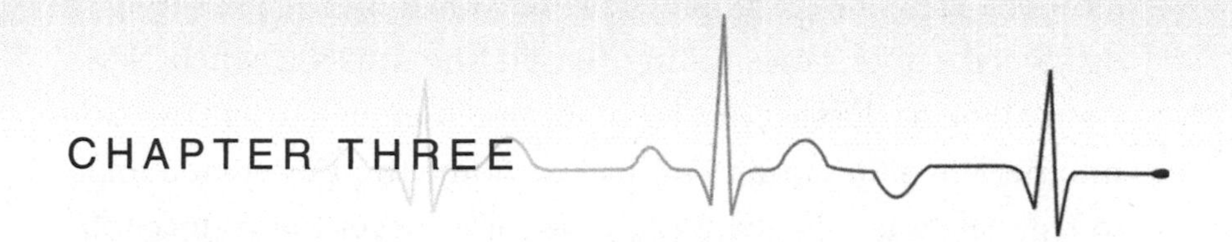

CHAPTER THREE

Erin turned the letter over in her hands, frowning at the name on the front. *Erin Anne Calloway.* Ten years and he still didn't get it. It wasn't her name anymore. She looked over to where her grandmother washed dinner dishes at the sink. "Why didn't you just throw this away? I won't read Dad's letters. You know that."

"No," Nana said slowly, drying the inside of a stoneware chowder bowl, "but I do know you." She gave Erin her famous I-have-faith-in-you look. The exact same expression she'd employed when, at age seven, Erin stubbornly refused to include the class bully on her list for homemade valentines. She'd pointed out all his nasty flaws, then politely listened to her grandmother's reminder about loving your enemies and turning the other cheek, all the while biting her tongue so she wouldn't say she'd rather punch his ugly nose. She'd grudgingly pasted his valentine. Last. With no glitter. Then picked through all the candy conversation hearts until she found a green one inscribed *Back Off*, spit on it, and sealed it in the envelope.

"Besides, mail tampering is a federal offense. My rap sheet is long enough already." Nana set her dish towel on the vintage Formica counter and reached for her cardigan draped over the back of a chair. "Let's take our tea outside. I need to check my hollyhocks.

And after all the hubbub at the hospital today, I think you could use some fresh air."

"Amen." Shower mold, pesticide scare, letter from Dad—ocean air was a great idea. Erin set the letter down on the glass-topped driftwood coffee table, telling herself she'd toss it when Nana wasn't looking. Just because Mom was weak enough to let Dad back into her life didn't mean Erin had to. Some things were too toxic to risk. She'd legally changed her name to sever the connection. And right now a change of subject would help keep that distance. She didn't even want to talk about Frank Calloway.

Erin grabbed the mug of herbal tea and followed Nana outside, thinking this might also be the perfect opportunity to broach the subject of volunteering at the hospital. She couldn't let her grandmother take that job. Hospitals were filled with pain and heartbreak. Not to mention frustration. The image of Scott McKenna intruded and she shook her head, thinking that over the course of the day he'd only managed to confirm her initial impression of him: rigid, humorless, stubborn. Although she'd been accused more than once of being too quick to judge when it came to men. Still . . . this firefighter already looked like a candidate for a menacing green candy heart. *Back off.*

She settled into a paint-layered chair on the small tiled patio and watched as her grandmother fussed with her hollyhock seedlings in the waning light. Then she drew in a breath of damp, salty air and closed her eyes for a moment, listening to the sounds of the ocean just a short block away. Some people found the waves soothing, peaceful. As a child, she'd found her own comfort with the sounds, often lying in bed at night imagining Jesus orchestrating the movement of the sea using a piece of driftwood like a conductor's baton. But now, the endless crashing seemed to stir Erin's restlessness and left her feeling even more unsettled . . . lonelier.

"Did you see the thank-you note from Claire and Logan?" Nana asked, settling onto the garden bench near Erin.

"I did. I can't believe they've already been married a month." A sigh escaped that she refused to call envy.

The truth was, fellow nurse Claire Avery deserved every speck of happiness that came her way. Falling in love with Dr. Logan Caldwell, after so much loss and heartache, was a miracle. Part of "the plan." Erin smiled, remembering Claire's passionate belief that meeting Logan had been God's plan.

She'd been convinced that something similar was in the works for Erin too. If only that were true. But unfortunately, Erin's track record with relationships butted right up against her friend's blissful enthusiasm. She was far more comfortable with a punching bag than any man she dated, and most of them had been knocked out of the ring after only a few awkward weeks. But "the plan" had indeed put her in a bridesmaid gown, with a bouquet of daffodils—and right back in the same Gold Country town as the long-wandering Frank "Flimflam" Calloway. Whom she'd artfully managed to avoid. *Back off, Dad.*

Her grandmother cleared her throat. "Your mother's planning a family dinner for Easter."

"Hmm. Better not count on me. I've got a lot of things going here." Erin turned to her grandmother, desperate to change the subject. "What else did Mom have to say?"

Nana hesitated, a maddeningly wise look in her eyes. "Only that she was glad I'm going back to volunteer work."

Bingo. Here was the chance. "You told her about applying at Pacific Mercy?"

"Yes." A smile spread across her face. "And I reminded your mother that the last year I worked at Pacific Mercy, I was pregnant with her. Of course, that was way back in the days when nurses were expected to stand when a doctor walked into the room, and bedpans were made of stainless steel. Drop one of those and they heard it in Cleveland." Her smile faded. "And those were the years of the polio epidemic."

Erin felt a rush of admiration for her gutsy grandmother. She'd endured plenty in her lifetime. And a polio epidemic certainly put Pacific Point's brief pesticide scare into perspective.

"Anyway," Nana continued, "thank heaven so many things have changed. Even in the twelve years since I retired."

"Still," Erin said, trying to segue as casually as she could, "a lot of it is the same. Despite better conditions and all the latest equipment, hospital work is still incredibly demanding, and—"

"Oh, darling," Nana interrupted. She set her cup on the table and reached over to take Erin's hand. "I wasn't saying you have it easy, for goodness' sake. Far from it. You know how proud I am of you. Don't forget I watched the nurses all those weeks your grandfather was ill. I'm so grateful for their skill and compassion and for the way they understood how much I needed to be there beside him. Right up until that last . . ." Her words faded off.

Erin's heart grabbed at the flicker of pain in her grandmother's eyes. Renewed interest in baking and planting flower seeds hadn't changed things; she'd been fooling herself about that. But spending time in a hospital could only make it worse.

She squeezed her grandmother's fingers. "I know you're proud of me. But what I was trying to say is that I don't think volunteering at the hospital is the best thing for you right now." A lump rose in her throat, and she swallowed it down. "It might be too soon after Grandy."

Erin saw her grandmother's lips press together and continued in a rush. "I didn't mean you're not strong enough. Or that they wouldn't be lucky to have you. Of course they would. It's only . . ."

"You're trying to protect me." Her grandmother let the pronouncement hang in the air for a moment, then shook her head. "You've always been that way. With your sister, your cousins, your classmates, your mother . . ."

Every time Dad let her down or disappeared. Or lied. Or cheated.

Nana chuckled. "Do you remember the Wonder Woman costume?"

Erin groaned. "I was six. Give me a break."

"Magic bracelets and the golden Lasso of Truth." Her grandmother laughed. "I'll never forget you standing there in those red boots with your little fist raised. Or what a dickens of a time your mother had convincing you the costume wasn't appropriate for Sunday school." She turned and grasped Erin's chin gently. "You're still a fighter, darling. For your patients, your coworkers, that new hospital fellowship. I love that in you. And I understand that this need to protect me comes straight from your heart. But . . ."

"But what?" Erin wasn't able to discern her grandmother's expression in the near darkness, but there was something in her tone . . .

"I can't be rolled in bubble wrap. Promise me you won't try."

Bleach alone wasn't going to do it. The grout still looked gray. Erin frowned as she inspected the toothbrush she was using to scrub the shower tile. The bristles were falling out. Third toothbrush in three months. What was this, supermold? She'd never had this problem at her apartment back in the foothills. Of course, the air was drier there. But there had to be a better way to fight it.

Erin smiled, thinking of Leigh's miracle answer to dingy tile grout: white shoe polish. Apparently she'd shared an apartment with two other med students, and one of the women tried daubing shoe polish onto the bathroom tile grout lines in a frantic attempt to tidy before her mother's visit. Instant fix. Erin tried not to imagine how this might extrapolate into how that doctor practiced medicine today. She worked for the CDC.

Shoe polish wasn't the answer. Maybe a stronger ceiling fan. And that all-natural eco-friendly cleanser she'd ordered on the Internet. She'd solve it. Like she'd solved the problem of the latest unopened letter addressed to Erin Anne Calloway. By stuffing it in the garbage can.

She stepped out of the shower stall, tossed the balding toothbrush into the wastebasket, and sighed. It felt like she'd been whacking a punching bag all day. The pesticide scare, Sandy's contamination, the run-in with the media, and then that irritating exchange with Scott McKenna. And there were still so many things left to deal with—Ana's uncertain prognosis, the interagency incident review, Sandy's recovery . . .

Erin had almost nothing left of what should have been her day off. She still needed to finish the homework for her nurse management classes and go over a new prayer she wanted to offer at the Faith QD fellowship tomorrow morning. After which, she would start a more normal workday of kidney stones, minor burns, migraines, and asthma; complaints about waiting room times; struggles with staff about vacation schedules; and a few laughs with Leigh. A routine day without the intrusion of outside drama. She was looking forward to it.

Erin moved to the doorway, hearing her grandmother's voice above the noise of the TV. "Are you calling me?"

"Yes, come look. They're talking about that pesticide problem on the news."

When Erin joined her grandmother on the blue-striped couch, an Action News reporter was speaking into the camera. The blonde that Scott thwarted with the threat of a public shower. But the news clip wasn't a replay, and Erin didn't recognize the background as hospital property. It looked dark and rural. "Where are they?"

"Out at that artichoke ranch. Where the plane crashed. Apparently they're still doing cleanup. Oh, look." She pointed to the TV. "Isn't that your fire captain?"

My captain? Erin started to protest, then stopped as she caught sight of him on the screen. Her stomach did an unexpected dip. It was Scott, all right, dressed in his regular uniform, blue shirt and twills and shiny fire-issue badge. But wearing the same expression she'd seen all day. Even in harsh camera lights that lit his rugged jaw like a kid playing monster with a flashlight, he still managed to look stubborn and calmly in control. He blinked as the reporter repeated a question.

"Captain McKenna, is it true that this cleanup—this very dangerous spill—is far more extensive than you'd realized?" She motioned toward floodlights and several vehicles in the distance. "Can you confirm that this morning's fire was a result of the pilot hitting a structure used for storage of agricultural chemicals?"

More chemicals? Erin leaned forward, waiting for his answer.

"I believe the sheriff will be making a statement in a few minutes. Now if you'll excuse me . . ."

"One more question, Captain McKenna. On a more personal note." The reporter raised her microphone and the cameras bore down, lighting an errant thatch of hair on the back of Scott's head. "Aren't you the son of Gabe McKenna, the hero firefighter who died in that hostage situation back in 1988? And you're now following in his footsteps at the Pacific Point Fire—hey, easy there. Don't touch the camera!"

Erin flinched as the blurry image of an outstretched hand obscured the lens.

Whoa. Erin held her breath as the picture angle widened and refocused on Scott. She caught a split-second glimpse of a man she barely recognized. His expression of calm control was gone, and his eyes were suddenly filled with what she could only describe as a mix of raw emotion. Smoldering anger, frustration, and pain, like a dental instrument scraping an exposed nerve. Scott's voice was a low growl. "No. More. Questions."

The camera refocused again, and he faded into the eddy of uniforms and newscasters.

The sheriff's face filled the TV screen. He squinted into the cameras. "I assure you that Pacific Point citizens will be kept informed of the results of this continuing interagency investigation. There is no cause for panic; this site cleanup is being performed according to strict protocols. Everything is under control."

The camera panned over the darkened rural landscape, then zoomed in on the crumpled single-engine ag plane, the remains of what looked like a storage shed, and at least a dozen workers, all outfitted in bulky hazmat gear. Her throat tightened. *"Everything is under control."* Why did she suddenly have the feeling the sheriff was rubbing shoe polish into tile grout?

CHAPTER FOUR

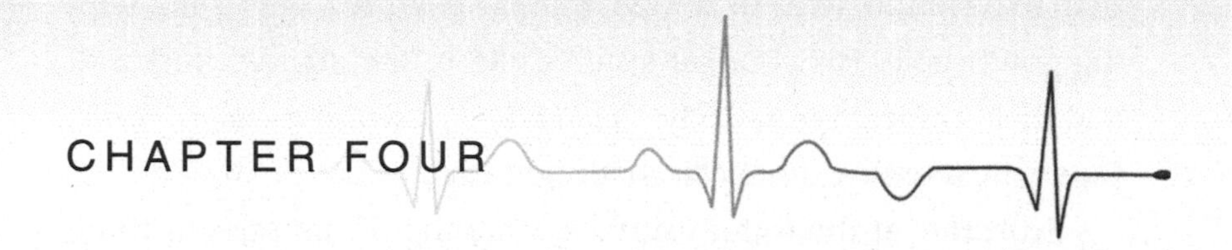

Scott waded deeper into the surf, blinking as the chill and briny water slapped against his sleeveless wet suit and splashed his face. A translucent green swell lifted his bare feet from the sand, and he thrust forward into it, stretching his arms in powerful strokes while kicking against the strong, insistent pull of the Pacific.

The tide was higher than he liked, but he could still get in a good half-hour workout before the sea reclaimed the rocky cove and its stingy stretch of sand. He needed the exercise, not only as training for the Pacific Point Ocean Rescue Team, but because it was better than slamming his fist against a fire station wall. He'd done that last year and spent six weeks in a fiberglass cast. Both humiliating and stupid. And Scott wasn't going to be stupid anymore; he'd keep everything in check. Move on with his plans, his life.

He sucked in a deep breath, then rolled his face back into the salty water as he swam farther out, telling himself to forget the TV reporter's unexpected and unwelcome question. *"Aren't you the son of Gabe McKenna, the hero . . . ?"* His stomach churned. He couldn't count the number of times he'd heard that. Along with comparisons to his own accomplishments, his career. He'd been living in that shadow since he was twelve years old, but . . . Scott's stomach tensed.

He had no doubt that the reporter's next question would have been about the other McKenna family tragedy. The accident almost a year ago along a darkened stretch of desolate coastal highway . . . with no hero to be found. Rain-slick road, intoxicated driver versus unyielding power pole. His younger sister, Colleen, her abusive husband, and their innocent son, Cody. *Could I have prevented it—saved them?* If only he'd returned her call that night . . .

Scott tore at the water's surface, straining his muscles until he felt a stab of pain deep in the shoulder joints. Still so much less than he deserved. The truth was, there was more than a chance that he'd failed his family that night. *Failed my own family.* The thought of it ate at him every day, devoured his sleep at night. And became unbearable whenever he looked into the eyes of his orphaned nephew.

So he'd thrown himself into Ocean Rescue, welcoming the challenge—the risks. He began volunteering for paramedic shifts in San Francisco, finding some measure of relief in the physical distance from Pacific Point. Enough to convince him to apply for a permanent position there as well as in several other neighboring cities.

And Portland? How will I explain that to my family? He pushed the thought aside. He'd interviewed for a position as Portland Fire's chief of emergency medical services but knew his chances for that position were slim. And even if his family didn't know about it, they'd long accepted his career ambitions. But right now all plans were on hold. Because of Cody's infection.

Scott kicked harder, pulling his arms through the dark water and keeping an eye out for floating beds of rubbery kelp. He swam parallel to the shore, pushing himself toward the limit of his endurance, until his pulse pounded in his ears and his lungs begged—burned—for air. Good. Just what he needed.

He'd swim another fifteen minutes, then towel off, pull on his nylon warm-up pants and a polo shirt, and grab some hot coffee at Arlo's Bait & Moor on his way to Pacific Mercy Hospital. Cody would have eaten breakfast by now and be awaiting another exam by yet another orthopedic surgeon. *To decide if he can keep his leg.* Scott fought a shiver. *My fault?* He stopped swimming, gulped for air, and treaded water, his body rising and dipping at the whim of the ocean's power. Guilt washed over him far more relentlessly than the swell of the rising tide. *No, don't do this. Think, don't feel.*

He'd get back to the hospital and visit with his nephew. Stay away from the merciless media. They could feed on speculation all they wanted to with the other agencies, but Scott's part in the pesticide incident was nearly complete. All that remained was completion of the crash site cleanup and the interagency review. He frowned. Not that the ER was going to like his take on their part in the incident; they could have handled things better.

He sputtered as a swell of salty water covered his mouth. Erin Quinn wasn't going to like the memo he'd be sending around today. His lips tugged toward a smile as he remembered the feisty charge nurse trying to force her way past him at the barricade, her fervor in defending her grandmother. And the way he'd had to take hold of her arm when she'd stumbled during the onslaught of reporters.

His low chuckle bubbled against the seawater as he began swimming back toward the cove. The beautiful redhead had a surprisingly powerful bicep. He'd be wise to keep that in mind. Not that he planned to see her again. Relationships were nowhere on his horizon now, and—

Whoa, what's this? Scott stopped swimming, his pulse quickening as he scanned the shoreline. The rocks? How'd he get this close so fast?

His body rose and fell on a set of larger swells, and he gulped air, then held his breath as a wave propelled him toward the small patch of remaining sand in the water-filled cove. The tide was coming far faster than he'd expected, and the surrounding rocks loomed way too close. The biggest one just yards away now. He kicked hard, hauling at the turbid green water with his arms, but he was slammed down, getting a mouthful of gritty, brackish water . . . and made little progress forward. He dived under, kicked furiously, and rose again, expecting to find his footing in the sand. Slipped under. And finally found the bottom, his feet clumsy, legs cramping.

He began jogging through the waist-deep water toward the diminishing patch of sand, but a wave broke over his head from behind. He staggered, belly flopped onto the water, and slid against the huge rock, shoulder first. Blunt impact, skin against stone, and pain—first sharp and then searing—as the frothy salt water sluiced across his torn skin. Blood streamed down his upper arm.

Scott regained his balance and stood, breath heaving as he steadied himself against the enormous algae-covered rock. Then he slogged through the water to the remaining sand before another wave could catch him. So much for his vow against stupidity. Did he think to check the tide table? He shivered in the morning air and rolled his shoulder to inspect the damage. After grabbing his half-soaked beach towel, he dabbed away the blood and looked at it again. A ragged avulsion below his right deltoid, embedded with sand. With any luck he could get one of the paramedics at the fire station to clean it and pull it together with butterfly bandages.

Meanwhile he had some duct tape and paper towels in his truck. That would stanch the bleeding for a while. Time enough to get his coffee and see Cody. And next swim he'd remember to check the tide tables. He wasn't going back to the ER.

+++

"Triage!" The registration clerk's bellow—like head wrangler on a cattle drive—echoed up the hallway and into the ER. It was followed immediately by a blinding red strobe light positioned above the nurses' desk.

Erin turned to Leigh with a groan . . . followed by an incredulous grin. "How on earth does Arlene do that? What does she weigh, eighty pounds?"

Leigh chuckled over the brim of her Golden Gate cup. "Yeah, after a quart of Starbucks. But then she's worked ER admitting for twenty years. Probably has calluses on her vocal cords." She pointed to the computer in front of them. "What's the triage?"

Erin ran her finger down the census screen. "Nineteen-year-old female. Headache."

She scanned the trauma room. Twelve gurneys with striped privacy curtains, one enclosed code room, a casting room, and an ob-gyn exam room. Twelve gurneys and only four patients by 8:15. Merciful, since they were one staff person short with Sandy still a patient in the ICU. But that meant Erin, in addition to her duties as charge nurse, was expected to handle triage. Still, it was nothing like the chaos of yesterday with all those victims, media, and agencies swarming.

She glanced at Leigh. "I'm going out there. You okay for a few minutes?"

"Sure." Leigh took one more sip of her coffee before rising from her chair. "I'm in a holding pattern for lab results, so take your time. The ward clerk's got the phones, and I'll call Judy from the break room if I need anything. Plus, Sarge is here somewhere if I need military muscle." She rubbed her neck and sighed. "Regardless, you won't hear any complaints from me. This is so much better than yesterday. I really needed a . . ." She didn't finish her thought.

A quiet shift. Erin nodded. *Quiet*—the Q word. No ER veteran ever said it out loud. Immediate jinx. Nothing made emergency department staff squirm more than a clueless rookie surveying a calm trauma room and quipping, "Wow. It's so quiet in here." It begged for a Code 3 ambulance. But Erin couldn't agree more with Leigh's wish. After yesterday, they all needed a breather.

"I'll be back in a few minutes, then," Erin said, striding toward the door. "And maybe we can go over that memo from the fire department. See what McKenna had to say about our day. Then we'll need to put something together for our part of the incident review."

Erin traveled the short hallway, popped her head into Arlene's cubicle, and switched off the strobe. "I've got it." She sniffed the air. "What's for breakfast?"

The clerk, hunched over her Tupperware, grinned. "Sausage and cheese biscuits. Two. And a prune Danish. I know; I know. I must have tapeworm. Everybody says that." Arlene's grin faded and her thin, penciled brows drew together. "Your teenager's eight months pregnant and is worried this headache has something to do with the pesticide spraying. She says she can't wear shoes because her feet are too swollen. But I couldn't fit all that in the chief complaint space on the census log." She pointed to the patient's information on the computer.

"Pesticides?" Erin asked, checking the patient's name. "That wouldn't cause swelling, but . . ." She stepped farther into the cubicle and squinted through the glass into the waiting room. "Who's her OB?"

"Nobody local. She just moved here from Oakland. I gave her

a list. And some paper surgical booties for her feet. Why do people think hospital floors are clean?"

Erin scanned the few occupants and spotted her patient in an instant. Dressed in striped pajama bottoms, a man-size T-shirt, and the elasticized paper surgical booties. She was pale, glistening with perspiration, and holding her head like it was going to explode. On her lap were a dish towel and a plastic wastebasket. Vomiting props. *Preeclampsia?* How high was her blood pressure?

Assessments already swirling in her mind, Erin jogged down the short hallway to the triage office and yanked the door connecting to the waiting room. "Heather?"

As the young woman stood, an elderly couple arrived through the automatic doors into the waiting room. The gray-haired woman carried a straw tote overflowing with yarn and magazines. She studied the room, grinned broadly, and turned to her husband. Her querulous voice carried over the noise of the TV. "Oh, look, Henry, no excuses for waiting this time. It's quiet as a tomb."

Erin flinched, then told herself that the superstition was ludicrous. She beckoned quickly. "Right in here, Heather. I'm ready for you."

When the lumbering teenager hesitated, Erin stepped out into the waiting room and guided her through the door and into the triage chair. She fitted the automatic blood pressure cuff around her patient's arm while studying her face. Then punched the Start button as she noted, with increasing concern, that the teen's lips and eyelids were also slightly swollen. As were her fingers. Had she had any prenatal care at all? "What's going on today? You said something about pesticides to the clerk. Were you near the spray area?"

"No, I live in town. But I got to thinking about it after I heard what those Safe Sky people were saying. How dangerous it could be if you're pregnant, and—" Heather groaned. "My head hurts. And I can't see very well . . . keep seeing sparkly lights. Can't think straight either." She rubbed at her nose ring, then squinted at the cuff on her arm. "Ouch, that's so tight. Do you have to . . . ?" She paused, and her eyes rolled upward, just as the alarm on the blood pressure machine began to shrill. The red digital display read 200/120. Critically high. Her eyelids fluttered again, and her head bobbed.

Erin ripped the Velcro away and shouted out into the hallway, "Arlene, get me a wheelchair—quick!" She patted Heather's arm. "Take a deep breath and hang in there with me. I'm taking you to see the doctor right now. We'll get you feeling better. Deep breath. Attagirl."

In scant moments Erin backed the wheelchair out of the triage office and hustled down the short hallway into the ER, managing to obtain a mumbled allergy status, medications, and due date on the way. She would likely get little other information. Heather's head sagged forward onto her chest. Erin headed straight for the code room, shouting breathlessly to Leigh as she passed by, "Hypertensive, 200 over 120, pregnant, severe headache, visual disturbance, and confusion. I'm thinking preeclampsia. Judy, give me a hand getting her on the gurney."

Leigh grabbed her stethoscope and followed. Everyone reached for the box of exam gloves and pulled them on.

From out of nowhere Sarge hurried over to help, and by the time they'd lifted Heather onto the stretcher, her eyes rolled back and her face began twitching. In an instant, she deteriorated into a full-blown seizure. Head, arms, legs rigid and jerking, saliva foaming from her mouth, lips dusky gray. Urine soaked the sheet beneath her.

"Watch her airway," Erin called out, protecting Heather's head as she thrashed. "Suction!"

Judy cranked the knob on the wall suction unit, slipped a stiff plastic tube into Heather's mouth, and cleared her airway, then fit a high-flow oxygen mask over her face.

Erin cut away the patient's T-shirt with trauma scissors so Judy could place the cardiac monitoring electrodes and Erin could get an arm exposed for an IV line. Judy ripped open a bag of saline and hooked up the tubing.

Erin wrapped a tourniquet around a flailing arm and uncapped a large-bore needle, trying to synchronize the sharp tip of the needle with Heather's thrashing. Her lips moved silently. *I'm working . . . on the back of a bucking bronco. Help me, Lord. Help me help her.*

"Let's get some magnesium on board!" Leigh ordered. "And pull out some Valium and labetalol, Judy. We'll need a Foley catheter when you can. Dip the urine for protein." She grabbed hold of the patient's arm to help steady it for Erin and nodded as the needle slipped into the vein. "Good job. Grab some blood for labs, okay?" Leigh turned and shouted over her shoulder toward the ward clerk, "Page labor and delivery stat. We'll want this baby monitored. Call respiratory therapy and anesthesia too. This woman's going to need an emergency C-section, fast as they can. Let's get it done!"

+++

Scott pulled his chair closer to Cody's bed, glad they'd stopped all those stat pages from the ER. His nephew had already asked at least twice if the poisoned little girl was going to die and if other people had been poisoned too. And "Are those people with the umbrellas right, Uncle Scotty? Is the air over Pacific Point poisonous?"

Scott glanced at the TV, now playing a sci-fi fantasy DVD he'd brought to keep Cody from having to watch the news. He frowned, angry once again with the media for feeding the pesticide scare. Didn't his nephew have enough to worry about, being poked and prodded for IV antibiotics, x-rayed, and swallowed up by MRI scanners? *He won't lose his leg. It can't happen.*

Scott's breath caught in a familiar jab of pain, and he reached over to pat the ten-year-old's tousled blond hair. "How're you doing there?"

"Good." He turned back to Scott with a smile. The smile widened and was punctuated by a single dimple at the edge of his mouth. Exactly like his mom's. "Thank you for bringing this. TV's pretty boring during the day. But this is great."

Scott's heart tugged at the gratitude mirrored in Cody's blue eyes despite all he'd been through in the past year. The loss of his parents in the accident, countless hospitalizations after surgeries for his crushed lower leg, physical therapy, and now an exhausting battle against infection. Yet somehow Cody still smiled, still laughed, and—Scott's gaze moved to a Sunday school workbook on the bedside table—still trusted God. *After all he's lost. How?* Because of Colleen's unshakable faith . . . and because at ten Cody was a far better man than his uncle.

"And thanks for this too." Cody lifted a gaudy fluorescent fishing lure with a rainbow of glittery streamers. "El Squid. I showed it to you at Arlo's bait shop, and you remembered. We'll catch big ones, won't we? Salmon and striped bass—maybe an albacore?"

"You bet. But meanwhile, promise you won't uncover those barbs. I put corks on them for a reason." Scott pointed to half a dozen Band-Aids on Cody's arm. "You've got enough holes in you, pal." He touched his own shirtsleeve and felt a twinge of pain over the wound he'd sustained in his run-in with the rock. He was a fine one to talk.

"I promise. I won't touch the hooks. And when my leg's better, we'll be going out on the charter boat. The big one out of Monterey Bay." His smile faltered. "You'll really take me?"

"Right." *Even if I'm living somewhere else.* Scott raised his fist, and Cody responded with a grin and an enthusiastic fist bump. Then the smile faded. "Hey, what's the matter, Cody?"

"I was just thinking . . ." The boy's eyes met his, and their vulnerability made Scott's heart ache. "If I can't stand up, I can still go on the boat, can't I? I could sit in a chair, and you'd help me pull the big one in?"

"Yes," Scott managed, summoning a reassuring smile. "I'll always help you."

When the tech came in to help Cody shower, Scott left the room and promised to come back the next day with a stack of charter boat brochures. Scott's mother would be in to visit tonight after she finished work. Scott's stepfather, Gary, wasn't feeling well, but he was still going to try to come for a while. Cody wouldn't lack company.

He'd grabbed his half-full cardboard cup of coffee, deciding to finish it in the elevator, despite the fact it was lukewarm. Then he'd go back home and shower off the sea salt and the sand that had been grating against his skin for the last hour. Afterward, he'd let one of the paramedics look at his arm, then make some phone calls to the county disaster agency to see how things were going with the cleanup. He was glad that, so far, there had been few reports of new victims—only a handful of people without symptoms wanting to be checked just in case. He'd also make sure Chuck, his firefighter paramedic, had an extra day off. Chuck's wife, Sandy, was being discharged today. Ana Galvez, however, remained in critical condition. He hated to think how frightened her family must be.

Scott took the last swallow of coffee just as the elevator door opened at the first floor. To reveal Erin Quinn. For some reason, his breath caught.

"Uh . . . hi," he said, reaching out to the hold the elevator door. "Are you getting on?"

Erin shook her head, and a tendril of her copper-colored hair slipped free from her topknot to trail along her jaw. Her cheeks were flushed and green eyes bright. "I'm headed down to OB. We just had a baby boy. Six pounds, four ounces."

"Baby?" Scott caught the door again, realizing he'd been so busy staring at the charge nurse he'd forgotten to step off the elevator.

"Teenage mother. Came in with a headache she thought was caused by the pesticide spraying. But it turned out to be eclampsia, with sky-high BP and seizures. We got her stabilized and into the OR for a C-section. That's the only cure, of course. Mom and baby are both doing fine. But remind me to strangle the next person who says the Q word in my department, and—" Erin tipped her head and pointed to Scott's cardboard coffee container. "Arlo's Bait & Moor?"

"I'm not much on fancy coffee."

Erin laughed. "Arlo's has great coffee. I just meant that I live maybe half a block from there. Bait and bakery and open until eight thirty. You don't know how many times I've run down there for emergency cookies." She moved out of the way of an X-ray tech pushing a gurney and ended up closer to Scott. "But it's such a hole-in-the-wall spot; how'd you know about it?"

"I lease a house about a mile down the coast from there, but the beach below Arlo's is better. For swimming," Scott added, realizing all at once that it was probably obvious, since he hadn't showered and probably reeked like a sea lion. "Training for the Ocean Rescue Team. I was doing that today, so I grabbed the coffee and came here because . . ." He hesitated, then decided he didn't mind telling Erin about Cody. "My nephew's up on pediatrics." He caught a sudden alarmed look on Erin's face. "What?"

"You're bleeding."

CHAPTER FIVE

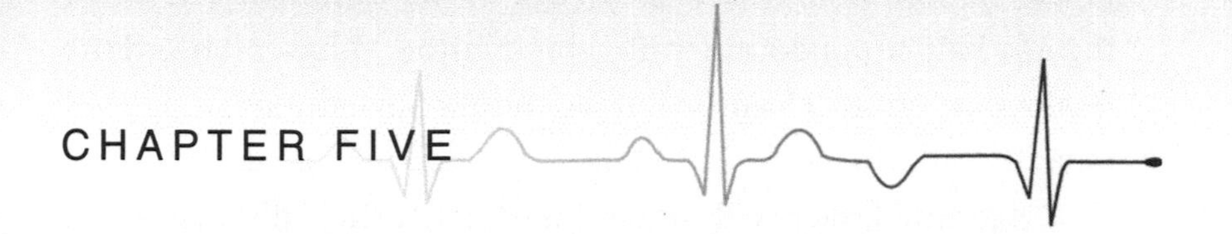

"This is going to sting a bit." Leigh Stathos raised the syringe and squirted a short stream of local anesthetic toward the ceiling to clear the air bubble, then looked at Scott McKenna. "You ready?"

"Go for it," he replied, glancing down at his arm exposed under the rolled-back sleeve of the patient gown. "I'm sorry about the sand. The hospital laundry won't like it."

Leigh chuckled behind her plastic shield mask. She'd been the one to insist the firefighter wear the gown after half a dozen young women—from the registration staff to housekeeping to an X-ray tech—had casually wandered by to ogle her patient. She'd never had so many offers of help. McKenna was incredibly fit and had come out fairly well in his encounter with that rock. And according to the nurse he'd dated in San Francisco, he had survived plenty of personal tragedy too. First his father, then his sister and her family in that car accident last year. Not that Leigh had ever asked for those details. The last thing she wanted to do was invade anyone's privacy. Some pain was too personal. Her own troubles stayed between herself . . . and herself, now that she'd let God off the hook.

Leigh's lips tightened behind the mask. This was no time to think about her marriage. There were no answers. She was relieved Scott hadn't asked why she'd left Golden Gate Mercy Hospital.

"Sand we can deal with. Just spare us the organophosphates." She sighed. "I want all that to be over with."

"Same here." Scott grimaced slightly as she inserted the needle of the syringe along the ragged edge of his wound and injected the first half-cc of lidocaine with epinephrine. "I haven't heard the final report on the cleanup, but we should have things completed today."

Leigh lifted the needle and reinserted it a short distance away, extending the injection through the already-numb tissue to lessen the pain of the stick. "I imagine if that pilot had survived, he'd be facing criminal charges. There have been ongoing protests against ag spraying for years. And valid concerns—yesterday proved that." She wrinkled her nose. "I heard that our Safe Sky folks have asked some of the national groups to fly in for a show of strength."

Scott snorted. "And you can imagine how much the media would love that. But I don't think this incident came from deliberate negligence. The pilot was freelance, and the sad fact is that he may have been willing to take some risks to get the job done quickly and move on to his next contract. We'll probably never know. But in this economy, I'd be surprised if his income hadn't dropped off. Hardships everywhere. Business and housing. Makes me glad I'm leasing my place." His eyes met Leigh's. "Did you and your husband have to sell a home in San Francisco before you moved here? He's a police officer, isn't he?"

Oh no. Leigh's stomach sank and she stopped, holding the needle forceps midair, nylon suture dangling. "No. I mean, yes, he's an officer. And we do have a house there, but—"

Judy arrived at the side of the gurney, and Leigh exhaled in relief. The truth was almost a corny cliché and still way too raw to talk about. *I left my heart, my home . . . and my husband in San*

Francisco. She blinked and nodded to the efficient middle-aged staff nurse. "Perfect timing. Pour me some saline, would you?"

+++

Erin glanced at her watch as she crossed the last stretch of lobby carpeting on her way to the gift shop. She still had ten minutes left on her break, and she'd grab a sack of trail mix to surprise Arlene. Never a bad idea to keep the registration clerk happy when you're stuck in the badlands of triage. All in all she'd made the most of her short break from the ER, seeing that Heather and the baby were doing well and checking on the status of little Ana. Erin's throat tightened. The child had worsened considerably.

She'd also briefly visited the ICU. Sandy would likely be discharged this afternoon. But there'd been a look in her eyes that worried Erin and a way-too-chipper quality to her voice when she tried to joke about being on the other side of the stethoscope. A bravado that somehow fell flat. Erin would check back with her later today.

Across the lobby she spotted Sarge Gunther, his gaze on the TV mounted overhead. He leaned his hip against the wall and then flinched with what looked like a spasm of pain. His expression was solemn, his eyes rimmed by shadowy circles. Erin wondered how difficult it was for Sarge to perform his duties—mopping, pushing heavy bins of linen, hauling sacks of trash—while dealing with the cumbersome prosthetic limb. Below-the-knee amputation, right leg. A land mine in the Gulf War, she'd heard through the grapevine. He never talked about it. Hardly talked at all, in fact. But he was always there to help—any shift, anytime he was needed. Maybe that helped Sarge too. People needed to be needed. God had an amazing way of orchestrating things like that.

Now, trail mix and then back to the ER to see if Rambo McKenna had traded his duct tape and paper towels for stitches and a tetanus shot. She shook her head. The incident commander wasn't quite as much in control as he'd thought.

Which reminded her that she needed to read the last of his memo; maybe she'd have a chance to go over it with him before he left the ER. She pulled it out of her tote bag as she walked through the doors of the gift shop. Then scanned it while she waited below a silver cloud of Mylar *Get Well Soon* balloons while the senior-age volunteer helped the customer in front of her. She traced a fingertip down the captain's neat outline of items he intended to bring up for discussion at the countywide review. The last several notations referenced the ER: *Need for additional public information officer. Need for training with the decontamination tent.* Erin grudgingly agreed with both. *Failure of basic security measures by emergency department staff (example: charge nurse, E. Quinn, identity badge).*

Her mouth dropped open. He was making a public issue about her missing name badge? Called in on her day off to work like a dog . . . and get reprimanded?

By the time she reached the ER, Scott was sitting upright and bare-chested on the gurney, awaiting his bandage and diphtheria tetanus booster. Erin couldn't think of anything she'd rather do more. She waved to Judy. "I'll finish up here."

He had sand in his hair. And she wished to goodness he were wearing a shirt. But she wasn't going to be distracted; she was having her say. Erin returned Scott's casual nod, pulled on a pair of gloves, and reached for a packet of antibiotic ointment. "I'll just bandage this up and give you your shot. And you can get out of here."

"Thanks. I need to do some paperwork at the station."

Erin's teeth clenched. She spread the ointment on the flat end of a forceps and smeared it along the dark line of sutures on Scott's upper arm. "Paperwork for the disaster review?"

"Right."

"I read your memo."

"Mmm." A muscle twitched along his jaw.

Erin tore open a package of gauze. "Your assessment of the ER's response." She motioned for him to lift his injured arm away from his side and began wrapping the gauze around his bicep. "Most of that was accurate. I'll be honest; we haven't used that inflatable tent before. And it would have been good to have at least one other PIO—the media was rabid." Erin smoothed the last of the gauze around his arm. "But that last bit about basic security failures. That wasn't fair."

"Security is a prime issue. 'Fair' doesn't figure in."

Erin tried to stay calm as she fastened paper tape across the bandage. She uncapped the syringe of tetanus vaccine and expelled the air. "Did you have to mention me by name?" She recapped the syringe.

Scott exhaled, his gaze following as she set the syringe back on the tray.

Erin crossed her arms. "Look. I was called in on my day off. I got here as fast as I could and had no idea there would be a barricade. With you manning it. Security knows me. I wouldn't have been stopped. You wouldn't have even been there yet if I hadn't asked my ward clerk to call for help."

"You're right. And you were eventually identified. But it took time. Which is a problem in those situations." Scott's brows drew together. "The memo's already out. Nothing I can do about it now."

Erin reached for an alcohol swab. "You can promise me you won't bring my name up at the meeting. Spare me that." She tore open the packet and gestured for him to turn so she could swab his opposite shoulder. She'd inject the medication there so any soreness could be differentiated from the tenderness of a possible wound infection.

He watched as she carefully prepped his deltoid for the injection. His gaze moved to the syringe in her other hand. "Under the threat of . . . ?"

"Oh, c'mon. I'm not threatening anything. I'm just saying, professional to professional, that we can have some respect for each other. We'll get through the review; we'll each go back to our own departments. We'll never have to cross paths again. One meeting. All done. No more drama. We'll both survive." She uncapped the syringe and stretched the skin taut across his shoulder. "I'll even sleep in my name badge from now on. Deal?"

Scott opened his mouth to speak just as Erin plunged the short needle into his muscle.

At the same instant Sarge hurried over to the ER desk. He was breathless and sweating. "Have you heard?" he asked Leigh. "They found a bunch of sick animals. Horses, cows, dogs, and even deer out at the crash site. When that ag pilot lost control, he hit a chemical storage shed and the spill contaminated a stock pond and a creek that feeds into the river. Our water supply."

+++

Scott stood, despite the fact Erin was holding the alcohol swab against his arm. He took a step toward the nurses' desk.

"Hang on. The injection site's bleeding a little." Erin held pressure on his deltoid with the swab, then lifted it away. "Did

Sarge just say what I thought he said? The water supply's contaminated?"

"That's what I heard." He watched the big man with the ponytail and rumpled tan scrubs move across the trauma room toward the door. "Is that guy one of the ER staff?"

"Not really. He's a tech with housekeeping. And he's assigned mainly to this first floor: ER, OR, radiology, and ICU. And up on second floor when he works nights. You know, taking care of the trash and biohazard bags and stocking the linen. But the staff counts on Sarge to do way more than he's required to."

"Sarge?"

Erin nodded. "I think his real name's Richard. *R* on his badge, anyway. But everyone calls him Sarge. He's a Gulf War vet. And disabled. Hard not to notice that limp. Frankly, I don't know how he manages all the heavy work with that prosthesis."

Prosthesis. "He had . . . ?" Scott bit back the rest of the question. He didn't want to know.

"An amputation of his lower leg," Erin answered, obvious compassion in her eyes. "Probably twenty years ago, but I don't imagine time makes it any easier. Something like that changes your life forever." She grasped his arm as he tried to step away. "Hang on. I'm going to put a Band-Aid on your shoulder."

"Don't need one," Scott said, fighting a sudden wave of nausea. *"Amputation . . . changes your life forever." Not Cody . . . no.* "I'm fine." He pulled his arm from her grasp and reached for his polo shirt. "But I need to get out of here. Am I finished?" He saw by the look on Erin's face that his tone had been gruffer than he intended. "I mean, I appreciate everything you've done. But I need to go. I have to confirm that information about the pesticide contamination."

Dr. Stathos arrived beside him. "Do you think it's true? Sarge said it was on the local news, but I couldn't pull up anything on my laptop."

Scott lifted the cell phone attached to his belt. He switched it on, despite the hospital rules. He'd be out of here in a minute anyway. No messages. Good sign. "I don't know. But even if it's only media speculation, that still needs to be stopped. The last thing we want is a citywide panic. My station provides incident command and coordinates with the Monterey County Health Department on issues involving biological and chemical agents; we'll get official information first. I'm heading over there now." He glanced toward the door. "I need to check with my nephew too. He's been upset about that little girl. I don't want him worried by this talk of dead animals."

Leigh grimaced. "Good idea. And I should make a call about my horse. He's boarded at a stable not far from the river."

Erin moved beside Scott. "Your nephew—that's right. I forgot. You were telling me that he's up on peds?"

"Yes, Cody's getting some IV antibiotics for an infection. Probably won't be there long." *Because he's going to be okay. He is.* Scott unfolded his shirt and began pulling it over his head, struggling a bit because of the bulky bandage. Erin reached out to help him. "Thanks."

He'd taken the instruction sheet from Dr. Stathos, agreeing to watch the wound for signs of infection and get the stitches removed in ten to fourteen days, and was turning to leave when his cell phone buzzed against his waist. The fire station. Before he could ask, Erin told him he could safely take the call from the outer hallway.

"McKenna," Scott answered, jogging out the trauma room doors. He leaned against the wall by the ambulance bay doors, looking up for a moment as the big housekeeping tech limped by, pushing a bin loaded with red biohazard bags. He listened to what the chief had to say, inhaling slowly with a small measure of relief. "Okay, Chief. Did animal control fax the information?" He nodded at the confirmation. "Good. How many barrels is he admitting to now? Is there any paperwork?" Scott spotted Erin walking toward him. Then listened as the chief relayed the last of the information. "I'm on my way in." He disconnected and turned to Erin, noting the worry on her face.

She glanced down the hallway, then lowered her voice. "It's true? About the animals, the water?" Her eyes widened, and for some reason Scott was reminded of the aching vulnerability in Cody's eyes when he'd inquired about the fishing trip. His question, too, was about frightening possibilities. *"If I can't stand up, I can still go on the boat, can't I?"*

Scott took a breath. "Yes, but it's fewer animals than the TV said. Probably drinking from the stock pond near the crash site. But it's true that it's close to a creek that feeds into the Pacific Point River. The rancher was stockpiling chemicals—far more than he'd admitted to last night. And in violation of county policies. Organophosphates, fertilizers, fungicides . . . No people seem to have been affected. But . . ."

"But?"

"They can't be sure yet how widespread the contamination is. How much of the chemicals were destroyed by the fire, how much saturated the ground. We thought we'd be wrapping things up, but the truth is that this mess is just getting started."

Erin shivered, then straightened her shoulders. "What's the next step?"

"Water resources is already performing tests on the water,

samples from every source including the river and bay. Meanwhile there'll be public service announcements, and the Red Cross will provide bottled water. You can bet the stores are already running out." He saw Erin's brows scrunch. "Don't worry. Your hospital keeps a three-day supply."

"Actually, I was thinking of my grandmother. I need to call her."

Scott nodded at her honesty and obvious concern. "Do that. But our primary focus right now is to avoid mass panic. The Office of Emergency Services will be coordinating a Crisis Management Briefing tonight at the town hall to provide information to citizens and control rumors. All services—police, fire, hospital, and so forth—will receive instructions regarding their own specific roles." He offered a half smile. "There's a book."

Erin gave a short laugh. "Which I'm sure you've committed to memory, Captain."

"Well . . . don't lose your name badge."

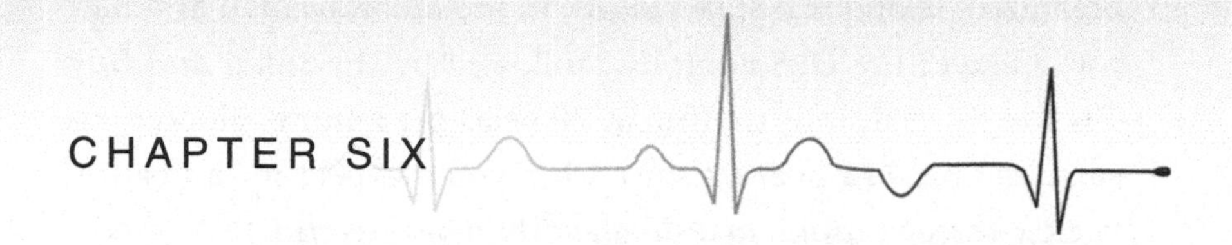

CHAPTER SIX

Erin paused outside the doors to the ICU, noticing the large linen cart pushed against the corridor wall. The dust cover was rolled back and the cart's metal shelves, usually stocked with neat stacks of freshly laundered patient gowns, pillowcases, and sheets, were now loaded with row after row of bottled drinking water. *"Don't worry. Your hospital keeps a three-day supply."*

Though she had no doubt Scott was correct, right now she was concerned about far more than drinking water. As day-shift charge nurse, she was responsible for her staff. And to them. They counted on her for fair scheduling, to act as liaison between staff and administration, to keep them informed of policy changes, to roll up her sleeves and pitch in alongside them with patient care. And to promote and safeguard the morale of her team. Erin had a nagging feeling that something wasn't quite right with Sandy. She needed proof her suspicion was wrong. Physically, the triage nurse was fine, but . . .

Sandy was sitting in a chair alongside the hospital bed, picking at the tape to her IV. She looked up as Erin tapped at the doorframe. "Oh, you caught me. I'm thinking about pulling this thing out myself. I want out of here in the worst way. All I hear are alarms beeping and people gagging and those ventilators."

"I'll bet." Erin nodded in sympathy and stepped closer, glancing at the cardiac monitor overhead. Sandy's heartbeat, in a fluorescent green tracing, marched across the black background in an organized, textbook display: short, rounded P-wave; tall and narrow spike of the QRS complex; followed by the small and tidy T-wave. Normal sinus rhythm at 70 beats per minute. Blood pressure reading: 113 over 62. Just what you'd expect for a healthy twenty-three-year-old. *In a situation she never expected.*

Erin studied her friend's face. Flushed skin, dry lips, but pupils far less dilated than before. "Looks like the atropine's worn off. Your heart rate's normal."

"Except that I still feel like I'm spitting cotton. My mouth's so dry." Sandy reached for the bottle of water on her table and hesitated. The dark centers of her hazel eyes were wide again, and Erin suspected it had nothing to do with drug therapy. "They took my water pitcher away this morning. They replaced everybody's water with these bottles. That was weird. Is it true what Sarge said about the pesticides and the river?"

"Sarge?"

"I cornered him when he was emptying the trash outside my room. I'd overheard one of the visitors talking with a nurse, and I had to know." Her fingers moved to the neckline of her gown. Then her voice lowered to a whisper. "Is our water supply contaminated?"

"No," Erin said quickly. Then amended it; she wasn't going to lie. "I mean, it's doubtful. Several agencies are investigating. They have to. But the spill was nearest to a stock pond. It's probably very isolated." She took Sandy's hand. "The important thing right now is that you're okay. You'll be back to work in the ER before you know it." Her stomach plummeted as she caught the look in Sandy's eyes. More than hesitancy. Fear?

"Sure," Sandy said, blinking rapidly before looking away. "As soon as the doctor clears me. But I'll need—"

"You'll have as much time as you need," Erin interrupted, giving her fingers a firm squeeze. "I've got plenty of coverage for the ER. Don't give it another thought."

Sandy's eyes brimmed with tears, and she exhaled a staggering breath. "You're sure?"

"Absolutely sure. And I'm the boss. So there you go."

"Thank you." Sandy reached for her bottled water, raised it to her lips, then startled, jumping at the sound of Sarge starting up a vacuum cleaner outside the room. Water sloshed onto the front of her gown. "Oh, for heaven's sake."

"Here, I've got the Kleenex," Erin offered.

"Thanks. Sorry I'm a little jumpy. Don't know why."

"No problem." Erin watched her dab at the spill, trying to tell herself that Sandy's nervousness was a side effect of the medications and the ICU atmosphere. Just because she was a nurse didn't mean she was immune to the disorienting effects of unnatural lighting, strange noises, the lack of sleep and privacy. It happened to almost every patient in every hospital. It was perfectly normal for a patient to feel jumpy. Even an unflappable nurse like Sandy. But if all of that were true, then why did Erin still have that nagging feeling something wasn't right? She nodded to reassure Sandy but told herself to accept the truth: *She's scared.* Scared to come back to work.

"And the little girl from the ER—our patient? Is she still in a coma?"

If ever Erin was tempted to lie, it was now. "Yes, but remember that Ana's condition is the result of pneumonia more than the initial poisoning. Because her airway was compromised for so long. It's not the same as your exposure."

"I know." Sandy's pupils were huge again. "I'm the lucky one."

Erin cut through the lobby on her way back to the ER, passing a cart filled with bottled water and Styrofoam cups standing alongside the drinking fountain. The fountain's spout had been covered with a plastic bag. An attached note read, *Please use bottled water.*

She slowed her pace, watching as a young mother helped her child reach a bottle before joining a small group of other visitors gathered in chairs in front of the TV. Erin stopped, mesmerized by the news clip. It showed a little girl about five years old, crying, followed by a close-up of a marmalade orange cat, its tongue protruding and eyes glazed. Obviously dead. The camera panned across the surface of what appeared to be a small pond, the lens zooming in on dozens of fish floating belly-up.

One of the children turned to his mother. "Did that kitty drink the poison water?"

The TV clip faded to black and was replaced by what appeared to be an interview with Pacific Point city officials, backed up by several police officers and firefighters, including Scott. He'd changed into his uniform, and his expression was all business. One of the officials gave a reassurance that the pesticide contamination was likely limited to the immediate dump site. No further animals or people had been affected. Water sampling continued. "There is no reason for panic. We repeat: no reason for panic." The clip finished with information regarding tonight's town meeting.

Erin crossed the last stretch of carpet leading to the ER's back doors, fighting the awful feeling that the dead cat and the bloated fish were only the beginning. And trying to forget the look of fear in Sandy's eyes.

+++

"Slow breaths, Mrs. Alton. Try to relax . . . your hand too, please. Ouch." Leigh grimaced.

"But I'm scared, Doctor. Please, you have to help me!"

"I'm trying. Nice, slow breaths. That's better. Let go of me, please."

The patient, a morbidly obese forty-eight-year-old blonde, dropped her death grip on Leigh's arm to reach for a yellow plastic emesis basin. "Oh . . . no," she continued, her moan interrupted by violent gagging. "Not again. I'm so sorry." She wiped her mouth on the towel Leigh offered, belched loudly, and then moaned again. "My stomach hurts so much. Do you think it's those pesticides, then? Have I been poisoned?"

Leigh glanced at the three patients on the other gurneys, hoping no one had heard. More panic was the last thing she needed; the hospital operator had been forwarding calls to the ER all morning. She'd moved to Pacific Point to find some much-needed peace in her life, distance from her problems. Dealing with citywide chaos wasn't conducive to any of that.

She patted her patient's arm, now damp with perspiration. "Show me again where it hurts. Put one finger on the spot where your pain is the worst."

Leigh turned and mouthed a thank-you as Erin pulled the privacy curtain around the gurney, then hastily called after her, "Start an IV here, would you? Normal saline. Let's give a half-liter bolus to start. Pull some blood for a CBC and chem-20. I'll write the complete orders when I'm finished here. Thanks." She turned back to her patient. "Now, where's that pain?" Leigh lifted the hospital gown.

Mrs. Alton's pudgy hand hovered over her abdomen for a moment, then indicated—with the tip of a raspberry-tinted acrylic nail—a spot at the base of her right rib cage.

Right upper quadrant abdomen. And colicky in nature. Leigh layered one hand over the other, then rocked her palm against the ample rolls of flesh, pressing her fingertips in as deeply as she could to palpate the organs beneath. "Deep breath, please." Edge of the liver, gallbladder . . . She watched her patient's face for a reaction and saw her pupils dilate.

Elaine Alton flinched with pain.

"I'm sorry. I don't want to hurt you. But tell me, why are you concerned this could be related to—" she lowered her voice—"a pesticide exposure?"

"The fish," Mrs. Alton explained, attempting to smother another bilious belch.

"You mean the fish that died? In the TV news report?" Leigh suppressed a groan. Why on earth did the station keep rolling the tape of that poor little girl and her dead cat? *And when is the stable going to return my call about my horse?* "You got worried after you saw the report about all those dead fish?"

The woman shook her head as Leigh lifted her stethoscope to her ears. "I mean the fish I ate. Last night."

Leigh stretched the earpieces away from her head. "You think you ate poisoned fish?"

"Maybe. How can I know? My hubby got it down at the pier, and he saw them taking water samples not far from there. The river runs to the ocean, you know."

"Ah," Leigh said as empathetically as she could. *Deep breath*

. . . *Patience, patience.* "And exactly what kind of fish did you eat last night?"

"Rock cod. Battered and deep fried. And clams. We had our five children over for the annual Alton fish fry. The neighbors too. You've never seen so much food—homemade onion rings, buttered garlic bread, cheese fondue, Boston cream pie. Oh, please, it's really hurting again." She squirmed on the bed, her skin paling. "And it's aching in my back now, up in my shoulder blade." She clutched at the gown over her right breast. "It's just like that pain I had a few years ago. Oh, Doctor, please help me."

"Nice slow breaths." Leigh lifted her stethoscope away from the woman's abdomen. "Did you say you've had this pain before?" *And didn't tell me or the triage nurse?*

"Oh yes. From my gallstones. I have one of them at home in a little jar."

Leigh nodded, trying not to imagine how someone would display a gallstone. HGTV would cringe. But the old med school gallbladder aphorism certainly fit here. The five Fs: fair, fat, forty, female, and fertile. Elaine Alton embraced them all with gusto—and a side of coleslaw.

The privacy curtain parted a few inches, and Arlene, the admitting office clerk, peeked in. "I'm sorry to interrupt, Dr. Stathos, but you have a phone call on line one. It's—"

"I know who it is," Leigh interrupted before Arlene could reveal the details. "I've been expecting this . . . consultation." *With the stable manager about my horse.* It wasn't a complete lie. "Transfer the call to my office and ask them to hold for a few moments, would you? I'm going to order some medication for Mrs. Alton's pain and nausea, and then I'll take the call."

Leigh exhaled softly, realizing that her call to Beachview Stables had little to do with serious concern over Frisco's health; the boarding stable drew its water from a tank filled prior to the accidental pesticide spill. And the big bay gelding was strong and healthy and completely full of himself these brisk spring mornings. No, this call to the stables was more about a connection to the peaceful, pastoral world that was Leigh's respite from the turmoil of her chaotic work . . . and her wounded heart. It had become a lifeline. After the events of the last twenty-four hours, she needed it more than ever.

In less than three minutes she was reaching for the phone, already imagining the sweet scent of alfalfa and pine shavings, the low snuffling of the stabled horses, and the chirps of barn swallows nesting in the rafters. Except that it wasn't the stable manager on the other end of the line. It was . . . *Nick.* Leigh's heart slammed against her ribs at the sound of her husband's voice.

"Leigh?" he repeated, his voice low and sleepy as if he were a rookie coming off a bruising night shift. She could almost see his sleep-tousled black hair, those heavy-lidded brown eyes, and the dark shadow of beard stubble. "Are you there?"

"Yes." She reached past her knitting tote and grabbed a bottle of water, hating that he had this effect on her. Still had the ability to turn her world upside down and fill it with a toxic mix of anger, pain, and hopelessness. *There is no hope for us.* "But I'm busy. Why are you calling?"

"I—hold on a minute." There was a muffling of the phone as if he'd pressed it to his shoulder and then whispered voices, one deep and one very insistent . . . and unmistakably feminine.

She's there with him? Leigh's stomach lurched until the familiar anger rose to shield her, like Nick's police-issue vest that had hung in the closet next to her scrubs for three long years. Thick, insulating anger. It was all she had. "No," she said after taking a sip of her water, "I won't hold on. I can't."

"Wait, please." The sleepy quality of Nick's voice was replaced by urgency. "I only wanted to say I heard about the pesticide spill, saw you on the news. Are you okay?"

Leigh choked. Whether that was because the second sip of water went down the wrong way or because of the ludicrous irony of her husband's question, she wasn't sure. Had he really had the gall to ask if she was okay? She gripped the water bottle as anger festered.

"Leigh?"

"I'm busy," she whispered through clenched teeth. "That's what I am right now. You shouldn't have called. I'm involved in something critical." *Like saving my sanity.* Leigh slammed down the phone, then hurled the water bottle against her office wall. *He's still with that woman.*

She sank into her chair and rested her head in her hands for a moment, blinking back tears. She took several deep, slow breaths and then smiled grimly, remembering how she'd advised Mrs. Alton to do the same thing for her pain. *"Nice, slow breaths."* It was sound advice. And Leigh was going to follow it.

Tonight she'd go to the stables instead of the town hall meeting. Erin was planning to attend, and she'd bring back a full report. Leigh would sit in a fluffy mound of pine shavings in a dark corner of Frisco's stall with her back against the oak-plank wall. She'd listen to her horse chew his hay and snuffle contentedly. She'd inhale—slow, deep, therapeutic breaths of sweet and pungent alfalfa, warm horse flesh, rubbing liniment, and saddle leather.

And then she'd start her plan to move forward with the divorce. End the pain once and for all. Otherwise her heart would end up in a specimen jar like Elaine Alton's gallstone.

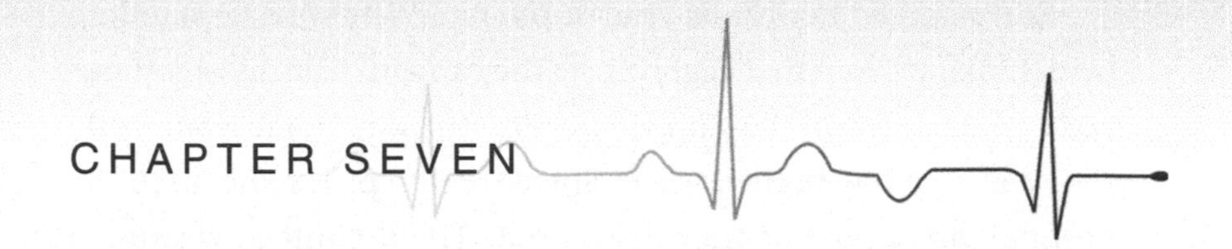

CHAPTER SEVEN

Erin parked her Subaru on the sandy asphalt outside Arlo's Bait & Moor. She opened the door, letting the salty and damp afternoon breeze toss her hair and fill her lungs. The distant call of gulls, scratchy and shrill, accompanied the relentless *draw-whoosh-draw* of the waves. She climbed out of the car, headed toward the red lacquered screen door of the coffee side of the shop, then changed her mind and walked to the metal railing overlooking the sea.

A handful of surfers, seal-like in their wet suits, dotted the gray-green water, some paddling parallel to the shore on their colorful boards, the rest sitting upright and laughing together, turning now and again to peer over their shoulders for waves. The narrow stretch of beach was empty of the usual shell-gathering young families and rapidly giving way to the rising tide. Frothy white water swirled around the pitted and sea-scoured rocks bordering the beach. *That big rock . . . where Scott injured his arm this morning.*

Erin's face warmed, remembering him sitting on the gurney in her ER, muscular shoulders, stony expression, and sand in his hair. *This is where he swims. And buys his coffee.* Erin bit her lower lip, thinking how close—within a short walk of her house—he'd been all this time. She'd walked this beach countless times, sat cross-legged on a blanket in the sand reading her Bible, joked with

Annie Popp about taking her coffee worldwide, and yet she'd never crossed paths with Scott. Not once. Until yesterday, when in the face of a community disaster—

Erin smacked her palms against the rail. Why was she standing here thinking about that aggravating fire captain? The disaster status was the exact reason she stopped here on the way home from work; she needed to buy bottled water. She'd tried to pick some up in the hospital gift shop, but they'd sold out. The volunteer, wearing a Pacific Mercy smock and rhinestone-embellished tennis shoes, had been chatty and sweetly apologetic to everyone, and . . .

Erin smiled as the thought struck her. Volunteer. In the Little Mercies Gift Shop. Why hadn't she thought of that before? It would be the perfect spot for her grandmother. She'd be helping at the hospital like she wanted, but she'd be away from direct patient contact and close enough to keep an eye on. A win-win all around. And after the past twenty-four hours, Erin could use a win.

She stepped away from the rail, then turned and glanced once more at the shoreline below, thinking of Scott being swept into the rock by the rising surf. She already knew him well enough to suspect he would have hated that loss of control. He liked to win too. Disaster, by the book. That's what he'd be offering tonight at the town meeting. She'd seen the goals on the fax sent to the hospital's chief of staff: provide information, identify leadership, disseminate information, and offer resources. All designed to "engender cohesion and morale, squelch rumors, and allay anxiety."

Erin's brows drew together as she remembered the hospital visitors watching the TV clip with the dead cat, the frantic voice of Leigh's gallbladder patient insisting she'd been "poisoned" by her dinner . . . and that anxious look in Sandy's eyes in the ICU. Erin hoped McKenna's book was big enough.

+++

Iris tapped at the thirty-gallon fish tank, watching as Elmer Fudd rose from the bottom, spat out a chunk of fuchsia gravel, and swam toward her fingertip, shiny as a newly minted penny. He was nearly nine inches long and had one opaque eye but was still spry considering he was . . .

Iris tried to remember Elmer's exact age. Was he turning eighteen this coming summer? Yes. Doug won him at the Monterey County Fairgrounds after spending thirty dollars on Ping-Pong balls to toss onto a table crowded with fish bowls. She recalled the determined look on her husband's handsome face as the plastic balls ricocheted off the rims. He'd been fifty-eight then, his thick hair more than a little gray at the temples. Iris's heart squeezed as she remembered the details of that day. He'd been determined, hurt, and angry because of what she'd told him. What she'd done. But there was no point in revisiting that now.

Iris sprinkled a pinch of food flakes into the tank and walked the short distance to the bathroom. "Erin?" She poked her head inside, wrinkling her nose at the scent of cleanser, cloying as sun-fermented grass clippings. "I hope that cleaner works better than it smells."

Erin turned away from the shower wall, her arms in opera-length flowered gloves and hair twisted into a haphazard topknot. "It's that eco-friendly stuff I found on the Internet. Nontoxic. But I'm still wearing the gloves. Considering what's happened lately, I'm not trusting anything. You know?"

"Yes, I know." Iris felt a rush of love for her strong and beautiful granddaughter. Mixed, as always, with a pang of worry. *You're not trusting . . . or forgiving, darling.* Erin's difficulty with trusting went much further back than the events of yesterday. It was born of all those disappointments with her father. Frank Calloway was the reason Erin spent so many summers here with Iris and Doug. Brooding, letting her wounds scab over. And her defenses deepen. *Always fighting.*

Iris glanced at the bathroom's small window, covered by the stained-glass panel that nearly obscured the sunlight. Jagged pieces of purple, scarlet, and green glass roughly soldered together to resemble a medieval shield and sword, tediously crafted by Erin the summer she was fourteen. Hours and hours of feverish work on a makeshift table out on the patio. Foil, glass cutters, pliers, solder—burns, cuts, and countless Band-Aids. She'd been so determined. Iris would never forget the look on her face. So much like Doug's the day he threw thirty dollars' worth of plastic balls to win a twenty-five-cent feeder fish. *My goldfish and that dismal window—both of them reminders of anger and hurt.*

"I couldn't reach Claire," Erin said, stripping off her cleaning gloves. "Did she say what she wanted?" She blew at a strand of hair falling across her eyes and grinned. "What do you bet Logan's trying to talk her into that motorcycle trip?"

"Actually, she saw the news coverage about the pesticide spill and wanted to know how we were doing." Iris tried to recall the exact words. "And she also wanted to know if you'd had to call together a CIS . . ." She frowned. "Anyway, some kind of employee counseling."

"CISM." Erin stepped out of the shower and set the bottle of cleaner on the sink. "Critical Incident Stress Management. It's a plan of action aimed at helping people cope in times of disaster to kind of boost their defenses and protect them from traumatic stress and burnout. That's how I met Claire, remember? She was trained as a peer counselor for critical stress and came in to help our staff at Sierra Mercy after that awful propane explosion at the day care." She pressed her hand to her chest. "Oh no."

"What?" Iris moved closer. "What's wrong?"

"Sandy. My triage nurse, the one who ended up as a patient. That's what I saw in her eyes: critical stress. And her husband . . . he's a paramedic but he's having to deal with his wife's being a victim. That's a whole different story. Why didn't I see this coming? I took the CISM course last fall, and I never stopped to consider that my team—the whole hospital—might be affected by this disaster. I need to go find my notes and figure out what I should do." Erin yanked at her topknot, and her hair tumbled down around her shoulders. "Can we drive separately to the town meeting?"

"Sure. But why?"

"Because I need to talk with Captain McKenna. And he's probably not going to like it that I'm bringing my book too."

+++

Sarge Gunther grimaced in the darkness against a jolt of searing pain in a calf he didn't have. Phantom pain, the VA called it. Even after twenty years, it still jabbed like an ice pick. And now, two full weeks after he'd stopped his medications—ending the suffocating fog the psych drugs induced—the pain was more noticeable. He didn't care; it was worth it. Because despite what the doctors said, Sarge knew he couldn't take the meds anymore. He had to stay sharp, focused on his mission, and alert to the dangers crowding in. Now more than ever before. Yesterday was proof.

He shifted his weight on the bulky prosthesis, then focused the penlight to inspect the water bottles on the closet shelf, looking carefully at the dates, the places of manufacture, the bar codes, and the lot numbers. He lined them up symmetrically and examined the tops to be certain they hadn't been opened and re-capped. Or pierced with a needle right through the plastic. They could do it to add the pesticides. He'd learned way too much about poisons during the war: nerve gas, blistering agents . . . the enemy had access to these and more. Look what they'd done to thousands of Kurds. He grimaced, remembering the photos. Bodies heaped high like so much garbage. And that little girl in the ER. She was still in a coma. He had to be careful. It wouldn't do anyone any good if the sergeant was out of commission. *My squad counts on me.*

When he finished checking the bottles, he'd mark each label with a tiny, inconspicuous dot of permanent ink. And then he'd know they were safe to drink when he returned to work the night shift. He was assigned to the south wing of the second floor, but it was easy enough to keep an eye on things here in pediatrics. He knew the nurses' routines, could slip down here and use this housekeeping closet as a base. Dark, contained—secure as a foxhole. It was worth the risk. He knew, more deeply than he'd known anything in years, that it was his mission. It felt good to have one again. Almost like . . . a second chance.

He would protect the boy. Only ten years old. He'd heard the whispers—they were trying to take Cody Sorenson's leg.

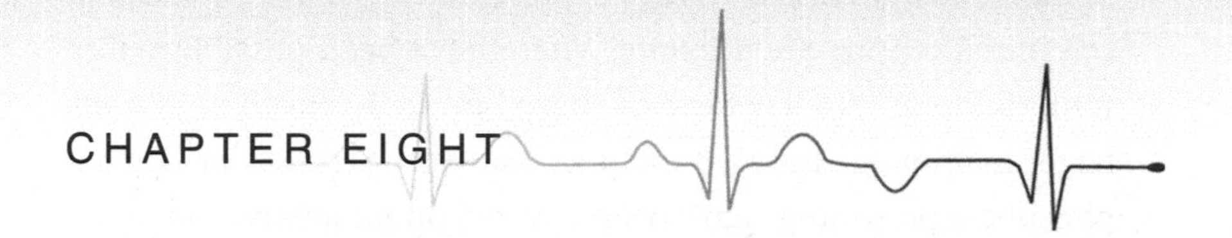

CHAPTER EIGHT

Erin squirmed with compassion. Scott's height and his unfortunate location on the raised podium put him at the mercy of the Pacific Point Butterfly Festival banner. Every time he moved, a gigantic orange and black rayon butterfly skimmed the top of his blond hair as if it intended to grasp him by the head and carry him off the stage. It was like some low-budget horror movie. Erin could almost see the caption on YouTube: "Killer butterflies terrorize coastal town." But there was nothing funny about tonight's town meeting. Bottom line, people were scared. She'd never seen so many people holding plastic water bottles. Or raising blue umbrellas—while wearing gas masks. The environmental group was well represented.

More than two hundred people filled the small auditorium to hear the assembled leaders from police, fire, water resources, animal control, and public health deliver information. And though the session was coming to a close, several hands still waved for questions. Erin turned as a balding man, one row behind her, stood.

"We've heard that it was more than a few fish and a cat that died." The man crossed his arms. "Is it true that facts are being covered up because of liability?"

Murmurs rose around the room, and the man blinked against

the sudden glare of camera lights as the TV news crews bore down on him. No Poison Rain placards waved overhead.

The public health officer approached the microphone after nodding at the animal control representative. "I assure you that the initial reports are accurate. There have been possible symptoms of illness in a few head of sheep but no deaths in any of the larger mammals. And that includes humans. No cases of organophosphate poisonings have been covered up for any reason."

"Don't you believe it!" A man near the middle of the room leaped to his feet, a gas mask perched atop his head. "This is exactly the same response the officials in New York City gave back in '06 during the West Nile spraying. They sprayed the streets without warning! Openly endangering children, blasting pregnant women, exposing innocent unborn babies to . . ." His gaze shifted sideways to the police officer moving closer to his row of chairs. The woman beside him tugged his arm, and he took his seat under the shadow of her umbrella.

The public health officer raised his hands in an attempt to silence the rumbling crowd. "Please," he said after gaining their attention once more, "let's not make comparisons that don't exist. This isn't New York. No one is spraying the streets. We're dealing with an isolated event, and I assure you we are doing everything we can to keep the citizens of Pacific Point safe. We're here to answer your questions." He pointed to a man in the front row. A look of relief passed over his face. "Yes, Doctor?"

As Erin tipped her head to watch, she was more than surprised to spot Sandy sitting in the second row. She'd been released from the ICU only hours ago, and her husband had his arm protectively around her. Even from a distance, Erin could see the anxiety on her face. *Critical stress.*

Erin turned her attention back to the gentleman rising from his chair. He was perhaps midseventies, sporting a silver mustache and dressed in crisp khakis and a denim shirt. Held close to his chest, in what appeared to be a sling-type carrier, was a dark-eyed Chihuahua. The dog stared at his owner, ears quivering and gaze unwavering, as the man began to speak.

"Thank you," the man began, acknowledging the attention of the public health officer. He then addressed the crowd. "If I may, I'd like to add my reassurance in response to these concerns."

Erin was surprised to see Scott offer the man one of his rare smiles.

"You see," the man continued while stroking the dog with one hand, "I have some experience with the subject of fish. I was long employed as a marine biologist and now volunteer my services to the Monterey Bay Aquarium." He chuckled. "And I'll confess to maintaining far too many personal fish tanks in my own home."

Erin's grandmother, sitting beside her, leaned forward in her chair.

"Anyway, the unfortunate demise of those fish you saw on TV was primarily due to the stock pond's small size and its very shallow depth at the point where the barrels were dumped. The fish in the deeper portion of that pond remain clinically healthy. I won't bore you with the mathematical equations, but significant dilution factors are involved. And fortunately, we humans are considerably larger than mosquito fish—" he patted his stomach—"some of us more so than others. And as a Pacific Point citizen, I'm heartened that our city put together this forum. If I can be of assistance to any of my neighbors, I most certainly will."

Then he brushed his hand against his hair in what appeared to be some sort of signal. Scott took a step away from the butterfly banner that rested menacingly atop his head. The elderly fish expert nodded with satisfaction and sat.

Scott took the microphone. He scanned the crowd and settled for an instant on Erin. He shuffled his papers. "In review, let me assure you that a multiagency task force is in place to protect Pacific Point citizens from any ill effects of the pesticide spill. This includes your local police and fire department personnel. Thus far it does not appear that any water other than an isolated ranch has been contaminated. And that is being cleaned up. Extensive water testing is ongoing, and nearly thirty-six hours post–initial incident no further contamination has been found. Bottled drinking water will continue to be supplied by the Red Cross and several local businesses free of charge."

He pointed to a desk laden with flyers and manned by volunteers. "We have lists of local resources available for you. Everything is being done according to strict disaster protocols, and—"

A young woman interrupted by shouting, "I don't care about your protocols and your papers."

TV reporters tripped over themselves to get her on camera.

"I want to know what I'm supposed to tell my six-year-old to help her sleep tonight. Can you tell me that? The little girl who got sprayed attends our school, and she's still in a coma. Now we keep seeing that dead cat on TV. And today I caught my daughter hiding stuffed animals under her bed. She begged me, 'Buy some of those blue umbrellas. It's going to rain more poison!'" The woman's eyes filled with tears, and she brushed them away, then planted her hands on her hips. "My baby's scared to death, and you're standing up there quoting some stupid government manual. What are you going to do about our children? Or don't you care?"

There was scattered applause and a wave of sympathetic murmurs.

Scott glanced at the other officials before leaning toward the microphone. "Ma'am, this forum is designed to provide basic emergency information. I'm afraid at this time we aren't equipped to address—"

Oh no you don't. "Excuse me." Erin leaped to her feet, waving her hand in the air. "Captain McKenna? May I help with this?" She blinked, blinded for an instant by the sudden glare of camera lights. She wasn't sure, but it looked like Scott was frowning. But then, she really didn't care. *Lord, I have to help these people. Help me help them.*

"I'm Erin Quinn," she said, turning to survey the audience. "Let me say first that I'm not a city official. I'm a nurse in the emergency department at Pacific Mercy."

Her name was repeated by a group of reporters, and there was an answering whisper, "Right. She's that charge nurse."

"I just wanted to say that certain feelings of anxiety and stress are normal during events like this." Erin glanced toward the podium and decided that Scott was definitely frowning. "And the county's multiagency task force mentioned by Captain McKenna does include resources to help any citizens who need emotional support, even if the agencies don't have a representative here tonight. It's all part of something called Critical Incident Stress Management, based on an international program put in place to assist victims after disasters like hurricanes and floods, and—" She bit off her words, not wanting to incite the umbrella crowd with further disaster images. "Anyway, what I'm saying is that there is help available through school counselors and volunteer pastors and family service agencies. Right here in Pacific Point."

She glanced at Sandy and her husband. "I've received critical stress training myself, and over the next few days I'll be coordinating with emergency physician Dr. Leigh Stathos and Pacific Mercy Social Services to offer assistance to our own staff as needed." She met the gaze of the young mother who'd spoken. "And I promise that you'll get help too. If you give me your name and phone number after the meeting, I'll see to that personally. Thank you for letting me speak."

There was a vigorous round of applause.

Erin sat, her face flushing.

Iris reached over and squeezed her hand. "Good job, Wonder Woman. But I'm not sure your fire captain is too happy that you commandeered his meeting."

Erin caught the look on Scott's face and groaned. She couldn't agree with her grandmother more. He was looking at Erin like he'd much rather share the stage with a gigantic man-eating butterfly.

She'd have to do some serious damage control.

+++

Get control! Leigh hauled on the braided leather reins, attempting to shorten Frisco's stride and pull him up as the big gelding galloped across the field toward the four-foot pasture fence, his ribs heaving beneath her. She leaned back but he yanked against her, eleven hundred pounds against 130, as the thoroughbred's power exploded vertically in huge up-and-down strides. She planted one fist against his neck and tried to muscle him headfirst into a turn, and he responded with a vigorous buck. *Oh, please, please let me stick. What good is a doctor with a broken neck?*

Frisco bucked a second time, and Leigh stretched tall in the saddle, centered her weight over her stirrups, gathered the reins, and made the only decision she could. They were taking the fence—splintered split rail and perfectly capable of entrapping a horse's leg, taller than anything they'd jumped together before—and had heaven only knew what on the other side. Leigh's stomach lurched. And it was now six strides away . . . five . . . four . . . three.

She rose in her stirrups to a half seat, then slid her hands forward and grabbed a hunk of Frisco's black mane. Two strides . . . one stride . . . Leigh held her breath as her horse's powerful haunches bunched under her before sending his big body spring-loaded into the air . . . and over the fence.

He landed in the soft earth on the other side and skidded sideways, throwing Leigh onto his neck, where she dangled helplessly as he trotted away. She let go and dropped on the seat of her riding breeches into a mud puddle.

Stunned, she sat there for a moment watching as Frisco, reins hanging, slowed to a walk, then stopped and turned to look at her, his dark eyes innocent and soulful. As if to ask, *What are you doing down there?* She stood and pulled off her riding helmet, not sure whether she wanted to laugh or curse. She'd survived.

She was still shaking her head when her cell phone buzzed against the belt loops of her riding breeches. The ICU? She'd asked the staff to let her know if Ana's condition worsened. Despite respiratory support and a second round of antibiotics, she remained comatose and had spiked a foreboding fever. The attending doctors were awaiting results on blood and sputum cultures, while Ana's family kept a vigil in the hospital chapel. It broke Leigh's heart every time she passed by there.

Or the call could be from her troubled half sister. Caroline always had some new drama. Leigh brushed the mud off the phone and answered.

It was Erin. "Leigh? Is that you? You sound funny."

"More like muddy and grateful to be alive. But I'm fine and it's a long story. I'll tell you over coffee—my treat. Any surprises at the town meeting?"

"Not too many. The umbrella people did their best to stir things up, just as we expected. And so far there have been no new exposures, animal or human. But trust me, people are still plenty worried." Erin moaned softly. "I sort of volunteered us to do some critical stress counseling."

"Us?" Leigh took a step to test her legs, and water sluiced in the bottom of her riding boots. "Meaning who?"

"Meaning you and me. And social services," Erin added. "Plus, I'm sure the chaplain would want to be involved with anything that benefited the hospital staff. It may not even be necessary to do a full debriefing, but I've got all the information to offer some one-on-one counseling—"

"Hold it," Leigh interrupted, walking toward Frisco. "You think the hospital staff needs critical stress intervention?" As soon as she asked the question, the image of Ana's pale and now sadly bloated face came to mind, and Leigh felt like a fool. *And how well did I sleep last night?*

"Yes." Erin raised her voice over a commotion in the background. "I do. And it's not only the staff caring for Ana in the ICU. And those last two patients in the telemetry unit. It's our ER team too. Sandy in particular. I saw her right before she was discharged, and she was nervous and panicky. When I said something about coming back to work, she reacted like I'd asked her to jump off a cliff."

Leigh glanced at the intimidating fence behind her. "I think I know that feeling. So what do we do?"

"I'm going to try to meet with social services tomorrow and hopefully get approval to do some initial staff interviews over the next several days. Sort of a pulse check to see how people are feeling and get a sense of whether or not a full department debriefing will be necessary. I think we need to identify any of our staff who might be at risk for critical stress." She sighed. "And at the very least offer some ways to boost resistance for the rest. Who knows when this incident will finally be over? We've all got to hang tough."

"Good point." Leigh looped Frisco's reins over his head and stroked his crooked white blaze. "Dare I ask who will provide stress intervention for the rest of the city?"

Erin chuckled. "Not us. Don't worry. That's the county's responsibility. But hold the good thoughts for your charge nurse, okay? I'm on my way to convince Scott McKenna that there are a few key chapters missing from his beloved book of rules. And I don't think our gladiator is going to like it one bit."

Fifteen minutes later, Leigh slid down from her saddle and ran up the metal stirrups. She led Frisco to the stable's grooming area, empty except for a barn worker pushing a cart piled high with soiled shavings. Located in the breezeway between long rows of stalls, the grooming area was equipped with thick, rubber-matted floors and lengths of chain attached to railroad-tie posts in order to secure horses safely. Nearby were wash racks, also fitted with rubber mats and ties, and hot running water—something Leigh could use herself right about now. She glanced down at her muddy breeches and boots with a grimace. Then pressed her palm against the big thoroughbred's chest and clucked, encouraging him to step backward into the cross ties.

Frisco did so obediently, and Leigh felt a rush of affection for the three-year-old bay, knowing that his earlier rowdiness was due to youth and inexperience and not any malicious streak. He was getting used to new surroundings, the same way Leigh was. Also not his fault.

She shook her head, wondering how many horsewomen she'd treated in the ER for everything from smashed toes to fractured ribs to a broken pelvis who'd insisted it was their fault, not their horses'. Only another horse lover could understand that logic. And then there was the paraplegic woman at the Santa Rosa horse show, reaching up to brush her horse from an electric wheelchair . . .

Nick's words drifted back before Leigh could stop them. *"And you complain that what I do is dangerous?"*

She complained because it *was* dangerous. But then Leigh didn't so much complain as worry. Sweaty palms, pounding heart, and antacids-by-the-handful kind of worry. Lying awake at 2 a.m. listening to the police scanner, knowing Nick was headed for a methamphetamine bust, hostage standoff, or a freeway sniper arrest. Horrible, danger-fraught situations, but she knew Nick would be pumped from the moment he got the call, eager to go and right the wrong, make the neighborhood safe. She'd seen that need over and over in his dark eyes. He'd almost tremble with anticipation, like her horse under saddle tonight.

But she'd seen Nick bristle defensively, too, when Leigh begged him to ask for a transfer and told him she couldn't bear the thought of getting a call saying he'd been shot, killed. She tried to explain that as an ER physician she'd been on the receiving end of too many tragedies and wouldn't even consider bringing children into that anxious existence. He told her she would never understand what only another cop could understand.

They began a downward spiral of pleading and arguments,

demands and ultimatums, slammed doors. Desperate need, aching loneliness. When Leigh finally mentioned separation, her indigestion turned to outright nausea and bone-deep fatigue. She had trouble concentrating at work. Then a fellow officer, Nick's best friend, was killed in a high-speed chase. And not long afterward Nick finally found the understanding he was looking for. In the arms of the slain officer's sister. During the humiliating and sleepless aftermath of that painful revelation, Leigh confirmed her suspicion that she was pregnant and then miscarried several weeks later. She didn't tell him.

Leigh grabbed a splintered post, dizzy for a moment, and gritted her teeth, determined to push the memories down. No good could come from remembering the past. It was why she'd left San Francisco. No husband. No baby. No reason to stay. And now she had things more or less under control.

Leigh groaned as she reached for a buckle on her horse's bridle. *Under control?* Right. Except for risking her neck on that fence, dealing with an ongoing chemical disaster, losing sleep over that child in the ICU, and watching her triage nurse collapse in the ER. And now she could be forced to participate in crisis counseling. *Crisis counseling.* She was laughing at the pathetic irony of that when her cell phone buzzed for a second time against the waistband of her breeches. What did Erin have up her sleeve now?

She smiled at a passing horse owner, then punched the button on the cell phone and leaned against Frisco's warm shoulder. "Speak to me," she growled dramatically.

There was a stretch of silence and then a familiar, deep chuckle. "Okay," Nick said slowly. "I will, then. I wanted you to know that my Guard unit is on standby in case things get worse with your pesticide incident."

Leigh's brain stuttered. "Guard?"

"National Guard. I'm still a reserve; you know that. A memo came out today. If those national environmental activists decide to fly in, or if you end up having to do evacuations—"

"We won't," Leigh said, not even caring that she sounded like a fool. *Don't come here.* "Why are you telling me this?"

There was another long stretch of silence, and Leigh hated that her hands trembled.

"Because I thought you should know there's a chance I may be coming to Pacific Point, and . . ." Nick sighed. "And I thought maybe I could see you."

Leigh wanted to throw the phone. To cry. But mostly she was afraid to know . . . "Why?" she asked, her mouth suddenly dry.

"Because it's been more than three months since you left." Nick's tone sharpened. "You loaded your horse into that trailer and took off without telling me. You left our house."

"I send you a mortgage check the first of every month."

"That's not what I mean." Nick voice softened. "I'm trying to say that we never . . . talked. We never really talked about all this. We need to. And it would be better face-to-face. Even if the Guard doesn't send me, I think I should come anyway. I want to see you."

Leigh forced herself to take a slow breath. Her heart thudded in her ears, exactly as it had when she'd grabbed Frisco's mane and prepared to face that terrifying fence. *I have to do this.*

"Leigh?"

"Don't come. I'm filing for divorce."

CHAPTER NINE

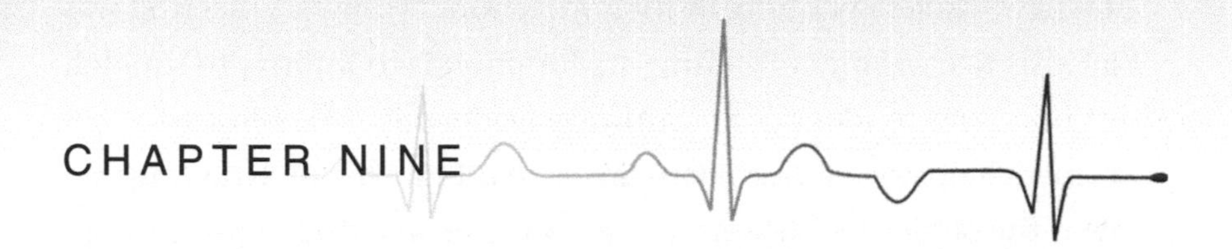

When Erin marched toward him, Scott reached up to gingerly touch his shoulder. Not the injury from his ocean skirmish but the site where she'd given that tetanus shot—it ached like a son of a gun. And after tonight's meeting, he sensed his discomfort had barely begun; this nurse could become a royal pain . . . Scott's throat constricted. *Ah, man. Does she have to be so beautiful?*

Tall and lean and dressed in jeans, with a sea green sweater over a simple white shirt, Erin looked fresh and wholesome. Like one of those women on the cover of a healthy living magazine. Or maybe a young mother headed to a PTA meeting. As she drew closer, her eyes narrowed. *Uh-oh.* Not PTA. And definitely not good for his health. But too late now.

"So," she said, arriving at where he stood beside the table of county brochures, "exactly how irked are you that I added my two cents to your meeting?" She raised her gaze to his and then, to Scott's relief, offered a slow smile. "On a scale of one to ten. Be honest."

"Ten being if you'd actually called me an insensitive clod?"

"Ouch. Good thing I reconsidered that." Erin crossed her arms, then seemed to think twice about it, letting her hands rest casually on her hips instead. "But you understand what I was saying?

Psychological support is an integral part of disaster management."

"I know that." Scott glanced away for a moment and spotted a TV news camera panning in their direction. "Tonight's meeting was a Crisis Management Briefing. Its function is to inform, to squelch rumors, and to identify community leadership." He blinked as TV camera lights swept past them and toward the mayor, who lingered near the podium. "We weren't here to offer any kind of psychological Band-Aid."

"Band-Aid? Is that what you think that young mother was looking for? Her daughter's afraid of poison rain!" Erin's eyes flashed. "How many more children are worrying about things like that? How many elderly folks? And have you thought about—?" She frowned as camera lights nearly blinded them both.

A reporter extended a microphone. "Amy Carson, Action News, here with Pacific Mercy nurse Erin Quinn and Captain Scott McKenna of the Pacific Point Fire Department. And it appears that they—"

"Have no comment," Scott interjected firmly. "We have no comment." He glanced at Erin, relieved that she appeared to agree. "And we're leaving now."

He waited beside Erin until the news crew stepped away. "I'm sorry, but I've had all I can take from those people."

"Me too. But I'd like to finish our discussion and maybe go over our disaster review. Are you really leaving now?"

"Actually, I said *we* were leaving. Meaning you and I." He shrugged and his shoulder cramped with pain, very likely a warning he was about to do something stupid. "How about if we go somewhere and get some coffee?"

"Sure." She looked around the room. "My grandmother and I

drove separately, but I should find her and . . . Oh, there she is." She clucked her tongue. "I knew it; she's cornered that cute old gentleman."

Scott easily spotted the elegant red-haired woman dressed in a long khaki skirt and boots. He chuckled. "Yes. His Chihuahua always draws the ladies. He's taught it to sort of . . . yodel." He saw Erin's brows rise. "I'm serious. He yodels."

"Well, regardless, I'm sure they're talking about fish. He said he was some kind of expert, and Nana probably has the oldest living goldfish on earth. I warn her all the time about trusting strangers. But at least that guy looks pretty safe."

Scott smothered a laugh. "I wouldn't be so sure about that. I hear he comes from a long line of insensitive clods."

"Huh?"

"That's Dr. Hugh McKenna. My grandfather."

She glanced over her shoulder, then back at Scott, a grin lighting her face. "You're serious?"

Scott smiled back, enjoying her delight. "Swear. And don't worry about your grandmother. Granddad is a far better man than I am."

"So you're saying I should be having coffee with him?"

"Probably. Except he thinks Arlo Popp has no business serving coffee."

"We're going to the bait shop?"

Scott's face warmed as he realized what a fool he was. He'd invited the most beautiful woman he'd ever met to a place that sold live sardines. "No . . . I meant I need to stop by there to pick up a tide table." He touched his bandaged shoulder. "Need to time my swims better so I won't take up valuable space on your ER gurneys. But we'll get coffee somewhere else."

"Arlo's is great. You can't beat the coffee. It's on my route home, and you live that way too. So we can meet there." Erin motioned toward the clutch of lingering reporters. "Besides, meeting at Arlo's means far less chance of being cornered by the media." Her eyes met his. "Thank you for agreeing to talk with me. I really do want us to try to be on the same page with our disaster support."

"No problem," Scott answered, realizing that he'd almost forgotten the reason they were having coffee together. For the last few minutes he'd only been thinking about spending time with her.

"Good. Not only because we need to get our tactical efforts coordinated for future events, but because I've seen the effects that traumatic stress can have on people. In my last job at Sierra Mercy, one of my staff nearly lost her life as a result." Erin winced. "You never know for sure who's at risk or what's the final straw for someone's ability to cope. I don't want that to ever happen here."

+++

Liars and worse. Sarge held the mop across his chest, shoulders squared and jaw tense as he gave the lobby TV his rapt attention. News clips from the town meeting, that blonde interviewing the mayor. The city official preened for the camera, his Adam's apple bobbing above a carefully knotted polka-dot tie. "This was an isolated event," he insisted, "and we have things well under control. My first priority is the safety of Pacific Point citizens."

Isolated event? A plane loaded with barrels of poison? Sarge's fingers clenched against the wooden mop handle. Did it have to crash into a building before anyone paid attention? Did the body count have to rise? He turned his attention back to the final clip, a young mother pleading for a child terrified by the poisonings. *"What are you going to do about our children? Or don't you care?"*

They didn't. But he did. The children had to be safe. Which was exactly why he'd be in that closet tonight, watching the boy. He turned at the sound of a voice.

"Hey, Sarge!" A male ICU nurse, wearing a fleece jacket over his scrubs, made his way toward the doors to the parking lot. He slowed his stride and tapped his watch. "Overtime again? You're too easy. Day shift, night shift. When do you ever sleep?"

"No problem. Anyway—" Sarge forced a smile—"I hear sleep's overrated." *Especially when there's a mission to accomplish.* He gave the nurse a sharp salute and watched him walk away. Then he glanced toward the Little Mercies Gift Shop. A few packages of beef jerky would be good to have on hand in the closet upstairs. He'd buy some, go to the apartment, grab a few hours sleep, then head back to the hospital. Night watch. He knew it well.

+++

Scott climbed out of his truck and leaned against its door, waiting for Erin. He could smell the coffee. He'd called his mother on his cell, and she'd had a good visit with Cody, though she'd kept it short because Scott's stepdad stayed home after all. Gary's diabetes was getting harder to control. But she said Cody was upbeat despite having his IV changed and still dealing with some leg pain.

The kid was such a trouper. And so mature for his age. Thoughtful too. He'd insisted that he was big enough so no one had to stay overnight with him. Scott's mother had been uncomfortable with the idea despite Cody's plea, "Please don't treat me like a baby." So Scott finally intervened, reassuring his parents that Cody was a favorite with the Pacific Mercy pediatrics staff. He'd get plenty of attention.

Scott turned as Erin's gray Subaru pulled up.

She rolled down the window and sniffed the air, then laughed, her eyes teasing. "Hey, Captain, think we can get a side of squid to go with that coffee?"

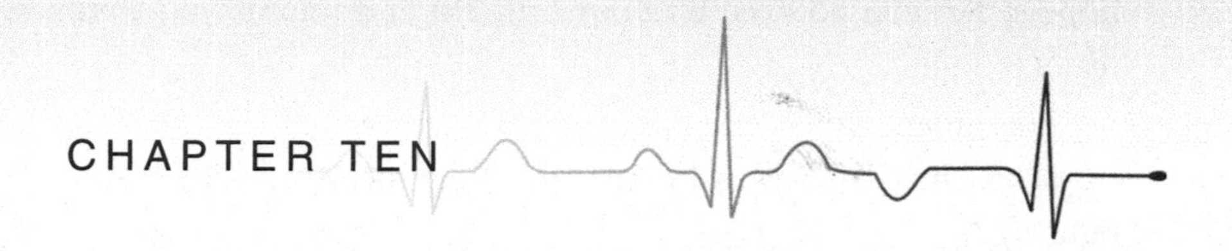

CHAPTER TEN

Annie Popp glanced first at Scott and then at Erin, and in an instant Erin felt strangely self-conscious in a bait shop she'd visited all her life. But then, she'd never walked in here with the best-looking man she'd ever met. *Don't say anything, Annie. Please.*

"Hey, Annie," Erin began casually, inhaling the rich scent of coffee and what she'd bet were fresh-baked lemon bars. "How's it—?"

"Well, would you look at this?" The gray-haired proprietress set down a pair of needle-nose pliers, and a grin lit her sun-weathered face. "My Sea Dog black and my Starfish Latte extra cinnamon. Together." She swept aside several pieces of sea glass and driftwood, then planted her palms on the counter, sighing as if the planets had finally aligned. "Praise God, it's about time."

"About time?" Scott asked.

"That you two met, of course." Annie nodded and her earrings, blue glass and silver beads, swayed back and forth. "I told Arlo it makes no sense, you battling that cold ocean like a tortured soul every morning. All alone. And you, Erin. How many summers have you been coming here with your grandmother? And your grandfather, may he rest in peace. I'll never forget that Labor Day weekend Iris was sewing your Wonder Woman costume. You paraded down here in your bathing suit twirling a gold lasso, with that crown sitting lopsided over your pigtails and all those 'magic' bracelets. Skinned knees, no front teeth, and knee-high to a grass-hopper. But you doubled up your little fist and told us you were ready to fight."

Erin groaned.

Scott chuckled low in his throat. "Trust me, Annie. She's still fighting."

"I am—we are, actually. That's why we're here. Trying to coordinate our disaster plans and help Pacific Point citizens deal with all that's happening right now." Erin glanced at Scott, wondering if there was really any chance he'd cooperate with what she had in mind. This meeting could be as misguided as hoisting an umbrella against poison rain.

"Good," Annie said, her grin fading into an expression of concern. "I saw that news piece with the young mother at the town meeting. Scared to death, poor dear." She grabbed a couple of Get Hooked on Our Coffee cups and then squinted over her shoulder. "You looked good on TV, Scott. Handsome as Superman. But be careful where you stand. It looked like a butterfly was having you for dinner.

"The fact is, this whole pesticide problem is hurting our little town. People aren't fishing as much, scared they'll pull in something poisonous, I suppose. I'm selling more bottled water than coffee." She waved toward the sea glass and driftwood mobiles dangling in the window. "And the art's for my soul, not income."

Annie checked the milk steamer. "Anything you can do to help our town through this mess would be a blessing." She turned back. "And you two take your coffee outside . . . enjoy the sea air. There's more to life than fighting."

Except they were sparring in less than fifteen minutes. Or so it seemed to Erin. Sea air, a glorious sunset looming on the horizon, and even Annie's lemon bars hadn't changed anything. They were sitting at a table overlooking the beach, but they might as well have been facing each other from opposite corners at Madison Square Garden. Too bad she didn't have her gloves. She should have stuck to discussing their incident review. He clearly wasn't happy she'd steered the conversation toward the subject of critical stress.

Erin shifted on the bench and glanced at Arlo's Bait & Moor, sighing when she saw the window blinds spring quickly back into place. Annie Popp, hopeless romantic, was undoubtedly expecting Erin to be holding Scott's hand right about now or feeding him bits of lemon bar while staring soulfully into his eyes. *Those eyes. As gray as a stormy ocean.*

Erin looked at Scott, who was, as usual, impossible to read and as rigid as his coffee choice. Sea Dog black. Why wasn't she surprised? The man was an emotionless robot. She frowned and touched her fingertip to the last crumbs of lemon bar. "Well," she began again, "at least it's good to know you're familiar with the various components of Critical Incident Stress Management, and—"

"I am. I told you that. But we've already accomplished what's called for in community disaster protocol." Scott raised his big hand, ticking off the items on his fingers. "Crisis Management Briefing: identify local leaders, provide information and resources, answer questions, quell rumors, and promote a renewed sense of community wellness."

"Wellness?" How many times had they gone over this? Erin willed herself to stay calm, tried to count to ten. And made it to four. Barely. "How do you suggest we check *wellness* off our list?" She leaned forward. "Have Tinker Bell come and sprinkle fairy dust?"

A muscle twitched along Scott's jaw, and he was silent . . . for ten full beats. "The town meeting isn't meant to address personal psychological symptoms. What you're suggesting now is a debriefing."

"Maybe. If it comes to that and only after the disaster response has completely ended. That could be several more days . . . or longer. I'm thinking more of one-on-one counseling at this point. Talking with staff, checking for signs of stress. With the help of social services and the hospital chaplain. For each affected department, like ICU and ER. We all dealt with Sandy's collapse. And Ana's still in a coma." She watched Scott's expression and continued warily. "Maybe you could offer the same assistance to the firefighters involved at the plane crash, with cleanup, and on-site at Pacific Mercy. Like Sandy's husband, Chuck."

Scott raised his brows but said nothing.

"You know, talk about symptoms of traumatic stress, offer ways to cope, and follow up if needed. That way, we could all get some closure." She saw Scott wince. "What?"

"Closure?" he asked with a barely concealed smirk. "You're offering Freud in place of Tinker Bell?" He raised his palm before she could speak. "Look, what I'm saying is that type of psychological first aid isn't universally accepted."

"Johns Hopkins isn't good enough for you?" Erin taunted, wondering if the peeping Annie Popp would call the police if she took a swing at the arrogant fire captain.

"I'm familiar with Hopkins's three *R*s: resistance, resilience, and recovery. I told you I've studied critical stress. On paper, I can understand the plan. Medical and rescue personnel are under the gun 24-7; I know that personally. And who doesn't want to protect themselves and their fellow coworkers from the effects of stress? What's that phrase used for medical personnel? 'Healing the healers'?"

"Yes," Erin answered, impressed that Scott had done his homework—or girded himself for battle against her. She still wasn't sure which.

He exhaled slowly. "Well, I'm not disputing the need for that. And I've seen plenty of good outcomes as a result of counseling. . . ."

"But?"

"But in some cases there's a risk." Scott's eyes seemed to darken, their gray less like the sea and more like a deep bruise. "Emotions are unpredictable. Sometimes you stir up the embers and everybody gets burned."

He turned and looked toward the beach below. The sun, dipping toward the horizon, cast an orangey gold glow over his features and broad shoulders, almost as if he were indeed battling a blaze.

"Everybody gets burned." Erin opened her mouth but wasn't sure what she could say. It was true; asking people to examine their feelings and express them in a group setting was uncomfortable at best. Health and rescue workers often viewed that as weakness. And some studies showed debriefings had in fact worsened symptoms in a small percentage of people. There was even reluctance to use the term these days. Scott was right about that. But she wasn't suggesting a full-scale debriefing at this point. Still, there was something about the look in his eyes just now that had nothing to do with statistics or his ever-present book of procedures. His wariness of counseling was personal for him. Why?

When Scott turned back, the bruised look in his eyes was gone. "Want to continue this fight on the beach?" He pointed at a large rock near the seawall. "Someone didn't douse that fire pit. I should put it out."

Erin shook her head slowly. "Sure. You, me, Tinker Bell, Freud, and now Smokey the Bear. I wouldn't miss that match."

She followed Scott to the steps that led down the cliff to the beach, pausing to glance toward the bait shop. Rosy sunlight glinted on dozens of sea glass mobiles dangling from the covered porch. Arlo Popp, his Einstein-wild hair as white as ocean foam, stood beside his wife, and they both waved with obvious approval. Erin could almost hear Annie boasting about her matchmaking success with Sea Dog black and Starfish Latte extra cinnamon. The woman couldn't know this beach stroll had nothing to do with romance and everything to do with dousing a campfire and continuing a skirmish.

Erin still wanted the captain's cooperation with counseling of affected staff—his as well as hers—but something about his earlier reaction made her think she needed to change her strategy. Sometimes you had to hold your punches and learn to read your opponent.

She waved to the Popps, then followed Scott McKenna into the sunset . . . for round two.

+++

"This is perfect." Iris lifted the framed message and smiled across the shop at Little Mercies' aging volunteer Helen Cary. "I'm going to tuck it away for my granddaughter's birthday next month. Erin wants new sparring gloves, but this is much more appropriate."

"One of the Scripture plaques?"

"No." Iris glanced down at the small frame. "It's an inspirational message called 'A Strong Woman vs. a Woman of Strength.' Just listen to this line:

"A strong woman works out every day . . .

but a woman of strength kneels to pray, keeping her soul in shape . . ."

"It reminds me of Erin." Iris's gaze dropped to another line, and a lump rose in her throat. She read it silently.

A strong woman makes mistakes and avoids the same for tomorrow . . .

a woman of strength realizes life's mistakes . . . thanking God for the blessings as she capitalizes on them . . .

She blinked against unexpected tears. *And that one's for me, Lord. Thank you.*

"So, now that we've got you squared away with your uniform," Helen said, glancing at the hanger she'd retrieved from the storeroom, "you'll be here tomorrow morning, then?" She tipped her head and her blonde wig shifted a little off center. "To start volunteer training?"

"Bright and early," Iris answered, realizing that she really was looking forward to it. It felt better than anything had in a long time. Maybe because she'd been a nurse for so many years, or because Erin hovered too much lately, but she needed to feel needed again. It was as simple as that. "And I've decided to make myself available for all the volunteer positions, not only the gift shop. I could deliver the flowers and mail or take the library cart around."

"Or help with the kids upstairs," Helen suggested. "One of our other volunteers is a retired nurse too, and she likes to work more closely with the patients. Up in pediatrics, there's this sweet little boy—" She stopped and smiled as a man walked through the doorway. "Hi there, Sarge. You're here late today."

"Needed a snack . . . for the road." The man, easily six feet tall and husky, maybe in his forties, had his hair in a ponytail and wore a battered leather jacket over tan scrubs. His eyes met Iris's for a moment before he glanced down and cleared his throat. Shy, she guessed.

Iris scanned the birthday cards, glancing occasionally toward the register as Helen, chatting away, rang up at least a dozen packages of beef jerky and some Twinkies. No . . . the man put the Twinkies back after turning the package over in his big hands a few times, like a factory worker doing a quality inspection.

"That ought to hold you," Helen chirped as she handed him his change. "Don't eat them all in one place, okay?"

"I'll ration them—promise." He turned, offered Iris the barest hint of a smile, then limped back into the lobby.

Iris shook her head as the thought struck her. Now that she was officially a volunteer, this shy man was a fellow employee. One of many she'd be meeting and working alongside. Getting to know. Wasn't that always part of the appeal when she was nurse? Never-ending drama, opportunities to be of real help, being part of a team of diverse people with a single mission. She was seventy-seven and still had adventures ahead. That could only be a good thing.

"I watched Erin on TV tonight," Helen said as she rang up Iris's purchases. "She's got spunk, that granddaughter of yours. For a minute I thought she was going to tackle that young fire captain." She giggled and ran a hand over her lopsided wig. "Of course, if I were ten years younger, I'd probably tackle him myself."

Iris raised her brows.

"All right, thirty years younger." Helen sighed. "But he's worth breaking a hip. Did you see those shoulders?"

+++

"How's your shoulder?"

Scott dumped the last of the seawater from a rusty coffee can onto the fire pit, then met Erin's gaze. There were tiny flecks of copper in the green of her eyes. He looked away to set the can down. "Which shoulder?" he asked, standing. He couldn't resist the smirk. "The one I bashed against the rock or the one you got ahold of?"

Erin groaned. "Touché. But, honestly, tetanus shots just plain ache. I wasn't trying to hurt you. . . ." Her words faded.

When he met her gaze again, her expression was so openly caring that he was caught completely off guard by her sincerity and the way she looked, standing in the sand in that green sweater with the sea breeze playing with her long hair and deepening sunlight turning it all shades of gold and red . . . like a California wildfire. Scott blinked. What was he doing? He'd come down here to put out a fire, not start one. And he needed to talk this stubborn nurse out of dragging him into a psychological circus he had no time for and no faith in. Besides, he wasn't looking for a relationship. He drew in a deep breath of briny sea air and was relieved when Erin broke the silence with a question.

"You swim here a lot?" she asked after scanning the shoreline.

"Yes. The currents are challenging. It's good training for Ocean Rescue."

"So you battle the 'cold ocean like a tortured soul'?" Erin's eyes crinkled at the edges. "Isn't that how Annie put it?"

"Annie Popp is prone to quoting Scripture and to colorful storytelling. But then you probably already know that, Wonder Woman." He chuckled, thinking of a little girl with pigtails, a crown, and a doubled-up fist. "Sounds like she had you pegged as a fighter from the start."

"You'll be relieved to know I gave up the Lasso of Truth. I think it turned into a dog leash." Erin lifted her chin. "But I've got red boxing gloves."

He raised his brows and she laughed. "Seriously. It's a great workout. And a good way to let off steam. Maybe punching my speed bag is like your swims." She sighed, and her expression grew serious. "But then some things are worth fighting for, and some . . ." She turned toward the ocean, took a step away, and the soft crashing of the waves muffled the rest of her words.

Scott wasn't sure, but he thought she'd added, "Things are worth fighting against."

Erin crossed her arms and walked farther; Scott followed, feeling certain that the tentative conversation was about to turn back to business. She was going to bring up the critical stress counseling again. He was surprised when she didn't.

"My grandmother's worth any fight," Erin said.

Scott drew alongside. He shortened his stride to match hers, and their feet sank side by side in the sand as they walked, hers leaving prints much smaller than his.

"She's an incredible woman, honest and loyal . . . a rock all my life. Nana marched in protests during the sixties, traveled with the Peace Corps, and volunteered at mission clinics in places that would scare the wits out of me. But she's been through way too many hard times these past few years. She's lost so much. Hurt too long." Erin glanced at Scott, and the look in her eyes made his breath catch. "It breaks my heart, you know?"

Scott stared out at the sea, struggling against a familiar ache. His family. Their losses. He turned back to Erin, and the words slipped out before he could stop them. "I do know. It's how I feel about Cody."

Erin brushed a strand of hair away from her face. "You said he was in the hospital for an infection. It was something serious, then?"

"They're concerned he might develop osteomyelitis. Be at risk for losing his leg." Scott jammed his hands into his pockets. "They've been fighting it for a few months now. He's only ten."

"Oh no. How did that start?"

"His leg was crushed in a car accident. Almost a year ago. He's had so many surgeries on the muscles, the vessels, the nerves. . . ." Scott swallowed against the tightness in his throat. "He's the bravest person I've known. Ever."

Scott faced the ocean and felt Erin's hand rest lightly on his arm. For a while they stood there silently watching the sun, huge and ember orange, slip under the purple edge of the sea, and for some reason a sense of peace washed over him. Not like a wave. It was more of an eddy . . . like one of those fleeting, inexplicable warm spots he'd enter while dragging his body stroke after stroke through the bone-chilling sea.

"I'm sorry," Erin whispered, her fingers warm even through his jacket sleeve. "His parents must be so—"

"They're dead. My sister and her husband were killed in the accident." Scott fought the pain and anger threatening to drown him like always. Her eyes widened, and he knew he was about to horrify her. "The car was traveling over ninety miles an hour. And the report confirmed that my brother-in-law swerved into that power pole deliberately. To kill them all. Colleen tried to grab the wheel, begged him . . . Cody remembers everything."

CHAPTER ELEVEN

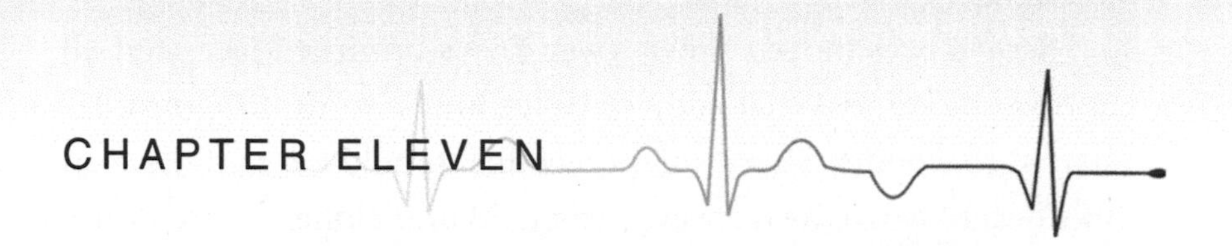

Erin gasped. "Oh, that poor boy. I don't know what to say."

Scott sighed, wishing he'd said nothing at all. Why had he done that? "You don't have to say anything, but . . ."

"But what?"

"Don't expect me to jump on board any of that psychological business. My brother-in-law had anger issues, was emotionally abusive. My sister tried to save her marriage, but everything only got worse and worse. They separated and he began harassing her. She was advised to take out a restraining order, but he volunteered to get counseling, so she held off." Scott swallowed hard. "Cody's father came directly from his therapist's office the night of the accident. He'd been going for months, and—" he stared into Erin's eyes and nodded to be sure she got it—"the doctors think he just snapped."

Erin hugged her arms around herself. "And you think something like that could happen because of peer counseling? That my staff, yours . . . Sandy, Chuck, any of them might be at risk? You think it's safer to let them work things out by themselves?"

He heard the skepticism in her voice and saw determination in the way she'd lifted her chin. The woman who'd challenged him that first day at the hospital barricade, a fighter for her staff and her grandmother. Wonder Woman with a splash of freckles and pair of red boxing gloves. What was he going to do with that? He wanted to shake sense into her, but at the same time, he wanted . . . *what?*

Scott's eyes moved slowly over Erin's upturned face, and all at once he wanted that eddy of peace and warmth to return. He started to wonder what it might feel like to hold her right here on this beach, where he'd always been cold and alone. . . . He nearly jumped when his cell phone buzzed on his belt.

"McKenna," he barked. "Really?" he said after listening for a few moments. Relief washed over him. "And what about the latest water samples? . . ." He nodded and paced a few steps as the fire chief went over the details.

Erin followed. The look on her face said she was ready to punch him if he didn't let her in on what was happening.

"So when does it go on the local channels? . . . Good. Thank you for the update." When Scott disconnected, he found Erin peering at him from mere inches away. So close . . . but taking her in his arms was never an option anyway. He'd settle for giving her some good news and avoiding a kidney punch.

"Well?" she asked, raising her voice over the sound of a boat engine in the distance.

"We've had some reassurance from the EPA. They feel that even if the farmer's records were off by several barrels, the contamination couldn't be as bad as we'd feared. And the newest water samples are clean. They'll continue to test for at least another week, and we'll still be drinking bottled water, but so far so good."

Erin's breath escaped in a rush. "Thank the Lord. This is such good news."

Scott barely had time to nod before Erin launched herself

against him in an exuberant hug, her arms around his back, her face against his jacket, and her silky hair brushing his chin. He felt, crazily, like a kid finding his dream gift under the Christmas tree. She was warm, soft, and smelled like . . . extra cinnamon. A rush of warmth made him dizzy for an instant. "Hey, what's all this?" he asked, his lips moving against her hair, as he wondered what to do with his dangling arms.

Before he could decide, Erin stepped away. "Thank you for telling me. I mean, I'm sure somewhere in some book, you weren't supposed to do that until it comes out officially on the news. My grandmother will be so encouraged. It's a glimmer of hope, and I'm so relieved. Thank you, Scott."

"No problem," he said with a casual shrug, trying to convince himself it was that boat engine, not his heart, pounding in his ears. "Let's get back up there. I want to call Cody. He won't admit it, but the news coverage has been worrying him. I want him to know things are looking safer."

+++

Sarge padded as quietly as he could across the darkened patient room, switched the water bottle for a safe one, turned to leave, then stopped, teetering for an instant on his prosthesis. Cody was awake. Even though Sarge waited nearly thirty minutes after the TV had been turned off.

"Rich?"

"Yes," Sarge whispered after glancing furtively at the doorway to the corridor. No sign of the night nurses. It was around eleven thirty; they were probably still in report. He'd be fired if he was found here. He'd never expected to interact with Cody—just protect him from afar. Check on him now and then as he slept.

Keeping watch, as much as he could, from his base in the housekeeping closet next door. When the boy awoke that first time and assumed he was one of the nurses, he didn't correct him. *Rich. The night nurse.* That's who Sarge was to Cody Sorenson.

The boy giggled. "I can tell it's you even in the dark. You have that squeaky shoe."

Squeaky plastic leg. "That's right. Maybe I need an oilcan, like the Tin Woodman in *The Wizard of Oz*. You know that story?"

"Sure. But that's kid stuff. I'm ten, you know. I like those old comic books you brought. They're cool."

"Good." Sarge searched his fuzzy memories, trying to recall his own son at age ten. *Does Ricky remember me?* He pushed the thought away. "Go to sleep, okay?"

Cody sighed. "Okay. But could you bring me that medicine first? My leg's getting sore again."

"You'll have to push the call button. Pills aren't my job."

"Only water bottles?"

"Mm-hmm." Sarge needed to get back to the closet before someone saw him. Then watch the hallway and slip down to the south wing when it was clear. "And keeping you safe. That's my real job. To keep you safe. Remember that."

Five minutes later, Sarge settled into the housekeeping closet. He had thirty minutes left on his scheduled meal break. The rest of the sparse night staff, if they even noticed his absence, would assume he'd gone to the cafeteria or lounge. He preferred it here—and the mission left him no choice. He had bottled water, beef jerky, and an aluminum baseball bat. If the enemy came for the boy, he was ready.

The town meeting was an obvious attempt at a cover-up, the officials either paid off or part of the conspiracy. But then Sarge might have believed that be-happy-don't-worry garbage himself a few weeks ago. When his brain was still full of those medications. A different kind of poison but a poison nonetheless, designed to dumb him down and keep him content with scrubbing toilets and mopping up delivery room floors. And to keep him unaware of what they were planning, make him forget he was a warrior. Flushing those pills was the best decision he'd made in years. He didn't care if the nightmares returned or if he heard the rocket fire, felt the stifling desert heat, inhaled the acrid rubber of the gas mask, or . . . *If I see the faces of the dead civilians.* Nausea rose and he swallowed it back. Saving this boy was worth the risk. Sarge leaned against the storeroom wall and pulled the bat onto his lap.

+++

Erin set her toothbrush down and glanced at the stained-glass panel in the bathroom window. Its purple, red, and green shards glistened with shower steam, almost as if the sword and shield were lifted in some stormy battle. How long had it taken her to make that window hanging? She wasn't sure, but it filled those awful weeks when thoughts of her father left her sleepless and agitated and unspeakably angry. The painstaking process of drawing a pattern, cutting the glass, wrapping the edges with foil, and applying the solder—building something instead of smashing things like she'd been so tempted to do—saved her life that summer. *And my soul?*

Erin sighed, thinking of Annie Popp working day after day with glass too. "Art for my soul," she'd said. But Annie's designs were so different, fragments of pale glass tumbled by the sea. Green, amber, a dozen shades of blue, bits that were once clear and now frosty opaque, all strung on fishing line, suspended in the sunshine and balanced by pieces of wood she'd collected from the beach. Driftwood. Like in Erin's childhood musings, when she'd imagine Jesus using a piece of driftwood to conduct the rhythm of the waves, the sound peaceful and comforting as she waited for sleep. And so very different from the way the ocean seemed now, restless and unsettling. And lonely. Although tonight, walking on the beach with Scott . . .

Erin raised a comb to her towel-dried hair, noticing in the mirror that she was flushing. *I hugged him.* Her stomach fluttered as she remembered being close to him, the solid muscles of his back, his warm breath against her hair. She chuckled, thinking of Scott's surprise at her spontaneous hug, how he'd stood there almost holding his breath, with his arms dangling at his sides. He'd be far more comfortable with a fire ax in his hands. The man didn't do emotion.

No, that wasn't true. He was clearly troubled when he'd told her the details of his nephew's medical problems. And that tragic car accident, which he felt was a direct result of counseling gone wrong. She grimaced, thinking of Cody hearing his mother scream, watching her struggle to gain control after his agitated, hopeless father pressed the accelerator down and aimed their car toward a power pole. Was it true? Had a psychological intervention pushed that man over the brink? And could peer counseling and a possible stress debriefing be similarly risky for Erin's ER staff?

She pulled the comb through her hair, encountered a snarl, and picked at it with the teeth of the comb. Scott could be right; maybe the counseling wasn't necessary. Maybe she'd imagined that fear in Sandy's eyes when they'd talked about her returning to work. After all, the TV news had already reported that the risk of water contamination was far less than what was feared, and recent testing showed no evidence of poisons. There wasn't any reason to believe her staff wasn't as resilient as she was. Maybe they could all just take a deep breath and forget this disaster ever happened. Go back to life as normal.

She turned at the sound of her grandmother's voice calling from the living room.

"Erin? Will you help me with this?"

She set her comb down and walked barefoot to the living room to find her grandmother kneeling in front of Elmer Fudd's aquarium. As usual, the old goldfish's nose was pressed to the glass, his mouth opening and closing placidly as he peered outward.

"The lid keeps dropping," Iris explained. "Will you hold it up for me so I can add enough water to—?"

"Water?" Erin's gaze darted to the pitcher on the floor next to the tank. "Which water? Is that from the tap? Oh no. Did you already pour some in there?" She hurried forward, stomach churning at intruding images of floating fish and a little girl sobbing over her dead cat. She was being irrational; she knew it. She'd just showered in the water. It was safe. But . . .

Iris let the tank cover close. "I didn't put any in yet, but I did get it out of the kitchen faucet. Isn't that okay now? The news said the water was showing no signs of contamination, so I thought . . . Erin?"

What am I doing? "Let's use the bottled water. Just until we get the last of the reports. I'll help you." Erin fought a shiver that had less to do with her wet hair and far more to do with a decision she'd just made. Her staff needed a stress check—maybe Erin did too. She'd get permission to go ahead with peer counseling this week whether Scott McKenna approved or not.

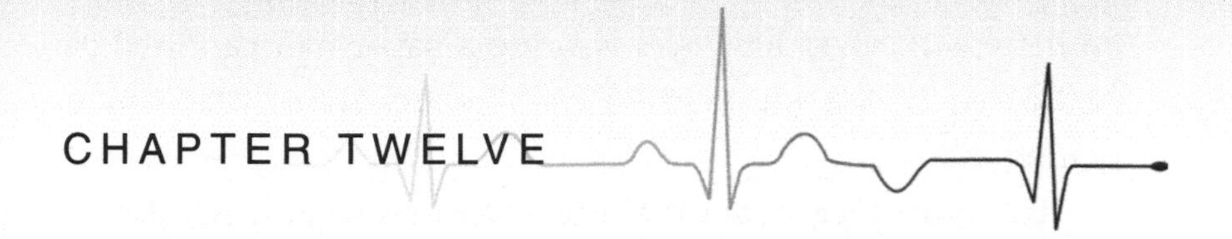

CHAPTER TWELVE

Iris smoothed the front of her crisp pink volunteer apron and smiled at Erin's expression when she caught sight of her grandmother in the hospital chapel. Iris had been the first to arrive at the Friday morning Faith QD gathering and had kept her plan a surprise, partly because it was her first official day and she wasn't yet sure of her duties, but mostly because she wasn't sure how her overprotective granddaughter would react. Erin told her more than once that these meetings, meant to "jump-start our shifts with an infusion of faith," often became emotional for staff who dealt daily with tragedy and death. Prayers were offered, encouragement given, but happy endings could never be guaranteed. It was the nature of their work. And Erin's plan, apparently, was that Iris's work never involved anything weightier than a giant cluster of Get Well balloons.

Erin gave Iris a hug as a few other employees filed in and walked toward the front of the chapel. "Nana, this is so great."

Iris returned her hug and stepped back. "The flyer outside said all staff welcome, so . . ."

"So then—" Erin's smile broadened as she gestured for the other employees to gather in a circle, then grasped her hand—"let's get started."

Iris glanced around the circle as the staff gathered hands: Arlene, the clerk Iris recognized from ER registration; a heavy-set blonde wearing the navy scrubs assigned to ICU; a nurse in teddy bear print scrubs; and—holding Iris's other hand—a young brunette with vivid blue eyes wearing a paper hair cap used in central service. She whispered to Iris, "I'm Brooklynn. Glad you're joining us."

Iris's heart tugged. She'd almost forgotten what it felt like to be part of a team.

Erin squeezed Iris's hand and looked at each face in the circle. "Any special prayers or concerns today?"

The blonde in navy nodded. "Our six-year-old from the pesticide incident. Ana's still on a ventilator, and her family keeps waiting for her to open her eyes, but it hasn't happened. I don't speak Spanish, but I see it in their faces. I watch her mother kiss her fingers. . . . I feel how much they're hurting. That poor family can use as many prayers as possible."

"And I'm still asking for prayers for ten-year-old upstairs. Cody's always so brave." The nurse dressed in teddy bears shook her head, her eyes suddenly shiny with tears. "He even tries to comfort me when I have to stick him for IVs. His antibiotics are nearly complete, and then he'll have the MRI. I can't bear the thought he'll have his leg amputated. My son's his age. It seems so unfair, and . . ."

Arlene slid an arm around the nurse's shoulders.

"Yes," Erin said gently, "sometimes it feels absolutely that way." She glanced at the others, and when no one had anything else to add, she bowed her head and the others followed suit. "Father, thank you for being here today. For entrusting us to do the work you would have us do and, in doing so, to know the joy that comes with giving. And when days are tough and we too are wounded, to know by faith that you intend healing for us as well. We ask special care for those patients we've mentioned today, that they, their families, and their caregivers feel your comforting presence and trust that you have a loving plan. . . ."

Iris prayed silently for an unconscious girl and a brave little boy she'd never met. And then added a prayer of gratitude for her granddaughter's gift to these courageous and caring people. Faith QD: faith every day. She'd learned long ago that's what it took.

+++

Leigh gulped coffee from a paper container as she walked toward ER, her third caffeine boost before 7 a.m. But even if she injected it directly into her veins, she doubted it would help. She'd been awakened by a call from her sister after midnight and spent more than an hour talking her down from her latest troubles. When Leigh finally got back to sleep, she'd dreamed Nick was on her doorstep dressed in his uniform and Kevlar vest . . . cradling a tiny baby in his arms.

Leigh groaned against the coffee's plastic lid. Three days since he called saying the National Guard might send him to Pacific Point—*and that he wants to see me*—and no further word since. It didn't look like they'd need the Guard, but the silence was like waiting for the other shoe to drop. No, it was like expecting a steel-toe Army boot to stomp on the remains of her heart. *Stay away, Nick.*

She passed by the closed doors to the chapel, knowing that Erin was there leading her Faith QD. A good idea, she supposed, but prayer was a thing of the past for Leigh. *Like my husband, my baby, my home.* In the last year her life had turned into what could pass for a bad country song—betrayal, loss, and unbearable confusion and grief. One punch after another since she discovered her husband's affair. She went from shell shock to anger to a sadness so deep she could barely drag herself out of bed. And then she'd miscarried, and the cycle started anew.

There finally came a point when she was certain even God was tired of listening to her misery. She reminded herself she was a doctor and there was work to do, lives to save; it was time to move on. She told herself to be grateful she wasn't pregnant. She stopped praying for miracles and started thinking about escape, first by leaving San Francisco and now by . . . Her throat squeezed unexpectedly, her stomach sinking. *I told him I want a divorce. I finally said it.* She was sure God would disapprove. It was good she wasn't talking to him anymore.

She took a long swallow of her coffee as she hurried on. No doubt Erin was asking God to "guide their day." She'd said that was the general idea. *God in the ER?* Leigh smiled ruefully. They were short staffed on a Friday, and this doctor was running on fumes. At the very least, they could use some mercy.

But it didn't happen. And in less than thirty minutes, adrenaline filled the gap where Leigh's caffeine fell short. Their first patient of the morning arrived swirling the drain.

"Talk to me," she told the husky and perspiring paramedic, her gaze never leaving the African American woman lying dentureless and somnolent on the ambulance stretcher. The woman's eyes remained fixed in an upward gaze, and an oral airway protruded from her lips beneath an inflated non-rebreather oxygen mask. Her respirations were deep and snoring, her breath sour.

"Charlene Bailey. Sixty-two-year-old type 2 diabetic, awakened at 6 a.m. by the worst headache of her life," the medic reported as his partners transferred the patient from their stretcher to the ER gurney. "Agitation, vomiting, history of hypertension. Those are her meds." He wiped his sweaty forehead with his hand and pointed to his notes. "We just got 240 over 110 as we pulled in."

"Blood sugar?" Leigh asked as Judy switched the oxygen from the portable tank to the wall source and checked the IV line. Erin attached the cardiac monitor leads and then the BP cuff and pulse ox finger probe.

"Glucose 140," the medic said.

"Still verbalizing?" Leigh asked, checking the cardiac monitor. *Rate a little slow at 58.*

"She was." The paramedic glanced toward the doorway. "Her family should be here any minute. Husband said she was holding her head, pacing around and 'talking kind of crazy.' He called their son at work to come over and help him figure out what to do. The son took one look and called 911. But she was incoherent by the time we got there and on the ride in she deteriorated to this. I gave her a Glasgow Coma Scale of 8. Maybe down to a 7 now—that posturing just started." He indicated the woman's right arm, bending at the elbow and curling stiffly inward. Her fist twisted against her chest in response to Erin's needle stick on the opposite arm.

Leigh looked at the woman's legs, extended and stiff. *Decorticate movements . . . increasing pressure on the brain.* Ominous signs.

"Pressure's 248 over 112, heart rate 56, respirations 24, oxygen saturation 99 percent on high flow." Judy pressed a handheld thermometer to the patient's ear canal. "Temp 99.2."

"I've got blood for all the labs," Erin said, collecting the last in a rainbow of capped tubes. "And the stroke team's on its way."

"Good." Leigh pulled off her lab coat, draped it over an IV pole, and moved to the head of the bed as she spotted a respiratory therapist arriving with the ventilator. "Let's get this woman intubated so we can protect her airway." She nodded at Erin. "We'll titrate nitroprusside for that blood pressure. I want something we can pull back on if she deteriorates and gets hypotensive." She sighed, catching a glimpse of a handsome, bearded African American man, his face etched with worry, pacing outside the room. "Slip in a Foley catheter when I'm done. Go ahead and get the Nipride on board. I want Mrs. Bailey on her way to the CT scanner stat; we need to know if this is a bleed. Time is brain, folks."

Leigh stepped aside as the respiratory therapist fitted an Ambu mask over the patient's face. He squeezed the attached football-size bag, hyper-oxygenating the woman's lungs in preparation for placement of the breathing tube.

Leigh turned at the sound of soft crying outside the code room and saw that more family had joined Mr. Bailey. A tearful young woman and a good-looking man wearing police blues. He was holding an infant. She struggled against the memory of her fitful dream. *Nick. Our baby.*

The paramedic spoke beside her. "That's Mrs. Bailey's son, the one who called us. He works nights for Pacific Point PD. And he's very worried about his mother's condition."

Leigh reached toward the tray Erin had prepared for her: stainless steel laryngoscope, a range of cuffed endotracheal tubes with a flexible metal wire guide, anesthetic lubricant, syringe for inflating the tube's cuff, and a CO_2 detector. Erin would stand by with suction, and with any luck Leigh would get the breathing tube properly placed—just distal to the white-edged vocal cords—on the first try. They'd tape it in place and get a quick portable chest X-ray to be certain of its position. Then Mrs. Bailey could go on to the CT scanner, with a nurse accompanying her.

Leigh glanced at her charge nurse. "Erin, I want you to go with Mrs. Bailey to the scanner."

"Sure."

"Thank you." Leigh positioned her patient's head into sniffing position. She lifted the laryngoscope and checked its light source, while trying not to hear the sound of the baby crying in the outer hallway. Erin would pray for this woman. She probably was right this moment. And that was good because Charlene Bailey's son had reason to be very, very worried. His mother's prognosis was grim.

Leigh stroked a gloved fingertip across her patient's cheek. *Stay with me, Charlene. I'm trying to save your life.*

+++

Iris stopped the library cart in the pediatrics department hallway, feeling a goose-bumpy wave of déjà vu. She'd walked this same corridor fifty years ago as a student nurse in a starched uniform and white stockings, with shiny bandage scissors, long hair swept high off her shoulders, cap pinned securely in place, and a sparkly new engagement ring on her finger. Iris's eyes misted unexpectedly. *Doug, I'm here again.* She sighed. Erin was wrong. It felt wonderful to be working in a hospital and completely different from the long, painful vigil she'd kept at her husband's bedside. *Because I'm beginning something, not waiting for an ending.*

Iris battled a twinge of guilt. She'd let her granddaughter assume she'd be working in the Little Mercies Gift Shop, away from direct patient contact. Erin was worried that being close to pain and tragedy would be too hard on Iris. She hadn't said so in words, but Iris saw it in her eyes. As usual, her granddaughter was fighting to protect her. *My little Wonder Woman.* But what Erin didn't know wouldn't hurt her. Or Iris. There was no risk in being here. Bottom line, she needed this. *And maybe somebody here needs me.*

Iris took hold of the handle and pushed the book-laden cart along the corridor, then stopped and backed up as a young voice called from the patient room nearest to the housekeeping closet. A blond boy, maybe nine or ten years old. With his leg on a pillow . . . *The boy we prayed for this morning?*

"Oh, great! Cool! I thought I was going to have to wait until this afternoon," the boy gushed, his infectious grin punctuated by a single dimple. He shoved himself upright in bed, wincing briefly as his bandaged right leg shifted with the movement. "I finished my homework, and there's nothing on TV except—" his nose wrinkled—"some girl thing about painting your toes. You're saving my life!"

Saving his life. Iris laughed and felt a second rush of goose bumps. "Good deal, then. It so happens there's nothing in this world I'd rather do." She pushed the cart into the room, then stepped close and extended her hand to the tousle-headed boy. "I'm Iris."

His blue eyes twinkled as he grasped her hand, small fingers warm against hers. "I'm Cody."

CHAPTER THIRTEEN

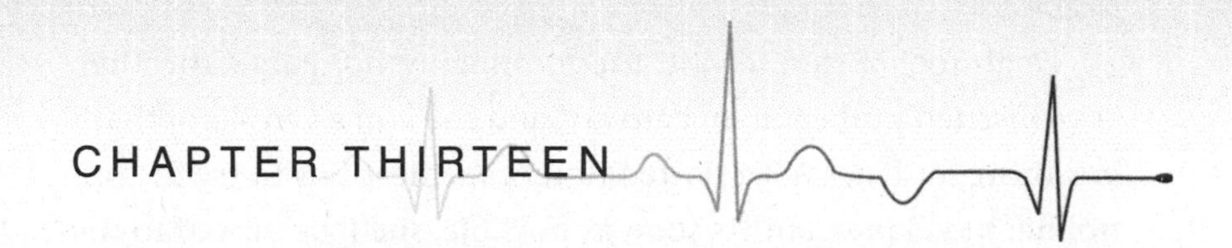

Erin stood in the quiet room holding a box of Kleenex—and her breath—as Leigh spoke with the Bailey family. Heart cramping, she watched their faces as their confusion turned to palpable despair over the doctor's words.

Charlene's husband obviously struggled to find words as long hours of hope began to dissolve into the unthinkable. "You're saying there's nothing that can be done?" he finally asked, voice barely above a whisper.

There was soft whimper, and Erin wasn't sure if it was the baby or his mother. Her fingers tightened on the tissue box.

"The hemorrhage is large and has spread deep into your wife's brain tissues." Leigh exhaled slowly. "I'm afraid surgery isn't an option."

"Then we have to wait for the blood to absorb?" the son asked. "Or . . . ?"

Erin's throat constricted at the sudden helplessness of this man so obviously used to taking control, making things right. *Lord, help them.*

"The bleeding has caused damage to the portions of your mother's brain that are responsible for vital life functions." Leigh's voice was gentle. "Including heart activity, breathing—"

The daughter-in-law gasped and clutched her infant close. "Mama's not breathing?"

There were voices in the outer hallway. *Please let that be their pastor.*

Leigh took a step toward them, bridging her palms together. "I've inserted a tube into her airway, and she's on a ventilator that's breathing for her. We've started potent medications to try to control her blood pressure. As soon as possible, she'll be moved to the intensive care unit and be examined by the neurology specialists, but I'm afraid—"

Mrs. Bailey's daughter-in-law cried out and lowered herself into a chair. "She can't die. Oh, please, Jesus, don't let her die!" She began to tremble uncontrollably.

In an instant, her husband lifted the baby from her arms, handed him to Leigh, then knelt beside the chair. He pulled his wife close, rocking her gently, as his own eyes brimmed with tears.

Mr. Bailey stood protectively over his family, a low, guttural sob escaping his lips as tears began streaming down his cheeks.

An hour later, Erin sat at the table outside the ER, grateful for a few minutes' respite. She broke her PowerBar in half and held the larger piece out to Leigh, waiting as her friend finished a row of knitting. The doctor looked tired and troubled. Erin sensed it went beyond the stress of delivering tragic news to the Bailey family.

Leigh drew in a deep breath of ocean air, then glanced across the table at Erin. She set her knitting down and took the piece of PowerBar. "Thanks for dragging me out here. I needed some sun on my face. Nothing worse than walking into the quiet room carrying boxes of Kleenex. The families know it's bad as soon as they see us coming."

Erin nodded, wincing at the memory. Mr. Bailey's sob, that heartsick look in Leigh's eyes as she held the baby. "Thank goodness their pastor arrived and that they have so much support from their family and church."

"It's going to be awful for them over the next several days. If she makes it that long."

"I don't want to imagine trying to handle something like that with my grandmother. At least with my grandfather there was time to be with him and say good-bye. But something like this, so horrific and coming without warning . . ." Erin shook her head. "Charlene's son said she and his dad booked a Mexico cruise for their fortieth anniversary next month. They'd been taking tango lessons."

Leigh took a sip of her coffee and was quiet for several seconds. "I saw Iris this morning. She looked cute in that pink smock, and she was all smiles. I'm glad you didn't talk her out of volunteering here."

Erin snorted. "Like I could. But I'm glad she'll be staying put in the gift shop. I still don't want Nana exposed to all of this tragedy and chaos."

"You mean the kind of chaos that could end up sending us to stress debriefing?" Leigh checked her watch. "You're still planning to talk with more of the staff today?"

"Yes, I think I'm almost finished. It took a few days to go through the list, but I'm glad social services agreed to this initial peer contact. I think it's really important to find out if they've been troubled by any symptoms of stress since this pesticide scare started. There's a nurse in the ICU who's had the CISM training as well, so she'll be doing the same thing. The social worker had some good pamphlets, listing symptoms and things to do to help. You know, like journaling, exercising, eating well, avoiding alcohol. And I'm reminding them about the employee assistance program in the event they feel the need for professional counseling." She frowned. "I sent information over to the fire station for Chuck, though his captain made it clear he's not a fan of counseling."

"Scott? Oh, that's right. You told me you were going to talk with him. When you called me that night . . . at the stables."

Erin paused, watching Leigh. There it was again—that troubled look in her eyes. It likely had something to do with her separation from her husband. Or new problems with her half sister in San Francisco. But Erin wouldn't pry. Leigh kept things pretty private. "Yes, we met for coffee. And sort of walked on the beach." Why on earth had she added that?

Leigh's PowerBar stopped halfway to her lips. "Oh?"

Erin raised her palms. "So he could play Smokey the Bear and douse a campfire. That's all. Really . . . don't do this to me."

Leigh was maddeningly silent, but a smile played at the corners of her lips.

"Besides, my current opinion of men in general makes real bears—maybe even Sasquatch—look like a far better choice." Erin's hand clenched before she could stop it, anger prickling. "My last boyfriend stole money from charity donations I'd collected and tried to use my grandmother's credit card number for online horse betting."

Leigh's eyes widened.

"I'm serious. I can really pick 'em." She shrugged. "But somehow it made the fact he was also cheating on me seem easier to accept."

Leigh picked up her Golden Gate cup and turned away for moment, glancing toward the corner of the building where Sarge smoked a cigarette. He was working a few extra hours to cover for a fellow housekeeper.

"Well, if it makes any difference," she said, turning back, "I never heard about Scott being anything but a decent guy. Maybe too decent. He wasn't at all like the other men the nurse in San Francisco normally dated. To tell you the truth, I never understood the attraction between those two."

Erin looked down at her coffee and tried to sound indifferent. "It wasn't something serious, then?"

"I only heard things on the periphery; I try to avoid getting involved in personal issues. But she complained that he was too involved with his career, that he was spending more and more time doing things like Ocean Rescue and didn't make enough time for her. She said he'd become moody and hard to be around. I didn't hear how it all ended and frankly didn't want to."

"Hmm." Erin chewed at her lower lip, remembering the pain and anger on Scott's face when he'd told her about the car crash that killed his sister and her husband and injured their son so badly.

"But on the other hand, you seem like the kind of woman Scott—"

"Hold it right there." Erin lifted her palms like she was stopping oncoming traffic. "I agreed to meet Captain McKenna. Once. At a bait shop. Where we managed to disagree on almost everything from that point on. Flavors of coffee, exercise regimens, Wonder Woman—"

"Wonder Woman?"

Erin rolled her eyes. "Long story. Just trust me. But the worst of it was that we'd met to agree on a plan to help the citizens of Pacific Point and especially the members of our individual teams, his firefighters and my ER staff. And we didn't. Scott's wary about counseling in general."

"He thinks it doesn't help?"

"He thinks it could make things worse, maybe even drive some people over the edge emotionally." *Like when Cody's father aimed their speeding car at a power pole.* "I don't think he'd interfere with Sandy's husband's participating in a hospital debriefing—if it comes to that. But Scott wouldn't be comfortable with offering counseling resources to his crew. You can bet your horse on that."

"Hey, leave Frisco out of this. He's all I've got." Leigh's expression faded into that troubled look again as she tucked her knitting into its tote. "Let's get back in there and wrap things up so you can do your interviews."

As Erin stood, she saw Sarge snuff out his cigarette and head toward the ER doors. He raised his hand in greeting and she waved back, feeling a stab of guilt. She'd almost forgotten to include the housekeeping tech on her list of employees to talk with. He'd been there the day of the disaster, quietly helpful as always. He deserved as much consideration as anyone else. It wasn't only doctors, nurses, and rescue personnel who could be affected by disaster situations. Everyone was at risk for critical stress.

+++

Scott glanced at the metal-framed wall clock, then back at the stack of paperwork on his desk—fire inspection reports and daily logs for review, budget requests to consider. He muttered under his breath as he saw the neat stack of CISM pamphlets Erin had delivered via the chief. She wasn't going to give up. He jabbed his pencil against the base of his desk lamp, remembering Erin's determination that night at the beach. Her protective insistence on providing closure for staff involved in the pesticide incident. And her compassion when he'd told her about Colleen and Cody.

Scott jabbed the pencil again, scowling as the tip snapped off and rolled beneath a framed family photo. The snapshot was taken in front of the giant octopus exhibit at Monterey Bay Aquarium: Scott's grinning grandfather in a volunteer's jacket, his mother holding a wriggling baby Cody, his stepfather, and Scott and Colleen mugging for the camera. Colleen's husband absent as usual. A lump rose in Scott's throat as he looked at his sister's teasing smile, her single dimple exactly like Cody's. Colleen Heather McKenna, two years his junior. Funny, smart, beautiful inside and out, and so brave. Scott swore aloud. Then his anger turned without mercy to guilt. Why hadn't he returned his sister's call that night? If he'd had a chance to talk her out of getting in that car with her husband, then . . .

He stared at the stack of pamphlets, which he felt certain included counseling resources. He'd meant what he said about the risks. Even if counseling was highly beneficial the majority of the time, emotions couldn't be predicted. *"Sometimes you stir up the embers and everybody gets burned."* He knew that only too well now. And yet . . .

Scott exhaled softly, recalling the tenderness in Erin's voice when she talked about her grandmother, the feel of her hand on his arm after he told her about the car accident, how she'd stood there silently beside him, and then how that strange sense of peace washed over him. That warm eddy after so much soul-wearying cold.

He reached for a pamphlet. He would read it, but he wasn't promising any more than that.

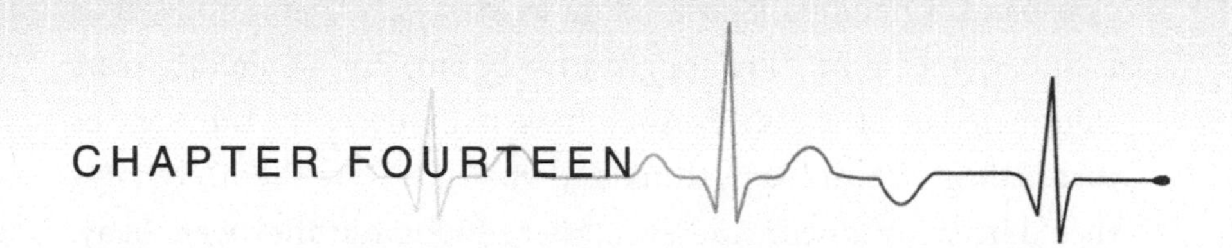

CHAPTER FOURTEEN

"I almost said something at Faith QD this morning." The registration clerk stared at the oatmeal cookie in her hand, then back at Erin.

"Yes?" Erin leaned forward in her office chair and nodded at Arlene, hoping to encourage her. She'd been surprised that the feisty ER veteran had volunteered for peer counseling, which only proved the point: *no one is immune to stress.*

Arlene shrugged, though the look in her eyes was anything but casual. "I felt selfish talking about my own problems. You know, when we were offering prayers for the boy who could lose his leg and that poor, sweet Ana Galvez." Her fingers trembled and she set the cookie down. "I've been at that ER window for twenty years now. I've seen stuff, you know? Like a guy who cut his knee with a chainsaw. And when that fisherman, who stank to death of mackerel, had that big hook stuck in the bridge of his nose . . . Ugly things, awful stuff. More than I can count. But that little girl getting poisoned . . ."

Erin reminded herself of the goals of this initial contact: *acknowledge, validate, reassure.* "Can you tell me about that day? When did you start to feel this case was affecting you differently than the others?"

"It was after I knew that Ana wasn't just sick. That she'd been poisoned by those pesticides. I mean, I'd even seen her having seizures. She had one when I was trying to fasten her identification band. I handled it fine, same as always." Arlene nodded as if to convince Erin. "I'm tough. I really am. But—" sudden tears shimmered in the clerk's eyes—"I have twin nieces the same age as that little girl. And I kept thinking, what if it were them? What if they'd been poisoned? And even after I found out they were okay, I couldn't stop thinking about it. I had a strange nightmare about my uncle who died from fumes in a mine cave-in when I was just a kid. I haven't thought about that in forty years."

Arlene glanced at the cookie. "No one will believe it, but I've hardly been able to eat. I listen to the news, even at work. I'm making my sister crazy by calling to be sure she's only giving my sweeties bottled water. I keep washing my hands, and I replaced all the pens in my cubicle. Don't tell my supervisor, but I threw away a couple dozen in case they're contaminated." She groaned and met Erin's gaze, her expression helpless. "I'm usually so tough."

+++

The last of the vodka went down in a single searing gulp, making Sarge's eyes water. He coughed and set the glass on the apartment's table, leaning heavily on a crutch to balance against his dangling stump. He hadn't touched alcohol in more than five years, but lately he needed something to take the edge off, to filter the brain-scalding glare—too much like relentless desert sun—that had replaced the fog of medication and lit dark corners he never wanted to see again.

He closed his eyes against a wave of dizziness, and in an instant the images intruded. A dead camel, bodies of civilians, bloodied and sprawled in the rubble of the shelled desert camp. Dark eyes, vacant and lifeless, staring skyward. Impossibly, some of them children. He flinched, hearing the echo of his own tortured wail that day, his tear-choked voice praying aloud again and again. *"Father God, not the children, not the children . . ."*

Gagging, Sarge grabbed for a chair and sent his prosthetic leg—abandoned on its cracked vinyl seat—clattering to the floor. He dragged the chair close and dropped down, burying his face in his hands as he recalled his brief conversation with Erin Quinn. She meant well; he didn't discount that. She was a good nurse and had always treated him kindly. Like he was more than the man who mopped the floor. But she'd been fooled too. She'd bought into that cover-up the mayor was spewing. Only instead of offering bottled water, she was offering advice.

He groaned, thinking of the pamphlet he'd tossed in the trash. Reassurances that it was "normal" to feel anxious or sleepless or depressed after experiencing stressful situations, that they weren't signs of "weakness." Too much like stuff the psychiatrists fed him at the VA while they were renewing his prescriptions. No one understood.

He shook his head, remembering the useless, printed advice: *"Listen to music, exercise—"* he glared at his prosthetic leg lying on the floor—*"eat well, write in a journal . . ."* He glanced at the spiral notebook he'd purchased at the Little Mercies Gift Shop. Not a journal. A tactical plan. For his mission. It was getting harder and harder to keep things straight in his mind. He'd make notes during his night shift tonight when he slipped into pediatrics to keep an eye on Cody's room from the housekeeping closet. His foxhole.

Sarge leaned across the table and grabbed the vodka bottle, fighting the returning images of the bodies. He'd nap until it was dark, then return to Pacific Mercy.

+++

Erin smiled at Sandy as she came through the doorway, relieved that the triage nurse looked more rested now and that she'd been willing to come in. She hadn't yet returned to work.

"This is the first time I've walked through that trauma room, since—" Sandy rolled her eyes and forced a laugh—"I did my little swan dive that day. Nothing like drooling all over yourself and becoming a public spectacle."

Erin recalled the self-defense mechanisms mentioned in her training. Humor—gallows humor, in particular—was often a choice of health care providers. She'd used it plenty of times herself. *Laugh quick so you won't cry.* "I'm glad you came in today. Like I told you on the phone, I'm touching base with everyone. Not for a critique or a performance review. Basically, this is a how-are-you-doing chat because you're my staff, my friend. And we've all been stressed by this incident. Bottom line: I want to know if there's anything I can do for you."

"I appreciate that. I'm embarrassed to admit how helpless this whole thing made me feel. I'm not used to that." Sandy attempted a smile. "Ask Chuck; I'm the worst kind of control freak. But that day . . ."

"You felt out of control?"

"Oh yes. One minute I'm triaging patients, making decisions, handing out basins. Then all of a sudden I'm dizzy and sick, and I start to worry I'll faint right in front of my patients. And then, of course, I did. In that child's room, with you and Dr. Stathos."

Erin nodded. "How did you feel when you realized what had caused it?"

"It's mostly a blur. I remember Sarge picking me up and Chuck being there. And all the firefighters and police coming in." Her pupils widened and she swallowed. "Then they paged Code Orange. I remember being really frightened. Because then I knew it was a hazardous material incident."

"What was the first thought that came to your mind?" Erin prompted, remembering the importance CISM placed on this key question.

"That I might be pregnant. And if I was . . ." Her eyes filled with tears. "You know Chuck and I have been trying to start a family for over a year. Last fall I had that miscarriage after I'd done everything I could to guard my health. So the thought of exposing a baby to . . ." A tear slid down her face.

Erin reached across the desk and took hold of her hand. "Are you pregnant?"

"No." Sandy's chin quivered. "Trust me, I never dreamed I'd be glad to see a negative test." Her voice dropped to a raw whisper. "And I never thought I'd be afraid to come back to work. I know it's irrational, and I can't explain it . . . but I'm afraid."

It was dusk by the time Erin gathered her belongings, and she was wrung out physically and emotionally. It had been her first experience with peer counseling, and she'd felt her way through—sending up more than a few silent prayers—but knew now she'd done the right thing by talking with her staff. Four days after the initial disaster, people were indeed showing signs of stress.

Her throat squeezed as she remembered Sandy's fear that she'd endangered an unborn child and Arlene's nightmare about an uncle who died decades ago in a mine. The impassioned and graphic warnings of the Safe Sky group could only have added to their anxiety. Equally distressing was that both Sandy and Arlene felt embarrassed and angry at themselves for being "weak" enough to experience stress symptoms. It was a common reaction for health and rescue workers who often hold themselves to unrealistically high standards. Erin was glad that Sandy and Arlene intended to contact employee assistance for counseling.

She reached for her purse, hesitated, and then shook her head. *Counseling.* How had Scott reacted when she sent those pamphlets via his chief's office? Had he tossed them in the trash? tucked them away where they'd never see the light of day? Probably.

But then, maybe it didn't matter anymore. She hadn't seen Captain McKenna in several days, and if things continued to improve with the community's water status, she'd have very little reason to connect with him again, beyond the paperwork required for the incident review, and they'd already discussed that. No. She'd have no reason—*no excuse?*—to spend more time with Scott. Erin ignored a confusing wave of regret and grabbed her purse, then stepped out into the hallway and nearly bumped into him.

"Scott." Her heart climbed to her throat without warning.

"Hi," he said softly. "I wanted to talk with you about those pamphlets you sent over."

"Please. Don't start on me. It's been a long day. And I've already heard your reservations about crisis counseling."

Impossibly, he smiled. "That bit in the pamphlet . . . about doing things that 'feel good to you'? Is that an important part of the process?"

"Yes. So?"

"Well, I'm doing that. Tomorrow. I can't swim because of the stitches, but I thought of something else."

What was she supposed to say? Bully for you?

"Come with me."

What? "Where?" Her heart did that foolish dance again. "To climb a fire ladder?"

"No," he said, his eyes lighting. "Nothing that tame. We'll go to the Santa Cruz Beach Boardwalk. I think we could both use some roller-coaster therapy. Ride the Giant Dipper with no hands. What do you say, Wonder Woman?"

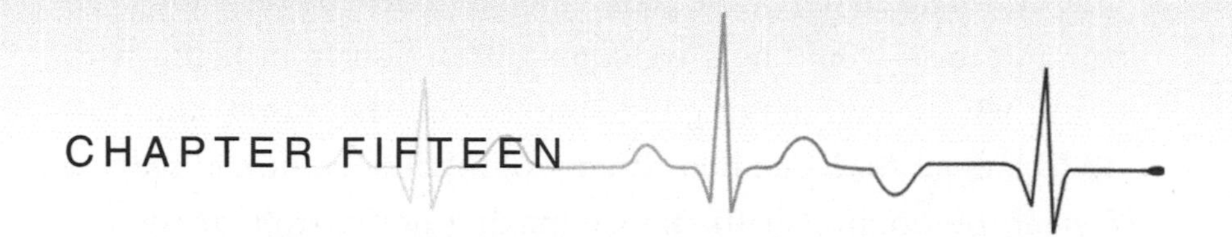

CHAPTER FIFTEEN

The morning breeze smelled of seaweed, hosed asphalt, cotton candy, and popcorn. Screeches from gulls blended with other sounds: laughing children, an electronic *ding-boing, pow-pow-pow* from the Casino Arcade, the relentless whoosh and pull of ocean waves, and a continuing chorus of screams from the Giant Dipper roller coaster.

If Erin kept her eyes shut a moment longer, it could be 1985 and she'd be perched atop her grandfather's shoulders, her nose sun-crinkled, feet bare and sand-speckled, fingers wonderfully sticky, and tongue half-numb from a frozen chocolate banana. Grandy's rumbling laugh would blend with Nana's, and Erin would throw her head back and add her own silly giggles. She'd be back in a time when she felt secure and loved, when life was simple and honest. Without threat of betrayal, heartache, death . . . or even poisonous disaster.

But Scott's voice hauled her back to the present as effectively as if he'd thrown her over his shoulder in a fireman's carry. "Always the same." He stared up at the towering Cocoanut Grove Casino, its neon-embellished facade freshly painted in orange, gold, and fuchsia. He clucked his tongue and looked at Erin, his expression giving no clue to whether he thought sameness was something good or bad. The breeze lifted a golden thatch of his hair, and she caught a subtle trace of citrus cologne. "Straight to the Dipper?"

"Sure," she agreed, pulling up the hood on her zip-front vest. The chug and clatter of the giant wooden roller coaster—and even the screams—would be a welcome distraction from being with Scott, which was anything but simple. And she wasn't sure how to feel about that. The hour drive from Pacific Point had seemed longer, his comfort with silence making her chatter, antsy as a prizefighter box dancing in the corner of a ring. He had rolled the truck's window down a few inches, while she sat with her chin tucked into the collar of her vest to keep warm.

Still, there were things about him that drew her too. Scott's quiet confidence, the way his arm sprang out to protect her when he'd had to brake suddenly, that smile when he mentioned his mother's upcoming birthday, and most of all, the small snipped photo of a blond-haired boy carefully tucked onto the truck's sun visor. Little things that said volumes about him. Seemed sincere. Warm. Like when she'd hugged him on the beach. But then Erin had been fooled before. There was so much about Scott she didn't know. And wasn't entirely sure she wanted to. She needed to remember she was here for a roller-coaster ride; that was all. It was a perfect prescription after the stress of the last week. If she could enjoy that without managing to butt heads with him, all the better.

"I'm surprised." He turned to look at her as they passed the colorful, shark-stenciled entrance to Neptune's Kingdom and walked toward the carousel.

"You mean that I'd ride the roller coaster?"

Scott shook his head. "That you agreed to come here at all."

She studied him for a moment, the silence filled by circus-style whistles and toots of the merry-go-round calliope. "I'm surprised you asked me."

"I wanted to make things up to you. I gave you a pretty hard time. From that first day, I guess."

"Yes, you did." Erin lowered her voice to a teasing mimic: "'I go by the book.' That's what you said. And you found out pretty fast that I do too. In my own way." She sighed, the urge for teasing—for her usual defensiveness—ebbing. "Seriously, I think we're both pretty stubborn. But about things that count. Doing the right thing at our jobs and for our families." She noticed his brows draw together, followed by something in his eyes that looked like a flicker of discomfort. "Honestly, I considered your concerns about peer counseling and the debriefing process as a whole."

Scott grasped Erin's elbow protectively as half a dozen giggling children ran from the exit of the Haunted Castle. He let go of her and started walking again. "And then you sent pamphlets to my chief and went ahead with peer counseling at the hospital this week. Chuck told me that Sandy met with you."

"Yes." She exhaled, relieved they were getting this dicey discussion out of the way. Maybe it would clear the air once and for all. "From the reaction of my staff, I think it served a good purpose. I don't know if it will be necessary to move forward with a more formal debriefing; that depends on feedback from the peer counselor in ICU. And how things go within the community. But in my book, the counseling felt necessary."

Erin raised her voice over a torrent of screams from the roller coaster. "I sent the pamphlets simply to share the information. In case you needed it. That's all." She stopped and stared upward at the towering stretch of red and white framework that supported half a mile of curving track. Her pulse quickened like a ten-year-old's. "Well, here's the Dipper."

"Front seat?"

"Of course," she agreed. It seemed far less daunting than this conversation.

In scant minutes, they purchased the tickets and hustled along the row of linked metal cars—bright yellow like a Wonderland caterpillar—and slid into the padded red seat. Ahead of them loomed the gaping darkness of the wooden tunnel and the first stretch of uphill track.

"I'm excited about this." She grinned, feeling girlishly giddy. "I'm glad you thought of it."

"Same here."

The warning bell sounded with a loud *brrring*, and the safety bar lowered over their legs. Scott's outstretched arm brushed her shoulder as he settled it along the back of the seat.

"And I'm . . ." Scott cleared his throat. "I'm glad you felt good about your peer counseling. Really. I know how much you want to help."

She smiled again as the line of cars lurched and moved forward slowly, wheels clacking. "Thank you for saying that."

The cars moved into the tunnel's inky darkness to begin the slow, upward chug, and Erin became way too aware of Scott beside her, the brush of his shoulder and leg against hers. She tried not to think of the giggling stories from her teenage years, girlfriends talking about stolen kisses in the Big Dipper tunnel.

When Scott spoke again, leaning close, she flushed. She was grateful for the darkness. "Chuck mentioned some other meetings that you hold regularly at the hospital and that you'd encouraged Sandy to come. What's that about?"

Erin blinked as gravity forced her back against the seat. "Oh, right. He was probably talking about Faith QD."

"What's that?" Scott raised his voice against the metal-against-wood chugging of the climbing coaster.

"A fellowship group. Nondenominational. I started one at my other hospital, and it caught on, so I—"

"Fellowship group?"

Erin's stomach sank, completely at odds with the car's upward climb. *Be careful.* "Yes. To start our shifts with prayer. I've found that it helps support staff, and . . ." Her words hung in the air, and Scott's silence felt like a third presence wedged between them in the coaster car. *Why do I care what he thinks?*

As they reemerged into the sunlight, she sneaked a look at Scott's expression. Stony as the first day she'd met him at the barricade.

He turned toward her as the cars climbed, *click-click*, high above the boardwalk and pressed them both backward into their seats. "Prayer?"

"Yes." Erin studied his face—the best she could with her head pushed back against the seat—and decided she had nothing to lose. "You're not good with that, either?"

His lips pressed together, and he was silent.

Erin glanced down, way down, a dizzying distance toward the tiny people on the boardwalk below, and then out across the sand to the sun-dappled sea. Her head felt at once both heavy and buoyant as a helium balloon. Her stomach fluttered.

When Scott finally spoke, she realized she'd been holding her breath for his answer. "Raise your hands."

"What?"

"Raise your hands—we're at the top!" He grasped her hand and lifted it high, and the world fell away in a torrent of screams.

+++

Disappointed, Iris wheeled the library cart out of the pediatrics room, then smiled at the gray-haired gentleman standing in the hallway. The Chihuahua dozed in the carrier on his shirtfront.

"Cody's down in X-ray," he said. "I just checked at the nurses' station. You're Iris, right? Proud owner of a goldfish called . . ."

"Elmer Fudd," she said with a laugh. "And yes, Iris Quinn. It's good to see you again, Dr. McKenna."

"A fish named Fudd. How could I have forgotten?" He extended his hand to her. "Please call me Hugh. There are far too many doctors here, and I hardly think anyone needs to be examined for fin rot." He glanced toward the empty room. "You've met my great-grandson?"

"Cody Sorenson is your great-grandson? I didn't know that. Then he's also Scott's . . ."

"Only nephew," Hugh confirmed, finishing her thought as he stroked the ears of the blinking dog. "Which reminds me how grateful I am that Scotty's spending the day in Santa Cruz with your lovely granddaughter." He caught the look on Iris's face. "Is something wrong?"

"Only that the world is suddenly shrinking. This is awkward, but I really don't want Erin to know I'm making visits up here. Not yet. I'm going to beg you to keep it quiet." Iris sighed at his confused expression. "It's a long story."

"Then we should go downstairs and have some coffee. Cody's going to be another thirty minutes, and Jonah here—" Hugh tickled the dog's whiskered chin—"is wild about the cafeteria's buttered rye toast. Aren't you, boy?"

The little dog perked his ears, then raised his nose . . . and crooned a long, warbling sound from deep in his throat.

"Was that . . . ?"

"A yodel," Hugh said, grinning. "His claim to fame."

They took the elevator to the lobby floor, returned the library cart to its closet, and joined the breakfast crowd—wearing scrubs or lab jackets, some in patient gowns—in the sunny cafeteria. The room smelled of coffee, toasted bagels, and bacon. Iris smiled as the PA system played its snippet of "Brahms' Lullaby" to announce a birth, struck once more by how very good it felt to be part of this again.

She followed Hugh to the coffee urn and filled a cup. "I'm surprised that they allow Jonah in the hospital," she said as they sat down at a table near the garden window.

"He's a certified therapy dog. Most of them are golden retrievers and Labs, so I tell folks Jonah is big medicine in a small package. Plus, he yodels. It never fails to make people smile."

Iris chuckled. "That's wonderful. Erin was involved in the dog visitation program at her last hospital. And the softball team, her staff fellowship, and a charity fund for burn victims. My granddaughter is a bit of an activist. She's determined to take up the gauntlet to help—or protect—everybody."

"Including you?"

"Especially me." Iris gave in to a withering groan. "She wants me to stay in the gift shop so I won't be exposed to the sadness involved with patient care. Erin's been so protective since my husband's death."

"Has it been long?"

"Two years, but . . ."

"It's still there with you. Every day." Hugh's eyes were filled with empathy. "I'm a widower myself. I understand that. I've lost a son too . . . and then there was the car accident a year ago.

Cody's parents—my granddaughter—killed." He exhaled slowly and reached down to pat Jonah.

"I'm so sorry."

Hugh gave an appreciative smile. "I've watched my family trying to put their lives back together. Each in his own way. It's been hard on all of us, but I've been most concerned about Scotty. He and his sister were very close. And since Colleen's death, he's changed. He seems intent on pulling away."

"From the family?"

"Family, friends, church. From Pacific Point too. Scotty's always been ambitious. More than ambitious. Driven, I'd venture to say. In sports, at school, in Scouts—he made Eagle Scout. And now he's pouring that drive into his career. Not at all unusual when one's father was a celebrated hero."

Iris remembered the news clip she'd watched with Erin. How the reporter had mentioned Scott's family and how he'd seemed so upset.

"The son I lost, Gabe McKenna, was also a Pacific Point fire captain. He was killed on duty when Scotty was twelve."

"How awful."

"Yes. And while we've always accepted Scotty's ambitions, this past year has been different. He's been working some paramedic shifts in San Francisco, traveling back and forth. But now he's applied for a full-time position there. In a few other neighboring cities as well. And for a position as chief of emergency medical services in Portland, Oregon. Portland! He thinks his chances are remote and hasn't mentioned it to the rest of the family, but still . . ." Hugh sighed, and then his expression brightened. "That's why I'm heartened to know he's taken Erin to the beach today. It's the first interest he's shown in anything outside work and his visits with Cody."

"Good, then," Iris said, raising her coffee cup. "I'm glad Erin's taking a day off too."

"Because she's not here to ride herd on you?"

She smiled. "And because I like visiting Cody."

"Well, then." Hugh returned her smile. "Jonah and I think you should. Our lips are zipped. Count on it."

+++

"What next? The Sea Swings?" Scott asked idly, distracted by the sun glinting on the gold strands in Erin's hair.

She shielded her eyes and gazed at the enormous tilting carousel, its riders sitting on individual swings as they hurtled, legs dangling, through the sky. "Not sure it's a good idea after lunch." She turned back to him, sun-pink nose wrinkling. "What do you think?"

"I think I'm relieved. Besides—" he nodded toward the Santa Cruz wharf in the distance—"there's a band. I've heard them before, great jazz."

"Jazz?" She looked mildly surprised, and he told himself this was all part of getting to know each other. Music preferences, coffee flavors, front seat or tail end on the Dipper, Boston or Manhattan style chowder. *Got faith . . . or not?* His stomach tensed.

"Let's go," she said, smiling. "I love the wharf."

They walked along the Beach Street promenade toward the pier, Erin talking all the while about how her grandfather fished from the wharf, how she once caught a starfish and hid it in her pillowcase . . .

Scott remained quiet, wrestling with his thoughts. He reminded himself that today was about diversion, not about pursuing a relationship. If he didn't have an arm full of stitches, he'd be out swimming. Alone. The way he liked it. If Cody hadn't been hospitalized, he'd . . . pursue moving away? He pushed away a niggling hint of guilt. His family knew his career goals, accepted them. Portland was a long shot at best. As for Erin, a new relationship wasn't something he could do right now. And he already knew she was the kind of woman who expected far more than he had to give.

"Wish you were swimming?" she said, breaking his reverie.

"No," he said, surprised to see they'd already walked a good distance of the pier and had arrived at the stage area. In front of them, the small jazz band—saxophone, bass, keyboard, and drums—had drawn a respectable crowd and competed with a background of barking seals, hungry cries of gulls, and the deep chug of idling fishing boats. He shuffled sideways to accommodate the crush of impromptu dancers—couples young and old, giggling teens, and a handful of children with painted faces and Day-Glo balloons. "No," he repeated. "I'm glad I'm here." Then he took a slow breath and a risk. "With you."

She gazed at him, uncharacteristically quiet, and he noticed for the second time since he'd met her that there were flecks of copper in the green of her eyes. The sun had deepened the faint splash of freckles across the bridge of her nose, and all of a sudden his mouth was going dry, and his pulse had begun to . . . "Dance?" he asked, filling the awkward silence.

"Sure."

He gathered her to him as the saxophonist began a solo, its rhythm smooth and slow, and they blended into the crowd, mindful of the knee-high children and occasionally buffeted by a helium balloon. Erin followed his lead as if they'd done this a dozen times before. Her hand felt warm and small in his, and despite navigating asphalt littered with popcorn and scrambling gulls, he knew in a matter of moments that she fit perfectly in his arms. Almost like it had been preplanned: the soft weight of her hand on his shoulder, the feel of his palm against the small of her back, and the way the breeze blew fine strands of her hair against his face. She smelled sweet, sort of like warm cinnamon toast. He heard her chuckle.

"I've never done this before. Dancing on a pier." She turned her head. "What's going on over there? See the crowd?"

"Probably nothing," he said without looking, refusing to allow anything to interfere with the moment. "Fishing boat maybe. Big rock cod—seen one, seen 'em all." He drew her close again.

Erin stopped dancing, slid her hand from his, and stepped away. "No, I think it's some kind of emergency."

Scott frowned, tempted to chide her about ER nurses' imaginations. But then the jazz combo stopped playing. The people in the crowd near the boat rental building began to shout and wave their arms. The saxophone player set his instrument aside and hopped down from the stage.

Scott squinted toward a roar of voices sounding increasingly frantic. Erin took a few steps closer.

And then one shout boomed above the rest: "Someone call 911!"

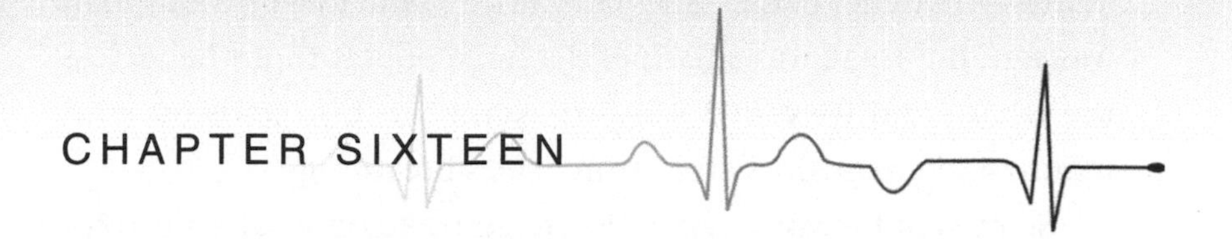

CHAPTER SIXTEEN

"Shocked—electrocuted. That girl's not breathing. Somebody do something!" The heavyset woman whirled, wild-eyed with terror, and stepped on Erin's foot.

"Please let me through. I'm a nurse," Erin grunted, breathless after racing down the pier. She pushed forward, clutching a fistful of Scott's jacket, and stumbled along behind him as he parted the gawking crowd like a running back. All she could see other than people's backs were glimpses of what appeared to be scattered construction equipment, electrical cords, and maybe a disassembled boat lift. She heard the stuttering sound of an engine coming to an abrupt halt, then breathed in the acrid scent of burning wire and plastic.

"Medic coming through! Everyone stand back!" Scott jogged a few more steps and stopped.

Erin bumped into him, then grasped his arm and moved aside to stare down at the scene. *Oh no.* A pretty young brunette in a thermal shirt, worn jeans, and a tool belt lay sprawled on the asphalt beside a tangled heap of electrical cords. Pale and motionless, eyes staring vacantly upward, lips dusky gray . . . *Not breathing?* Erin started forward.

But Scott grabbed her arm. He pointed to a burly, gray-haired man standing in front of an anxious group of laborers. "Have you cut the power?"

"Yes, as soon as I saw the problem. I'm the job foreman. Mattie—that's her name—she had the drill, and maybe the asphalt was wet. But there was a flash and a huge pop. It threw her across the wharf, and we called 911." He scrubbed his hands over his mouth and groaned. "I don't think she's breathing."

Scott kept his voice calm. "We're going to do what we can for Mattie; you keep the crowd back. That's your job now. Give us room to work."

In an instant, they rushed to the woman and knelt beside her, Erin at her head and Scott alongside her torso. Erin shook her gently and called her name without a response. Then she brushed aside Mattie's dark hair and lifted her chin to open her airway. She leaned close—*look, listen, feel*—checking for signs of respiratory effort.

"Not breathing," she reported, dread making her mouth dry. "Got a pulse?"

Scott pressed his fingers into the side of their patient's neck, repositioned them, and concentrated for a few more seconds before shaking his head. "No pulse. She's probably in V-fib from the alternating current." He rose onto his knees and positioned his hands, one on top of the other, over their patient's sternum. "She's young, and time's on our side if we can keep her going until the medics get here with a defibrillator."

"I'm starting ventilations." She pinched Mattie's nostrils, inhaled deeply, lowered her mouth to give a first rescue breath, and then stopped as Scott grasped her arm.

"Wait. I hope that's what I think it is." He pointed to a middle-aged woman barreling through the crowd, holding a plastic case over her head.

Erin held her breath. *Please, God, let that be an AED.*

"Here! Will this help? It's one of those HeartStart machines. We keep it on our charter boat." The woman hurried forward, puffing and red-faced, to hand Scott the case.

"Oh, thank heaven." Erin's breath escaped in a rush as she began furiously hiking Mattie's clothing up to expose her skin.

Her heart tugged as she heard the protective foreman warning people to stand back. "Hey, give my girl some privacy, would you?"

In the distance, a sound like approaching sirens mingled with the screams from the Giant Dipper. Hopefully the paramedics were close. But there was no time to wait.

"Great. Here we go," Scott said, pulling the release handle to start the device.

In seconds he'd pressed the two large, adhesive-backed pads onto Mattie's chest and abdomen, well ahead of the AED's calm, verbal instructions: *"Place pads exactly as shown in the picture."* The triangular yellow warning light flashed. *"Analyzing. No one should touch the patient."*

They leaned away, watching as the machine began to automatically analyze the heart rhythm.

Scott nodded at Erin. "At least with fib we've got something to work with. Sure wish we could see the rhythm."

She knew he was feeling as helpless as she was, waiting for a machine to make the diagnosis instead of reading the monitor display themselves. So different from the equipment at hospitals and on ambulances. But the beauty of the AED was that it had been designed for use by the general public; it was simple and incredibly efficient and was responsible for saving many people.

The orange warning light flashed and the machine spoke:

"Shock advised. Stay clear of patient. Press the flashing orange button now."

Scott depressed the button, and Mattie's body jerked in response to measured joules of electricity.

Erin held her breath, praying as the rhythm was analyzed again. Then groaned softly as the orange light flashed a second time. Still in V-fib.

"Shock advised. Stay clear of patient."

Scott pressed the button and delivered a second shock to the stubbornly fibrillating heart. He glanced up at the sound of sirens and an enthusiastic murmur from the crowd.

"Shock delivered. . . . It is safe to touch the patient."

Erin pressed two fingers on the side of Mattie's neck. "She's got a pulse! It's strong and regular. Good girl. C'mon, Mattie. Stay with us now. . . ."

Voices in the crowd drowned her out. Sirens filled the air and the crowd began dispersing.

Erin pulled off her vest and draped it across Mattie's chest, then looked at Scott. Her head felt suddenly light, legs wobbly as Jell-O, the adrenaline rush receding like low tide. His eyes held hers for a long moment before he slowly smiled. Goose bumps rose and her eyes filled with tears. She bowed her head ever so slightly. *Thank you, Father. Thank you for saving this woman.*

In seconds, the ambulance braked to a stop and the medics hit the ground running. Only moments later, Mattie's dark and expressive eyes fluttered open behind an oxygen mask, and she spoke a few words. Confused, but miraculously alive. Her foreman hunkered close, tears streaming down his weathered cheeks. Several people in the crowd applauded. Then someone cheered . . . as Erin stood and moved into Scott's arms.

"Nice job, Wonder Woman," he murmured, his breath warm against her hair.

"You too." She shivered and he tightened his arms around her. "That sure topped the Giant Dipper."

A laugh rumbled deep in his chest. "Let's get out of here. This is too much like work."

+++

Leigh sighed, and her breath fogged the viewing window for an instant before fading away. Only four newborns this morning—three blue blankets, one pink—all of them wearing standard white polyester infant caps. Not like the ones she'd been knitting for the Save the Children project, with lollipop stripes, shimmery pompoms . . . *"Knit One, Save One."*

She told herself not to do the math, not to count the months. *Our baby would be born in June.* Her hand drifted down the front of her scrub dress, palm spreading across her flat abdomen, and she closed her eyes for a moment to buffer the hollow and confusing sadness. She hadn't wanted a baby; the timing was all wrong, but . . . No good came from dredging up what-ifs. She was having a divorce, not a baby. She'd be content with her work, escapes to the stable, knitting caps for Save the Children, and—

"Morning, ma'am."

Leigh turned and smiled. "Good morning, Sarge."

He shifted his weight to peer through the nursery glass. "Four babies this morning. And three kids up on peds."

Her brows drew together in mild surprise that Sarge would know the pediatric census since he wasn't assigned there. By the wrung-out look of him, eyes rimmed with shadows, a hint of beard growth, he'd probably been volunteering for extra shifts again. Maybe he needed the money. You never really knew about people.

He turned away from the window, nodded at Leigh, and began walking away.

"Oh, Sarge, I forgot. Will you do something for me when you go back to thc ER? The drug reps brought microwave popcorn and one of the packages was torn. It spilled all over my office floor. I tried to get it up, but I'm still skidding on those things. Will you sweep it for me, please?"

"Yes, ma'am, I'll do that for you before I leave."

"Leave?"

"I worked a night shift on the second floor. South wing," he added. "Stripping the floors, cleaning the baseboards . . ."

She apologized, realizing why he looked so tired. And trying not to imagine an amputee struggling with those arduous tasks. "Go home. Don't bother with my office. I thought you were on duty now."

"No problem. I'm glad to do it—I want to help." Sarge raised his hand and touched it to his brow in the familiar salute. "That's why I'm here, ma'am."

+++

Scott ran his thumb over the broken shell, walked a few yards, then hurled it through the darkness toward the sea. The stitches over his wound pinched with the motion, reminding him that if it weren't for the injury he wouldn't be here. He'd have stayed home to swim, to go over B shift's new training schedules, and maybe to tackle the equipment budget again. Still, being with Erin . . .

"Wait," she called out, "let me dump my shoes. They're filling up again."

He turned and saw her grinning at him from where she'd plunked herself down on the sand.

"Besides, I want to stop for a minute and see the boardwalk lights." Erin emptied her shoes, slipped back into them, and stood. "My grandfather used to say the bulbs on the Dipper looked like a million lightning bugs in a conga line." She chuckled. "Of course I'd never seen a firefly. Still haven't, except for fake ones at Disneyland. But Grandy was stationed in San Antonio for a while, so he knew. He knew everything."

Scott crossed the stretch of sand to stand beside her and forced himself to look away from her face long enough to scan the boardwalk. Ropes of colored neon, illuminated flags and striped awnings, the white bridgework of the coaster track, and the Ferris wheel with lighted spokes in green, yellow, and red. "You always talk about your grandfather. Not your father." He saw her expression change and wished he'd stayed quiet.

"That's true, I suppose." She leaned down to roll up the bottoms of her jeans.

He moved alongside her, and they walked down the darkened beach.

"I never knew him very well—my father. Good old Frank Calloway."

"Calloway?"

Erin nodded. "I took my grandparents' name."

"After your father died?"

"Not exactly . . . dead." Her voice took on a surprisingly bitter edge. "But it sure felt like it sometimes." She stopped and kicked a dark mound of seaweed. "My father's been trying to leave us all my life. I never knew what was worse: seeing him take off to chase his newest harebrained idea . . . or having him come back and promise he'd never do it again. Or that time someone spray-painted 'Flim-flam Calloway' on the side of our car after he scammed the neighbors in an investment scheme. Then there was the joy of my entire Brownie troop seeing him at the movies. Kissing the secretary from our school."

Scott winced.

"And now," she continued, "he's back again. After more than twenty-five years of bouncing around, he's suddenly . . . sorry. Sending letters and e-mails to tell me he's a new man, that he's finally seen the light. And found God. My sweet, deluded mother believes him."

"And you don't?"

Erin looked at him like he'd lost his mind. "He's *found* a lot of things before: Ponzi schemes, miracle diet programs . . . He even found a way to profit by reselling life insurance policies on cancer patients." She swiped the tears from her eyes. "Do I believe Frank Calloway's found faith? No. He spent his whole life chasing his ambitions—his self-righteous sense of personal glory—at the expense of his family. He's never going to change, and I won't ever trust him."

Scott hadn't a clue what to say, so he didn't say anything.

"But I do believe, with all my soul, that my grandparents were the biggest blessing in my life. They really loved me. And they had the best marriage I've ever seen, faithful and honest and kind. They were each other's world. Now that Grandy's gone, all I'm thinking about is helping my grandmother put her life back together. Not living down my father's reputation." Erin reached out and touched his arm. "I'm sorry, Scott. I shouldn't have dumped all that on you."

He shrugged, relieved to see that her tears were gone and very aware of her touch. There it was again, that warm eddy in a cold ocean. "It's okay, really. You and I have a strangely similar problem."

She let her hand drop away. "What do you mean?"

"My father's reputation followed him too."

"Wait . . . did I hear something about him on the news? The night the reporter interviewed you at the ranch where the plane crashed? She said your father was a firefighter, right?"

"Yes. Gabe McKenna. He was with the Pacific Point department too. Killed on duty when he caught gunfire in a hostage situation. His crew was doing medical backup. And he tried to rescue a child." Scott shook his head. "Mistaken for a cop. Happens too often."

"That's horrible. How old were you?"

"Twelve. My sister was barely ten. Some of it's sort of hazy now. But for some reason I mostly remember the bagpipes at the funeral and the huge line of cars and police motorcycles following our limo. Firefighters and police officers came from all over the state. A hero's send-off. And I remember how hard it was on my mother. That day and for a long time afterward."

"Did she remarry?" Erin asked as they started walking again.

"Yes. Fifteen years ago. Things have been good for them, except that my stepfather's started having trouble with his diabetes. Then last year they had to deal with my sister's death . . . and now Cody's situation."

His throat tightened, and he told himself he should never have started this turn in the conversation. He couldn't talk about Colleen. *Or how I may have failed her and how Cody's paying the price.* Erin seemed to sense his hesitation and was quiet.

They walked on toward the darkened pier, with only the sound of waves filling the distance between them. He inhaled the scents of sea-scrubbed wood and brine, trying to dispel the troubling sensation of riding a roller coaster to the top of the first hill, then hanging there endlessly—

"You were close?" Erin asked gently. "You and your sister?"

His stomach dropped like the front car on a coaster.

+++

The pain on Scott's face broke Erin's heart. Why had she asked about his sister? It was too new, too raw, and far too soon after the tragedy. She saw that now. She had no right to pry into his private life. Even if they'd shared this wonderful day, worked side by side to save someone's life, it still didn't give her the right. Did she think this tough fire captain had some by-the-book policy for reacting to painful personal loss? that it wouldn't hurt?

"Colleen was my best friend." The dim lights on the wharf above heightened the strong angles of Scott's jaw. "My mother used to say that God . . . She said Colleen was sent to help balance the scale for her big brother's stubborn broodiness. She was joking, but I know it's true. My sister was everything I'm not—funny, good, and giving."

"I shouldn't have asked you to talk about her. I—"

"She shouldn't have died," he growled. "She didn't deserve to be treated the way she was by that guy. It should never have happened. I should have seen it coming. I . . ."

"Oh, Scott." Tears sprang to Erin's eyes. She stumbled forward in the sand and wrapped her arms around him, aching to comfort him. "I'm so sorry it happened." She rested her face against his chest, sighing as his arms closed around her. His heart thudded against her cheek as the sea continued its restless rhythm. Somewhere in the foggy distance a ship's horn gave a low, mournful blast. They stood there in silence for a long time.

Scott's hands slid away; then he tenderly brushed his lips across her forehead. "Thank you," he whispered. "For today."

When he stepped back, her heart began to move to her throat. "Scott, I think . . . you are."

"You think I'm . . . ?"

"Good. And giving and funny and—" She stopped when he moved close again. Her pulse quickened as he traced his fingers along her jaw and searched her eyes. She smiled and gave the barest nod.

Scott cradled her face in both hands and touched his lips lightly to her cheek and the corner of her mouth. She held her breath as he drew back ever so slightly, then covered her lips with his own.

+++

"Why are you checking under the bed?"

Sarge bolted to his knees in the darkness, blood surging to his head as he brought the broom's wooden handle sharply across his chest. He rubbed his head, then groaned as he struggled to stand. Cody's wispy blond hair was barely visible in the glow of the corner night-light.

"Why, Rich?"

"Dust," he said, finally settling his weight onto the prosthesis. "You're supposed to be asleep. It's past ten. Homework, prayers, teeth brushed. Bedtime."

"I . . . don't do that anymore."

"You should. Or you'll end up with cavities like I did."

"No." The boy struggled to pull himself up in bed, murmuring as he dragged his injured leg under the sheets. "I meant that I don't say bedtime prayers anymore. I hardly pray at all now." His eyes looked huge in the dim light. "Do you?"

Sarge grasped the broom handle against a wave of dizziness. The bodies, the children's faces reappeared. Then the echo of his voice. *"Father God, not the children . . ."*

"Do you pray?"

"I have. And you should." He wondered briefly if it would have made any difference if he'd done that more. "Just do it, Cody. That's an order."

"I don't think my uncle says prayers anymore, either. He doesn't come to church with us. And—" his voice quavered—"I don't think he wants to be around me anymore. I don't know why. But it makes me feel so . . ."

The pain in the boy's voice brought the images of the bodies back again, and cold sweat pricked Sarge's skin. "I have to go now. Talk to your folks about that."

"I can't."

The tremble in the boy's voice made Sarge's heart stall. He tried not to wonder who his own son may have confided in over the years.

"They're dead," Cody whispered.

Sarge swore under his breath, stomach roiling as the shaky little voice continued.

"Now I'm afraid my uncle's going away too. I don't know what to do."

He swayed against a vicious wave of dizziness, then checked his lighted watch. Fifteen minutes until the nurses made their next rounds, unless . . . "You didn't call for medicine or anything, did you?"

"No."

"So the other nurses aren't coming in?"

"No."

Sarge walked to the doorway to check the darkened corridor beyond. Empty. He reached for a visitor's chair.

"You still there, Rich?"

"Yes," he answered, dragging the chair toward the bed.

"I'm glad."

He adjusted his leg and sat down. "I'm listening, Cody."

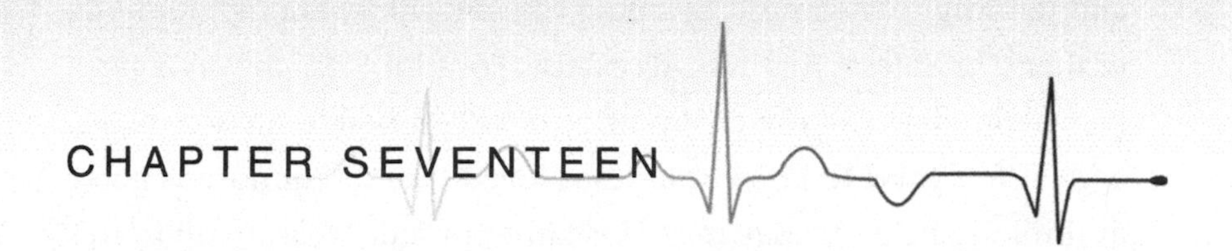

CHAPTER SEVENTEEN

Scott knelt at Colleen's headstone, a speckled pink granite called Morning Rose, chosen by his grandfather after his grieving mother couldn't. Scott had mumbled, "Fine. She'd like it," telling a small lie rather than the larger truth that would rend his heart like the cold spade that opened her grave. *Her favorite flowers are sweet peas, not roses, and any morning without my sister should never come. Maybe I could have prevented this.*

He drew in a slow breath of sea air made smoky sweet by the cemetery's aging stands of cypress and waited for the pain in his chest to dull. His gaze shifted. The next stone was gray and taller, its weathered bronze plaque embossed with a firefighter's hat, shield, and ax. His father and his sister resting side by side. Scott shook his head. He'd talked about them both with Erin on the beach last night. Why? He'd always been more careful than that. But there was something about her . . .

He thought of Erin's excitement when she'd found the pulse on the woman they'd rescued on the wharf, then her rush of tears and her discreetly bowed head. Praying. He hadn't missed it. Scott shifted on his knees, glancing at the headstone again.

Colleen had been the one with stronger faith. Somehow it had always been a part of her, way back to when they'd sung together in Sunday school. *"This little light of mine, I'm gonna let it shine."* His chest tightened at the memory of Colleen, strawberry blonde curls and missing front teeth, waving her little finger like a candle flame and swaying to the music, beaming. She did shine. Enough for both of them, or at least that was his excuse. For him, church was a great part of Sunday, like the crispy strips of bacon beside his scrambled eggs. It felt good to know that Jesus loved him . . . almost as good as thinking he'd one day make his father proud. Measure up to the man Gabe McKenna would want him to be. After his death, Scott had prayed for that above all else. But for Colleen, Sunday worship was one day of seven, all filled with unwavering faith. And with trust.

He gritted his teeth. She'd married far too young, trusting her heart to a husband who'd never deserved her. A rage-filled, controlling man who'd battered her emotionally for years, until he'd finally slammed that car into a power pole.

Colleen's voice mail that afternoon had been nothing out of the ordinary: "Give me a call, big brother. I want to run something by you, okay?" Logic told him that it could have been anything. Any ordinary thing. She'd always valued Scott's advice—teased him, in fact, that if she were on that game show to win a million dollars and wasn't sure of an answer, he'd be her lifeline call. His stomach twisted at the irony as he asked himself the question that had haunted him for nearly a year: Was she going to ask his advice about going on that drive with her husband? *I would have stopped her. Saved her life.* If he'd only returned her call.

He checked his watch. Ten thirty. His grandfather, mother, and stepfather, if he was feeling better, would be here soon. After church let out. They'd finally stopped asking Scott to go with them. Even though he could see the need in their eyes, he couldn't. Couldn't sit there this past year without Colleen. Missing her and knowing that she'd been the one with the stronger faith. And he was the brother who'd skated by, huddling just close enough to catch a glimmer of his sister's redeeming light.

But mostly Scott couldn't sit in church anymore, expecting God to listen, if he'd been responsible for snuffing that beautiful light forever. The gut-wrenching pain of that was what kept him from joining his family at church and from praying. But he was glad that Colleen had passed her faith along to her son. That was what mattered now. Cody would keep her light alive.

Scott stood, wondering again why he'd talked to Erin about Colleen. And remembered how she'd moved into his arms to comfort him. The warmth in holding her close, kissing her, was unlike anything he'd felt before. Maybe because Erin was different. Passionate, fearless. He pictured her expression as the Giant Dipper's track dropped away in front of them. She had such gutsy devotion to her career, her grandmother . . . her faith.

There it was again. He'd seen the look in her eyes when she'd asked him about prayer: *"You're not good with that, either?"* She'd be as forgiving of his doubts about faith—his neglect of his sister—as she was of her reckless and irresponsible father. He'd never be the kind of man she wanted.

The stitches were coming out in a few days; Scott could swim again. Then he'd follow up on his job applications. It was best for everyone.

He set the bouquet of sweet peas in front of the pink headstone and walked away.

+++

"I think Elmer needs a friend." Iris tapped the tank, smiling as the old goldfish rose toward her fingertip. He stared out at her, his mouth forming a perfect, plaintive O. She glanced toward the bathroom, raising her voice. "He looks lonely."

"Right." Erin's voice echoed through the short hallway. "Or maybe hungry. He ate that last friend you bought him. And all the snails too, remember? Nana, you can't force relationships." Her tone was decidedly cynical. "Sometimes alone is better."

Iris sighed. *That's our girl, Doug.*

She headed back to the couch, shaking her head. She'd bite her tongue, of course, but Erin had no business being pessimistic. Not at thirty-one and not an hour after attending church. Especially when last night she'd seemed so . . . different. Iris lifted the newspaper onto her lap. It was true. Erin had come home from her day at the beach with more than a sunburned nose; there had been a new quality to her voice, breathless and warm, with something in her eyes . . . *Dreamy* was the word Iris would have used to describe it back in her day, though the word would make her granddaughter, the boxer, cringe. Still, she was certain the look in Erin's eyes had everything to do with Scott McKenna. Even if she'd talked mostly about the roller coaster, a new ride called the Sea Swings, how the clam chowder tasted exactly the same, and about that awful electrocution.

Iris's gaze fixed on a newspaper photo, and her eyes widened. She studied it again to be sure, then walked toward the bathroom. "Erin?"

"I'm cleaning the tile. Twenty bucks' worth of Eco Cleaner and this mold is still so stubborn."

"Oh, heavens." Iris walked through the doorway, immediately blinded by the glare. She squinted toward where Erin stood in the shower stall. "Why are the lights so bright?"

"Hundred-watt bulbs. Four of 'em." She pointed her flowered

glove at the overhead fixture. "The window's too small, and mold thrives in darkness, so . . ."

Iris glanced at the bathroom's solitary window. And the stained-glass sword and shield which obliterated the morning sun. She bit her tongue for a second time. Sometimes the obvious remained elusive. Even in the light of 100-watt bulbs. She lifted the paper. "It looks like you and Scott made the *Sentinel*'s Metro page. At least I think that's you." She pointed at the photo washed gray by the too-bright bulbs.

"Really? Let's see." Erin stepped out of the shower and took the paper. "Yes, it's from far away, but that looks like my hair. Probably taken with a camera phone. The foreman tried so hard to keep everybody back." She scanned the short article and sighed. "Good. No mention of our names. Scott made them promise. He's had all he can stand with Pacific Point media."

And Pacific Point itself? Iris thought of her coffee conversation with Hugh. He'd said his grandson was pulling away, and the paramedic shifts in the Bay Area might evolve into something more permanent. Even as far away as Portland, Oregon. And then Scott would be gone. She fought the image of a heartbreaking Christmas Eve. Six-year-old Erin, sitting on the porch step, waiting for her father. Maybe her granddaughter's wariness about relationships—as much as Iris hated to see it—was a good thing this time. She couldn't bear having her disappointed again. Or hurt.

"But I'm sure glad he was there," Erin said, a hint of last night's softness returning to her eyes. "We're good together. I mean, we work well together. I'd thought since he acts mostly as a captain, managing things at the station, that Scott would have been more hesitant with medical procedures. He surprised me."

"Do you think you'll be seeing more of him?"

"Oh, I don't know," she said, her tone a touch too casual. "We're both so busy. I've got my work, Faith QD takes time, and I . . ."

Have a grandmother to protect? Iris reminded herself to avoid the topic of her volunteer work.

"Scott's schedule's really demanding," Erin continued. "Plus, he's part of the Ocean Rescue Team. And then there are the problems with his nephew, Cody."

Iris caught herself before she could nod. Erin had no idea she'd met Cody Sorenson. Guilt prodded her. Lying . . . within an hour of attending church. And she'd asked Hugh McKenna to cover for her. She was a fine one to point a pious finger.

"He's ten, and he's a patient at Pacific Mercy. It's fairly serious. The whole family's had some . . ." Erin hesitated, and Iris knew it was out of respect for their privacy. She felt a rush of pride for her granddaughter's integrity. "Anyway, it's been a tough time for Scott."

Erin inspected the shower one last time and frowned, then removed her cleaning gloves before switching off the glaring lights. "Besides, I'm not sure if it would work out. We're different in a lot of ways."

Iris's eyes adjusted as she entered the hallway. "I think God planned it that way, darling. Difference can be a good thing."

Erin followed her into the kitchen, and Iris was fairly certain she'd grumbled something under her breath, probably about her father. There'd been another e-mail from him this morning. Along with a conciliatory plea from her mother. Both immediately deleted, of course. And just as quickly added to Iris's prayers. *Gracious Lord, help our little fighter learn that forgiveness shows strength, not weakness.*

Erin folded her arms across her chest. Then she chuckled. "It's your fault, of course."

Iris turned, brows raised.

"My pathetic lack of a love life." Erin sighed, her expression as wistful as a six-year-old's. "I'm holding out for what you and Grandy had. I can't settle for less." She rested her palms on the chipped Formica counter, gazing around the small space. "You used to dance right here in this room. Start out washing dishes, end up dancing. Or arguing about politics."

"Discussing." Iris shook her head. "Your grandfather and his convictions—stubbornly loyal no matter how the wind blew."

"Exactly. That's what made it so great. You were both that way—about your relationship most of all. Solid, always there for each other no matter what happened."

Iris looked away, her stomach beginning to sink.

"Faithful and honest. That's why I know it's possible. That's why I can't accept—" Erin touched Iris's shoulder. "Is something wrong? I'm sorry. I shouldn't have gone on and on about Grandy."

"No. It's not that." Iris pressed her fingers to her chest. "Really, I was just thinking I should make another pot of coffee." She reached for the bag of beans. "And shouldn't Annie Popp have some of those triple chocolate . . . ?"

"Brownies." Erin glanced at the wall clock. "You're right, and she just opened. I'll walk down there and get some."

Iris exhaled, relief making her shoulders sag. "Good."

Erin tugged her sweatshirt over her head, grabbed her purse, and opened the door. She looked over her shoulder. "We'll sit outside. It's gorgeous out. I'll water your hollyhocks; then you can tell me how things are going with the volunteers. I want to hear everything."

"All right then."

Iris ground the coffee, filled the coffeemaker, then waited

while the pungent brew streamed through the brown paper filter. Erin's words repeated over and over in her head. *"It's your fault, of course."*

Was it? Her intelligent and compassionate granddaughter had become cynical, defensive, untrusting . . . and lonely. Erin was so quick to blame her father. Frank Calloway was an easy target. And Brad, that last boyfriend, had been so appallingly dishonest. But if Erin was basing her faith in successful relationships solely upon . . . *Is it my fault?*

Iris walked over to the fish tank and knelt down beside it, watching Elmer root through the pink gravel, always searching for something better than his food pellets. Nearly two decades since that day Doug pitched all those Ping-Pong balls in an attempt to win so much more than a goldfish.

Tears welled. Erin would soon be home with a sack of Annie's brownies, and she'd want to hear all about Iris's volunteer work. Which was worse: hiding the fact she'd been spending afternoons sitting with Scott's nephew or that her perfect marriage to Erin's beloved grandfather would never stand up to inspection under 100-watt bulbs?

+++

The Sunday surfers were out in force, at least a dozen straddling their boards in the cove below Arlo's Bait & Moor. Kids scurried along the sand chasing skimboards, dodging an older man as he tossed a stick for his tireless black Lab. Alongside parked vans, groups of young people stood talking and listening to music, women wearing smocked dresses and skirts in hibiscus prints and tie-dye, men in sunglasses and neon wet-suit jackets over plaid shorts, sand clinging to their tanned legs.

Sand. Erin sighed. She'd had sand in her shoes when she got home last night. Had shaken them out over her grandmother's hollyhock bed, but she was having less success shaking the confusing tumble of emotions left in the wake of her day with Scott. The Giant Dipper paled in comparison. He'd kissed her. *No, we kissed.* It had been as mutual and unexpected as their rescue of that victim on the wharf. Her face warmed, remembering Scott's arms around her, the soft thudding of his heart as he held her against him, and that look in his eyes the moment before he leaned down . . .

And then they'd driven that endless hour home in maddening silence. Scott watching the road, occasionally switching the jazz tracks on his iPod, Erin antsy to fill in the pauses with disconnected chatter. Anything to end the silence, quell her whispering doubts. The same anxious energy kept her awake long after midnight and then had her up early. Too early to slam the speed bag around, so she'd changed lightbulbs and pulled on cleaning gloves to scrub the shower tile.

Would Scott call? *Do I want him to?* That was the real question. Because what she'd told her grandmother was true—she and Scott were different. Except for what she'd seen of his concern for his family; she admired that. Her throat tightened, recalling the pain in his voice when he'd talked about his sister. It was the reason she moved into his arms in the first place. And his selfless need to protect his nephew was so very obvious. She felt exactly the same way about her grandmother. Erin groaned. Her grandmother who was waiting for brownies.

She opened the screen door and was greeted by the aroma of freshly brewed coffee and decadent fudgy chocolate and by Annie Popp's engaging grin. From a boom box behind the counter, a very young Elvis crooned truly vintage Southern gospel.

"Smells like heaven," Erin said, sniffing the air.

"Someday maybe. Not ready to sign my recipes over yet." Annie winked. "Not that the angels haven't been twisting my arm." She set down a piece of driftwood knotted with lengths of fishing line. "Starfish Latte extra cinnamon?"

"Yes, please. And some brownies, if you have any left. I should have come right after you made your rounds." Erin felt a rush of warmth for the bait shop couple who carved time out of their precious Sundays to gift local nursing homes and shut-ins with fresh-baked treats. The remaining few dozen were sold first come, first served to the always-hungry beach crowd.

"For Wonder Woman? Always."

The teasing nickname made Erin remember Scott's hug on the wharf after they'd rescued Mattie. His whisper against her hair, *"Nice job, Wonder Woman."* It wasn't even a week since they'd met here to talk about the incident review . . . and battle over the critical stress counseling. It felt like so much had changed.

"Great. Four then, please," Erin said, pushing the thoughts of Scott aside. "Nana will be thrilled." She stepped close to the counter, regarding the weathered pieces of driftwood, spools of transparent fishing line, shells, and beautiful sea-tumbled bits of glass. She touched one with a fingertip. "I tried glasswork once. Stained glass."

Annie reached for a Get Hooked on Our Coffee cup. "I remember."

"You do? Did I bring it down here to show you?"

"I remember the Band-Aids," Annie explained, her kind eyes saying much more. "Your fingers were covered in them that summer."

Erin hated that her father's morning e-mail came to mind. "Yes. It was really hard. Stained glass, I mean. Those sharp pieces and the hot solder. Getting it perfectly matched up, making it all fit." She lifted a piece of the sea glass, opaque and wonderfully smooth. "This seems so different."

Annie raised her head at the sound of belly-deep laughter outside.

Erin glanced through the screen. Arlo was on the wooden porch holding his tall, hand-carved walking stick. He stood with two of the young surfers, nodding as he listened intently. His white curls moved in the breeze, making him look almost like King Neptune, while above him a galaxy of sea glass mobiles twirled and tinkled. Annie had always said that listening was Arlo's gift.

"And it's easy. The mobiles, compared to the stained glass." Annie handed a short piece of sun-bleached driftwood to her. "Do you know what I like best about them?"

"No Band-Aids?"

Annie smiled. "That too. But I think the best part is that each piece is worn smooth by the sea. By time. Sort of the way people are shaped by life experience. And by tests of faith." She lifted her unfinished mobile from the countertop, some of the strands of fishing line still hanging loose, several shells and pieces of wood clumped awkwardly together on one side. "The trick is to get the balance right. Balance, counterbalance. It takes some trial and error. You need to find that one point of support—a fulcrum—and then it all comes together." The breeze swept across the porch, and the mobiles tinkled again. "Then there's the sound, of course. Silence . . . sweetened." She reached for a pastry sack. "Now, brownies. Four fat ones."

Erin reached into her tote for her wallet.

"Oh, by the way—" Annie filled the sack and set it down—"was that you on the Metro page today?"

"Um . . . yes. I guess it was."

"I thought so. Arlo owes me a foot rub. And was that Scott?"

Erin hoped that her face wasn't as red as it suddenly felt. "Yes. We were . . . It was lucky we both . . . happened to be right there on the wharf."

Annie's eyes twinkled. "Amazing how those things happen."

Erin lowered her gaze, taking longer than necessary to pull the bills from her wallet. If she was this clueless and confused about Scott, no way would she try to explain it to Annie. "An incredible coincidence."

"Well, I'm not much on coincidence," Annie said, raising her voice as the laughter on the porch rumbled again. "To me, it's all about balance—that all-important fulcrum. It's a larger plan than we can know, my dear."

"What?"

Annie chuckled, then nodded toward the doorway.

Scott.

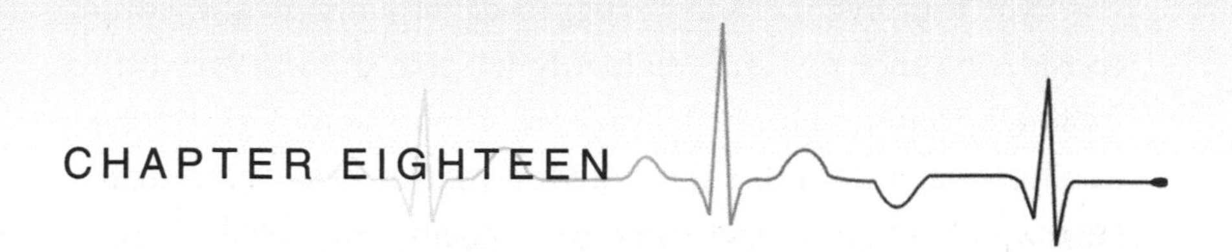

CHAPTER EIGHTEEN

Erin told herself to breathe. It was ridiculous to feel nervous and self-conscious. Even if Annie's bemused gaze made her personal life seem as transparent as . . . Elmer Fudd in his tank. *Breathe.*

"Uh, hi." Scott smiled, glancing first at Erin, then toward the counter. He rubbed his hand over his hair. "Sea Dog black. And a tide table if you've got one, Annie."

"Coming right up."

"Tide table?" Erin asked, relieved when Annie moved toward the coffee machine. She took in his San Jose State sweatshirt, mussed hair, light beard stubble, sleepy eyes, lips . . . Her heart thudded, and she could almost feel sand in her shoes again. "You're swimming?"

"In a few days, I hope. I'm stopping by the ER tonight to have the sutures checked. I'm hoping they can come out a couple of days early." He shook his head. "Man, going without my workouts has been making me crazy. You know?"

Yes, I know. She looked away, stomach sinking. He'd just explained it perfectly: temporary insanity. That impulsive, crazy kiss last night. A mistake. Which was why he hadn't—

"I tried to call you," Scott said, lowering his voice after a glance to where Annie still fussed with the coffee cups. "This morning around nine thirty."

"I was at church." Erin wasn't sure whether she felt relieved or simply more convinced of the chasm between them.

His lips pressed together. "Right. I should've thought of that."

"Not a problem." She shrugged as casually as she could, considering that her arms suddenly felt like she was laced into weighted training gloves. It was clear from the look in his eyes that he felt as awkward as she did. More than awkward . . . *regretful.* He regretted what happened between them. *Don't I?* She turned toward the counter, hoping her order was ready. She wanted to get out of here.

Scott cleared his throat. "I'd planned to call again, but—"

"It's fine," she said, cutting him off. "You don't need to do that. Really."

He crossed his arms, and for some reason she felt a wave of déjà vu. As if they were arguing over that disaster barricade again. She in her scrubs, he in his smoke-stained jacket. At odds with each other from day one. Why hadn't she left it that way?

He sighed. "What I'm trying to say is . . ."

A roar of laughter from outside the screen door swallowed his words.

Then Annie called out, "Here's your coffee. And if anyone's interested, I've still got plenty of bottled water. More than enough, if those water tests keep looking good. Thank the Lord. I'll sure be glad when things are back to usual."

"Some things already are," Erin mumbled as she paid for her order. Why would she think that last night had meant something to Scott? Hadn't she learned her lesson with her father? The minute you start counting on a man, trusting him to be there, to really care . . . that's when you're vulnerable to a sucker punch. Erin wasn't making that mistake again.

Annie signaled to Scott. "I've got to run back to Arlo's bait counter and grab your tide table."

He stepped up alongside Erin and her stomach fluttered. She turned to leave.

"Erin, wait."

"Can't. Sorry."

"I want to explain."

That you kissed me out of temporary insanity? "No need," she said, forcing a smile. "I've got to go. My grandmother's waiting. But I hope you're able to swim soon. That everything's back to usual. Just like Annie said."

"Uh . . . right."

Erin walked straight out the door, under porch rafters tinkling with sea glass, and kept going until she reached the railing overlooking the beach. Then she squeezed her eyes shut and exhaled the breath she'd been holding. It would be a blessing if things were really headed back to usual. It would be. For Pacific Point, for Arlo and Annie . . . and for Scott. He was ready to go back to his swimming and to a life that didn't include Erin. The pesticide scare might still spin some things out of control for a while, but then it would be over. Back in balance. Wasn't that what Annie had said was so important with the mobiles?

It was the same with boxing. Being strong was nothing without balance. It was exactly what Erin's trainer had always said: assume a proper stance, keep your feet shoulder width apart, knees slightly bent. Have someone push you relatively hard. *"If you lose your balance, you're not solid."*

She nodded; she needed to find balance. Stay solid. Not only in boxing, in her whole life. Remain focused on the things that counted—keeping her grandmother safe and happy, doing the best she could for the ER, and growing in her faith. *Have someone push you relatively hard . . .*

The fact was, she'd been pushed hard. By her father's return, the pesticide event . . . even by that wonderfully warm and completely crazy moment with Scott last night. She couldn't let those things throw her off. She had to keep her stance, stay strong and balanced. On her own two feet.

Scott stepped out onto the porch, and she started walking toward the road. Her grandmother was waiting. They'd have coffee and brownies. And then Erin would glove up and spend some quality time with the speed bag. *Strong, balanced . . .*

She nodded at Scott's tentative wave, then picked up her pace. She'd avoid him for the next several days; they'd both get busy with their lives, and that would be the end of it. Crazy could only lead to heartache.

+++

"It's past reveille, Sarge. Heads up, or you'll fall over."

His eyes snapped open in semidarkness, hands gripping the wooden handle as he stared at the young bearded man, confused for several seconds. Navy blue scrubs, stethoscope . . . ICU nurse? Right, that new hire. Sarge groaned under his breath; he'd been mopping the vacant patient room and must have dozed off. Leaning against the wall. Working overtime onto day shift wasn't such a great idea.

"Yeah," he snapped, "fall over and then lie there while you stepped around me. Like I'm collateral damage in some . . . forgotten war."

"Uh . . ." The nurse backed up. "Hey, I was just joking. Take it easy. Well, I'd better go check that ventilator. See you."

"Yup." Sarge snapped a half salute and then frowned as the nurse disappeared, his freshly ironed scrub pants making a swishing sound as he hurried away. Scared probably. Not that Sarge cared.

He shook his head, trying to get rid of the ugly, confusing anger that had suddenly begun choking him—gritty and suffocating as a Persian Gulf sandstorm. He didn't like it, didn't understand it . . . and knew it could jeopardize every good thing he was trying to do. *I'm trying to save that boy.*

He groaned again, shifting his weight away from the wall and back onto the bulky prosthesis. Stupid to fall asleep. Stupider to smart off to the nursing staff. He needed this job. That nurse had done nothing to harm him. But being dressed down like that had made his gut churn, especially after what his landlord did yesterday. Let someone into his apartment. He didn't remember asking anyone to check the heating system. It had to be an excuse, a reason to get inside his apartment for surveillance. They were on to him, had probably gone through his things—food, garbage, papers, and medicine bottles. Maybe even handled the only photograph he had of his son. He knew they'd done that, even if they hadn't left any visible evidence.

Sarge clenched the mop handle, anger pricking his fatigue. He hadn't slept even an hour before going to his night shift—and to watch Cody. He'd checked everything. Threw out food that might be poisoned, searched for listening devices, even dismantled the toilet with that useless pair of pliers.

He rubbed at his scabbing knuckles. They hadn't found what they were looking for. He'd hidden the mission journal in the storeroom up on peds, zipped into the musty bag of an old vacuum cleaner behind the linen bins. The notes were his way to stay focused—harder and harder now that the VA's medicine was out of his system and the nightmares were back. Faces. Dead eyes. The squeal of Scud missiles streaking across the night sky. The horrifyingly simple click in the vast desert silence . . . an instant before the land mine took his leg.

He reached into the pocket of his scrubs, grasping his nearly empty cigarette package with trembling fingers. He needed a smoke. He'd make it a short one, a few drags to take the edge off. His gaze moved to the ceiling. Smoke detectors, sprinkler systems everywhere. If he lit up, they'd alarm and staff would come running. Along with security and engineering and maybe even the Pacific Point Fire Department. The operator would Code Red over the PA system, and in minutes it would be completely crazy, and . . .

Sarge lifted the military Zippo from his pocket. He ran his thumb over the smooth metal surface of the lighter while looking up at the smoke detector system. Distraction was a good tool to have in a war arsenal—along with the aluminum bat tucked into the vacuum cleaner bag with his mission journal and the stash of beef jerky. The enemy might have been able to break into his apartment, but no one was going to hurt Cody. He'd see to that.

+++

"Para . . . el bebé." Leigh presented the knit cap to Ana Galvez's very pregnant mother. Then she pointed at the doors of the ICU, her brain scrambling to come up with a translation. "And *espero que* Ana soon . . . *se sentirá* . . . better." She nodded and clasped her hands over her heart, resorting to mime as her Spanish failed, but saw that Mrs. Galvez understood completely: *I hope your daughter will feel better soon.*

The young mother's eyes filled with tears and she grasped

Leigh's hand, pressing a kiss onto it. *"Usted, Doctora, es un ángel de Dios. Muchas, muchas gracias."*

I'm *an angel of God?* Leigh smiled at the irony of those words. God would hardly consider her an angel; over the past few months they hadn't even been on speaking terms. She was more than happy to let Erin be the resident angel of the ER. But still, Leigh was trying to find encouragement in Ana's response to the newest antibiotic. Her white blood cell count looked better, though she remained on the ventilator. But she'd opened her eyes, and that small response was enough to convince her family that their beloved child was on her way to a full recovery.

Leigh wanted to believe it, especially in light of the sad news that Charlene Bailey, the woman with the hemorrhagic stroke, had worsened. At one point yesterday, this waiting room was filled with members of both families, the Baileys trying to accept that they'd soon be saying good-bye, and the Galvezes welcoming what they believed was a miracle from God. Long and painful vigils . . . relief coming in two vastly different ways.

Leigh was relieved, too, that things were moving toward normal after the pesticide incident. People were still drinking bottled water until the water testing was completed, but no more gallbladder attacks had been blamed on poisoned fish. And panicky phone calls to the ER were dwindling. The two organophosphate victims on the telemetry unit had been discharged. Sandy's name had been penciled in on the upcoming work schedule. Closer and closer to normal every day. It felt hopeful, safer.

Ana's mother finally released her from a second smothering hug. Leigh said good-bye and started back down the hall toward the ER after adding, *"Sí. Gracias, gracias,"* to the woman's animated narrative containing the words *muchos tamales*. She hoped it meant she'd be eating them in celebration of Ana's recovery, not helping to cook them. If anything was worse than Leigh's Spanish, it was her kitchen skills. The cooking had always been expertly handled by . . . *Nick.* The image came before she could stop it: her husband at dawn, handsome and sleepy-eyed after a night shift, puttering around the kitchen to prepare her favorite omelet.

Does he do that now for her? Leigh's heart cramped in that way which refused to go away. And reminded her of the biggest personal reason she was relieved things were improving in Pacific Point: the National Guard wouldn't be needed. Her husband didn't have an excuse to show up. She winced at the memory of his words that night at the stable. The urgency in his voice. *"I want to see you."*

He'd said they hadn't talked. That wasn't exactly true; he'd said plenty, leaving voice mail and text messages, sleeping outside the house in his car to try to catch her. Always attempting to somehow explain away what he'd done; Nick had been relentless—until she threatened a restraining order. He was wrong. Talking wouldn't fix anything. Back then, and certainly not now. It would only tear the scab off the wounds she'd been trying so hard to heal with time and distance. Distance from Nick. And . . . Leigh passed the open doors of the hospital chapel, and her lips pressed tightly together. Yes. Distance from God too. Though she wasn't sure who was most responsible for that separation—she, by slogging through prayerless weeks of depression and hopelessness; or he, by deciding she should lose a baby in addition to her husband. Either way, the result was the same. A disconnect, same as her marriage.

She nodded and picked up her pace as she crossed the lobby, reminding herself she still needed to make an appointment with the lawyer. The mention of it had stopped Nick from contacting her again. Good.

Leigh flinched as loud screeching sounded overhead. *What's that, the fire alarm?* She stopped, her gaze traveling across the lobby.

A second alarm joined the first in an earsplitting crescendo, and visitors scurried toward the exit, holding their hands over their ears. The Little Mercies volunteer rushed from her shop just as the operator page shrilled overhead: "Code Red area one. Code Red main lobby."

+++

"Uncle Scotty, if it was a real fire, the sprinklers would put it out, right?"

"Right." He watched as his nephew scanned the ceiling. Trying to act brave, while lying in bed attached to an IV, with his leg pieced together like welding shop project. Scott's chest constricted. He'd gotten upstairs as quickly as he could, but he still wasn't sure he'd convinced Cody he was safe. *Safe* . . . Guilt stabbed him. *Now I worry about keeping him safe?* Scott made himself nod confidently. "I had two of my men crawl up into the space over the lobby. Everything looks okay. The alarm was tripped by accident. Promise."

Cody gave an exaggerated shrug. "I'm not worried."

"Good, then." Scott's gaze lingered on his nephew's face for a moment, noticing how the boyish roundness was gone. Cody's chin seemed sharper, his cheekbones more prominent. There was pallor in place of his usual sprinkle of freckles and a pinched look to his expression. Tragedy, loss, and pain had aged him far too much this past year.

Scott swallowed against the ache in his throat. "What if I come back tonight? We'll play one of the DVDs. I'll sleep in the chair like I did that other time. Keep you company. I don't know as many jokes as your grandpa, but—"

"Is he better?" Cody interrupted, his features pinching again.

"That's what your grandmother told me," he said, realizing that though it was the truth, he'd be willing to stretch any truth to ease the look in Cody's eyes.

"Were you there?"

"Where?"

"At church, when Grandpa started feeling worse."

"Uh . . ." Scott's stomach churned, and for some crazy reason he saw Erin's face.

"You don't come with us anymore," Cody added. A statement, not a question.

"No." Scott scraped his hand across his mouth. "I don't." He realized with another sickening wave of guilt that the past year's tragedies had made this boy not only older but far wiser. He looked down, hoping that Cody wouldn't ask—

"Why not?"

"I . . ." Where did Scott find the answer for that? How could he say his sister died when Cody lost both of his parents—worse, saw his father try to kill them all? explain that he was hurting too much when his nephew was lying there hoping to keep his leg? or admit to Cody that he couldn't face God, because he'd failed his family, and now nothing felt good anymore, except swimming? Fighting those cold currents and sometimes finding a rare, merciful warm spot . . .

Cody met his gaze, the impossible question still in his eyes.

Scott's breath escaped. "I don't know why. I have a lot to figure out, I guess."

Cody was silent for several seconds, then nodded. It almost looked as if he understood.

"So," Scott said, after clearing his throat, "movies—sleepover?

I have to go to the ER and get my stitches checked, but I'll come back."

"Don't you have to work in the morning?"

"I can go from here. I know you're not a little kid anymore, but I could keep an eye on things."

"The night nurses do that. They're great. Especially one of the guys. He's pretty cool."

"Oh yeah?" Scott smiled, despite a small stab of jealousy. "Well, that's good."

"So you can go. It's okay."

Once again, Scott had the feeling Cody had matured far beyond his years . . . maybe beyond his uncle. He stepped close and ruffled the boy's hair. "You get rid of that IV pretty soon, don't you?"

Cody's eyes lit for the first time. "Yes. On Wednesday. And the doctor said I could leave the hospital for a few hours once it's out. If I promise to stay in the wheelchair. Grandpa's picking me up." The pinched look returned. "Do you think he'll be better? that we'll still be able to do that?"

"Sure," Scott said. "Now where's my hug?"

Cody's arms closed around him, and Scott shut his eyes for a moment, letting the brief, sweet connection stretch the truth about his lonely life.

+++

Erin stilled the speed bag, then glanced down at Elmer Fudd. The goldfish, transparent fins swirling, stared placidly out at her. No tsunami waves. She'd finally figured out how to punch the bag without shaking the wall behind his little glass condo. It had to do with her foot position and the arc of her swing. Balance. Just like Annie said. Erin needed to stay balanced over her feet, be strong and consistent, and stick to the moves, the routine . . . no crazy stuff. *Crazy.*

She pressed a towel against her damp forehead. She wasn't going to think about Scott. She'd eaten two and a half brownies, whipped her heart rate up to 140, and was sweating right through her Faith QD T-shirt. Chocolate and endorphins—he was supposed to be banished. It wasn't fair. All she was asking for was a little bit of peace.

Erin stepped close to the window and smiled. Now *there* was the perfect vision of serenity. Her grandmother, auburn hair tied up with a batik scarf, sat on the garden bench in the rosy gold sunset, her back straight, hands resting palms up on her thighs, and eyes closed. Her breathing was rhythmic and intentional. Beside her lay her well-worn Bible. Centering prayer. She'd done this for as long as Erin could remember. She explained it alternately as "my quiet time," "Christian meditation," "listening with the ear of my heart," and—when her life was particularly hectic and her temper short—"my only sliver of sanity. Now scoot and leave me be!" Sometimes, during those awful months of her husband's illness, this daily silence had seemed exactly that. Her sanity and her strength.

Since childhood, Erin had tried over and over to emulate Nana's peaceful repose. And failed completely. The truth was that profound stillness made her edgy. Silence prompted her to . . . fill it. Her work, the chaos of the ER—sirens, nervous chatter, beeping alarms—felt far more normal. On her days off, she whacked at her speed bag, shadowboxed on the beach, or jogged along the sand, listening to her iPod instead of the waves. Even when she curled up to read, she tapped her foot to an endless stream of music. Deprived of that, she'd hum. Always moving, never silent; it was who she was. If she were a goldfish, she'd welcome the tsunami.

Erin saw her grandmother open her eyes and stepped out to join her on the small patio. "Psalms?" she asked, pointing at the open Bible before settling into the old painted chair. She breathed in the salt air, catching a whiff of the neighbors' barbecue.

"Yes. A verse kept running through my mind—" her grandmother laughed—"which is getting more and more filled with cobwebs, I'm afraid. But I finally found it."

"Which one?"

"Psalm 28:7. 'The Lord is my strength and my shield; my heart trusts in him, and I am helped.' I saw it on a bookmark at the hospital."

Erin leaned back in the chair, stretching her legs out in front of her. She closed her eyes, idly wondering how to resurrect their own rusted barbecue. The air smelled like grilled chicken. "So how are you getting along with Helen in the gift shop?"

"Fine."

Erin waited a few moments and then opened her eyes. "That's it? Just fine?"

Her grandmother closed her Bible. "Was there something specific you wanted to know?"

"No. I just expected you to sound more enthusiastic. These days you spend almost as many hours at the hospital as I do."

A sudden, radiant smile lit her grandmother's features, and Erin realized she hadn't seen that in a very long time. *Thank you, God.*

"I love working there," her grandmother said. "It's wonderful."

Erin chuckled. "I'm not so sure you would have thought so today. I heard the fire alarms went off. Leigh said Helen sprinted out of Little Mercies so fast her wig flew off." Her grandmother's eyes widened, and she hurried to explain. "It was a false alarm. No smoke. The fire department came, though."

"Scott?"

Erin picked at the hem of her T-shirt. "That's what Leigh said. And I guess he stopped by the ER afterward to get his stitches checked. He's anxious to get them out so he can start swimming again." She noticed her grandmother staring intently. "I'm not going to be seeing him anymore. If that's what you're wondering."

"No," she answered, her gaze drifting. "I was only thinking about how concerned he must have been for his nephew when that alarm came in."

Erin nodded. "I'm sure he was. I know how I'd feel if you were in danger."

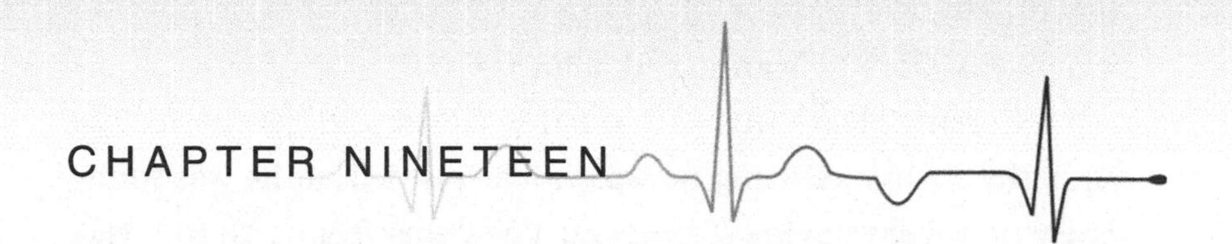

CHAPTER NINETEEN

"Are you okay, sir?" Erin's gut instinct told her that he wasn't. She'd been heading toward the administration offices when she saw him leaning against the wall beside the elevators. A muscular man maybe sixty years old, salt-and-pepper hair, dressed in a blue work shirt layered over a thermal one—and in obvious distress. She had a feeling that the ER's laid-back Wednesday morning was about to change gears. "Can I help you?"

"No, really . . . I'm fine," he said, telling a complete whopper. "Just a little stomach upset. It caught me by surprise; that's all." He forced a smile that did nothing to change the look of pain and anxiety in his eyes. His skin was ashen, and sweat beaded on his forehead. The stitching over his breast pocket read, *Wells Bros. Electrical.*

"It looks like more than an 'upset.' When did this start?"

"On the drive over. I was going to visit my grandson upstairs before work, and—" He pressed his palm flat over his sternum and groaned softly. "I'm sure . . . it's . . . nothing."

Erin reached for his wrist. "And I'm not so sure." *Skin damp, cool, pulse steady, but . . .* "Any health history? Heart trouble, diabetes, high blood pressure?"

"Diabetes and some pressure problems."

Two out of three. "I'm Erin Quinn, the ER charge nurse. And I want to take you down there to check things out. To be safe. Really. I think this is necessary—you're pale and sweating and short of breath. Mr. . . . ?"

"Wells. Gary." He grimaced. "But I—"

"No buts. Please trust me on this," Erin said gently, feeling empathy for him, sensing he was embarrassed. That he was someone who valued staying strong. She knew that feeling all too well. But if she was right and his pain was of cardiac origin, every minute counted. "Stand right here while I grab a wheelchair."

"I'll see the doctor. But I can walk; I don't need—"

"Wheelchair, Mr. Wells," she said, tempering her firmness with as much compassion as she could. "We're playing this by the rules."

Within five minutes, she got Mr. Wells on an ER gurney and alerted the physician, and in the next ten they'd obtained a history and vital signs, done a twelve-lead EKG, and begun routine cardiac protocols.

Erin finished prepping his arm for an IV. "You're going to feel a needle stick, sir. I'll be as gentle as I can."

"It's okay." He watched his heart blip in neon green across the monitor screen. "But I still think if I'd had some Tums I would have been fine."

Denial. Still. *How many patients do we lose to that?* "Maybe. But we always play it safe with chest pain. And your diabetes does add risk. Now here comes the needle; bear with me, please." Erin poked the 18-gauge needle carefully through his skin and into the forearm vein, confirmed a blood return, and then inched it forward a bit more before threading the plastic cannula into place. "All of these things—the monitor, EKG, oxygen, aspirin, and this IV access—are routine." She secured the needle with tape and drew several vials of blood before flushing the attached tubing with saline, then plugging it with an access port. "I'm sure your family will want us to take good care of you."

"I appreciate all that's been done, and you've been especially kind. It's only that I hate to burden my family with this. They've had too much to deal with lately. Way too much." His voice thickened with emotion. "I'd do anything to spare them."

"I can see that," she said, touched by his concern for his family. *What a blessing to have a father like that.* She shoved the thought aside. No time. No point. "And so far, so good. The doctor said your EKG looks great. And—" she checked the cardiac monitor—"your rhythm's as good as mine, your blood pressure's back to normal, and your pain's subsided. Right?"

He nodded.

"Great. We'll check your cardiac enzymes and get a chest X-ray." Erin picked up the blood vials and pulled off her gloves, then caught sight of an attractive middle-aged blonde standing in the doorway. "Hi. Are you . . . ?"

"Lynda Wells. That stubborn man's wife." The woman's smile faded, and her eyes brimmed with tears. "Oh, Gary—" her fingers moved to a small silver cross at the collar of her denim shirt—"I should have stopped you from going to work this morning. I was afraid you weren't feeling as well as you said you were. And when they called and told me you were here in the emergency department . . ."

"I'm sorry, sweetheart."

Erin waved her forward. "Come in, please. I was just telling your husband that everything's looking good so far." She stepped aside as Mrs. Wells took her husband's hand and pressed it to her lips.

"His pain is gone," Erin continued, "and nothing yet points toward a serious cardiac problem."

"Thank goodness," the woman said, settling into the chair beside the gurney.

"Mostly," Erin added, "he seems to be worried about worrying you."

Lynda Wells shook her head. "That's my Gary." Affection warmed her eyes. Beautiful, expressive eyes with dark lashes, a striking smoky gray . . . and somehow familiar, though Erin couldn't recall having met her before. "But when our son arrives, he'll have plenty to say about Gary pushing himself so hard, taking chances with his health. He's a paramedic with Pacific Point Fire Department."

"Really?" Erin said. "I've probably seen him here."

"Maybe not." Mr. Wells lifted himself up higher on the gurney. "My stepson doesn't work the ambulance much since his promotion, and . . ." He glanced toward the doorway and his face lit with a smile. "Scott, we were just talking about you."

+++

Iris inched the library cart closer to the doors as the elevator settled to a dipping stop at the third floor. Then smiled as the doors opened to reveal Hugh McKenna.

"Well, good morning, Iris. What a pleasant surprise. Here, let me hold that door for you." He slid his arm through the open doors, the movement shifting the bright-eyed Chihuahua tucked against the front of his corduroy blazer. "Jonah and I took the stairs." Hugh chuckled. "He's watching my cholesterol."

Iris laughed, then eased the cart out into the pediatrics foyer. "Thank you. Both of you. I was bringing Cody a magazine, but if I'm interrupting a visit . . ."

"No, no. Not at all." A flicker of concern crossed his face. "In fact, your being here could be a blessing. Scotty and I were in Cody's room, and—"

"Scott's here?" Iris glanced warily down the corridor.

"Don't worry. I meant that he was here a few minutes ago, but he got a call on his cell. His stepfather, Gary, is down in the ER. He was on his way to visit Cody and started having chest pain."

"Oh, I'm sorry to hear that."

"So am I." Hugh stroked Jonah's head. "But I just phoned my daughter-in-law. She's been assured that Gary's out of danger."

"You can't help but worry. Does Cody know his grandfather's ill?"

"Not yet. He got his IV out, and he's expecting Gary to pick him up for an outing. I'm not sure how we'll handle it. That's why I'm glad you're here. I told Cody that Jonah was needed for a pet therapy visit, but actually I wanted to slip down to the ER myself."

"Go. And take your time." She touched his arm. "I'm always glad to sit with Cody."

"Thank you." A smile spread across his face, and his eyes held hers for moment. "What would we do without the Quinn women?"

Iris raised her brows.

Hugh chuckled. "I hear your granddaughter is Gary's nurse. Strong team, you two."

Her face warmed unexpectedly, and once again she felt that wonderful sense of being needed. *Strong team?* She liked the sound of that.

"Well, Jonah—" Hugh tightened the straps on the dog's carrier—"ready to jog the stairs?"

Iris waved as they disappeared down the corridor, then pushed the cart to Cody's door. He was sitting in a wheelchair, leg extended, and his immediate grin made her heart soar.

"Iris! Cool—you found my magazine?"

"Yes," she said, glad she'd made the trip to Arlo's Bait & Moor. The hospital selection offered donated paperbacks and very limited magazines. Fashion, sports and fitness, *Bon Appétit* . . . But *Sport Fishing*? Not exactly. "You're quite the fisherman, then?" she asked, handing him the magazine.

"Trying, anyway." He shrugged as his gaze moved from the glossy photo of a marlin to his propped leg. "Not so easy right now."

Her throat tightened.

Cody looked up. "But my grandpa's coming to pick me up. He's taking me to the wharf."

Iris nodded despite her stomach's descent like the hospital elevator. How disappointed was this child going to be if the outing was canceled?

"I'll have to stay in a wheelchair and be back in time for my whirlpool treatment, but we'll still have plenty of time to watch the fishing boats. I'm taking my camera. You never know what they're going to catch out there." Cody's smile faded, and there was a flicker of discomfort in his eyes. Along with a sudden shimmer of tears.

"What is it, Cody? Are you having pain? Should I call the nurse?"

"No," he said, taking a shuddering breath. "I'm okay. I just remembered the time my mom caught her first halibut. It was a nice one, maybe thirty pounds. They've got both their eyes on one side, you know?"

"I've heard that," Iris said softly.

"Well, Mom did this big girly squeal after she hauled it onto the boat and got a look at it. So Uncle Scotty started teasing about how its eyes were that way 'cause she'd pulled up too fast. Her mouth dropped open really wide . . . then he started laughing and I did too. My uncle laughed so hard his sunglasses fell overboard. Mom said it served him right; see if he got any when she cooked it. It was so funny, a great day, and . . ." Cody's voice cracked, and the look on his face broke Iris's heart.

Father, help me comfort this child.

He swallowed and the tears slid down his face. "I miss her . . . all the time."

She stooped down and he flung his thin arms around her neck, burrowing his face against her shoulder. She patted his soft curls and rocked him ever so slightly, murmuring soothing sounds. And let him cry.

When Iris began to push the library cart down the hall, she remembered what Hugh said earlier. That she and Erin were a strong team. Though she'd loved the sound of that, it wasn't true. Not if one team member was sneaking around behind the other's back. Nothing strong there. It was ridiculous—and wrong. She had to tell Erin she'd been visiting Cody. Explain that instead of being exposed to heartbreak and tragedy, her time with him made her feel better than she had in a long while. And next time she'd bring Elmer Fudd along, just the way she'd promised before she left today.

There was nothing for Erin to worry about. No need for her to be so overprotective, always imagining dangers. Iris stopped abruptly alongside the door to the housekeeping closet, frowning. It felt like she'd rolled over something on the floor, and now the cart refused to budge. She wanted to get downstairs and find Hugh, see if Cody's grandfather was being discharged. But this silly cart . . .

She tried again, pushing hard against the heavy weight of the books. The cart creaked sideways and faltered. It felt like something was . . . Iris knelt and checked the wheels. Yes, something had wedged itself into one of the casters. She peered closer. What was that? It looked like a half-chewed, sticky strip of . . . beef jerky?

+++

Sarge grabbed the sack of OB department trash and hurled it onto the pile near the huge hospital trash sanitizer at the north end of the hospital, feeling heat through its iron doors. He'd seen it in action these past nights when he slipped out for a smoke during his watches for Cody. From the closet to the stairwell, only a few paces. And not hard to sneak by the pediatric nursing staff—all staff levels were down, especially on nights—but he'd also had to figure out a way to bypass the outside door alarm.

It had been worth the risk. Smoking and drinking were the only things that eased the gut-gnawing edginess that replaced the dulling effects of medication. No, not the only things. The boy made him feel better too. *More than anything has . . . since I last saw my son.*

He hefted another sack, heavier than it should be, from the cart and pitched it onto the growing pile. He frowned; the orthopedics staff was probably dumping half-empty irrigation bottles again. Water bottles. He thought of Cody and how he was replacing the boy's drinking water from the supply he'd stocked in the housekeeping closet. The hospital provided bottled water, but he didn't trust any bottle he hadn't inspected himself.

He'd learned that only too well in the Gulf. The lives of his squad had depended on it. Only bottled water shipped from the States was safe to drink, snort up their noses—sputtering, coughing—in futile efforts to wash the gritty, all-invasive sand from their sinuses, and for saturating pieces of wool blankets they'd stuff under their gas masks to filter the noxious stench of hundreds of burning oil wells. Black, sulfurous, and suffocating as the very air of hell—toxic.

He clenched his teeth. Mustard gas, sarin, Ebola virus, anthrax. The fear was that the enemy had it all. In the Persian Gulf . . . *and here now?* If you watched the news these days, you knew what else they had: ricin, botulism, nuclear. He glanced around the trash bin. Radioactive materials were supposed to be disposed of separately, but you couldn't trust anybody. Not when they were strapping explosives to women, hijacking ambulances and fire trucks to carry terrorists, using innocent little children . . . *Ah, no. No.*

Perspiration beaded on his forehead as the sounds, smells, and images returned with an ugly vengeance—high-pitched squeal of missiles, oily smoke, pillar after pillar of orange fire rising in the blackness . . . Then the discovery in pale morning light . . . bodies of civilians, nomads who'd pitched their tents in the dark in the strike zone. The coppery stench of congealing blood, staining the sand . . . so much of it, all mixed together: from camels, men, women . . . children. Those tiny faces, pale hands, those dark, unseeing eyes. *"Father God, not the children . . ."*

Sarge's stomach lurched and he retched, leaning against the brick wall until the nausea finally subsided, the heaves mercifully dry because he'd eaten little more than beef jerky. He tried to remember Cody's whisper in the darkness of his hospital room. *"You still there, Rich? . . . I'm glad."*

He folded his hands to his chest for a moment, holding his

breath. When was the last time anyone had been glad to see him? needed him for anything more than mopping up a mess, lifting something heavy, or emptying the trash? When had anyone cared enough to ask him something like . . .

His chest constricted as he remembered the boy's words. *"Do you pray, Rich?"*

Sarge opened his eyes at the sound of distant sirens and fumbled in the pocket of his scrubs for his cigarettes. He was running low. Better run by the gas station. Get some jerky too. That old woman in Little Mercies was looking at him like he was nuts for buying so many. *Ever heard of C rations?* It didn't matter. But he couldn't risk the mission by having her get suspicious.

He flicked his Zippo, touched the flame to the end of his smoke, and inhaled deeply. Then pinched the cigarette between his lips and reached for another sack. Red plastic. Pathology lab, he could tell from the faint, sickly sweet smell of formaldehyde. Specimens, tissue. *Body parts?* He yanked the cigarette from his mouth and cursed as the new, toxic anger swirled.

No one was taking Cody's leg. No one was hurting that kid. He'd do whatever it took to keep him safe. And he'd take out anyone who stood in his way.

+++

"Well . . ." Scott shook his head as Jonah's yodel receded down the ER corridor. He glanced back at Erin. "Can't say you haven't been warned about the McKenna clan."

"No, I can't." She blinked at him, studying his face long enough to make his pulse quicken. "And I like what I've seen—" she glanced down—"I mean, your parents are great. I'm glad things look so encouraging for your stepdad."

"Yes." Scott glanced toward the doors to the ER, the mix of dread and relief swirling again. "You made all the difference, Erin."

"I didn't do that much. Fortunately he was fairly stable and the ER wasn't a madhouse, so I was able to whisk him right in. Once we got his blood pressure to settle down, it was simply a matter of—"

"Hey. Hold it." Scott grasped her shoulder. "I'm saying you were good to my parents. Explained things, took time. Cared how they felt. It meant a lot to them after all they've been through." He took a breath and released it slowly. "It means a lot to me too. Thank you."

"Well, good, then; I'm glad." She raised her arm to look at her watch, and he realized his hand was still on her shoulder. He lifted it away reluctantly. He hadn't seen her in three days and hadn't known until just this moment how much he'd missed her.

"What's next?" he asked, suddenly unsure whether he was asking about medical treatment . . . or about where things stood between them.

"Gary's almost ready for discharge; he'll go home and rest. Tomorrow morning he comes back for the thallium treadmill and more labs. With orders to return here if anything changes in the meanwhile, of course."

"How likely is that?"

"Not very. You heard the doctor say that his symptoms are probably gastric and point more to the effects of stress."

He nodded, his stomach churning at how tough things had been for his parents this past year. For his grandfather, too, and especially for Cody.

"And I'm afraid," Erin continued, "the doctor nixed the idea of your stepdad taking that outing with Cody this afternoon. He was really disappointed."

"They were going to watch the fishing boats come in," Scott said with groan. "Ah, man, I forgot. Cody hasn't been farther than the hospital's sunroom in nearly two weeks."

"Your grandfather was going back up to his room; maybe he's going to take him."

"Can't. Doesn't drive much anymore. Takes the bus most places. And he'd have trouble with a wheelchair." He scrubbed his hand across his mouth, remembering Cody's pallor and pinched expression, the feel of that frail hug last night, his plaintive voice when they'd talked about church. *"You don't come with us anymore."*

"Then you'll take him. It's the only solution."

"I'm working," Scott blurted, his mind already ticking off the list of things he had to accomplish at the station. *That follow-up phone call to Portland . . .* "Today's not a good day. The chief is counting on me to . . ." His words trailed off as he caught her expression. So much like that night she'd talked about her father.

"You can't take some personal time? explain things to your chief so he understands that your family needs you?"

"Right. Okay . . . I'll make sure my parents are settled at home, check a couple of things at the station, and—" He stopped, noticing that she'd begun to smile.

"I love it," she whispered. "I love that you'll do this for him."

"Then come meet him," he said in a rush, needing to share the sweetest part of his family with . . . *the most caring woman I've ever met.* "After Gary's discharged, come upstairs. Okay?"

"I . . ." Her fingers moved against his, and he was surprised to realize that somehow he'd taken hold of her hand. "Sure," she said, her smile widening. "I guess I can handle one more branch of the McKenna family today."

+++

When Erin arrived at the peds room thirty minutes later, she found Scott and Cody poring over a magazine, blond heads together. Both with Lynda Wells's expressive eyes. She pushed aside the doubts that kept trying to creep in. Would he have chosen to disappoint this boy if she hadn't pressed him? *Could he really do something like that?*

"Good. You made it." Scott rested his hand on his nephew's shoulder, his expression clearly proud. "Erin, this is Cody. Cody, Erin. She's a nurse . . . and a boxer."

Erin laughed. "Your uncle exaggerates. But I hear you're a fisherman."

"Yes," Cody said enthusiastically, despite the wheelchair and bandages. Her heart squeezed, knowing he'd suffered far more than physical wounds. "When I'm better, Uncle Scotty and I are going out on a charter boat. Maybe we'll pull in some of the big ones, like the pictures in my magazine." He tipped his head as if he were studying Erin's face. "Hey, you look kind of like her—my library lady."

"Librarian? I don't think so, buddy. Erin's more the adventurous type—roller coasters and . . ." Scott's voice faded as his eyes met hers.

Erin was glad Cody broke the silence. "Do you fish, too?" he asked.

"Sure. My grandfather used to take me." She wrinkled her nose. "Lingcod—those guys have teeth."

"Cool." Cody glanced at his uncle. "We're going out to the wharf today. I can't fish this time, but I get to watch the boats."

"Right," Scott answered, still watching her face, "and maybe Erin could come along."

Her eyes widened.

"Oh yes!" Cody's grin spread. "Could you?"

"Well . . . I'd have to get someone to cover for me. But Judy's been wanting some extra hours, so maybe . . ."

"See if she'll do it," Scott said, "and we'll all go watch the boats."

+++

Iris stepped around a bobbing cluster of balloons, smiling at her granddaughter. "What 'little mercy' brings you in? PowerBars, trail mix?"

"No." Erin smiled back. "I wanted to tell you I'm leaving early."

"Oh?" Iris asked, knowing the telltale flush springing to Erin's cheeks had nothing to do with sudden illness.

"I'm going to the wharf with Scott and his nephew. He's being released for a few hours, and I thought . . . we thought it seemed like the right thing to do. For the boy."

"Of course." Iris nodded, remembering the child's mournful tears. *Good plan, Lord.* "I have my car, so don't worry about me."

Erin tugged at the string on a balloon and watched it bob for a moment, the look in her eyes almost wary—like a child afraid it would sail away. She sighed. "He wants to take me out for dinner after we bring Cody back to the hospital. Would that be okay?"

"You're asking permission?"

Erin's flush deepened. "No. I was thinking about your evening."

"Pooh. It gives Elmer and me an excuse to order Chinese. He loves bean sprouts."

"You're sure, then? I won't be out late."

"Perfectly sure," Iris assured, then wrapped her granddaughter in a tight hug. "Don't give me another thought. I'm fine. Now scoot. I've got work to do."

She watched Erin head toward the ER, then stepped into the back room to grab her sweater. When she returned to the counter, she was surprised to see a customer standing there. The big man with the ponytail, that employee she'd seen the day she'd bought a gift for Erin. "I'm sorry. I didn't hear you come in. You're Sarge, right?"

"Yes, ma'am," he answered politely. He set a spiral notebook on the counter. "I'd like to buy another one of these, please."

CHAPTER TWENTY

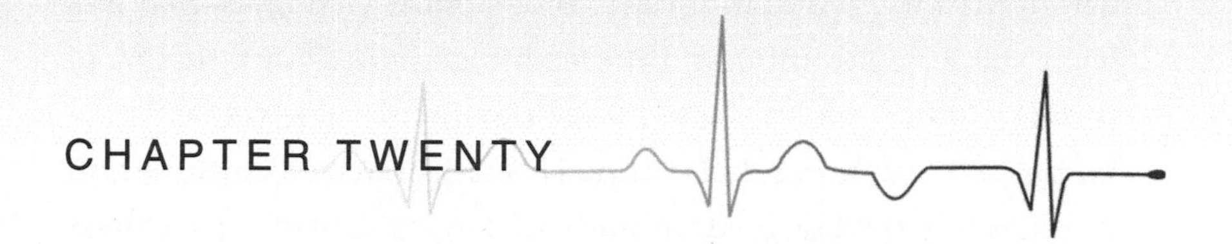

Erin hadn't been kidding about fishing—she knew her stuff—and Scott wasn't sure who was more impressed, he or Cody. She knew her way around little boys too. His nephew had a crush. Couldn't blame him.

"Squid, slimy mackerel . . . bloodworms?" Cody taunted, continuing his litany of gross bait and blinking into the afternoon sun.

"No problemo," Erin insisted, planting her hands on the hip pockets of her jean skirt. "Can't make me squirm. I told you." She checked the brake on the wheelchair.

"Chicken guts, liver, kidney?"

She rolled her eyes. "Nurse?"

Scott snorted, biting his lip to keep from laughing. He watched her point toward the ocean and hand the binoculars to Cody as the breeze flirted shamelessly with her hair. In the distance, the sharp bark of sea lions rose above the soothing push and pull of the waves. Erin's perfume, cinnamon sweet, mingled with the salty air. More effective than any bait. He reminded himself that he'd invited her along because Cody had seemed taken with her, because Grandma Lynda couldn't make it today, and because it had been so long since his nephew had laughed in the sunshine, joked, and been fussed over by a young woman.

Erin patted Cody's hair and then stooped to peer through the binoculars. Sunshine on her hair, long-legged stance, athletic, and so very confident. She was an amazing combination of strength, determination . . . and innocent vulnerability. Genuine—that was what she was. Beautiful and incredibly genuine. Warmth spread through him. Who was he kidding? Having her here was as much for him as it was for Cody. Scott had been deprived of sunshine and laughter too. He'd slogged through long months of cold loneliness this past year, limited himself to work and intense training, pushing aside all hope for happiness. But did it have to be that way? Didn't he deserve to feel alive again?

"Scott?"

"Yeah?"

"Cody's tired. And his leg is hurting," Erin said, her concern palpable. "Maybe we should get him back to the hospital."

"Right," Scott said, glancing at his watch and feeling the cold swirl back as mercilessly as the tides below Arlo's Bait & Moor. *His pain, my fault.* "It's time."

And time he stopped kidding himself. He wasn't the right kind of man for Erin. It was foolish to even think of that. The important thing was to get Cody well and settled back with his grandparents . . . and then move ahead with his career goals. It had been the plan all along.

+++

Our lemon tree. Leigh stared at the e-mailed image on her cell phone. The dwarf fruit tree in its beautiful hand-painted pot. It was blossoming, dozens of delicate white and purple blooms. *Like on Capri.* No message. But then, there didn't have to be. An ache spread from her throat to her chest. Why would Nick do this? The first time he contacted her since she mentioned divorce, and he reminded her of their honeymoon? They'd planted the tree as a memento. She sank into her office chair, telling herself it could have been worse. He could just show up here, and—

"Ma'am?"

Leigh spun toward the door, startled. "Oh, Sarge. Need to sweep up?"

He glanced over his shoulder, then back at her, hugging his broom handle close to his chest. His eyes looked tired. "I wondered if you could spare some heartburn pill samples?"

"Sure." She rose and walked to the shelving near the door. "I should have some. Yes, here we go." She grabbed a package, then hesitated. "Indigestion, not chest pain? I don't have to worry about you, do I?"

"No, ma'am," Sarge said. "Don't worry."

"Good." Leigh handed him the antacids. "If this keeps up, you'll give your doctor a call?"

"Yup. Thanks."

She watched as he peered at the sample for a moment, turning it over and over in his hands. "That's what you wanted, isn't it? Antacids?"

He nodded, headed toward the door, and stopped. "That girl," he said, twisting around to meet her gaze again.

"Girl?"

"The one they poisoned. She's better?"

"You mean Ana Galvez?"

"Yeah."

"There are signs of improvement. That's encouraging."

Sarge sighed deeply. "They won't win. We'll save her."

"Yes . . . we're doing our best." Leigh returned his salute and watched him walk across the trauma room. *"We'll save her." We.* This housekeeper felt part of the team working to save a little girl's life. How great was that? If everyone thought like Sarge Gunther, the world could be a better place. But . . . Her brows drew together, recalling his words. *"They won't win."* Who were "they"?

She shook off the thought, picked up her phone, and deleted the lemon tree.

+++

Erin glanced around the casually upscale restaurant, voted Best Seafood on the Monterey Peninsula, glad she'd slipped into the ladies' room for a quick trace of shimmery lip gloss and grateful for the hammered silver earrings she'd tucked into her purse. With those touches and the white cotton sweater she'd layered over her shirt, she didn't look completely like a deckhand. After all, she could be picking anchovies out of her hair. She chuckled.

"What?" Scott asked, buttering a last chunk of sourdough.

"Cody and his bait talk." She shook her head. "He'd have given anything for a handful of slimy stuff to tease me with."

"That's the job of a ten-year-old. Though Cody hasn't had much opportunity to enjoy it lately."

His gray eyes grew shadowy somber, and Erin was reminded of all the family had endured . . . were still enduring. It was troubling Scott; she'd seen that today. Along with something more that she couldn't quite put her finger on. A sense, though it was obvious he cared for his nephew, that he'd needed her there, almost as some kind of buffer.

"He lives with your parents?" she asked, nudging a grilled shrimp with her fork. Somewhere across the room, waiters finished singing an anniversary tune. People clapped.

"Yes." A muscle twitched along Scott's jaw. "His father's family is scattered. They've hardly been in contact since the accident. My mother works from home, so she's freer to get Cody to his doctor appointments. And to help him with his studies so he won't get behind in school. It's the best solution . . . for Cody, I mean."

"And having you close by, being able to count on you, must be a huge blessing for your whole family. It's obvious how much Cody admires you, and—"

"Coffee?" he asked, cutting her off. It was there again, that look in his eyes.

"Um . . . sure," she answered, certain now that he was struggling with more than he'd made known. That look reflected far deeper pain than when he'd ripped his shoulder open on the ocean rock. He was still hurting from his sister's death and because of Cody's uncertain outcome. It was the reason she'd tried to comfort him that night by moving into his arms, and . . . She raised her brows, realizing he'd asked something. "I'm sorry. What?"

"Key lime pie. It's good here."

"Absolutely, then," she said, anxious to put him at ease. "And thank you for this wonderful dinner. It's been a treat for me."

"And the least I could do after you helped my parents today."

She glanced down, hoping the disappointment didn't show on her face. "Well, I told you I was glad to help. You didn't have to—"

"Erin," he said. "Hey, wait."

When she looked up, her breath caught at the change in his eyes.

He reached across the table and took hold of her hand, his expression earnest. "I said that all wrong. Asking you to dinner has nothing to do with paying you back for what you did for my parents. Or Cody. Or any of that. I asked you here tonight because I wanted to be with you again."

"Oh." Erin sighed with relief.

The waiter interrupted to pour their coffee and Scott let go of her hand. She met his eyes. The tender look was still there. On the rugged and handsome face of a man who stirred her, whether she wanted him to or not. A kind, selfless man, who cared for his family. *But wouldn't be here for Cody if I hadn't pressed him?* The doubt rose again, and she hated the fact it made her think of her father. Scott wasn't anything like Frank Calloway. He was one of the rare, good guys. *Believe it.* She cleared her throat and smiled at Scott. "So, then . . . key lime pie?"

They ordered dessert and sipped their coffee while they waited. Erin was quiet, feeling Scott's words hanging in the air like a gull over the Pacific Ocean. She stirred more cream than she wanted into her cup as the sun dipped gold and lavender toward the sea. Beautiful and as seemingly serene as Nana's silent repose on her garden bench . . . except that Erin's thoughts tumbled in new confusion. While her heart boxed against a hundred little doubts. All waving red flags.

"I wanted to be with you again."

How on earth was she supposed to trust that? Did she want to?

Bait was so much easier.

+++

They'd snatched the boy. Right under Sarge's nose.

He hunched over the employees' lounge table, pretending to read an article on deer hunting while he strained to hear the conversation at the lockers beyond. The voices rose over the rattle of metal doors and the canned laughter from the lounge TV. Lupe and Claudia, housekeepers assigned to the pediatrics floor talking about Cody Sorenson.

"I tell you, girl, that boy breaks my heart. I keep praying he won't lose that leg. Ten years old, same as my oldest grandson. Such a shame."

"Do they know yet? If the infection's spread?"

"I think they have to do that MRI before they can tell."

"And decide if he should go off to that oxygen chamber. Didn't Michael Jackson sleep in one of those things?"

What? Sarge patted his pockets for the antacids, his stomach roiling. He leaned forward and tipped his head as he listened for more.

"If you believe the tabloids. *Hyperbaric chamber* is what it's called. Like the divers use if they get the bends. I guess it helps wounds too. But it all sounds wrong to me. Squeezing a kid into an MRI tube, then shutting him into that oxygen chamber. I'm glad they let him go out with his uncle today."

"That was his uncle? My, my, I didn't think he'd make it through the doors with those shoulders." Claudia's voice whooped loudly, then dissolved into giggles.

"Yeah, and the spitting image of his father, Gabe McKenna. You remember the story. I swear that family's going down the road of the Kennedys—one sad thing after another."

"Oh, I didn't make the connection. That's too bad. Well, the boy's tucked in bed now. I brought him a granola bar. Have to leave the rest to God."

"Amen." The lockers rattled. "Safe to clock out now?"

"Yeah, four minutes after. Don't forget that key—someone might steal your moldy old Tupperware."

There was a groan and more laughter as the voices began moving closer.

Sarge sat back in his chair and raised the hunting magazine, his stomach still churning. *An outing with his uncle.* What was to stop someone else from taking the boy? Could the hospital be trusted to check identities? And the oxygen chamber. What kind of garbage was that? Were people fooled that easily? He'd been wrong to think that watching the boy at night was good enough. He needed to be upstairs during the day too. But he was scheduled off tomorrow.

"Hey, Sarge. Time to clock out." Lupe pointed at the magazine cover. "Or are you gonna hang around here and hunt somethin' down?"

"Nah. Only killing time."

"I'm not wasting another lousy minute." Lupe sighed. "Tomorrow comes too fast. And I'm back upstairs, mopping floors and emptying trash instead of watching my grandson's spelling bee. He's gonna win, and his grams will see it on a camera phone . . . if I'm lucky. I requested Thursday off before the schedule came out, but you think the boss could give me a break?"

His breath snagged, and he forced himself to wait several seconds before speaking. *Easy does it. Be casual.* "What time is his spelling bee?"

"The assembly starts at two. It'll be over by the time I'm out of here."

Sarge shrugged. "I'll come in, cover a few hours for you."

Lupe's mouth dropped open. "Hey, don't kid a grandma like this. Heart can't take it."

"Not kidding." His pulse quickened.

"I can't believe this. Why—?"

Claudia nudged her. "Tell the man thanks, honey. Then run before he changes his mind."

"Okay." Lupe nodded. "Sarge, I could kiss you for this."

"Do it and I *will* change my mind."

Lupe laughed. "Well, thanks. You're a lifesaver."

The woman had no clue how true that was.

+++

"When are you bringing Elmer Fudd?" Cody asked.

Iris pulled a chair close. "Next time. I thought you'd had enough excitement today."

He snorted. "I want to see him, but I wouldn't call a goldfish exciting. Small shark or a jellyfish, maybe. My great-grandpa's a marine biologist. I've seen stuff."

"I'll bet." Iris thought of Hugh McKenna with his yodeling dog and how concerned he'd been for his family today. She was glad things were working out. And that Cody had his outing. The sun had raised a smattering of freckles over his nose. "You had a good time at the wharf?"

"Better if I could have fished, but we'd get in big trouble if my bandage got wet or if I bumped it or . . ." Cody's gaze flicked to his propped leg, and he sighed like he'd long ago tired of the subject. He glanced back at her. "You've never come after dinner before and without your books."

She shrugged. "Time on my hands tonight. Plus, a little bird told me you wouldn't have many visitors."

He rolled his eyes. "I'm too old for that 'little bird' deal."

Iris laughed and smoothed his thermal blanket. "Okay, then, your great-grandfather told me."

"You know him?"

"Yes." She'd almost said, "Small world," but decided it was as clichéd as gossipy little birds. "I met your uncle Scott too." She shook her head, thinking that day seemed so long ago. The day of the pesticide poisonings, the day she'd applied as a volunteer here. And Erin tried to talk her out of it.

"He was working today at the fire department, but he asked for the time off to take me to the wharf. My grandpa was supposed to take me, but he's sick. Grandma called a little while ago. She said he's better, but she was using that voice."

"What voice?"

"The one people use when they say things to make you think everything's okay."

"What kind of things?"

"You know. Like just now when she said, 'It's nothing serious with your grandpa.' Or when people tell me, 'They'll get your leg fixed this time' or 'Your mother's watching you from heaven.' And 'We'll take that charter boat, Cody.' Those kinds of things."

The pain in his eyes made her heart stall and she searched for words, afraid she'd come up with another cliché or use "that voice." She finally picked the subject that sounded safest. "Charter boat?"

"With Uncle Scotty. We're supposed to take a fishing boat out of Monterey when my leg's better. He bought me this cool deep sea lure called El Squid, but . . ."

"But what?"

"Sometimes I'm not sure we'll really go. Because—" Cody picked at a thread on his blanket—"he's not around as much as he used to be. Not since the accident." His shoulders lifted and fell in another sigh. "Today was good, though. And I'm glad Erin was there. He invited her to come with us. She's a nurse."

Iris nodded, a wave of guilt washing over her. If she told Cody about Erin, then he'd mention it to Scott, who'd tell . . . She was going to have that talk with her granddaughter. Cliché or not, it was a small world. And it was past time that she cleared things up. *A lot of things, Lord.* Tomorrow . . . Friday at the latest. She'd do it.

"Erin's pretty. Nice too," Cody said. "And knows about bait—can't say that about most girls. She makes my uncle smile. I think he likes her."

+++

Scott ended the cell call, then glanced at Erin standing a few yards away. She'd stepped away from the truck to give him privacy and was gazing at the ocean.

He inhaled slowly, watching. The sunset's burnished glow, orangey bright, splashed across her cheeks and tinted her sweater coral pink, almost like a reminder of her incredible warmth. Not that he needed a reminder. He'd been steeped in it all day—when she'd cared for his parents in the ER; the good-natured teasing with Cody; a discreet bowing of her head before beginning their meal; and the feel of her skin when he'd briefly taken her hand across the table. Her warmth . . . warmed him. Like nothing had in so long. Made him want that. No, worse, made him *need* to feel it again, and—

"How's Gary?" she asked, walking back toward him with the breeze in her hair.

"Good," he said, trying to ignore his mouth's going dry. He cleared his throat. "He's sleeping." Down the beachfront street, there were the faint sounds of music and laughter mixed with the far-off chug of boat engines.

"I'm glad. And I'll say a prayer for his tests tomorrow. He's going to be fine, Scott." Erin's eyes met his. "Thank you for all of this today. I loved meeting Cody, and dinner was wonderful." She chuckled and pointed down the long wharf. "But I should force you to walk the entire length of this thing with me, after you tempted me with that key lime pie."

"No problem. I could use the exercise myself," he said, realizing that while he'd had the stitches removed earlier than expected and would be able to swim tomorrow morning, he suddenly didn't care. For the first time in a year he didn't feel the need for it. He wanted warmth, not cold. "Besides, I hear music down there."

"Sounds more like a hungry sea lion to me."

"No. I heard music a minute ago. I swear. Which also means dancing."

"Dancing? The last time we tried that someone got defibrillated."

"We'll be more careful."

"Well . . ." A surprising wariness came into her eyes.

"C'mon," he said, reaching out to her. "Let's risk it."

She took his hand and the warmth swirled.

CHAPTER TWENTY-ONE

Erin leaned back in the creaky rattan chair and laughed at the look on Scott's face. Pure exasperation. It turned out the elusive music had been coming from a karaoke party, a Hawaiian-themed fund-raiser for a senior citizens' recreation center. They'd set up on the deck outside a cheesy seafood bar, with clusters of brightly colored tables, swags of party lights, neon palm trees, tiki torches, fruit punch, a bubble machine . . . and row after row of double-parked walkers. Plastic leis required; glow-in-the dark hula skirts optional. Erin tied one around her hips just to see Scott cringe. She glanced around the tables, shaking her head. They were the only couple under sixty. By a long shot.

"So," she said, raising her voice over a trio of oldsters singing a rousing rendition of "Tiny Bubbles," "shall we review our ABC's?"

"Huh?" Scott fussed with his triple leis.

"Airway, breathing, circulation. If they start the 'Hokey Pokey,' we'll be doing CPR again before you can count to ten."

He flipped through the songbook and frowned. "This isn't exactly what I had in mind."

"Really?" she teased. Then her heart tugged. The man had wanted a chance to dance with her. He'd sprung for the tickets anyway because she'd hated to disappoint the eager senior at the doorway. Captain McKenna *was* looking more and more like a good guy. She popped a glistening bubble and smiled at him. He stood up. "Hey, where are you going?"

"To put in our song request."

"What? Wait, I don't sing."

"You do now."

"But—"

"No buts. It's for charity. And your idea. If I'm willing to make a fool of myself for a good cause, you can too."

Before she could break out in hives, the balding man at the microphone called for a round of applause. "Let's hear it for Scott and his . . . Wonder Woman."

The crowd hooted and Erin's face flamed. *No way*. She sank low in her chair, but Scott tugged her to her feet. The crowd applauded again, and the opening notes of Sonny and Cher's "I Got You Babe" blared from the speakers. Then somehow they were suddenly holding microphones under a decrepit disco ball. She grimaced, hiked up her glowing hula skirt, and squinted at the hot pink lyrics on the TV monitor, then reminded herself that Scott was making a fool of himself too. *Charity, charity, charity.*

She croaked out the first line like Kermit the Frog with a bad case of laryngitis: "'They say we're young and we don't know. We won't find out until we grow . . .'" She pressed her fingers to her lips and looked at him helplessly.

Scott winked through a glistening spray of bubbles, then responded . . . in a rich and completely confident baritone: "'Well I don't know if all that's true. 'Cause you got me, and baby I got you . . .'"

She stared at him, mouth open, as a dozen silver-haired women scrambled to their feet and squealed with delight, "Ooh, honey, sing it!"

"You sing?" she mouthed.

He smiled.

She'd been hustled, big-time. Erin stared into his eyes, her heart thrumming. Not sure if she was furious or completely blown away by this handsome and unpredictable fire captain.

Scott nodded and pointed to her mike, signaling her to start.

She blinked against another release of soapy bubbles and then joined him in the silly vintage refrain: "'I got you babe. I got you babe.'"

+++

Sarge switched the water bottles as quietly as he could in the darkness and turned to leave.

"Rich?"

"Yeah?"

"I knew it was you." The smile in the boy's voice made his chest feel full.

Sarge returned to Cody's bedside. "Here," he said, pointing to the bottles. "Good water. If you get thirsty."

"There was still . . . half a bottle . . . ," Cody said, his words stretched by a yawn.

"This is fresher." *And safer. Can't trust what the evening staff left.* Sarge watched the night-light play across the boy's sleep-mussed curls as he moved in bed. It gave him a sort of halo. Like God's angels in that bedtime story that . . . *I always read to Ricky.* For a blissful second, he could feel his son's downy hair beneath his fingertips. He winced at the bittersweet memory. Things had started to come back like warped jigsaw pieces this past week. Not all of them good.

"You're not like the other nurses," Cody said, sounding like he'd given the idea some serious thought. "You never check my blood pressure or ask me those same dumb questions over and over. Like, 'Can you give me a number for your leg pain? Is it a three or a seven?'"

Sarge grimaced and shifted his weight on the prosthesis. "That's not my job."

"Right. You're here to keep me safe." There was a soft chuckle. "It makes you sound like some kind of superhero. You know, like Batman."

"No." The nausea swept back without warning, along with the images of the bodies in the desert. Sweat prickled above his lips. "No hero. Not even close. I'm . . . just here. For you."

"You probably won't have to do that much longer."

Sarge's stomach tensed. "Why not?"

"After the MRI, we'll know."

"Know what?" Dread rose with bile.

"If I go home. Or to Rohnert Park. That's where the hyperbaric rooms are. Oxygen treatment. My great-grandpa says they use it on scuba divers that come up from the ocean bottom too fast. Pretty strange. But better than surgery."

Amputation. Sarge fought the image of the red plastic pathology bags piled beside the trash sanitizer. The sweet stink of formaldehyde filled his nostrils. His mind whirled. "But what if you didn't want to?"

"The oxygen treatment? Or the surgery?"

"Any of it."

Cody shifted on his bed. "If the infection's in my bone, I have to. No choice."

Sarge's temples pounded as the children's faces intruded one by one, lying milky pale and still on the sand beside the tattered tents.

"What about your family?" he asked, hands trembling. "Wouldn't they help you get away from the desert?"

Cody peered at him, his hair lit once again in a halo. "What do you mean?"

"If your family thought you weren't safe, wouldn't they take you out of the hospital?"

"Oh. You said *desert*."

"Huh?" Sarge choked.

"*Desert*. You asked if my family would help me get away from the desert."

He groaned, battling a wave of dizziness that nearly buckled his good leg. "Forget it. Stupid mistake. I'm tired. And old."

"How old?"

"Old enough to be your father."

"Are you? A father, I mean?"

Sarge decided not to answer. How did you tell a kid like this . . . *I don't see my son anymore*?

Cody was mercifully quiet and then yawned. "It seems kind of funny that I've never really seen you. Not in the daylight, anyway. I can tell you're tall and that your hair's sort of long, but I'm not sure I'd recognize you." He chuckled. "You know, if I had to, say . . . pick you out of one of those police lineups like you see on TV."

"All you need to know is that I'm always here."

"To keep me safe."

"Yes. Remember that."

"I will." His blond halo bobbed.

Sarge glanced at the doorway and saw that the corridor was clear. He went back to the closet—his dark, secure foxhole—grabbed a piece of beef jerky, and opened his notebook.

Change in mission: Get the boy out.

+++

You could count on Sinatra. Scott knew if he waited long enough, a string of balding seniors would capture the karaoke stage for an endless tribute to Ol' Blue Eyes, and Erin would be in his arms. They did, and she was. *Worth the wait.* He steered her around a silver-haired couple wearing matching Hawaiian shirts, then whispered against her hair, "Still thinking about punching me?"

Erin leaned away and peered at him, the party lights reflecting in her eyes like glass beads in a kaleidoscope. "I should, but I'm afraid your fan club would tackle me." She nodded toward a table. "Word to the wise: every time we pass that woman with the pineapple hat, she makes a grab for your back pockets."

He chuckled. He hoped Sinatra never ended. This felt good. Laughing, holding her, and forgetting everything else. It was like the world was suspended. Right now crew schedules didn't matter, the job follow-ups could wait, and there was even respite from Gary's medical problems and worries about Cody.

"Where did you learn to sing like that?" she asked.

His heart cramped. He exhaled softly as the karaoke singer began crooning a new song: *"I wanna be around to pick up the pieces when somebody breaks your heart . . ."* "Colleen," he said, drawing Erin close again. "She was the singer in the family. Even when she was a little kid. I remember her standing in the kitchen, wearing Grandma's high heels and Mom's lipstick, holding an old strainer, pretending it was a microphone. . . ." He tried to swallow down the rising ache.

"And you sang with her sometimes?" Erin's voice was gentle.

"She was always twisting my arm. Signing us up for the school talent show, karaoke duets . . . our church worship team. Her favorite song was 'Amazing Grace.' I don't know how many times she made me sing it. I couldn't say no to her." His stomach sank, and he closed his eyes. Why had he started this? All he wanted tonight was to finally escape.

"Scott?"

"Yeah?" He opened his eyes. The music had stopped.

"They're starting the raffle." Erin pointed. "That golf cart. With the fringe."

Scott smiled, partly because of the look on her face. Partly because she was so beautiful. But mostly because she'd been such a good sport all day—pushing Cody's wheelchair and discussing mackerel and fishing hooks, standing up onstage bravely squeaking out that duet. He suddenly wanted to kiss her. Long and sweet. Right there on the dance floor, beside the woman in the pineapple hat and under the strings of colored lights, and while they were calling out the winning raffle number. Reach out, cradle her face in his hands, bend down, and—

"No golf carts," he said, touching his finger to the tip of her nose instead. "No fringe. No way. Turn in your hula skirt, and let's get out of here."

+++

Erin walked beside Scott down Monterey's Old Fisherman's Wharf, past still-bustling restaurants, dimly lit souvenir shops, and whale-watching headquarters, in a long row of weathered buildings thickly layered in paints the colors of bakery frosting. She sidestepped a cluster of noisy gulls scrambling for popcorn on the damp pavement and brushed against him. He took her hand.

Her face warmed despite the chilly fog, proof positive that her traitorous senses intended to defeat her logic. *Why, Lord?* Why should this fire captain seem so special? Why on earth should she risk feeling like this? She was nearly thirty-two, smart, independent, strong. So deliberately strong. She'd learned the hard way to be wary, but . . .

"Coffee?" he asked, facing her as they passed under a wharf light. His eyes, the same misty shade as the fog, held hers, and her resolve hit the mat with a thud. "Cappuccino on the Wharf is just a little ways down."

"Only if you let me pay this time," Erin insisted, aware of the feel of her hand inside his.

"Can't let you. Against the rules."

"Which rules?"

"Dating book," Scott said, not cracking a smile.

"Dating . . . ?" Her brows scrunched for a split second until he laughed. "Oh, brother. Your books."

"Which reminds me," he said as they approached the small coffee kiosk painted red, green, and white like the Italian flag. His expression sobered. "I finished that report."

"Report?" The rich scent of coffee permeated the damp air, and spotlights shone on bottle after bottle of Italian syrup, glittering like jewels. She caught a waft of chocolate.

"My summary of the incident review, including the information you passed along regarding CISM," he explained.

"Oh." Erin released a low sigh, not sure if it was because he'd let go of her hand or because he'd changed the subject. He'd had issues with the subject of stress counseling. But no matter what his report said, he wouldn't change her mind. She'd been right to try to help her staff. His too. And she'd do the same thing again in a heartbeat. Still, she didn't want to argue tonight. For the first time in so long, she didn't want to raise her gloves against—

"My conclusion was overall positive."

"What does that mean?"

His gaze moved to the penned list of gourmet coffees, then back to her. "That the hospital's initial response was adequate. And that your suggestions for critical stress intervention are valuable."

"Wait. You mean, you concluded that stress counseling should be included?"

Scott smiled. "Yes. I'll tell you more after we order. You're buying me a brownie too."

She placed their order while he made a quick cell call to his family; then they continued their walk down the wharf. She couldn't believe what he'd said.

"What changed your mind?" Erin asked after taking a bite of her macaroon. "You were really wary about counseling."

He lowered his coffee container and waited a moment before he answered. "I'm not saying I'm convinced of the process overall. I still have serious concerns about side effects of psychological intervention in some cases."

Erin saw a muscle tense along his jaw and knew he was thinking of his brother-in-law's violent and tragic actions. Which may or may not have been spurred by his therapy. She drew a breath through her teeth.

"But Chuck tells me that your peer counseling made all the difference for Sandy. He'd been really worried about her. And I saw his face when she collapsed in the ER." Scott shook his head. "I've worked with Chuck during incredibly tense rescue situations, watched him stay calm when most guys would choke. But . . ."

"He loves her." Erin met Scott's gaze, and her stomach quivered.

"Yes. He does."

They walked on for a while in silence. Erin heard the distant bark of seals and realized they'd come to the end of the wharf, marked by benches, a few coin-operated viewing scopes, and a dizzying view of the marina with hundreds of masts bobbing silently in the black waters. Far away, lights dotted the outline of Monterey Bay. A foghorn sounded, long and low. The salty and damp breeze lifted her hair. She shivered.

"Cold?" he asked.

She crossed her arms, rubbing at the sleeves of her cotton sweater. "I'm okay. California girl—tease me with a little March sunshine, and I'll leave my coat in the car every time."

"Here." Scott pulled off his jacket and insisted that she slide into it despite her weak protests.

It was fleeced-lined, prewarmed by his body, and smelled like . . . She chuckled.

"What?"

"Everything you have smells like a campfire."

"Sorry. It was in my locker at the fire station along with my turnouts." Scott pulled up the collar. "Is that better? You're still shivering."

Erin nodded, hoping to goodness he wouldn't figure out that he was the cause of her shivers. His closeness, his eyes, and the way she was starting to feel despite all common sense. *Lord, make me strong.* "I'm fine now."

"Good," he said, letting his hands drop away. "Cody would have my hide if I let anything happen to you. He told me you're very cool."

"Oh, all the guys say that when I talk about mackerel." She took a sip of her coffee and set the cup back on the railing next to his. "He's having his MRI tomorrow, isn't he?"

"Yes, in the afternoon." Scott sighed. "My stepdad's treadmill in the morning, Cody's exam in the afternoon. Mom will wear her knees out praying."

Erin thought of Lynda Wells's tearful and loving expression when she'd seen her husband in the ER this morning. How her fingers moved to the small cross at her collar. *A woman who prays.* But what about Scott? Her curiosity got the better of her. "You mentioned before that you sing with your church's worship team?"

Scott glanced away. "Not anymore."

Don't sing, or don't go there? Erin told herself not to ask, not to push.

"I haven't been to church since Colleen's funeral. I can't sit there . . . after what happened." He winced. "And seeing Cody go through everything that he's going through—it shouldn't have been this way."

Erin nodded, her heart going out to him. His pain was apparent, still raw. He'd lost his father so young and grew into a man focused on fixing, protecting, and rescuing. Then things had swung so far beyond his control. She took a step closer and touched his arm. "Sometimes, for me, even praying all alone can—"

"I don't," he said, cutting her off. "I don't pray anymore. I can't talk to God. I don't expect him to listen." His expression held no criticism for her offering, only a gut-wrenching honesty. "The only thing that's helped is my work. And swimming. That's all." He brushed the back of his hand very gently along her cheek. "Until now. Until . . . you."

Erin's heart climbed into her throat, and the shivers returned. "Me?"

Scott smiled. "Yes. I don't know how you do it, but you do. Even that first day at the hospital when you tried to bully your way past me."

"Bully my way?" she said, trying to find an ounce of indignation. And failing utterly.

"That's right. You and your grandmother both. Now there's a team."

"Hey, now—"

"And then you threatened me with a tetanus shot, took over my town meeting, and . . ."

Erin grimaced. "This is not sounding good for me."

His smile broadened. "I know. I keep thinking that too. If I listed it all out on a spreadsheet—and I've thought about doing that—it would sound like you're the most aggravating woman I've ever met. But the fact is . . ." He stopped, and the look in his eyes made her stomach quiver.

"What's the fact, McKenna?"

"Since I've met you, I've felt better than I have in a long time." Scott's voice dropped to a whisper, and he moved close again. Close enough that she could feel his breath on her face. "I'm not sure why that is, but I like it. Even if you could probably nail me with a right hook."

"Definitely could."

"So warned." He chuckled low in his throat, then lifted a strand of hair away from her face. "Even so, I'd like to see you again. Is that all right?"

Oh yes. Erin nodded or hoped she did. It was hard to tell with her heart pummeling her ears.

"Great. And . . . there's one other thing I'd like. Right now."

She wasn't sure how to handle another thing with her knees giving way. "What?"

"I want to kiss you."

"Oh."

Scott tucked his fingers under her chin, stooped down, and hesitated, his lips mere inches away. "It's okay?"

"Of course."

He touched his lips to her forehead. "Just checking. Right hook. Been warned."

"Good point." She grinned, her skin tingling. "Permission granted, Captain."

Scott kissed her cheek, moved on to the corner of her mouth, then touched his lips to hers. They were soft, gentle . . . and tasted wonderfully like warm chocolate. He leaned away and sighed. Then drew her closer and kissed her again, longer this time and more deeply.

She slid her arms around his neck, sweetly dizzy, and returned his kiss.

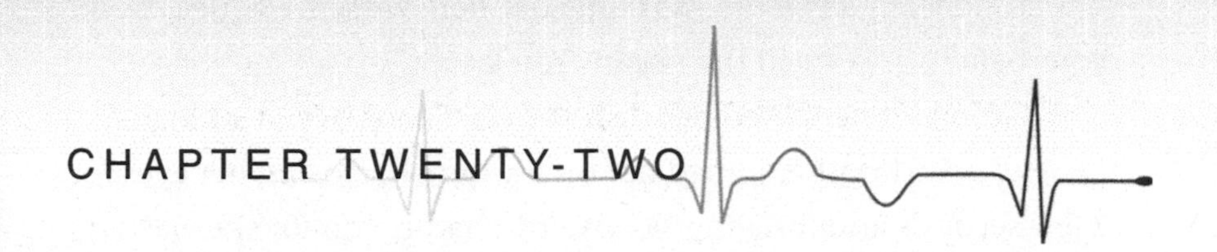

CHAPTER TWENTY-TWO

"Scrambled egg whites and turkey bacon?" Nana's voice carried out through the patio door. "Or are you going to blend one of those protein shakes?"

"Mmm . . . how 'bout pancakes?" Erin leaned back against the garden bench, her mind still tumbling memories that had kept her awake half the night. Scents of citrus and smoke, the feel of Scott's arms, the brush of his beard growth, the soft texture of his hair under her fingers . . . those incredible kisses. His caring heart. She wanted to hold on to it all, feel optimistic for once. *Please, Lord, let me have this a little longer.* Even if only for this morning.

"Pancakes? Did I hear that right?"

Erin cupped her hands around her mouth. "Yes. Oatmeal pancakes, with chopped pecans and real maple syrup. I could cut up those strawberries, and—"

Her grandmother appeared in the doorway, striped dish towel in hand. "Do we need to check your temperature?"

"Oh, for goodness' sake." She drew her knees up, hugged her arms around her baggy plaid pajama bottoms, unable to smother a smile her grandmother would undoubtedly call dreamy. "Can't someone want pancakes without . . . ? Can't I hide anything from you?"

"Never. Though I hesitate to question anything that quiets your punching bag. Or keeps you from scrubbing the shower and filling our house with fumes. Praise God, that's a blessing in itself."

"Touché. I just wanted to come out here with my coffee, sit on your bench, and smell the ocean. You know."

"I know." She waved her dish towel. "Scoot over a smidge."

Her grandmother joined her on the bench, closing her eyes for a few seconds and inhaling slowly. Erin had no doubt she was saying a prayer—it came as naturally as breathing to her. Nana opened her eyes. "I'm assuming this all means you had a good time with Scott and Cody."

"We took him to watch the fishing boats, and apparently he thinks I'm cool."

"I'm sure of it. And his uncle? He thinks you're cool too?"

"Probably." She saw her grandmother's brows rise and laughed. "Okay, he does. Definitely. Of course, I'm already fighting doubts about trusting him."

"But . . . ?" The sea breeze lifted a wavy tendril of her grandmother's hair, and she searched Erin's eyes with the loving concern Erin had counted on all her life.

"I want to believe Scott's different. He seems that way. Real and sincere and caring." She grimaced. "Even if he's maddeningly quiet."

Her grandmother smiled with obvious amusement.

"And I have to believe he's devoted to his family. I don't think you can fake that sort of thing. If they needed him, he'd be there. No matter what. They can count on him. I think that's what I like best about Scott. I keep telling myself he's not at all like . . ."

"Your father?"

She shrugged, deciding not to pursue the point. Her grandmother wasn't going to give up hope for a family reconciliation. "And he sings—you can't believe how well. Used to be part of his church worship team." She remembered what he'd said about singing "Amazing Grace" for his sister. But then the doubts tiptoed back as she remembered the rest. *"I don't pray anymore. I can't talk to God. I don't expect him to listen."* She sighed. "Anyway, I've decided I like him and that I'll go out with him again. Not sure how smart that was, considering my track record."

"Well—" her grandmother slid an arm around her shoulders—"I'm proud of you."

"For what?"

Her grandmother winked. "Lowering your boxing gloves a few inches. I'd call that progress, darling."

"Hmm." Erin rested her head against Nana's shoulder, and for a fleeting moment she felt six years old. Safe. Loved. Certain of everything. "Here's hoping it doesn't end up being called down for the count."

Her grandmother patted her hand. "Pancakes?"

"Absolutely," Erin said, unable to stop last night's warm memories from swirling back again. Still tempered by a smidgen of doubt. "But I'll add a tablespoon of protein powder."

+++

Scott dragged a palm powerfully through the dark water, stretching his other arm forward and kicking hard. His body rose and fell on the building waves as he swam parallel to the shoreline below Arlo's Bait & Moor. He hadn't missed that much training, but the ocean already seemed strangely unfamiliar.

Scott stilled his movement, blinked against the sting of salt, and scanned the shore. Same empty shore, same early morning fog. No reason that this swim should feel any different from the hundreds he'd done before, except . . . for Erin.

He shook his head as he bobbed up and down, not at all surprised by the warmth that flooded through him. The difference in the way things felt today was because of her. She was the reason he'd lain awake hours last night too. Remembering her laughing with Cody, the look on her face when she held that karaoke microphone . . . the way she'd kissed him. *Ah, man.* His mouth dipped below the sea's cold surface and he sputtered, kicking his legs to rise higher in the water before it was over his head. He groaned at the thought. *In over my head.*

It was another reason he'd lost sleep last night: Did he know what he was doing? Did it even make sense to start having feelings for Erin when things were so unsettled, when he was trying so hard to move on with his career . . . his life? Though Portland was likely out of the equation, he still planned to take a position outside of Pacific Point. The timing was wrong for a relationship. But Erin was special, different from anyone he'd known. Fiercely protective of her grandmother, strong despite the heartache she'd endured with her father, generous, committed to her career . . . and to her faith.

Scott sputtered again and started to swim, remembering what she'd said about prayer. How it helped her. He'd been honest when he said he didn't pray anymore, that he didn't expect God to listen. But he hadn't told her why . . . *that maybe I let my family down. And Cody deserves more than a man like me.* His issues with God would complicate things between them, but even still, being with Erin made him feel better. Like she accepted him for who he was. Not because he was Gabe McKenna's son or Colleen's brother . . . and even if he didn't reach all the career goals he'd been striving for. It felt like she could care for him, just for himself. He needed that. So even though the timing wasn't completely right, even if they had to work around the faith issues, and even if they had to deal with some geographical distance, it still seemed worth the risk to—

He stopped swimming and treaded water, scanning the misty beach. He'd heard something, and . . . *yes.* He waved one arm over his head and shouted, "Erin!"

+++

Erin watched, heart in her throat, as Scott jogged through the foam and across the stretch of wet sand toward where she stood beside his mound of gear. His grin answered the question she'd wrestled with while walking from the beach house. *He's glad I'm here.* She picked up his towel and held it out as he got closer. Black wet suit across broad shoulders, blond hair standing up in wet clumps, eyes meeting hers . . . When he stopped in front of her, the towel slipped from her fingers, forgotten.

"Hi," he said, voice low and breathless after the run. "I was thinking about you."

"You were swimming."

"I multitask."

"Why am I not surprised?" Her heart quickened as he pulled her gently to him. "You probably have a book on it."

His strong arms encircled her, impossibly warm through the spongy and sea-soaked neoprene. "You were nowhere in my books. But I'm beginning to think that could be a good thing."

"Oh? Want to know what I think?"

Scott leaned back and tucked a finger under her chin. "No."

"No?"

"Right now, I only want to kiss you." He pressed his lips—gentle, warm, and salty—against hers. "There. Now I can concentrate. What were you thinking?"

Erin glanced up at the cliff. "That Arlo and Annie are watching."

+++

Sarge frowned. The boy's MRI was scheduled for 3 p.m. He'd have to think of a way to hang around the radiology department for a while, since Lupe's shift would technically be over. And it cut into the sleep he needed to get before his night shift tonight. But it didn't matter; he could barely close his eyes now without hearing the missiles overhead, smelling the burning oil. Seeing the children's faces. Remembering how he stood there in the sand, looking down at them as the words tore free, half prayer, half howl: *"Father God, not the children . . . not the children."*

Sarge peered down the pediatrics corridor toward the boy's room. Strange to be here during the daylight and without hiding. Although, in truth, he was. From Cody. Taking part of Lupe's shift gave him a legitimate reason to be here, but he'd had to watch the boy from a distance. Safer that way. Cody might call him Rich in front of the nurses, mention his being here during the night, or . . . Sarge's jaw tightened. *See me the way everyone else does?* Crippled, emptying trash, and pushing a mop. His chest constricted at the memory of the boy's words. *"You're here to keep me safe . . . like some kind of superhero . . . like Batman."*

He glanced toward the housekeeping closet, thinking of his stash in the old vacuum bag. The beef jerky, his mission journals, and—the grim irony struck him: *Batman*—the aluminum bat. There for a reason. No one was taking the boy away. Or cutting off his leg. He'd save him, the way he wished he'd saved those children in the desert.

The MRI was at three. Then he'd know what he had to do.

+++

Iris laughed as the little dog yodeled for Hugh's sandwich crust. She watched Jonah enjoy his reward, glad Hugh had found her in the Little Mercies Gift Shop and asked her to join them for lunch. "Gary's been discharged, then?"

"Yes." Hugh smiled and his silver mustache stretched. "Good news about his heart. But apparently the doctor really laid down the law about the diabetes and blood pressure. And all the stress he's been under."

Iris nodded. "I can imagine. The economy must be affecting electricians too."

"It is. Although I suspect Cody's situation has provided the majority of Gary's stress. It's not easy being a full-time parent at sixty years old. That's part of the reason I'm still here. The doctor told Lynda to take him home and stay there, so I'm waiting with Cody during the MRI."

"That's right. It's today." Her heart tugged. "He's been in my prayers. I don't think I've ever met a sweeter or braver boy. I'm glad you and Scott will be there for him."

Hugh cleared his throat, disappointment coming into his expression. "Scott's gone to follow up on a few of his job applications; he said he'd be driving to Monterey and then on to San Jose. He promised Cody he'd be back in time. But you never know with traffic. Moving forward with his career has become more important than . . . anything."

Iris remembered Erin's words this morning about Scott's devotion to his family: *"If they needed him, he'd be there. No matter what."* She'd said it was what she liked best about him.

"I may have mentioned it before," Hugh continued, "but I'm concerned that Scotty's pulling away from the family. Until the accident, I don't believe he'd have agreed to move from Pacific Point. He and Cody were inseparable. Now all he can think about is finding a new job. If you'll pardon the pun, my grandson suddenly seems far more intent on climbing the ladder in his firefighting career. I'm afraid he inherited more of his father's ambition than I realized. And maybe some of his foolish grandfather's."

"You're talking about yourself?"

Hugh nodded. "I hate to admit how much time I spent away from home when my son Gabe was a boy. At sea, attending academic conferences, and even holed up in my university office a few miles away. But still . . . away. From my wife and my family. I wasn't the best example."

Iris winced, wondering again about her effect on her granddaughter's life. Erin's stubborn need to be strong above all else, her hesitancy to trust . . . and to forgive. Could Iris have prevented that?

"Sometimes I wonder," Hugh said, stroking Jonah's head. "If I'd asked the good Lord to help me get my priorities straight earlier, then passed those good values on to my son, if it could have changed things that day."

"What day?"

"The day everything began sliding downhill for my family. Gabe volunteered for an extra shift the Saturday he was killed; he wanted to catch the chief's eye for a promotion. He should have been home. It was Scotty's birthday."

+++

"I am. I am listening." Erin propped the stained-glass window hanging against the garden bench and pressed her cell phone to her ear.

Her mind raced ahead, formulating responses. Boxing against her sister's tentative pleas. *Lord, help me stay strong.* The family was ganging up. Big-time.

"Okay," Debra continued breathlessly, "good. So you'd be doing this for Mom. You wouldn't even have to talk to him. It will be the same old Easter dinner. Just show up, kiss your niece and nephew, pet the dogs, and eat your roast lamb. Simple."

Erin pushed the Windex bottle aside and sat. "Eat *what*?"

"Lamb. Roasted or braised maybe. Um . . . with turnips and baby carrots. And snow peas, I think. Anyway, it's a French recipe. I'm sure it's good, and—"

"Hold it," Erin interrupted, familiar wariness making her skin prickle. "Turnips?"

Debra moaned. "Yes. Oh, why are you doing this?"

Erin rose, her cheeks stinging. "Because our family's only vegetable is Tater Tots. Because we always have a store-bought ham for Easter, and the only thing French in Mom's kitchen is the label on that squeeze bottle of mustard." *Same old dinner? Yeah, right.* She knew the answer before she asked the question. "Why all this sudden interest in fancy cooking?"

"She's taking classes." Her sister's voice dropped to a mumble. "With Dad. They joined Dinners for Eight at the church. And go shopping together at the natural food co-op down in Folsom. Dad's the assistant produce manager there now. He bought her a special set of saucepans, and they're digging up a space for an herb garden. I've never seen Mom this happy—"

"That's enough." Erin pressed her fingers to her forehead. "I do *not* need to hear this."

The silence made Erin think she'd lost the connection.

But then Debra spoke, and the change in her tone hit like a

sucker punch. "Maybe you do need to hear this. He's her husband. Our father. You were born a Calloway."

Aagh . . . stay strong. "And you've forgotten everything he's done to her? to us? Why Mom's worked two jobs the last ten years? *He's* the reason she never had time to learn to cook. I'm sorry, but he can't change everything by just showing up."

"No. *You* can't change things by dumping our family name, deleting Dad's e-mails, or even hijacking Nana to the beach."

"Hijacking?" Erin whirled around, and her foot bumped the stained glass she'd leaned against the bench. She dropped to one knee, steadying it with her free hand before it could fall over and shatter. "How can you say that? I brought her here because of the tax situation; if Nana doesn't occupy this house for two years, she loses money when she sells. She can't afford the loss. You know that. I moved here for her—*for her.* It's what she needs to do."

"What she *needs*—" her sister's voice gentled again, and Erin felt a rush of homesickness—"is her family. Together again. All of us."

Erin's fingers clenched, at odds with the tightening of her throat.

"Erin?"

"I'm here."

"Hannah's started smiling now. Not those gas bubble thingies—real smiles. It melts my heart. And her bald spot's coming back in reddish, like her auntie Erin's. I don't want you to see all that on a video clip; I want you here. I want Nana here and all of us around Mom's table after Easter service. Please. Please say you'll come."

"Oh, Deb, I . . ." She choked and shook her head.

"It's *Easter.* And . . . he's changed. I was skeptical too at first. But Dad's really changed this time. He's doing great at that job. He's making Mom happy, and he wants to tell you he's sorry."

Her stomach twisted.

"All you have to do is listen."

Erin glanced down at the stained-glass sword and shield. How could she make her sister understand she couldn't bear any of this again? She couldn't take seeing fragile hope in her mother's eyes, hearing her father's inevitable excuses, then remembering the promises he'd break in the wake of his leaving . . .

"Can't you do that? just listen to him?" Debra prodded.

"No," Erin said after swallowing softly. "I'm sorry, but I can't."

After a few seconds of polite, disconnected conversation, Erin ended the call, certain she'd heard tears in her sister's voice. And not entirely convinced she'd be seeing her nephew and her baby niece on her next visit to Placerville. Debra was capable of hijacking too, it seemed. *"We'll be eating lamb on Easter. You know where to find us."*

Erin sat on her grandmother's bench, tore a paper towel off the roll, and picked up the Windex. She'd shine the window hanging until it was as beautiful as Annie Popp's sea glass. Then she'd hit the punching bag for thirty minutes straight. She'd sweat, get her heart pumping, her muscles strong, and her guard firmly back in place. Later she'd meet Scott at the marina near his house for a late lunch. She'd taken a vacation day and planned to meet him for a picnic when he got back from his errands. Then they'd drive together to the hospital; today was Cody's MRI.

Scott would be there because he was the kind of man a family could count on. Unlike Frank Calloway, Scott was solid and stable. Her pulse quickened, remembering how he'd kissed her on the beach this morning. How it had felt like the beginning of something real, lasting. *Finally, Lord, finally.* Amazingly, she'd started to count on him too. Step by step and slowly, because it was the first time she'd allowed herself to do that in a long time. *But it feels so good.*

+++

Scott checked the truck's clock—2:30—then revved his engine as he idled in traffic at the stoplight. *C'mon, c'mon. Hurry up.* When he'd called the hospital, they'd already taken Cody down for his MRI, and the way this commute was going, it looked like he was going to miss being there with him after all. But they'd said his grandfather was there, so that was good. The meeting in San Jose had taken longer than expected. It was obvious they were interested in hiring him. But even that didn't matter now, because . . .

His grin spread as he stepped on the accelerator and moved forward again. He still couldn't believe what he'd heard when he checked his phone messages at home. They were offering him the job, chief of emergency medical services for Portland Fire. *Chief.* It was the opportunity of a lifetime, a dream he'd thought was far beyond his grasp. A chance to prove himself. Colleen had understood how much he wanted that; she'd have been so happy for him. *Ah.* Scott's stomach plunged, sadness twisting like a snarl of barbed wire. She was gone, the one person he wanted most to share this news with.

No, not the only person. Erin would understand. She was as ambitious about her own career, and . . . she cared. She really cared about him. The familiar warmth flooded back as he imagined telling her the news.

+++

Scott's not coming. Erin checked her cell phone one last time, then dropped it onto the picnic table she'd set with a tablecloth, bright Mexican napkins, and a last-minute addition: a few daisies tucked into the shell-embossed vase she'd given her grandmother years ago. She wasn't sure which felt worse, the fact that Scott had stood her up without bothering to call, or that it all felt so very, very familiar.

She took a slow breath of sea air that did nothing to stop the intruding memory. She'd been ten, gangly, freckled, and so awkwardly in between childhood and puberty. But the night of the Girl Scout Troop 687 father-daughter dance she felt like a princess for the first time in her life. She didn't even mind that she'd had to ride to the church hall with the other girls and their fathers. Everyone knew that Frank Calloway, movie-star handsome, was flying in after very important business. On the phone the night before, he'd told Erin that he'd soon be crowned king of West Coast Insurance. He joked that next week she'd be riding in a Mercedes convertible; they'd buy a house in Granite Bay with a pool and join the country club.

She didn't care about any of that. She only cared that this time he'd be there. Finally be there. Time would be tight because of the plane schedule, but he'd come. He promised. He'd teach her the fox-trot and twirl her in front of all the other girls. This time it would be true. He'd ordered the corsage of gardenias, hadn't he?

When the hours passed, she'd told herself planes could be late, that traffic was fierce that time of the evening . . . and so what if the gardenias had started to turn a little brown around the edges? And then Pastor Ted began looking at her with the same woeful expression he wore with the bereaved, and the other girls put their heads close together, watching her and whispering, "He's not coming."

Erin stood, took a deep breath, then began stuffing everything back into the picnic basket—sandwiches, fruit, Mexican napkins, tablecloth. No, wait. She picked up her grandmother's vase and dumped the daisies onto the ground. They'd already begun to remind her of gardenias. But mostly they told her she'd been a fool again.

+++

Scott stepped out of the elevator and strode down the pediatrics corridor, his thoughts tumbling. There were details to work out, of course. He'd be flying back and forth to Pacific Point. Or he could drive sometimes. Twelve hours, wasn't it? But that was okay. He'd figure it out. Cody would be discharged soon, his stepfather was out of the woods, his grandfather would fill in the way he always did, and it would all be good. So good. Erin could even come to Portland for visits. There was the Mount Hood Jazz Festival, great hiking trails, museums, and . . .

He halted, confused for a moment as he caught sight of a man standing outside his nephew's room. Why was he familiar? Tall, with broad shoulders, tan scrubs, hair pulled into a ponytail . . . Yes, that housekeeper from down in the ER. Sarge. Leaning on a broom with his back to Scott, his head cocked as if he were listening to something.

Scott's chest squeezed as he heard the sound too. Cody. *Crying?* His grandfather would be there, but . . .

He crossed the last stretch of carpet at a jog, saw the housekeeper scuttle away, then hurried through the doorway, his heart in his throat. "Cody?"

His grandfather wasn't there. Erin was. Sitting on the bed and holding Cody as he sobbed against her shoulder.

"Erin, what . . . ?"

She raised her gaze to his, her disappointment in Scott palpable. "He's been waiting for you for more than an hour. There's been some tough news."

CHAPTER TWENTY-THREE

Erin watched as Scott talked with Cody, her stomach in knots. *Why wasn't he here? What could be so important that he'd break his promise to Cody?* Her heart ached as she saw the boy struggle to put on a brave face for his uncle. His chin quivered.

"Great-grandpa went to make a call," he said after wiping his nose on the sleeve of his hospital gown. "They want to take me to that hyperbaric chamber. Tomorrow, I guess."

Scott turned to look at Erin, his eyes clearly troubled. "Tomorrow?"

"He'll have his IV restarted tonight, a first dose of new medication. Then he'll get a cool ambulance ride to Rohnert Park. They want to start the first treatment tomorrow afternoon. There was some evidence of early osteomyelitis," she added, praying she didn't sound as worried as she felt. "With the infection spreading to the bone, they don't want to delay. At least that's what your grandfather understood."

"My parents know?" Scott asked.

"That's the call he's making now. He was hoping you'd be here to explain it to them, but . . ." She shrugged, her stomach churning again. *You promised to be here and you weren't.*

Scott squeezed Cody's hand. "I'm sorry I'm late, pal."

Hugh appeared in the doorway, Jonah asleep in the pack strapped to his chest. "Scotty, my boy. Good." He smiled though concern was evident in his age-lined eyes. "I told Cody he could count on you."

"I'm going to leave now." Erin nodded at Cody. "Hang in there, okay?"

"I will."

She grabbed her purse and headed down the corridor.

Scott caught up with her. "Wait. Please."

Erin wished she could stop the old familiar doubts from flooding back, wished he could say something that would change how she was feeling. "How could you do that? How could you promise that little boy you'd be there for him and not show up? Blowing me off for our lunch date is one thing, but—"

Scott's mouth dropped open. "Lunch—I completely forgot. Things got crazy, and time slipped away. I haven't even checked my messages. Did you call?"

"It doesn't matter now. But things 'got crazy' enough that you couldn't even make it in time for Cody's MRI?"

Scott took hold of her hand. "That's what I want to explain. Something did come up suddenly. I didn't expect it would go anywhere, so I haven't said anything to you. Or my folks yet." He smiled, his thumb brushing her palm. "They're offering me a position. Chief of emergency medical services at Portland Fire. I'm flying up Sunday afternoon. And I'll meet with them first thing Monday morning."

Portland . . . Oregon? Her breath caught. "Wh-what?"

"Chief of EMS," he repeated, taking her other hand as his eyes lit. "I still can't believe it myself. You're the first person I've told."

Erin pulled her hands from his. "You're moving away?"

"It's not that far. A couple hours by air. Drivable, even. It's only like—"

"I know where it is. I own maps." She knew how stupid she sounded, but somehow her brain and tongue had disconnected . . . and her heart flopped uselessly in her chest. *He's leaving them. Leaving me.* "I need to go home," she finally whispered. "Right now."

"I can tell you're taking this wrong. I've got a plan. I'll tell you all about it. Can you please listen?"

Listen? Erin crossed her arms, remembering her sister's voice on the phone. Pleading on her father's behalf: *"All you have to do is listen."* No. She'd already heard all the excuses for leaving your family, for breaking promises . . . for not caring enough to stay. She began to tremble, suddenly as cold as she'd been that Christmas Eve she'd waited on the porch for her father to come home. But now she was so much stronger.

"Erin? Will you listen to me?"

"No," she said, anger mercifully replacing the cold. Bolstering her defenses. *Stay strong.* "It doesn't matter to me whether you go or not. It's not about me. But it's not about *you,* either." She pointed down the hallway toward Cody's room. "They're the ones who count on you. That wonderful old man in there, your parents who've been sick with grief and stress, and—" she was helpless to stop the tears that came despite the anger—"that sweet, sweet little boy who needs you to be there for him. Who pretends to be brave and cool, while he's really feeling small and alone. He's scared. And he has a right to be. There's no guarantee that the hyperbaric treatments will stop the infection. He could lose his leg!"

Scott's face paled.

"That's right," Erin continued, dismissing a stab of guilt. She caught sight of someone at the water fountain across from them.

Sarge? She lowered her voice. "Cody could be facing surgery, and you're making plans to move away. I don't understand. I can't understand. Ever." She saw the pain on his face, but anger made her continue. "Cody wasn't crying because of his leg. He was crying because he's afraid of losing *you*."

She stared at him for a moment, then hoisted her purse over her shoulder and strode toward the elevator.

+++

Leigh held the Kleenex box on her lap and gazed up at the altar. It was more of a raised podium, since the hospital's chapel was non-denominational, and even more a multipurpose room these days. The morning of the pesticide disaster they'd tucked a family of nine in here, all clutching emesis basins. Chapel turned sickroom. But then, she had a hunch God would be okay with that. *Even if he's not okay with me.*

She glanced to where the afternoon sunlight shone through a modest panel of stained glass near the ceiling—pale, translucent amber, with a simple white dove. It was the one element that made the room seem like a church, and she was grateful for it today, because—

"Leigh?"

"Don't get your hopes up; I wasn't signing your fellowship roster. I've been sitting with a patient's family." She sighed. "Charlene Bailey was taken off life support and died about an hour ago. No brain activity. It ripped their hearts out to let her go."

Erin's faced pinched with empathy as she walked to where Leigh sat. "I saw them outside the ICU and thought that might be happening. Her brain hemorrhage was so sudden. I can't imagine losing someone that way. This is turning out to be one miserable day all around."

Leigh raised her brows, noticing as Erin sat down beside her that her eyes were red-rimmed. "I can see that. Why are you here on your day off? Last time I saw you, you were taking off early for a date with Scott, and—" She stopped, alarmed as tears sprang to her friend's eyes. Erin hardly ever cried. "What's going on?"

"I don't know." Erin pressed her fingers to her forehead, then groaned. "Yes, I do. It's me. I'm a fool. Why did I think things could be any different this time?" She pulled a tissue from the box on Leigh's lap. "Scott's taking a job in Portland. He's flying off Sunday to seal the deal. Then he'll move there."

Leigh grimaced.

"I'd actually convinced myself that he was special," Erin said, dabbing at her eyes. "After all this time, I thought I'd finally found one of the good guys."

Leigh tried not to think of Nick.

Erin folded the tissue, her gaze faraway. "All I ever wanted was to have what my grandparents had." She faced Leigh. "I know that sounds completely corny and Old World. But what they had was real. They were there for each other no matter what. They didn't put anything ahead of their relationship. Except God. And Nana always says that faith was the glue that held them together. You know?"

Leigh nodded, even though she didn't know. She only knew what tore couples apart. "So because Scott's going to be living in Oregon, you don't think there's a chance for . . . ?" She let her words trail off when she saw the look on Erin's face. It was clear that this was about much more than geography.

"If you're going to say that it's only a short flight away, don't bother. I already heard that one. Even under the best circumstances, most long-distance relationships are doomed." She caught Leigh's flinch. "I didn't mean you."

"I know. But you're right. I'm seeing a lawyer on Monday."

Erin gasped. "Oh, Leigh . . . I'm sorry."

She shrugged. "You were telling me about Scott."

"It's complicated," Erin continued, concern for Leigh still visible in her eyes, "but I think the real problem is that we're too different in too many important ways. I guess I needed to see that. I was crazy to let my guard down. I won't do it anymore."

Leigh had been in medicine long enough to tell when someone was being stoic in the face of pain. Erin was hurting far more than she let on. But what could Leigh offer? Some placebo cliché about darkness before dawn, being grateful for unanswered prayers? The fact was she'd pulled the plug on her own belief in happily ever after. And she was the last one who should offer advice. "Are you okay?"

"Of course. You?"

"Absolutely." Leigh gazed at the peaceful dove soaring in sunlit amber glass, wondering if God could hear little white lies drifting upward from a multipurpose chapel.

+++

Scott sank into the lumpy vinyl chair, relieved Cody had finally dozed off. The night nurse had a difficult time restarting his IV; his veins were fragile after the antibiotics. Scott's gaze moved to the series of bruises on his nephew's arm, some fresh, some the yellowish brown of overripe fruit. He winced. Cody had squeezed his hand, trying hard to be a man and not cry. Scott was glad he'd been here for him. His jaw tensed as Erin's angry words flooded back. *"How could you promise that little boy you'd be there for him and not show up? . . . He's afraid of losing you."*

She was wrong, and he wasn't going to let her words eat at him. He'd tried to get back here for the MRI. And he was here now.

That's what mattered. Cody wasn't losing him. Scott was as much a part of his nephew's life as he'd always been. He could easily do that from Portland. His family had always counted on him as the backup, the pinch hitter in an emergency. And he'd done that for his parents, his grandfather, Cody . . . Colleen. His stomach sank.

He shook his head, remembering the look on Erin's face. Anger and disappointment. And worse. It was the same look she'd had that night on the beach in Santa Cruz when she'd talked about her father. About how he'd abandoned his family. She'd never believe Scott wasn't doing the same thing. She'd refused to listen, or . . .

Scott leaned forward as Cody lifted his head. "I'm here, pal."

"Oh." He blinked, his eyes heavy lidded and sleepy. "I thought you left."

"No. I'm staying."

"All night?"

Guilt washed over Scott at the surprise in Cody's voice. "Of course."

Cody yawned. "You don't have to. The nurses watch me at night, remember?"

"I remember. But I'm still staying. I'm family," he added, then felt immediately foolish. Why had he suddenly needed to say that?

"Is Erin coming back too?"

Scott swallowed. "I don't think so."

"Will I see her before the ambulance picks me up tomorrow?"

Ambulance. Erin's words rushed back. *"He could lose his leg."*

"Uncle Scotty?" Cody's voice prodded his silence. "Will we see her?"

"I don't know. But I'm glad she sat with you during your MRI. That was nice of her."

Cody bit his lip. "She wasn't sure you'd be back."

"Well, she was wrong." *She's wrong about me.*

"I told her you'd come. You always do, if Grandma and Grandpa can't or if Great-grandpa can't or . . . you know."

His nephew had just confirmed his credibility. Uncle Scotty could be counted on as backup. It had always worked that way. So what was suddenly making him feel strangely defensive about that setup? He glanced toward the hallway, where he'd stood just hours ago, sharing the news about his new job with a woman he thought would understand.

Erin was the reason he was feeling edgy. He'd never met someone so sure of her opinions. But she was wrong about Scott. About his move to Portland and about his family. His stepfather would be fine—stress wasn't the problem. Grandpa Hugh was a rock, and Cody's leg would heal and he'd go home. Scott wasn't abandoning anybody. He was doing what he had to for his career. He had it all worked out. If only Erin would listen.

+++

Erin pulled her fleece jacket closer, goose bumps rising as the damp ocean breeze swept over her perspiring skin. The molten sun sank toward the sea, so much like a match dunking into a bucket of water that she half expected to hear a hiss. She thought of the first time she'd stood on this beach with Scott, when she'd teased him about playing Smokey the Bear with the beach campfire. It seemed so long ago and, sadly, so full circle. Because now they were at odds again. Maybe for the last time. Her chest cramped. Was what she'd said to Leigh true? Were she and Scott just too different about too many important things?

She shifted her weight, her running shoes sinking into the sand as she scanned the darkening ocean. It seemed impossible that she'd stood in this same spot with Scott this morning; that he'd emerged from the sea and wrapped his arms around her. Kissed her and joked that *"You were nowhere in my books. But I'm beginning to think that could be a good thing."* It had been wonderful and hopeful, but now . . .

Erin tried to blot out the pain of holding Cody as he'd cried this afternoon. It tore her heart apart to see him watching that door, waiting for his uncle. He'd pretended the broken promise didn't hurt. But she knew it did. She'd felt that way herself far too many times. That awful Christmas, the night of the father-daughter dance . . . too many times before and after. How could Scott expect her to accept that his career plans justified that kind of pain for Cody? that anything took more priority than love of family and faith in God?

"You were nowhere in my books." She nearly groaned at the irony. Scott McKenna would never be on the same page as she was. Because they were following different books. Her book would take her to church with her grandmother Sunday morning, would help her write a new prayer to support her coworkers at Faith QD. The same book brought her to Pacific Point to help her grandmother. It was the reason she was here. Scott's book—full of spreadsheets and policies and career ambitions—would take him to Portland. Away from his family . . . *and me.* She'd met men like that before. The first one she'd ever loved broke her heart and had just moved back in with her mother. How could they all be so foolish? Her mother, her sister . . . all of them. Again. She swiped at her eyes, refusing to give in to tears.

"Please, Lord," she whispered, lifting her gaze to the sky, "help me stay strong when everyone around me is so weak. You know how hard I'm trying to make things right, to protect Nana and my family. You know I'm tough, but I need you to help me. Don't let me make the wrong decisions. Keep me strong. I need your help."

She stood still for a moment, letting the breeze sift through her hair, then turned and glanced up the wall toward the sound of soft tinkling. Annie's sea glass mobiles. She squinted in the deepening dusk. Arlo stood on the porch with a few of the young people from the beach crowd. Listening probably. Annie said it was his gift. For some reason, it made Erin think of her grandmother, sitting on her garden bench each day with her Bible open beside her. Eyes closed, face lifted . . . listening with the ear of her heart.

She was struck by a breath-catching wave of homesickness, zipped her jacket, and headed back toward the beach house. She could hardly wait to get there. Nana would understand everything. She counted on that.

+++

Sarge took a throat-scalding swallow of vodka, set the glass on the cluttered dresser, then limped to the closet. He slid the cheap, plastic hangers along the rod, searching through his meager clothing: two sets of tan scrubs, the frayed cotton robe he'd taken from the VA hospital, a wrestling team jacket, half a dozen shirts he'd picked up at a Sears clearance sale . . . the sport coat he'd worn to church that last Christmas Eve with his wife and son. He couldn't start thinking about that. He had to find . . . He grabbed a fistful of hangers, dropped them to the floor, then peered into the darkness toward the back corner. *Where the—?*

There. He hadn't seen it since he'd last moved. But he'd never have lost it. He pulled the Army fatigues from the hanger, his stomach tensing at the feel of fabric in his hands. He laid them carefully on the unmade bed, took another swig from the grimy glass, and lurched toward the bathroom. One more thing left to do.

He checked the equipment he'd smuggled from the OR: scissors, electric clippers. They'd do the trick. He'd look the part as he made up for the past. For all that had happened way back, when . . . A wave of nausea made him clutch his belly as the images returned. The tents, the desert sand . . . children's sad, lifeless faces. He swallowed hard and stood upright, back rigid and shoulders squared. At full attention. For one last mercy mission.

Sarge raised the scissors, slid it against his scalp, snipped hard . . . and then dropped his ponytail into the toilet.

+++

"Rich?"

"No. It's me," Scott mumbled, squinting at his nephew in the darkness. "I didn't mean to wake you. I was trying to get comfortable in this chair."

"That's okay. Has the night nurse been here yet?"

"I haven't seen anyone in a while." He checked his lit watch—2 a.m. "Maybe they came in while I was asleep."

Cody raised himself on his elbows, blue eyes luminous as he looked at the bedside table. "He hasn't come. I can always tell by the water bottles. He brings fresh ones." He turned toward the shadowy doorway, and the night-light illuminated his blond curls, so like Colleen's that Scott's chest constricted.

"Maybe it's his night off."

"No. He's always here."

"No one works seven days a week." *Except me, lately.*

"It sure seems like it. He brings the water or books. Or sometimes we just talk. Well, mostly he listens. I talk."

"Oh yeah?" Scott tried to ignore a wave of regret. He and Cody used to talk a lot more.

"Yeah. You know, I tell him about my homework. Or about how I used to play soccer or how funny it was when Great-grandpa was teaching Jonah to yodel. And . . . about Mom sometimes."

Scott's heart wedged into his throat. *You've never talked about her with me.*

"Anyway, he'll be here. You'll meet him."

CHAPTER TWENTY-FOUR

Grace, peace, grace . . .

Eyes closed, Iris inhaled slowly, ended her quiet time, and welcomed the morning with all her senses—the texture of the sun-warmed wooden bench, scents of salty air and sweet narcissus, twitters of a house wren, and the lingering taste of vanilla coffee. Gratitude filled her. *Grace, peace—*

Her eyes snapped open at the sound of clattering in the kitchen beyond. Erin. She closed her Bible and set it on the tile-topped table. After her granddaughter's mood last night . . . *Father, give me strength.* For long-term peace, Iris was willing to risk this fray.

"Nana?"

"I'm out here." She raised her cup. "Bring the carafe and join me."

Even if Iris hadn't heard her during the night, she'd have known Erin slept fitfully the instant she saw her. She was still dressed in her running clothes from the night before, hair tumbled, eyes red-rimmed and smudged faintly with mascara. She filled Iris's coffee cup, poured her own, and then sighed and sank onto the bench beside her. The scent of vanilla steam wafted between them.

"I'm sorry," Erin said, peering over the rim of her cup. "Maybe you should go to that garden tour without me. I'll never get myself together in time."

"No, they're holding it tomorrow too. Right now I think I'm right where I'm supposed to be." Iris pursed her lips for a moment. "No messages from Scott?"

"I wasn't expecting any." Erin lifted her chin, the streaky mascara making her look like a tough little clown telling a sad lie. "But I got three more texts from Deb. And an e-mail from Mom. You know what that's all about."

Iris nodded. "But you still don't think you should call Scott?"

Her granddaughter moaned. "Are you going to start this again? I told you all that because I thought you'd understand."

"All he asked was that you listen."

"To what? His plans to move away? How this new career opportunity is so important that nothing else matters?" She stared into Iris's eyes. "You can't imagine how awful it was to see Cody watching for him, waiting and waiting. And see him cry like that, and—"

"Yes, I can. Because I did it. Over and over." Iris gently grasped her granddaughter's chin. "With you."

"This isn't about Dad."

"Isn't it?"

Erin pulled away but not before Iris saw pain and familiar anger in her eyes. *Please, Father . . . strength.*

"I don't get it," Erin said. "Mom is your daughter. You know how many times Dad broke his promises. To her, to us, to everyone. You know how many times he left us waiting and watching and . . . hoping." Tears shimmered in her eyes. "You know how much it hurt me."

Iris took hold of her granddaughter's hand. "Of course I know. I was there, darling. And here in this house, all those summers."

"Then how can you expect me to give him another chance, to listen to what he has to say now? or to what Scott has to say? How am I supposed to believe that any of that would be the truth?" She shook her head. "I thought you'd understand. All I've ever wanted was what *you* had. It was everything . . . everything right. That's why I changed my name to yours; that's why I came here all those summers. To be part of what you and Grandy had, to be where everything was always happy, and—"

"Don't!" The word came out sharper than she'd intended, and she winced at the look on Erin's face. "I'm sorry. I only meant that I can't let you hold me up like some paragon of virtue. I'm afraid I've made it harder for you."

"What do you mean?"

Iris took a slow breath. "I let you run away from your parents and run to us. Maybe I even encouraged it. So I could protect you, comfort you, dry your tears, and bandage your fingertips. All because I loved you."

"I know that, and I'm grateful. It was exactly what I needed."

"I don't think so anymore. I think what you needed was a grandmother who helped you face your problems, not run away from them. You needed to learn that people, especially family, can be flawed and fallible and that they make mistakes. Hurt each other. And need . . . forgiveness." Iris expected the look she saw on Erin's face. It only proved she needed to tell her everything. No matter how hard it was.

"Are you saying you think Mom's right to take him back? that she should forgive him?"

Iris nodded.

"But how can you say that? After the kind of marriage you had, the kind of man Grandy was?"

"Because of that. Because your grandfather was the dearest man alive and our marriage was a blessing." Iris forced herself to look directly into Erin's eyes. "But mostly because it was only an act of forgiveness that kept us together. I nearly lost it all."

"Lost it?"

"My marriage. My husband."

"I still don't understand. I . . ." Erin's eyes widened. "Wait, do you mean . . . ? No, I can't believe this. Are you saying Grandy was unfaithful to you?"

"Not your grandfather," Iris whispered. "I was the one."

+++

Erin's breath caught, and she let go of her grandmother's hand. "What?"

"It's true. I wish it weren't. I wish I didn't have to tell you this now." Her grandmother shook her head. "Right here, where you used to dress in that costume and wave your Lasso of Truth. I'm finally giving it to you. I hurt your grandfather terribly. I made a selfish, awful mistake that I'll always regret, but—"

Erin clutched the edge of the wooden bench. "I don't want to hear this. I can't."

"I know you don't want to, but you need to."

A splinter pierced Erin's fingertip and she flinched. She stared at her grandmother, a confusing snarl of anger making her stomach churn again. "Why? So you can take away the last hope I have about honesty, family loyalty . . . lasting love?" She choked and her eyes blurred with tears. "How can you do this to me right now?"

"Oh, Erin," her grandmother groaned softly. "I'm not trying to take anything away from you; can't you see that? I'm trying to give you something I should have given you a long time ago. My own experience with grace. That's where our real hope is. Your grandfather's forgiveness after I told him—"

Erin stood up, shivering. "I'm s-sorry. But I need to go. Take a run or . . . go out awhile." *God, keep me strong . . . oh, please.*

Her grandmother reached for her hand. "Sit back down. A few minutes more, that's all. I want to explain things. Will you please just listen?"

Erin rubbed her arms but the shivering continued. "I can't. This . . . and Dad, Scott, everything . . . it's too much right now. Maybe later. I don't know." She took a step away, then turned back. "Can I ask one thing, though?"

"Anything," her grandmother answered, pulling her Bible onto her lap.

"When did you tell Grandy?" She steeled herself, knowing any answer made it real.

Tears brimmed in her grandmother's eyes. "That summer you were working on the stained glass. The day he won Elmer at the county fair."

Erin stopped in the kitchen to grab her purse, then hurried out, head down, before she could imagine her grandparents dancing there in each other's arms.

+++

"You look beat, Scotty."

Scott ran his fingers across his beard growth, then looked across the cafeteria table at his grandfather. "I'm okay. Thanks for insisting on this breakfast. I missed dinner last night. All I had was the granola bar a housekeeper brought for Cody."

His grandfather studied him for a moment, and Scott noticed—

with a pang of sadness—how much older he seemed lately. "Was it worth it?"

"The granola?"

"The trip to San Jose. Your meetings at the fire departments." He rubbed a fingertip across his little dog's head. "Was it all you'd hoped it would be?"

Scott hesitated, remembering Erin's reaction to his news, then pushed the memory aside. "Actually, I had some even better news, and I'm still trying to take it all in, but they're offering me the position in Portland. Chief of emergency medical services. I'm flying up there Sunday afternoon so we can finalize things Monday morning. After that, I'll tell the rest of the family. The fact is, there's no real opportunity for career advancement here in Pacific Point. Not for several years, anyway. And you know how important that is to me."

"I do," his grandfather said, lips tugging toward a smile that did nothing to change the look in his eyes. "You've worked toward this for a long time. You must be thrilled. Congratulations." He reached across the table and gave Scott's forearm a firm squeeze.

"Thank you. I didn't think it was going to happen. But . . . they'd want me to start in three weeks. Move there." The concern in his grandfather's eyes deepened. Scott wasn't imagining it. His stomach twisted. "Do you think Cody and Mom and Gary will be . . . more settled by then?"

"Hard to say. I suppose that depends on the outcome of this new therapy." His grandfather checked his watch. "The ambulance is coming at one; is that what you heard?"

"Between one and one thirty. How much time should we give Iris for her visit?"

His grandfather shook his head, a sudden smile erasing the

concern in his eyes. "She promised to show Cody that geriatric goldfish of hers. And that grand lady keeps her word."

Scott nodded. He'd been surprised by her arrival, pushing a cart topped by an oversize fish bowl. "Erin didn't mention that her grandmother had been visiting Cody."

His grandfather tickled Jonah's ear. "She doesn't know. Apparently Erin has strong opinions about what her grandmother should and shouldn't do. All well intentioned, I'm sure, but—"

"A complete pain in the backside nevertheless," Scott interjected with a groan. "I've been the bull's eye for a few of her opinions recently. According to Erin, I'm not the kind of man who can be counted on." His heart cramped unexpectedly.

His grandfather stayed silent, but he held Scott's gaze.

"She thinks that if I move to Portland, I'll be letting Cody down. And Mom and Gary, you too." Scott glanced down at his plate, suddenly finding it uncomfortable to meet his grandfather's gaze. "She had some issues with her father. Still does. That woman's a lot faster with a right hook than forgiveness. Trust me."

Jonah gave a yawn that ended in a soft yodel. Scott chuckled, his tension diffusing.

"You like her a lot." It was a statement, not a question.

"Yes." Scott sighed, unable to deny how much he already missed Erin—and how important her opinion of him felt. "I've never met anyone like her. But I don't know if she wants to be with me. I thought she did, but now I'm not sure. She's got these expectations, these values . . . and it's clear she doesn't think I measure up." He caught his grandfather's gaze again and made himself ask, "What do you think? Is she right?"

His grandfather was quiet for a moment, regarding Scott with a look that made him feel both loved . . . and around eight years old. His throat tightened, and for some reason he remembered standing in the cemetery beside him amid an endless sea of blue uniforms. And listening to the mournful sound of bagpipes.

"I think," he said finally, "you'll need to answer that one. How do you see yourself measuring up? And more importantly what do you measure yourself against? That's where you'll find your answer."

+++

Leigh set her stethoscope on the office desk and picked up her knitting, glad for the break in the morning's patient load. It was nearing 10 a.m., so food had likely become more of a priority than aches and pains. Or pinkeye.

She shook her head; her last patient—after missing three days of work for an itching eye—insisted she see someone else first so he could finish his Egg McMuffin. Then left a trail of ketchup-soaked hash browns across the exam room floor when he left. Judy had grumbled aplenty, but Leigh was grateful it wasn't anything more challenging. Fast-food spills were a blessing in the wake of their pesticide disaster, and ketchup was her preferred shade of red in the trauma room today.

She wasn't up for drama. She'd slept only a scant few hours last night, and most of those were filled with confusing dreams. One of Charlene Bailey's funeral, family praying beside a casket covered with blossoming lemon branches—Leigh on her knees, sobbing. And Charlene's police officer son holding his infant child. Then he'd somehow turned into Nick, wearing his uniform, pleading with Leigh, dark eyes intense. *"You're wrong, wrong. . . . You can't bury this. I won't let you."*

She dropped a stitch, picked it up again, her pulse quickening at the memory of the dream. It had to have been spurred by her appointment with the divorce attorney Monday. Or the e-mail from Nick: *Wait, please. We'll talk. I'm making that happen.*

It almost sounded as if he knew about her appointment with the attorney. She'd only told Erin, but . . . "Law enforcement is a brotherhood. We watch each other's backs," he'd told her. Over the years she learned it was true. Cops knew attorneys, firefighters, and medical people; it was a tight, interconnected world.

She sighed, knowing she was being ridiculous. Nick hadn't heard about her appointment. But he'd always been able to sense her feelings. Read her heart. That was the risk. She couldn't see him until she was less vulnerable. That would take time. Meanwhile . . . *"We'll talk. I'm making that happen."* What had Nick meant by that? He wouldn't just show up, and—

Someone tapped on the doorframe, and she jumped, dropping her knitting needles into her lap.

"Sorry, Dr. Stathos," Judy said. "I didn't mean to scare you."

"You didn't," Leigh fibbed, ignoring the hammering of her heart. "Got a patient for me?"

"No, I don't. Amazingly." She dragged her fingers through her short, spiky hair and smiled. "But I wanted to let you know that I talked with the ICU nurses. Ana's awake, and they're weaning her off the ventilator."

"Oh, thank heaven!" Leigh exclaimed, clasping her hands together.

"And to celebrate, I've made a fresh pot of coffee to go with the goodies one of the nurses from the medical offices offered us. I just met her outside and snagged a few. Thought I'd refill your cup and threaten those hips with a few calories. Homemade lemon bars?"

Lemon. In an instant the dream was back, lemon blossoms, her tears, Nick's pleading eyes. She pressed her fingers to her forehead.

"Dr. Stathos? Are you okay?"

Leigh met her gaze. "Sure. Just tired. Didn't sleep all that great. I'm glad today's quiet."

Judy groaned.

"What?"

"I can't believe you said that."

"Said what?" Leigh reached for her coffee cup.

"The Q word. You said it out loud. You've doomed us now."

Leigh grimaced. "Sorry. Good thing we're not superstitious." *About jinx words or dreams or . . . a soon-to-be ex-husband who can read my heart.*

Judy smirked. "Oh yeah, that would be which nurses? You want a lemon bar to boost your energy before people start dropping like flies?"

"Only coffee, thank you. And I promise that the only mess we're having today has already happened. Ketchup and hash browns. Did housekeeping answer your page?"

"Finally. I hate it when Sarge isn't working."

Leigh handed Judy her Golden Gate coffee cup. "His weekend on nights?"

"I think he's doing some Army Reserve time."

"Really?"

"I know. I'm surprised too. Because of his leg. But I saw him outside just now. He was getting out of a car by the trash management area. I don't think it was his car, but I'm sure it was him. I almost didn't recognize him, dressed like that."

"In uniform?"

Judy nodded. "But the weirdest part was . . . he shaved his head."

+++

Sarge grabbed a cleaning rag and mopped it across his brow, startled again at the stubbly feel of his scalp. Twenty minutes since he'd sneaked up the back stairs to the housekeeping closet and he was still sweating. Like those 115-degree days in the desert, when he'd pour the sweat out of his gas mask so he wouldn't drown in it.

Had that nurse recognized him in the parking lot? She'd done a double take, but he wasn't sure. He'd kept his head low and hurried. And he'd used his landlord's car, the one abandoned behind the apartment complex. Hot-wired it, because he couldn't use his own for the mission. At any rate, it was probably better if the nurse thought he was someone who belonged at the hospital. Not a stranger intent on child abduction—Code White.

He rubbed the rag across the back of his neck. They wouldn't be paging Code White right away. First, it would be Code Red—fire. He dropped the cloth, pulled the old Army Zippo from his pocket, and tested the flame. In a very short while he'd complete his mission. Save Cody. He opened the closet door half an inch and peered toward the boy's room. That man—a relative, he'd heard someone say—had slept in the chair all night, completely out of character. Who knew if he could be trusted? So it had to be done now. Risk or not. Sarge couldn't allow the boy to be taken away and his leg sawed off. Wasn't going to happen on his watch, daylight or not. He'd set off the fire alarm, get the boy, smuggle him down the stairs, and . . . His brain stuttered. Where was his war journal?

Sarge shoved a mop bucket aside, pulled out the old vacuum cleaner, the journal, and the aluminum bat. A package of beef jerky fell from vacuum bag, and he retrieved it from the floor. He ripped it open with his teeth, then chewed the salty meat as he flipped the pages of the journal, looking for the mission outline. He skimmed page after page, concrete plans . . . but so much about Cody too. Their conversations in the night. *"I hardly pray at all now."* His chest constricted. The boy had no one he could count on. Sarge had to do this. It wasn't Code White; it was mercy.

He patted his pocket to be sure the Zippo was there. Then pulled an OR gown over his uniform and peered down the hallway. Now or never.

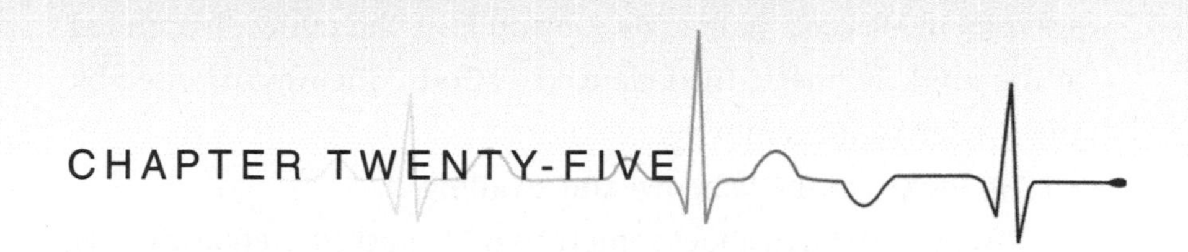

CHAPTER TWENTY-FIVE

"Elmer doesn't look so old," Cody said, peering through the glass at the goldfish. "Except maybe around the gills."

Iris laughed softly. "Happens to the best of us, I'm afraid." She watched Cody spread his fingers alongside the fish. She was glad she'd come. This boy had made her feel welcome and needed from the moment she first met him. "I figure Elmer Fudd measures around nine inches now. I doubt he was even two inches when we got him."

"You won him at the county fair?"

"My husband did." The hurt on Erin's face came to mind, and she sighed. "It took a lot of trying, dozens of misses, but good things are worth the effort. Elmer helps me to remember that." Her gaze moved to Scott's jacket draped across the chair, a discarded snack wrapper, folded into a neat square, lying on its seat. "Your uncle stayed with you?" she asked, thinking that she'd finally have to explain things . . . to everybody. Scott had seen her arrive at Cody's room this morning.

"Yes. He stayed all night," Cody said, his dimpled smile leaving no doubt how pleased he was. "I told him he didn't have to, that the night nurses watch me, but he really wanted to stay. I was hoping Rich would be working last night. He must know I'm leaving today. And I wanted Uncle Scotty to meet him."

Iris nodded. Cody was fond of the hospital staff, this night nurse in particular. Though she'd never met the man, after hearing Cody mention him—his patience, obvious kindness—she'd begun to imagine the nurse like a burly guardian angel. Perhaps like John Travolta in *Michael*, that movie she and Erin had rented. Iris smiled at the unlikely image, then glanced at Cody. She was surprised by the sudden sadness in his expression.

He looked at the fishbowl and swallowed.

"Are you worried about something?" Iris asked, stepping closer to the bed.

He bit his lip and nodded. "If the oxygen chamber doesn't work, if they have to operate on my leg . . ." Tears welled in his eyes. "I don't want to be so much trouble for everyone. My great-grandpa's old, now Grandpa's sick, and Grandma's worrying . . ."

Iris took a deep breath, her heart aching for this selfless child. Losing his parents, at risk for losing his leg, and worried about being a burden? *Dear Father, help me find the words*. But Cody continued before they came.

"You see," he whispered, "I think that's why Uncle Scotty stays away so much. I think I'm messing things up for everyone. And if I only have one leg, then it will get even worse." A tear slid down his cheek.

"Oh, Cody . . ." She reached for his hand and then stopped as an alarm began to sound.

A deafening series of staccato blasts, fast as a panicked heartbeat. "Code Red third floor south. Code Red."

+++

Scott rose from the cafeteria table, glanced toward the PA system speakers, then back at his grandfather, raising his voice over the din of the alarm. "Did they say third—?"

The operator's voice repeated the page before he could finish. "Code Red third floor south. All staff, be advised. Code Red. This is not a drill."

His grandfather pushed back from the table, his expression anxious. "That's Cody's—"

"No," Scott interrupted, "his room's at the north end, and it's probably a false alarm, but I'm going up there to check things out."

"I'll go with you." His grandfather rose and tightened the strap of Jonah's carrier.

"No, stay here. Just in case." He read the concern on his grandfather's face and tried to reassure him, despite the quickening of his own pulse. "It's probably nothing. I'll call you from Cody's room."

He took off, barely making it to the south stairwell before the radio buzzed on his belt. Fire dispatch was rolling an engine to Pacific Mercy Hospital. He yanked the stair door wide and took the steps two at a time.

+++

Erin slowed from a jog to a walk for the last half block, finally convinced—after a thirty-minute run on the sand and one of Annie's cinnamon lattes—that she could face her grandmother without bursting into tears or punching a hole in the wall.

She'd given the Lord an earful down there on the beach, about her doubts regarding Scott, the continuing frustration with her family, and now this with Nana. *"I made a selfish, awful mistake."* Her throat squeezed. God knew how badly she needed to believe it wasn't true. And how sick with guilt she felt about the confusing mix of anger and heartbreak that slammed her when she heard those words. She could count on one hand the number of times she'd been really angry with her grandmother.

But God understood—even if her grandmother didn't—that what she'd confessed threatened Erin's belief in honesty and loyalty . . . and love. How could it not? All her life, she'd wanted nothing more than to be exactly like her grandmother. The wave of sadness returned. How could Nana have thought it would help Erin to hear that? How did she expect her to sit there and listen? She couldn't.

But now she'd had her run, her coffee, and her talk with God. She'd laid it all out for him point by point and reconfirmed her commitment to stand firm—strong and balanced—no matter what anyone threw her way. Even her grandmother. Erin loved her so much. But she couldn't listen to anything more about Grandy, her father, or Scott. Or be pressured about forgiveness. She'd draw the line, loving but firm. God understood that. She'd done everything but shout it to him from the sea cliff a few minutes back.

And now . . . Erin caught sight of the house. Now she'd give her grandmother a hug, tell her she loved her. And that she was starving. Maybe they'd go out to breakfast at that place with the salmon latkes. And then try to catch up with the garden tour. Great idea. Erin opened the door, stomach rumbling, and called out.

But her grandmother wasn't there. Not on the patio either. Her Bible was gone from the bench. The coffee cups cleared away.

Erin walked into the tiny living room and spotted the note on the coffee table.

Darling,
Needed at hospital. Back soon.
XXX

Kisses, so wonderfully Nana. But a strange sense of foreboding swept over her. *Needed at the hospital?* She looked toward the front door key rack, where her grandmother hung her hospital ID badge, and her gaze fell on the aquarium beside it. Top open. Net floating. The tank was empty. Where was Elmer? The odd sense of foreboding raised goose bumps as she headed out the door for her car.

+++

It all happened so fast that Iris was caught completely off guard. The deafening din of the alarm, her hurried attempt to reassure Cody, her sprint to the half-closed door, then surprise as it slammed open hard enough to knock her off-balance. And now she stared at the man in the military uniform. Shaved head, wild eyes, completely filling the doorway. Stunned, she inhaled sharply. *Don't let this man in here.* She stretched tall, squaring her shoulders and hoping she looked authoritative. Her stomach shuddered. There was something familiar about his face. Still . . . "I'm sorry, but . . . what's going on? Who are you?"

"Out of my way!" he rumbled. "Move it."

Her body trembled with dread. The man wore a burgundy backpack and held an aluminum baseball bat. *A bat?* What was going on? National Guard? But surely they wouldn't—

"Please," she insisted, stepping backward but raising her hands in what she knew would be a futile attempt to keep the huge man at bay. "Just tell us what's going on first."

Cody called, "Who is it? Is there really a fire?"

The man peered past her toward the bed, and though his expression softened, her dread remained.

She raised her voice. "Cody, push your call button. Push—"

The intruder shoved her backward, and she lost her balance and fell.

Cody screamed, "Iris!"

"Push the button!" Iris scrambled to her knees, heart thudding. She shouted out the doorway, over the relentless din of the fire alarm, "Help! Someone, help us!" Then watched in horror as the man strode toward the bed.

Cody hunkered down behind the fishbowl, and she caught a glimpse of his terrified expression magnified by the glass. He screamed again as the man shoved the table aside. The fishbowl slid across the surface, teetered on the edge, then hit the floor and shattered. There was another scream. Her own.

"Stop!" she yelled, back on her feet. "Don't touch him!"

The man whirled, baseball bat clenched tightly across his chest, and stared at her. Perspiration streamed down his face, and his expression was pained, frantic . . . but determined. "Stand down. I'm taking the boy to safety. We're leaving the desert. Please . . . please. Don't try to stop me. Don't make me hurt you."

"No," she begged, trying to calm her voice, "listen to me for a minute. Can we just—?" She turned toward a sound in the hallway. *Oh, Father, please let it be the staff.* Then she turned back in time to hear closer sounds: a grunt, followed by a sharp swish of air, and Cody's scream as the aluminum bat slammed into the side of her head. A sharp crack, exploding pain, then strange debilitating numbness, weakness, and an angry buzzing in her head . . . as she staggered and fell. A stream of liquid, warm and sticky as syrup, filled her ear and pooled in the hollow of her collarbone.

Cody's screams ended in a sob.

Please, Lord! She tried to lift her head, to see, but she couldn't focus her eyes. All she could make out were dim shapes. The man lifting Cody. There were faint shouts from outside the doorway.

Then Cody's voice—frightened, confused. "Don't take me, Rich. Please."

Rich? Nausea gripped her. She heard heavy footsteps, a curse, more shouts . . . before the vicious buzzing in her head obliterated everything else, and the darkness was complete.

+++

Scott raced toward the pediatrics corridor, his heart slamming against his ribs as the new page repeated overhead. The wastebasket fire was out, but now . . .

"Code Blue pediatrics. Code Blue."

A resuscitation? He'd passed the nurses' station, empty except for a lone ward clerk, before he saw a crowd at the end of the hallway. *Cody's room, the room next door? Which?* He pushed harder, his shoes pounding against the vinyl flooring, eyes focused on his nephew's door. Was that security there? There were nurses pointing, and then a crash cart emerged from another doorway.

The PA blared again: "Code White pediatrics. All staff on alert. Code White."

He stopped in disbelief, lungs heaving, then grabbed the first person he saw. "What's happening?"

An aide in pink scrubs gave him a wary look.

He dug into his pocket for his wallet and flipped it open to his ID. "Fire department. Captain McKenna. What's going on down there?" *Please don't say it's Cody. It can't be Cody.*

"A woman's been assaulted," she said. "A visitor or a volunteer, we're not sure. The police are on the way."

Scott tensed, searching the crowd of staff at the end of the corridor. "But that page just now, Code White. Doesn't that mean—?"

"Child abduction," she confirmed with a grimace. "A precaution. We can't find the boy the woman was visiting with."

His heart wedged into his throat. "What boy?"

"Cody Sorenson."

+++

By the time Sarge got to the first-floor landing, he was panting and queasy. The boy weighed more than he'd figured. His muscles were shaking. If his prosthesis slipped, they'd both be at the bottom of the steps in a bloody heap. No. He'd do this. He had to. If only Cody would stop crying.

He hoisted Cody higher against his shoulder and started down the next step, hanging on to the rail. He'd tried to wedge the baseball bat to block the stair door, but if anyone had seen him with the boy, it wouldn't be long until—

"Rich, my leg's hurting. Please stop."

"Can't. There isn't time." The boy struggled in his arms, and he fought to maintain his balance. "Hold still. You'll make us fall." The boy's sob, close to his ear, tore at his heart.

"Please," Cody begged. "Please . . . it hurts."

Sarge turned awkwardly and returned to the landing. "Okay, we'll rest. But only for a second." He glanced up the stairwell, listening. "They'll be coming for us."

"Will you set me down? I can balance on one leg. I'm good at it now."

One leg. No one should get good at that. Sarge lowered the boy onto the landing. He set his backpack down too, relieved to shed its weight. "But hang on to the rail." His gaze fell to the boy's bandaged leg and the fresh red stain wicking through the layers of gauze. Blood. In an instant, he saw the children's faces. Their eyes. The pale hands. "Let's go," he said, more gruffly than he'd intended. He glanced back up the stairs and reached for Cody. "C'mon. We're going."

"No. I won't." The boy slid his arm through the handrail, then sat down on the landing. His face was tearstained, his expression a mix of confusion, fear, and defiance. "I'm staying right here."

"You're coming. Now." He reached out again.

Cody threw his head back and yelled, "Help, help! I'm—"

"Stop it!" Sarge clapped a hand over the boy's mouth, hard, his heart pounding. He stared up at the door, then down the last flight of stairs. *Were those sirens?* Cody's lips quivered under his palm, and his small shoulders shook. Sarge softened his voice. "Don't scream. Okay?"

Cody nodded. He let go.

"You're . . . kidnapping me, aren't you?" He stared at Sarge, his eyes filled with terror.

Sarge's gut twisted. "No, I'm keeping you safe. You know that."

"I used to. But you hurt Iris. You hit her with that bat. I saw you."

Had he done that? hit someone? He couldn't remember. "Collateral damage. Happens on a mission. I can't let them kill you."

"Who?"

"The enemy." Sarge grimaced. They had to go. If he could make the boy understand, he'd cooperate. "The people who poisoned the water . . . the ones who want to take you away today. It's all a lie. They kill children. I've seen it."

Cody shook his head. "I'm only going to the oxygen treatment place. They want to fix my leg, and—"

Sarge grasped the front of Cody's hospital gown, causing his head to thump back against the wall. "Don't be stupid! You want to see what they'll do to you? Look. Look at this—" He yanked up his pant leg, exposing the prosthesis, then rapped it hard with his fist. Cody gasped, and he hated himself instantly. But he had to make the boy understand, make him cooperate. "They'll cut it off. Is that what you want? Is that—?" He stopped short at sounds coming from up the stairs. Someone banging on the door. He let his pant leg fall and reached for the boy. "Let's go."

"No," Cody whimpered.

Sarge shook him. He didn't want to hurt the boy, but the images were swirling back. The flattened tent, the dead camels . . . the children. And the smell of sulfurous burning oil . . . Sarge retched, tasted bile, and pulled at Cody's arm. "Don't make me fight with you." He stared at Cody. Saw him splay his pale palms, cowering, begging. Eyes so big.

"Don't," he pleaded. "Please don't take me. . . . Don't take me."

Sarge winced against the high-pitched squeal of a Scud missile . . . No, sirens. *Were those sirens?* His body began to shake; he pressed his hands to his ears to block the sounds.

"Don't do this, Rich . . . please."

He stared at Cody Sorenson and saw the children's faces again. Innocent children camping in his strike zone. His squad, his orders to fire, and—

No. No . . . Father God . . . I've killed the children! His body went slack and he closed his eyes, a mournful groan escaping his lips.

The door opened at the top of the stairs, and a deep voice shouted Cody's name. Footfalls pounded down the steps, coming closer.

Sarge struggled to stand, grabbed for the rail, and missed. His prosthesis twisted under him, and he pitched forward onto the steps.

+++

"Get that backboard down here quickly—and toss me a cervical collar!" Leigh dropped to her knees on the hospital floor, her mind still reeling in disbelief. *Erin's grandmother?* Beyond her at the doorway, security officers talked rapid fire into their radios over distant shouts from the hallway. *Keep that maniac away, please.* "Iris? Don't move your head. But can you hear me?"

"Mmph . . . yes. Oh . . . it hurts. My head."

"Don't move," Leigh advised, relieved to hear her respond. The peds nurses reported she'd been unconscious initially. Her gaze swept over Iris's face, noting the eye nearly swollen shut, a gash on her forehead that had filled her ear with blood. Blunt impact from what? She pushed the horror aside, trying not to think of Erin and only of the treatment plan. *Airway okay, reasonably alert . . . immobilize her neck and get her down to the ER.* "Stay still now. We're sliding a foam collar under your neck—don't try to help me. Nice and still."

She steadied her patient's head, holding light spinal traction, as one of the nurses slid the collar into place and fastened the Velcro. Then Leigh stepped aside so the aides could align the backboard alongside Iris and logroll her onto it, very carefully to protect her spine.

"Okay, then," she said, as they lowered a transport gurney to the floor beside Iris. "Let's get that portable oxygen in place and hustle down to ER."

In less than two minutes they were rolling out the doorway and past Scott McKenna. Who was . . . kicking in the stairway door?

+++

Erin hurried through the lobby doors and toward the PBX office, the sense of foreboding worsening with every step. The parking lot was full of police and fire vehicles, and a helicopter hovered overhead. Another disaster? She'd stop by the ER after she located her grandmother. She'd have the operator page her.

"Hi," Erin said, stepping through the door and catching the eye of the snowy-haired hospital operator. "My grandmother said she was working today. Could you page her for me, please? Iris Quinn."

"Um . . ." The operator paused, and several of her coworkers raised their heads to glance at Erin and then at each other. "Dr. Stathos has been trying to reach you."

"I had my cell phone turned off," Erin explained with stab of guilt. She'd done it to avoid her sister's calls. Her stomach sank at the growing concern in the woman's eyes. "Why? Is something wrong?"

The operator winced. "I'm afraid your grandmother's in the trauma room."

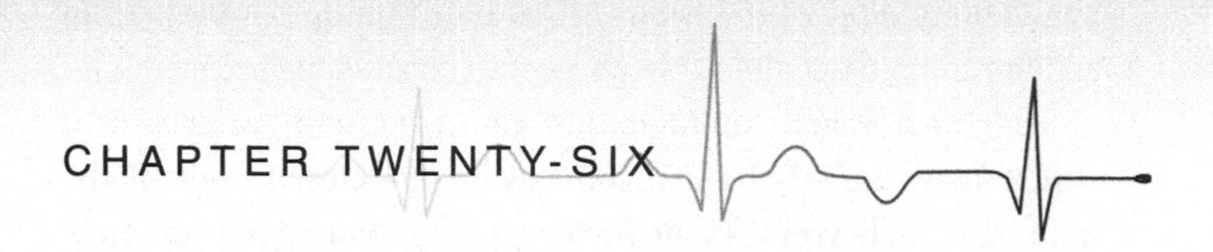

CHAPTER TWENTY-SIX

Leigh signaled across the trauma room. "How long till she goes for the brain CT?"

"Ten minutes or less." Judy affixed a label to a blood tube. "I want the clerk to run these to the lab. And I'd like to give that med a few minutes to work so she won't vomit in the scanner. Her stomach's been pretty touchy. Plus, I'm hanging on, hoping that Erin will . . ."

"Is my Erin here?" Iris Quinn asked the question she'd voiced at least twenty times in the short span since her arrival in the ER. Repetitive phrases, short-term memory loss—all evidence she'd suffered a significant brain concussion. And likely far worse. "It's . . . Friday?" Iris queried once again. She reached up to touch the stiff foam cervical collar fastened under her chin.

"Yes, Friday morning, Iris. And she'll be here soon. Don't worry." Leigh adjusted the oxygen cannula in her patient's nostrils, then gently palpated the head injury site with gloved fingers. A linear wound above the left ear, the surrounding scalp swollen and as mushy as a ripe melon. Hair matted with congealed blood. Did the underlying skull seem a bit depressed, right there? She moved her fingertips, and—

"Oh . . . it hurts." Iris blinked up at Leigh, and her right pupil—dark against the brilliant blue—widened with pain. The left eye was swollen shut, a mere slit in a purple expanse of bruising. An injury to the temporoparietal skull, top of the ear, and the fragile bony ridge of the brow. Brutal blunt trauma. A blow from an aluminum baseball bat, swung with considerable force.

Leigh's stomach shuddered as the incomprehensible horror struck anew. *Sarge?* She glanced toward the closed door of the holding room beyond. At the police officer stationed outside. How could this have happened? And how on earth was she going to explain it to—

"Is my Erin here?" Iris asked, confusion making the question sound urgent, raw, and new. Like the first panicked gasp of a mother missing her child in a department store. "It's Friday?"

"Friday morning, dear," Leigh said, brushing a strand of hair away from her patient's face. Copper colored like her granddaughter's, only softened by gray and stiff with dried blood. She checked the trauma room clock. How long since they'd put the first call out to Erin? Maybe thirty minutes. It wasn't like her to be out of reach. But Leigh had utilized every second of that time. She'd done an initial exam, a detailed neuro assessment; ordered IVs, labs, meds, X-rays. And seen Sarge too.

The shudder in her stomach returned. Arrangements were under way to transport Sarge to the locked unit at the psychiatric hospital in San Jose. The Haldol injection had settled him down somewhat, but he still ranted incoherently about the enemy, chemical warfare, and dead children. They'd handcuffed him to the gurney and asked Judy to remove his prosthetic leg so it couldn't be used a weapon. Leigh's chest constricted. They were treating Sarge like . . . *the dangerous assailant he is.* A man who'd always been here, quiet, powerful, and so willing to help, was now a prisoner in this

ER only yards away from his victim. Had Sarge Gunther been this disturbed all along? Were there signs? *Did I miss them?*

"I'm sorry to be such a problem," Iris whispered. Her sparse brows drew together, as if she was struggling to remember. "But I was needed here today, and . . . it's Friday, isn't it?"

"Yes, it's—" Leigh heard the monitor alarm sound. Was it a rhythm disturbance, low oxygen saturation, or a change in vital signs? Her gaze moved across the digital displays. Yes, blood pressure.

"Her pressure's reading higher," Judy acknowledged, stepping to the bedside. "It's 187 over 94. That's not what she's been running. Let me recheck it with the manual cuff."

"Thank you." Leigh watched the cardiac monitor; the rhythm still looked good, but the rate had dropped from the steady eighties to the low sixties. Not dangerous in itself, but combined with the rising BP it could be a sign of increasing pressure on the brain. Bleeding beneath the skull. Cerebral hemorrhage. She didn't like it. They needed to get Iris to the CT scanner.

"Is Erin here?" Iris asked, wincing as she rubbed her swollen brow.

Leigh opened her mouth to answer and then caught sight of Erin in the doorway. Relief flooded through her. "Yes," she said, her voice choking as she met her friend's frightened gaze, "it's Friday, and your Erin's here now."

+++

Scott shifted on the hospital bed, holding Cody in his arms. Thirty minutes since he'd scooped him up from the stairwell, and he could still feel his nephew's heart pounding. Or maybe it was Scott's. He wouldn't doubt it. He swallowed and shut his eyes for a moment, feeling the soft brush of Cody's curls against his face. He'd never been so scared, even on the roof of a burning building. The thought of losing Cody . . . Scott exhaled slowly. Taking him home to Mom and Gary tonight was a good idea. They'd get him to the oxygen treatment center first thing tomorrow. It would all work out.

He whispered against Cody's hair, "How're you doing, champ? Think we can let Teresa fix your bandage now?"

He heard him sniffle, felt him nod, the little body mercifully relaxed at last. The pain medicine was kicking in.

Scott looked up at the young staff nurse. "I think we're good now."

"Thank you," she said, her expression filled with sympathy. "I've brought the dressing cart from—" she lowered her voice—"his other room. Most of his personal belongings too. I had to get permission. The officers are working in there now."

Scott nodded, knowing she meant they'd strung up yellow crime tape, were taking photographs and collecting evidence. He pressed his lips to Cody's forehead, then slowly slid his arm from under his nephew and adjusted the pillow. He'd fallen asleep. Scott stood and checked his watch. "We're still on schedule for his discharge home?"

"Yes. I'll get the paperwork together as soon as I finish his bandage. Praise God you were here, Captain. That you found Cody in time. I still can't believe what happened. Sarge, Erin's grandmother, and . . . I can't seem to take it in, you know?"

It was impossibly surreal to him too. He'd had a glimpse of Sarge—Rich, as Cody knew him—when the SWAT team stormed the stairwell. And of Iris Quinn when they'd wheeled her toward the elevator. She'd been barely conscious, bleeding from the head. Battered with that stained baseball bat he'd found when he kicked open the door to the stairs. It made him sick to think of it. And of what could have happened to Cody. He pushed the thought away. *He's safe now.* Leigh had been there with Iris, directing the staff for her transport, but what about Erin? She hadn't even known her grandmother was coming here today. Or that she'd ever visited Cody. Was she down in ER now? How was she handling it?

"Scotty?" His grandfather beckoned from the doorway. "Can you help me for a minute?"

"Sure." Scott glanced at Cody, still asleep, and then joined his grandfather outside the door. He studied the plastic trash bag he held away from his body and just inches from Jonah's nose. It was dripping. "What is that?"

"Heavy, for one thing. Take it for me, would you? Careful, it's full of water."

"Sure, but . . ." Scott reached for the bag. "What is this?"

His grandfather sighed, sadness flickering across his face. "It's Elmer Fudd. The goldfish. He's quite traumatized; I'm not sure he'll make it. But I'll take him home and do all I can. Jonah spotted him flopping on the floor under Cody's bed." Tears filled his eyes. "That poor, dear woman . . ."

Scott squeezed his grandfather's shoulder. "I'm going to get down there to find out how she's doing," he said, Erin's image coming to mind again. "If I can, before Cody's discharged. Did you get ahold of Mom and Gary?"

"Yes. Thankfully they hadn't seen it on the news yet. I told them about the change in plans, that you'd drive Cody home before you go to the fire station. They're relieved. And tomorrow we'll get him to Rohnert Park. I can help get him settled over the weekend; I know you need to catch that flight to Portland on Sunday."

"Right. Sounds good," he said, ignoring a vague uneasiness.

"The nurse got Cody's belongings from the other room. And I grabbed his backpack from the stairwell—I gave it to you, right?"

"Yes," his grandfather said, concern deepening the lines around his eyes, "but it's not Cody's backpack."

"It was beside him." His eyes widened. "You think it belongs to that guy?"

"I'm sure of it. I looked inside." He glanced toward the police officers across the hallway. "They'll want it for evidence."

Scott's jaw tensed and he felt a wave of queasiness, remembering the blood-smeared baseball bat. "What's in it?"

"Not much. Some bottled water, beef jerky, cigarettes, an old Zippo lighter, and . . ."

"And what?"

"A journal, it looks like. But more of a military plan. Detailing his 'mission.' I didn't look at more than a few pages, but it really seemed as if he believed he was rescuing Cody. As strange as it sounds after all that's happened, I think it's possible that this man really cared for our boy."

Cody's words about Rich came back to Scott: *"Mostly he listens. I talk."*

"Should I take the backpack to the officer over there?"

Scott hesitated. "No," he finally said. "I'll drop it off on my way to the car. You should get Elmer home. Iris will be asking about him."

His grandfather rested his palm very gently on the plastic bag, and suddenly Scott remembered him doing that same thing before—on his grandmother's waist as they danced, on his father's casket while the bagpipes played, on Colleen's abdomen, blossoming with Cody. And these days, on her pink granite headstone every Sunday after church. He looked at Scott. "I'll be praying she will."

+++

Erin grasped her grandmother's hand as the gurney rolled to a stop at the door to the CT room. Her fingers were warm as she returned Erin's squeeze. A little weak but definitely there. Her confusion had cleared, a very good sign. So, though her blood pressure was still too high—and even if Leigh was right about a skull fracture—there was plenty of room for hope. Her grandmother was the strongest person she knew. Erin shivered, suppressing a moan. *Lord, why? Why did this happen?*

She pressed her lips to her grandmother's fingers, then leaned over the gurney. "I'm right here. We're going to get that CT done. Judy's letting them know you're here. Won't take long." She saw her grandmother try to nod—impossible while immobilized in the stiff collar—and then settle for blinking the eye that hadn't swollen shut. It almost looked as if she were winking at some silly joke they were sharing over breakfast. A breakfast they should be having right now, if only . . . Erin's throat constricted. "I won't leave you, Nana." *And please don't leave me.*

"I know," Iris whispered. She closed her eye for a moment and swallowed, then gazed up at Erin again. "I want you to bring my Bible. I'll need it in the morning."

Erin's throat tightened. Her grandmother was planning to begin tomorrow like all of her days, with her quiet time with God. But there would be no garden bench, ocean breeze, hollyhocks . . .

"It's in my top dresser drawer." Her grandmother brought her palm to her chest. "And one other thing. It's about what happened with Cody."

Erin winced. "Everything's okay, remember? Cody's safe. The police have Sarge in custody." Her brain struggled to grasp the reality. "He can't hurt anyone now. You don't need to worry."

"It's funny." Iris shook her head very slightly, the translucent green oxygen tubing shifting in her nostrils. "I'd begun to think of him as a kind of . . . guardian angel."

"Angel?" Erin gritted her teeth, anger rising. "Hardly. He could have—" She stopped herself. *He could have killed you.* "He's right where he belongs. All that matters now is you."

"I hope . . . he'll get help. I don't think he meant to hurt anyone. I think he really cares for Cody, darling. The authorities must consider that. Please tell them that I—"

"Shh." Erin touched her grandmother's lips, stopping her. *Forgive him? Is that what she's trying to say?* She wasn't listening to that. "You need to rest. Everything's being taken care of."

Her grandmother pulled her hand away. "But there's another thing. Cody told me something. Right before the fire alarm went off. That poor boy was so upset. He's afraid that—"

"Nana," Erin said, interrupting, "there's nothing to worry about. I told you. Cody's safe. And it's not good to get yourself all worked up. I can't let you do that."

"You don't understand. This is important. You need to tell Scott." She struggled to sit up. "Erin, please . . . listen."

"Don't move." Erin caught a glimpse of Judy and called, "Help me, would you? She's getting restless." She pressed her hand against her grandmother's shoulder, trying to ease her backward as one of the monitor alarms sounded.

"I'm okay," Iris insisted as Judy joined Erin. "I just—" The color drained from her face, and she grimaced. "My head . . . oh, it hurts." She sank back against the pillow.

"BP's climbed some," Judy said after reinflating the cuff. "It's 210 over 98. Heart rate's 58. Sinus rhythm. Oxygen's good. Iris, I'm ready to move you in for the CT. Can you hang in there?"

"Nana?" Erin touched her grandmother's face. Anxiety—and a sudden intrusive memory of Charlene Bailey's fatal hemorrhage—made her legs weak. "Can you hear me?"

"Yes, but I'm a little sick to my stomach." She licked her lips and groaned.

"I've got something for that." Judy released the brake on the gurney and nodded for Erin to open the door into the scanner room. "I'm rolling you in; then I'll fix you right up."

Her grandmother was in the scanner within three minutes and lay quietly after an IV dose of medication for nausea. They called the ER as soon as the tech was ready to start the films, and in mere minutes Erin was sitting between Judy and Leigh in the darkened imaging room. Behind a large window of viewing glass that looked onto the scanner. If she were a family member and not a nurse, she'd be pacing the waiting room. They were bending the rules.

"We're scanning now, Mrs. Quinn," the tech announced through the microphone. "Stay still, please." He pressed a button, and initial gray and hazy images began to appear on the viewer in front of them. Impossibly, layers of her grandmother's head peeled slowly away, skull to brainstem, like an onion readied for Sunday supper.

Erin watched her grandmother's vital signs glow neon bright in the dim light of the scanner room, fighting a wave of dizziness. She'd had little sleep, nothing to eat, and every second that passed made her feel more and more . . . helpless. *Not helpless, please, Lord.* The thought was foreign, frightening—she couldn't let it happen. She'd keep herself together, be rational, clearheaded. *Stay strong. I can do it.*

The images continued to fill the screen, slice by slice. Then Leigh hunched abruptly forward, pointing at an image and talking to the tech.

But Erin's gaze was riveted on her grandmother. Something was wrong. She'd begun moving around. *Oh no. No!* "Stop scanning! She's having a seizure!" She leaped to her feet and bolted from the room.

Leigh followed, shouting orders back to Judy and the tech: "Grab the crash cart and page surgery stat!"

The table slid electronically backward, moving her grandmother's body out of the scanner, and Erin grasped her hand. The full body jerking had ceased, but . . . Erin's breath caught at the sight of her grandmother's eyes rolled back, mouth grimacing in spasm, the frothy sputum . . . "We need suction!"

"Here, I've got it." Judy slid the rigid plastic suction tip into the corner of Nana's mouth to clear away the saliva and protect her airway.

Erin reached for a high-flow oxygen mask and cranked up the liter flow, then replaced the nasal cannula . . . holding her breath as she watched her grandmother's chest rise and fall and the color return to her face and lips. *Thank you, Lord.* "I think it's stopped now." She turned to Leigh as Judy began to take a set of vital signs. "What do we—?"

Her question was cut short by a shout from the CT tech. "Surgery's on the line, Doctor!"

Erin's heart wedged into her throat. "Surgery?"

Leigh nodded, her gaze holding Erin's. "She has a traumatic brain bleed."

+++

"Gunther, Richard M., sergeant, United States Army, 557-82-53 . . ." His words dissolved, tongue sticking to the dry roof of his mouth. *Where am I?*

"It's okay, Sarge. I got it the first time. Just relax. We'll have you out of here real soon. You'll get some help."

Help? He squinted in the dimly lit room, making out a figure of a man in uniform. Short and pudgy. Boyish face, peach-fuzz mustache. One of the men in his squad? No, the uniform was blue. Sarge tried to lift himself up on one elbow, but metal dug into his wrist. He shook it, and it rattled—metal against metal. Handcuffs? And leather restraints too. He thrashed and his stump flailed uselessly. His prosthesis was gone. He groaned, then swore.

"I hear ya, Sarge. I'm not one to cuss, but I can't blame you this time." The man in the uniform stepped cautiously closer. "Do you remember me now? Curtis. Pacific Point PD. We talk sometimes when you're out having a smoke. You carried my boy in from the car last Christmas after he fell off his bike and broke—" He frowned. "Hey, don't try to get up. I can turn the lights on if you want, but my orders are to call the nurse for more meds if you don't stay quiet. I don't want to do that."

Nurse? Meds? Sarge struggled to cram facts together, mushy as jigsaw puzzle pieces swollen by unexpected rain. He glanced around the room: sink, surgical light, wall monitor, overflowing linen bin, and his leg, propped against the wall by the door. *I'm in the ER shackled to a gurney*. He groaned again.

Sarge lifted his head and felt the room swirl, then rattled the handcuff on his wrist. The pieces, beginning to fit now, made cold sweat bead on his forehead. His breath quickened. "Why?"

"Why are you handcuffed?"

"Yes."

"You don't remember?"

Sarge shook his head, and a rivulet of sweat ran down his temple. His heart thudded.

"Assault." Curtis rubbed his hand across his mouth. "You hit a woman with a baseball bat. She's in bad shape. And kidnap. A little boy from up on the third floor. You grabbed him, and—"

"No!" Sarge's stomach heaved. He spit and struggled to sit, the restraints digging into his wrists. "You're lying!" He flinched against a barrage of intruding images and then opened his mouth to shout again. But all that came out was a low, keening howl as the desert images rose again, followed by new truths . . . *the children, the boy. No, please . . .*

Curtis shouted through the doorway, and people came rushing in. Arms held Sarge down, turned him sideways. A needle pierced his hip. There was burning, a woozy sensation of swimming, gray fog seeping into his brain, then gradually . . . darkness.

When he opened his eyes again, he was in a different room, a different place maybe. Smelled like a hospital; he wasn't sure. And he didn't care. He'd remembered what he needed to. He still couldn't recall the details about that woman. But the boy was safe now. He knew that. Because the man he'd seen with the boy on the stairs was the same man who'd sat with him the night before. All night. Listening, like Sarge did. Something about that felt right. Like this man was on the same mission as Sarge . . . to save Cody.

He hoped it worked out. Maybe he'd help Cody pray again too. And he'd stop feeling so lost, so alone. Start feeling better about everything. Yes, the man would help Cody. He had to.

Because living with that kind of pain was the worst kind of poison. And harder than losing a leg.

CHAPTER TWENTY-SEVEN

Scott took the south stairs to get to the lobby; the investigators had closed the north stairwell, and truthfully he couldn't have stomached being there again. Not after he'd kicked in the door, vaulted down those steps to find Cody huddled, trembling, and clutching the railing like a life preserver in a cold ocean. Scott shivered and descended the last flight of stairs, shifting the weight of the bulky pack he'd looped over his shoulder. The backpack that belonged to Sarge Gunther. Containing, among other things, a journal detailing his "rescue" plan, which according to his grandfather, showed evidence that he'd somehow had Cody's welfare at heart. *"I think it's possible that this man really cared for our boy."*

Scott clenched his teeth, biting back a curse. Granddad, as usual, was too kindhearted. Gunther was a kidnapper. And maybe even a murderer. His chest squeezed, remembering the rapid-fire overhead pages he'd heard earlier. For respiratory therapy stat to the CT scanner. Then for surgery staff and anesthesiology. He'd had a horrible feeling it had to do with Iris Quinn. In fifteen minutes he'd get Cody into the truck; there was time to drop the backpack off with the officers outside the ER and find Erin. After their last conversation, he had his doubts about whether she'd want to see him. But he had to know how she was doing.

He caught Judy outside the doors to the emergency department.

"Erin's not here," she explained in answer to his question. "She was waiting outside surgery, but . . . I'm sure it's all over the news already. And you're part of this whole awful thing anyway, so I guess privacy issues are hardly—"

Scott interrupted, his stomach sinking. "Her grandmother?"

"Yes. A subdural bleed, putting pressure on her brain. She had a seizure during her scan. Thankfully the neurosurgeon was doing rounds upstairs. He took her right to the OR. It gives her the best chance possible, but still . . ." Judy groaned. "This is all so unbelievable. Sarge, Erin's grandmother, and your nephew, of course. How's he doing?"

"Good, considering. I'm taking him to my parents' in a few minutes, but I wanted to see if I could find . . ."

"You might try the chapel."

+++

"I should be *doing* something," Erin said, pressing her hands to her forehead. She rocked forward, then back, in the chapel chair. "Not sitting. Waiting feels so frustrating, so . . . fruitless, so . . ." She turned to Leigh.

"I know. But I also know that you're exhausted. When did you sleep last?"

"I don't know, don't care." Erin jumped, startled, as a page sounded overhead. Newborn nursery. Not surgery. *Get a grip. Stay strong.* "I don't get it. How did this whole mess happen?"

"With Sarge?" Leigh shook her head. "I've been asking myself that too. When I examined him, he was ranting on and on about chemical warfare, missile strikes, and needing to save the children.

And the police officers said he'd started reciting his name, rank, and serial number. So I'm thinking this has to be related to his military experience. Which would explain the uniform and the shaved head. I've called for his VA records."

"So he thought he was saving Cody." Erin winced, knowing how frightened the boy must have been. Scott too. *Where are you?*

"I imagine so. And unfortunately, your grandmother happened to be there."

"Happened?" Erin spread her palms with exasperation. "That's another thing that's making me crazy. She leaves me this note saying she's needed at the hospital. And takes off—*with her goldfish*—to visit Scott's nephew. And not for the first time, either, I hear. Why didn't she tell me she was sitting with patients?"

Leigh was quiet for a moment, then looked into Erin's eyes. "I think I remember you trying to discourage her from working here altogether."

"Because I'm responsible for her. I was sure being here would be too hard on her after Grandy's illness. I wanted to keep her—" Erin's voice broke—"safe." She pressed her hands to her forehead again, the irony making her queasy. "I promised my family I'd do that."

"Have you called them?"

"No. Not yet." Now wasn't the time to admit that she was barely on speaking terms with them these days, because she couldn't listen to anything they had to say. It was the reason she'd turned off her phone this morning. And missed the call after Nana was attacked. "It's so hard to sit here waiting. There must be something I can do to help."

Leigh laid her hand over Erin's. "You can go home and rest."

"What? Leave her? When she's having a hole cut in her skull? I could never—"

"Easy now," Leigh said, squeezing her hand. "I meant after she comes out. The last report was that there were no complications. So it shouldn't be long. You'll see her in recovery, give her a kiss—" she smiled—"count her fingers and toes if you want to. Talk with the doctors. Ask questions. But then I think you should go home for a little while. At least long enough to take a shower and eat something. It will be hours until she awakens from anesthesia. And she'll need you then. Meanwhile I'll be sitting there, knitting, until you get back. Right beside her. Watching everything myself. I've already arranged for the on-call doctor to take over the ER."

"Oh, Leigh." Erin fought tears. "I . . ."

"Don't trust me?"

"Of course I do. But . . ."

"But nothing," Leigh insisted. "You need a break, and your house is five minutes away. I'd call you stat if anything changed. Besides, didn't your grandmother ask for her Bible?"

"Yes." Erin tried to swallow a huge lump in her throat. "She did."

"There you go, then." Leigh glanced at her watch. "I've got to meet social services back in the ER. Of course your grandmother is your priority, but I'm certain they're going to want your help in planning a full staff debriefing this go-round." She sighed. "I understand Cody's going home today. I hope he'll be talking with a counselor too. After all that boy's been through—"

Her cell phone buzzed in her pocket, and she pulled it out. "I'm sorry. I need to return this call. It's personal." She pushed the phone back into her pocket, then wrapped her arms tightly around

Erin, whispering against her ear, "Call me when your grandmother goes to recovery, and I'll run right down."

"Thank you," Erin murmured, returning the hug, "for everything. You're a blessing."

"You'd do the same for me, my friend."

"That call . . . You look worried. Is it a problem with your sister?"

"No." Pain flickered across Leigh's face. "It was Nick."

Erin waited until Leigh left, then called the OR on the house phone. Her grandmother's vital signs remained stable, and they were evacuating the last of the blood putting pressure on her brain. No further seizures. No signs of complications. They expected to send her to the post-anesthesia room within the half hour. They promised to call Erin immediately.

When she hung up, she realized her hands were trembling. Legs too. Leigh was right. She'd feel stronger after some food and a shower. And she'd do that after her grandmother was in the recovery room. Meanwhile she'd sit; she'd wait. She wouldn't fall apart, even if this whole ordeal still seemed so incredibly unreal. For everyone involved. Social services was right; there should be a debriefing. Full scale, not simply peer counseling like she'd done with the pesticide scare. The pediatrics staff had been badly affected by this incident, and everyone knew Sarge. All his coworkers would be in shock. To have someone you know go completely off the deep end, start ranting about chemical warfare and . . .

Erin bit her lip as she remembered the height of community panic just last week during the pesticide incident. All that talk of chemical threats by the Safe Sky group. More than enough to give Arlene nightmares, frighten Sandy about pregnancy, and make that woman at the meeting fear for Pacific Point children.

Erin's heart wedged into her throat. Sarge had seen all the media coverage, and he'd been in the ER when little Ana Galvez and all the other victims came in. He was always in the background. But always there. A Gulf War veteran who'd lost a leg. And maybe suffered other debilitating traumas no one realized. Post-traumatic stress very likely. Had the pesticide incident caused him to snap?

+++

Scott shifted the weight of the backpack and peeked through the chapel door, watching Erin. She sat near the front, hands in her lap and head bowed. Praying maybe. She'd said it helped her. He hoped that was true. Her grandmother was lying in surgery with a cerebral hemorrhage. Erin was strong; maybe sometimes she even *was* Wonder Woman. But right now . . . His heart ached at the sight of her tumbled hair and sagging shoulders. She looked alone and lost.

He took a slow breath, telling himself to risk it. To go in there and put his arms around her. Hold her. Tell her he understood how she was feeling; he'd been there too. And that she could count on him for . . . He flinched. That was the problem, wasn't it? Last night she'd made it more than clear that she didn't think he measured up to the kind of man anyone could possibly count on. And obviously not the sort of man she could really care for. Maybe that was true, but Erin looked like she needed a friend. Plain and simple. And he could be that for her. He could—

"Scott McKenna. East lobby. Scott McKenna, please."

He glanced at the overhead speaker. They'd changed the location to pick up Cody because of the media, no doubt. He'd have to bring the truck around. He looked at Erin. He could still run in there and say . . . what? *"I'd like to be here for you, but I can't stay?"*

He shook his head and sighed. That would only prove her point. He didn't measure up. She couldn't count on him.

He slung the backpack over his shoulder and headed for the lobby.

+++

"Nana? Can you open your eyes for me?"

Erin's voice was soft, hazy, faraway, and sweetly concerned. But the poor darling didn't understand that it wasn't necessary to have her eyes open. Iris saw everything very clearly. Clearer than ever before, and it was even more breathtakingly lovely than she'd imagined. Light, nurturing as morning sun on hollyhock seedlings, sweet and pure. Warm light that came from inside somehow—inside her very soul—and shone outward in an offering to others, until she felt transparent, glowing, completely lifted by it. Peaceful and loved . . .

"Do you need something for pain?"

Pain? Iris tried to laugh but heard a groan. It couldn't have been hers because there wasn't any pain. No more headache. Not so much as even a twinge of her pesky arthritis. She was free of it all now, as if it never existed. Free to enjoy the light, the loving warmth, the peace and the beauty. Oh, the beauty, so much deeper when seen through a lighted soul. Colors—tabernacle hues—scarlet, purple, blue, sea foam white . . . She stared, awestruck at something coming into view. Was that really . . . ? It was. Delight filled her, and she was tempted to giggle as she watched. Elmer Fudd swimming, free of his bowl, fins swirling, young and sleek, body glinting with gold, piece by glittering piece, layered as if it were scales. But real gold, like the glorious streets of heaven. Warmth enveloped her, inside and out.

"There you go. Nice, warm blanket. Can you squeeze my hand, Nana?"

She thought about doing that for Erin, but then she saw him. Her breath shuddered, and a tear slid down her face. *Doug.* Healthy, strong, handsome as the day she'd married him. He watched her with love in his eyes, then stretched out his hand . . . asking her to dance. The light within her softened like the glow of candles. Her heart blossomed, and she wanted to reach out. But it wasn't time yet to dance, because . . . *our granddaughter still needs me.*

She opened her eyes as best she could, then heard Erin's soft cry.

"Thank you, God. Oh, Nana, Nana, I love you so much. . . ."

Her granddaughter's warm cheek, wet with tears, nestled against hers, and Iris sighed.

+++

Scott slammed the journal down, shoved it across his desk, and stood. Why had he brought the stupid thing in here? What sense had he expected from a deranged lunatic who set a fire in the hospital, bashed an elderly woman with a baseball bat, then snatched Cody? He fought an alarming wave of nausea and bit back a curse. *Could what he wrote be true?*

He walked to the window, stared down at the orderly fire station compound. Engines gleaming, floors hosed, ambulances restocked, checklist complete. By the book, just as Scott always insisted. The same way Gabe McKenna had from this same office some twenty years ago. Everything was orderly, exactly as it should be. So why did Scott suddenly feel so restless, out of sorts—*out of control*? He crossed his arms and glanced at Sarge Gunther's spiral notebook, lying facedown next to the enlarged snapshot of his family at the Monterey Bay Aquarium before the tragedy of Colleen's death.

Not wanting the journal's demented lies anywhere near his family, he marched back to the desk and snatched it. His fingers sank into the coil of metal holding the notebook together. *No, it's not true. It's not.* He wasn't going to read any more of it. If he hadn't had to hurry to take Cody home from the hospital, he'd have dropped the thing off with the police. Where it belonged. A prosecutor's evidence of insanity. Not proof that . . . *Erin's right about me. I've failed my family.*

He set the journal down and reached for the phone. In moments, he had the chief on the line.

"Scott, what can I do for you?"

"If it's all right with you, I'm going to take off. I can be available by phone, but things look good here."

"Of course. I understand. Don't know why you came in the first place, after what happened with your nephew. Family takes priority, and—"

"Thank you," Scott said, cutting him off. *"Family takes priority."* He squeezed his eyes shut, battling defensive anger . . . and something far worse. "I'll go, then."

"No problem. Your family's in our prayers."

Scott hung up the phone and scrubbed his hand across his mouth. Cody was fine. He'd checked. He was asleep at his grandparents' house. There was nothing more Scott could do. He was available as backup, the way he always was. Besides, he had to fly to Portland on Sunday. He'd tell his family all about that soon, and they'd understand. They always did. Meanwhile . . .

His gaze moved to the framed photo. And over Colleen's face, her hopeful smile. The same smile as when she was a little girl. At

Sunday school. Waving her finger and singing. *"This little light of mine, I'm gonna let it shine."*

Scott strode to the door. He needed to get out of here. Get some air. He yanked open the door, then stopped, went back, and grabbed Sarge Gunther's journal.

+++

Erin rubbed steam from the bathroom mirror, squinting against 400 watts of glare. Two o'clock in the afternoon, broad daylight, and The Home Depot's brightest bulbs, yet somehow it still felt dim and dank, and—she glanced at the shower tile—*moldy*. In all the months she'd lived here, nothing she'd tried had ever fixed it. And now . . . Her throat squeezed as she tugged a comb through her wet hair. Now everything felt that way. Dim, unfixable.

She forced her sleep-deprived brain to concentrate on what she had to do. Finish her peanut butter sandwich, find Nana's Bible, get dressed and back to the hospital. Coffee would help. No reason to fix a pot here; she'd stop at Arlo's. She didn't want to waste time. Leigh was standing watch in the ICU and had practically forced Erin to take a break. But her grandmother would need her when she fully awakened. *If she wakens . . .* No, she would be okay. She'd come out of anesthesia successfully. She hadn't talked and had drifted off to sleep again, but she'd known Erin was there. Erin felt sure of it. The surgeon said it would be several days until they could be certain of her prognosis, but that he was very optimistic. There'd been no evidence of brain damage, and her vital signs remained stable.

Erin cinched the belt of her robe and padded barefoot through the living room. She caught sight of Elmer's tank, empty in its space below her punching bag, then realized that she had no idea where the old goldfish was. She'd only heard that his bowl had been shattered in Cody's room when . . .

Tears she'd fought all day welled in her eyes. *Oh, Lord, how could this have happened?* Yesterday morning they'd fixed pancakes right here; she'd told her grandmother about her date with Scott. And afterward, she'd walked down the beach and right into his arms. She'd finally dared to hope. What had her grandmother said? Yes, that she was proud of Erin. Because it had seemed as though with Scott she was lowering her boxing gloves a few inches. It had felt that way to Erin too. That she could trust him enough to . . . She told herself to stop thinking about it. She'd raise her fists back up before she made another awful mistake. That was smart. And now all that mattered was her grandmother. Doing what she'd asked.

She walked into the bedroom, tugged at the old dresser drawer, and lifted the worn Bible from where it lay. She held it close, letting her gaze drift to the photo atop the dresser. Her grandparents dancing at her sister's wedding. Dressed in a lacy gown and white tuxedo, but the happiness on their faces was exactly the same as when they'd waltzed barefoot in the kitchen of this beach house.

She'd started to close the drawer when she spotted a gilded frame tucked toward the back. Beautiful calligraphy verses, with a tiny gift card from Little Mercies Gift Shop tucked along its edge. Nana's handwriting: *"Happy birthday, darling. This reminded me of you."* She lifted the frame, read the first lines, and her eyes filled.

She carried them both, Bible and birthday gift, to the porch. Sat on Nana's bench, read for a moment . . . and cried.

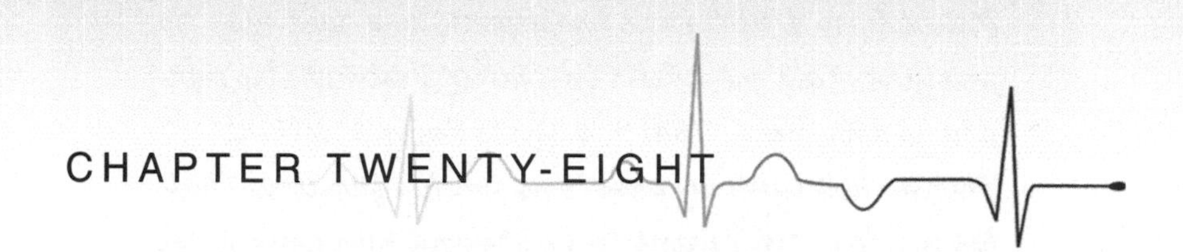

CHAPTER TWENTY-EIGHT

Scott shifted his position on the rock and gazed out across the waves. The first twenty minutes of his swim, he'd felt better. Icy water, gritty sand, salt stinging his eyes, the relentless need to fight the current, muscles straining, and lungs heaving. It had been exactly what he'd needed this past year . . . since Colleen. And what he was certain he needed today, when the walls of his office began closing in and suffocating him.

So he'd pulled on his wet suit and waded out into the sea to drag his body through the surf, stroke by stroke. For the challenge, the striving, and the solitude. And as a balm to ease the edginess he'd felt these last few days, from new whispers deep inside that said he'd abandoned his family. That he'd taken the easy way out. Used his grief as an excuse to stay away. The whispers became an ugly, angry shout when he'd held Sarge Gunther's journal in his hands. When he'd read the man's scrawled words: *"The boy says he knows he can count on me to be here."*

He'd swum for the twenty minutes, then stopped, buoyed by the water. Remembering a demented man's words . . . and feeling the truth in his soul. Colder than the ocean. And far, far deeper. Then he'd hauled himself out the water, returned to this big rock.

Scott forced himself to reread the journal entry. He inhaled slowly, feeling the choking sensation again despite the sea breeze.

> *Asked boy if he'd done homework and said his prayers. Told me he sits in church but hardly ever prays anymore. That his uncle doesn't, either. Thinks he's causing problems for his family. That his uncle doesn't want to be around him anymore. Cried hard. Kid has nobody he can talk to. Now he'll lose his leg. Must get him out.*

Scott traced his finger down the page, past what looked like a shopping list—*"jerky, water, comics for boy."* Then found the entry he was looking for.

> *Boy calls me a superhero. Counts on me now. Must save him.*

As Scott shoved the journal into his swim bag, his grandfather's words—impossibly, only this morning—echoed in his mind. What he'd said, after Scott told him about that last conversation with Erin. How she'd said he couldn't be counted on and implied he didn't measure up to the kind of man she could care for. He'd asked his grandfather if he thought she was right, and he'd answered with questions of his own: *"How do you see yourself measuring up? And more importantly what do you measure yourself against? That's where you'll find your answer."*

Scott shivered as the breeze moved over his damp skin. The truth was that he'd been measuring himself against Gabe McKenna's legacy for as long as he could remember. A legend, a hero . . . the man lying in a grave next to his sister. So he'd chased a career and basked in the light of his sister's faith and her goodness. Without ever completely stepping up. For Colleen, when she smiled bravely despite her heartaches, for his parents in this long, stressful year since her death, and for Cody, who'd been heartsick and lonely. And now he suddenly measured his success by a job in Portland?

He started shaking. The ugly truth was that Sarge Gunther stepped up . . . *when I failed.* Erin was right. About so many things. He needed to finally get it right. With his family, his life . . . and with God. If he didn't do that, his life would be worthless.

He bowed his head, tears sliding down his face as he whispered against the soft rush of the waves, "Lord, I hear you now. I've had it all wrong. I want to measure up to be the kind of man you're asking me to be. Please help me do that."

+++

Leigh set her knitting in her lap and raised her arms, stretching in the chair beside the ICU bed. Iris had slept since they'd moved her from the recovery room. Erin had been there to see her grandmother open her eye—one was still swollen shut—and follow a few simple commands. She'd stood by when they took the endotracheal tube out of her throat before moving her to ICU. But then Leigh had insisted she go home to get that Bible and take her time.

She glanced at the clock. Two thirty. Erin had made it almost twenty minutes without calling. Hopefully, that meant she'd taken a nap; the woman was running on fumes. Or prayers, more likely. That was Erin. And that was fine, but she still needed food and sleep. People couldn't function without those bases covered. Leigh knew—she'd tried it last year. And very nearly came undone.

She picked up the baby cap she'd been knitting, worked for a minute, dropped a stitch, and set it back down. Why had Nick called? The message had said that it was urgent he talk with her. She'd wrestled with whether to ignore it, then tried his numbers, home and cell, twice in the hours since she'd received his message. No answer. There had been something in his voice . . .

Iris moaned softly beside her.

Leigh stood and touched the woman's shoulder; she was still asleep. Leigh checked the monitors: BP normal, heart rhythm, pulse, and oxygen level . . . *better than mine, probably.* She glanced at Erin's grandmother, her heart tugging for this elegant and courageous former nurse, missionary, recent widow, and faith-filled firecracker just like her granddaughter. Now lying with her head wrapped in bandages, bruised and swollen.

Leigh looked up as someone called her name from the doorway. "Judy. Hi. How's my ER doing without me?"

"Fine. But there's someone here to see you."

Leigh shook her head. "Well, I can't leave now. I promised Erin I'd stay. Who is it?"

"He says he's your husband."

+++

Erin read the words a second time, her heart crowding into her throat.

A strong woman works out every day . . .
but a woman of strength kneels to pray, keeping her soul in shape . . .

A strong woman isn't afraid of anything . . .
but a woman of strength shows courage in the midst of her fear . . .

A strong woman won't let anyone get the best of her . . .
yet a woman of strength gives her best to everyone . . .

A strong woman makes mistakes and avoids the same for tomorrow . . .
a woman of strength realizes life's mistakes . . . thanking God for the blessings as she capitalizes on them . . .

A strong woman walks headfirst with no doubt in her mind . . .
but a woman of strength knows God will catch her when she falls . . .

A strong woman wears the look of confidence on her face . . .
but a woman of strength wears grace . . .

A strong woman has faith that for the journey she'll have enough . . .
but a woman of strength knows it's in the journey she will become strong.

She set the framed poem down, the bittersweet irony making her eyes fill again. She'd hinted she needed a new punching bag—after nearly slamming the one she had to smithereens—and instead her grandmother planned to gift her with a lesson for her soul. *"A strong woman won't let anyone get the best of her . . . but a woman of strength gives her best to everyone . . ."*

Her grandmother had listened patiently to her angry rant last night. About Scott, how he'd abandoned Cody, how he was like every other man she'd ever known, the same as all the weak and flawed men who'd lied to her. Hurt her. Nana hadn't judged her, and then this morning she packed up her goldfish to go visit a boy who needed comfort.

Erin hunched forward, hugging her arms around her stomach, remembering how she'd stalked off this morning when her grandmother tried to explain what happened in her marriage. She'd refused to listen. Because it hurt to hear it, because . . . She groaned, recalling her own selfish words: *"How can you do this to me . . . ?" To me.* She'd made it about herself.

She squeezed her eyes shut against a painful rush of memories seen in new light. She'd run to her grandparents—to this house—all these years, expecting them to bandage her wounds. And to validate her angry disappointment in her father's repeated betrayals, in what she saw as her mother's weakness in always, always offering him another chance. Loving him . . . forgiving him.

And all the while, her grandparents had their own troubles, their own private pain. Such heartbreaking pain that summer Erin was fourteen. They were trying to save their marriage during those very weeks she was chipping away at the stained glass right here at the beach house. Cutting her fingers, cursing the unfairness of life while piecing together that soldered testament to her all-consuming anger. The sword and shield that still hung in bathroom window, shadowy and dark, and—

The truth hit home again. *Dark* . . . She stood, legs weak, and walked back through the living room, past Elmer's empty tank and her punching bag. She grabbed her grandmother's step stool and carried it into the bathroom with the moldy tile she'd been fighting against for six long months. She set the stool in front of the window, stepped up, and lifted the stained glass away . . . letting the sunlight flood in.

Erin paused just long enough in the living room to take down the punching bag, then went back to her grandmother's bench and sat, eyes closed and palms up. She took a breath of sea air and let it out slowly, lifting her face toward the heavens, the way she'd seen her grandmother do for as long as she could remember.

"Heavenly Father," she whispered, "please give me the strength . . . to finally hear you."

+++

Nick Stathos stood with his back to her, in worn jeans and an old leather flight jacket, and the sight of him made Leigh's breath catch. It had been that way the first time she'd met him, but now—after what he'd done to her heart, *her life*—the reaction seemed like sacrilege. As if her very senses were taking his side. Anger, as effective as a Kevlar vest, rose to protect her as she strode through the door of the chapel, arms crossed over her white coat.

"I'm here," she said, voice curt, "but only to tell you that I have nothing to say, so—" He turned, and her heart climbed her throat, choking the words. *Nick*. He'd lost some weight, his hair was a little too long, but he was the same. So much the same. *Please go away.*

"Leigh . . ." He took a step toward her, then stopped, arms dropping awkwardly to his sides as if he'd forgotten everything for a moment and had almost wrapped them around her. His eyes, dark as his leather jacket, met hers. "Thank you for seeing me. I didn't think you would."

"Don't thank me," she said, glancing at her watch, more to avoid his eyes than check the time. "I'm not staying to talk. I have a patient in the ICU. And . . ." She looked back at him, willing herself to find the right words, summon the anger, and remind herself she had an appointment with a divorce lawyer Monday. "There's nothing to discuss. I won't talk about us. I don't even *think* about us anymore. Nothing you can say will change my mind, so don't—"

"Stop. I'm not here to harass you about your decision. You don't have to threaten me with a restraining order again." Nick regarded her as if he were negotiating a hostage situation. "I came here as a favor. Period. It's Caroline. She's in a mess again. She got arrested."

Leigh's stomach sank. "No . . . when? Why?"

"Last night." He sighed, his concern obvious. "A DUI. And she sideswiped a parked car. So . . ."

"You mean she's in jail?" Leigh gripped the neckline of her scrub top, her mind whirling. This couldn't be happening.

"She was. They kept her overnight. I picked her up this morning. She made me promise that I wouldn't tell her parents. Or you. But there'll be a hearing. And I think you should be there." His eyes filled with compassion. He cared for her sister. Leigh knew that.

"She's being reckless again," Nick continued. "She needs treatment, not jail time. Maybe even inpatient for a while. I think, between us, we have the influence and the resources to make that happen."

"Where is she now?"

"At our house. Her nurse friend—you remember Angela—she's with her. But she needs you. I'll go . . . somewhere else. If you'll come back."

Come back? Leigh stared at him, the protective anger replaced by stunned confusion at what Nick had just proposed. All of it. That they try to have her sister admitted for substance abuse treatment, that Leigh return to San Francisco and live in their house, and that Nick would go somewhere else. *Somewhere else? With . . . ?* Her heart gave a dull thud. She wasn't sure which of those things sickened her most.

+++

Erin opened the Subaru's door and sat there for a moment, staring at the porch of Arlo's Bait & Moor with its dozens of sea glass mobiles and wind chimes, reflecting the light and dancing in the breeze—seeing them in a way she never had before. Then she closed her eyes and listened to their sound with *"the ear of my heart."* The way Nana listened to everything, everyone. Especially God. Erin had discovered that he had plenty to say about strength and forgiveness. He'd given her an earful today.

She shook her head. It would take practice—putting down her iPod, sitting still, and biting her tongue sometimes—but she was going to try. To really listen. She'd already made a good start on Nana's bench and afterward. When she phoned her mother . . . *my parents*. Her heart crowded her chest at the memory of their voices. And her own tears. She'd left a text message for Scott too. Asking him to call her. If he did, she'd tell him how wrong she'd been, that she was the last person who should judge anyone about family loyalty. About anything. *And that I wish we could* . . . No, he'd be finalizing things in Portland on Monday. If he called, she'd wish him well and leave the rest in God's hands. Meanwhile, she was here on a mission.

Annie hurried from behind the counter and grasped her hands. "Erin, child, we saw it on the news. We've been praying. And now that I see you, I'm hoping that Iris . . . ?"

"Came through surgery well. And the doctors say there's every indication she'll do fine." Erin smiled through a sudden shimmer of tears. "More than fine, if I know my nana."

"Amen to that." Annie grinned, her eyes shiny as well.

Erin's smile spread. "I'm on my way back to the hospital. And I thought I'd . . ." She glanced toward the counter.

"Starfish Latte extra cinnamon—to go?"

"Yes." Erin felt a rush of affection for her old friend and for this special place that offered coffee, sweets, bait . . . and blessings. "But I want to buy one of your mobiles too. A gift for my grandmother. And for me. I remembered what you said about the sea glass. How it's shaped by the sea, the way people are by tests of faith. And all those other things you told me about getting the balance right. How you have to try and make mistakes. But once you find that point of support, the . . . What's that thing called?"

"The fulcrum?"

Erin nodded, the day's revelations bringing a rush of goose bumps. "I get it now. God is the fulcrum." *And my shield, my strength.* "Faith in God. You're so brilliant!"

Annie laughed and raised her palms. "No, please. I make a decent cup of coffee, but I'm not brilliant. Just old—worn smooth like that sea glass. And happy for you. You've grown far beyond that little girl with the raised fist and red boots."

"I just want to finally find the balance, you know? Faith, family, work . . ."

"And love?"

Erin sighed. "I'm not sure that's possible right now. Maybe someday."

"Come with me," Annie said, tugging her across the porch to the railing that overlooked the beach.

Erin's heart cramped. *Scott.*

"Arlo says the boy's been sitting on that cold rock for nearly an hour. I say he needs—"

"Pour me a Sea Dog black, Annie."

CHAPTER TWENTY-NINE

Scott's bare feet sank into the sand as he slid from the rock; he was certain he was seeing things. It couldn't be . . . He blinked, tilted his head, and his breath stuck in his chest. It was. *Erin.* In jeans and that sweater the color of her eyes, walking down the path from Arlo's, carrying two containers of coffee. He reminded himself to breathe. *Please help me get this right, Lord.*

"For you," she said, stopping in front of him and holding out the coffee. "Sea Dog black." Her gaze flickered across his wet-suit vest. "Annie was afraid you were getting cold out here."

"Thanks." He took the container, feeling the familiar swirl of warmth she always brought with her . . . even empty-handed. Cold wasn't possible. "Judy told me that your grandmother had to have surgery. I saw you in the chapel. I wanted to talk with you, but I had to take Cody to my folks' house."

"It's all right. She's going to be fine. I'm on my way back. She'll be waking up soon, but I saw you down here and . . ." Erin hesitated. "I sent you a text a little while ago."

"I had my phone muted. What did you want?"

"To find out how Cody is doing, first of all."

"He's okay. Considering. But . . ." Scott dragged his fingers through his salt-stiffened hair. "I was going to call you. Those things you said the other night, when I didn't make it back in time for his X-ray—"

"Wait," she insisted. "That's the other reason I wanted you to call me. I shouldn't have said those things."

He wanted to explain that it was the best thing that could have happened, but she shook her head as soon as he opened his mouth.

"Please, Scott, I need to say this. Can we go sit somewhere for a few minutes? Do you have time?"

"Sure."

She followed him back to the rock and he grabbed his swim bag, then quickly checked his messages before spreading his beach towel on the sand near the cliff wall. Except for a pair of elderly women walking near the water's edge, the beach was deserted. They sat together and sipped their coffee, and Erin didn't say anything for a while, closing her eyes as if she were listening to the waves beyond. She seemed different somehow.

She turned to him. "It's been quite a day. And it took my grandmother being nearly killed to make me finally face some big truths. About myself. It wasn't pretty."

Scott had no idea what to say or where she was going. But he could see that it was important to her. He listened.

"I had no business telling you how to deal with your family. Not after how I've behaved with mine. I jumped all over you for 'abandoning' Cody because you were a couple of hours late for an MRI. One single MRI. While Wonder Woman—" she tapped her chest and grimaced—"dumps my father's name, calls Mom weak because she stuck by the man she loves, and then 'hijacks' my grandmother to the beach. My sister didn't mince words, and she was right. I brought Nana here because I wanted to run away. The way I always did when things got tough. I convinced myself I was doing it to protect her and ended up putting her right in harm's way."

"No." He grasped her hand. "Don't do this to yourself."

"I'm just being honest. Finally. The truth is, I've been pushy and unforgiving and horribly selfish. I understand now, and I'm working on it. I just wanted you to know that I'm sorry. Really sorry." She looked into his eyes. "I wouldn't blame you if you didn't want anything to do with me ever again. I had no right to force my opinions on you about your family, the job in Portland, or . . . about my faith."

"But you were right," Scott said.

"I was right?"

He chuckled at the confusion on her face. He knew the feeling. "You're *wrong* that I don't want to see you again. Dead wrong. I want that more than anything I've wanted in a long time. What I meant was that you were *right* about those other things. Especially about God. And praying." He'd begun to tremble inside.

"Praying?"

It was all he could do not to stop talking and kiss her. But he wanted her to know this. He needed her to. "Yes." He glanced toward the rock, and the sensation came over him again. That warm eddy in a cold ocean. "That's what I was doing out there—talking to God. Finally connecting with him again. It's hard to explain. It was more like . . . listening."

She gasped softly, and then her sweet smile melted his heart. "I understand," she whispered. "I do."

He released the breath he'd been holding. "I was hoping you'd say that. I want to keep listening to God, change things in my life. I could use your help." He watched her eyes. "What do you think?"

"I think you should count on me. I'll be here. Like you said, Portland isn't so faraway. We can talk when you get back."

"I'm not going."

"You mean you changed the date of your meeting because of Cody?"

"No," he said, his resolve as firm as the rock he'd sat on for the past hour. "I'm not taking the job. I won't be moving."

"You . . ." Her mouth curved into an incredulous smile.

He'd never wanted to kiss her more. He lifted her hand to his lips, then smiled back. "Cody needs me. I need him. It's time I stepped up. And—" he brushed a strand of Erin's hair away from her face—"I don't want to be away from you. I've never met anyone like you, Erin. I . . ." He searched her eyes, hoping he was making sense.

"I'm listening."

"I'm saying that I care for you. That I want to get to know you better. And I'm hoping there's a chance for us." He saw her answer in her eyes before she said a word, and his heart filled his chest.

"Yes," she said, reaching up to rest her palm against his face. "More than a chance."

He rose to his knees in the sand and drew her to him, wrapping his arms around her and closing his eyes. Feeling her warmth, smelling her hair, suddenly dizzy from everything that had happened, never wanting to let her go, but . . .

He whispered against her ear, "Ah, I hate it that there's no time. You have to get to the hospital. And I need to see Cody." His heart pinched, remembering the words in the journal. His nephew's pain and loneliness. He knew too well how that felt.

Erin drew back, eyes shiny with tears but still smiling. "I do have to go. Leigh's there, but I want to be with my grandmother when she wakes. She'll need me, have questions . . ." She groaned softly. "I don't even know what happened to Elmer Fudd. He's her—"

"Goldfish. About nine inches, pretty long in the tooth." Scott laughed at the surprise on her face. "Don't worry. He's fine. Jonah found him under Cody's bed. Granddad's been working miracles." He laced his hands together low on her back and sighed. "It's been one big day for miracles."

"It has. And one of them is that my family's on their way to the hospital. My dad too."

He raised his brows.

"I told you I was working on things. And with my family here—and if Nana's doing well—I can probably sneak away for a while after dinner tonight. If you can, then maybe we—"

"I can," he said quickly. "Where should we go? The Giant Dipper?"

She looked at him like he was crazy.

He laughed. "Right. It feels like we've been on a roller coaster for days. I'll think of something. In fact—" he pulled her closer—"I just did."

She narrowed her eyes. "Karaoke?"

"Not karaoke. And no roller coasters."

"So then . . . what are you thinking of?"

"Kissing you."

"Good idea, Captain."

He cradled her face in his hands and kissed her gently at first, then slid his arms snugly around her, drawing her closer. Erin twined her arms around his neck as their kiss deepened, her fingers at the nape of his neck. She was sweet, warmly responsive, and—

As she leaned away, he opened his eyes.

She started to laugh. "Do you hear that?"

He shook his head, idly wondering how corny it would sound if he said he couldn't hear anything over the pounding of his heart. "No. What?"

She pointed and waved up toward the top of the sea cliff. "It's Arlo and Annie." Her laugh tinkled like wind chimes. "They're clapping."

+++

Iris shifted in the hospital bed and ran her fingers over the cover of her Bible, the worn leather as familiar as her family's faces. *My family. Here. Together*. Warmth filled her at the image of them, her daughter; oldest granddaughter, Debra, with her husband; their son, Peter; and baby Hannah, giggling and bright-eyed; and her son-in-law, Frank Calloway. Newly returned to the fold. She remembered the look in his eyes as he gazed at his family . . . including his younger daughter, Erin. A man grateful for his blessings and for God's saving grace.

It would take time. They were all out having dinner together. It was a start. Erin was moving with baby steps, still so wary, but the hope was there. For forgiveness and healing. Oh . . . at long last. So much good news, including what she'd heard from the nurses only a few minutes ago—that the final testing of the water system had been completed. And Pacific Point was safe.

She moved her head and felt the huge pressure bandage brush against the pillow. And the dull throb of the headache. Healing. She'd have some of that herself. She glanced toward a sound in the distance, different from the beeps, buzzes, and whirs she'd come to recognize in the ICU. She focused her nonswollen eye in the direction of the sound . . . a doggy yodel. Jonah and Hugh. A tear slid down her cheek.

"Quite a shiner you have there," he said, stepping close. "I think Mr. Fudd fared better."

Iris smiled, and more tears came. "Oh, dear, I'm sorry about these waterworks. They tell me it's common to cry at the drop of a hat after they cut a hole in your head." She sighed. "I'm so grateful to you for helping Elmer. Erin said he was under Cody's bed. That his bowl was broken by . . . I keep having these images of tall angels playing baseball. I can't remember much of what happened. It's sort of crazy."

Hugh rested his hand over hers. "I'd call it a blessing. We've had more than a few today."

"Cody. How's my Cody?"

"That's one of those blessings. I'll tell the whole story another time, but Cody's feeling better than he has in a long time. He's going to Rohnert Park tomorrow for his hyperbaric treatment, and he's offered to take Elmer along with him. He thinks your fish needs watching, but I think my great-grandson needs to feel useful."

"I know the feeling." Iris swallowed softly, aware of the comfort from having this kind man's hand over her own. "Is Scott driving Cody to Rohnert Park?"

"Yes. He's taking a leave from the fire department for the week that Cody's there. Although—" Hugh chuckled—"we'll be relieving him now and then. He's going to want to see Erin. I think our grandchildren are smitten, Mrs. Quinn."

"I believe you're right." She spread her palm across the cover of her Bible. And left the other hand exactly where it was. *Thank you, Father.*

+++

Leigh burrowed her face against Frisco's satin-soft neck, inhaling the scent of him. Sweat after their long gallop, pine shavings from his stall, warm leather . . . blissful, musky horse. She leaned back against the tie post and sighed. It had been an endless and draining day, full of events she would never have expected. Being in the quiet solitude of the stable was exactly what the doctor ordered. She was glad she'd stayed with Iris for Erin but relieved to leave. She stooped down, picked a curry brush from her grooming box, and began rubbing in slow circles over Frisco's damp back. His skin quivered.

After Erin returned, she'd stayed in the ICU long enough to watch their tearful and loving reunion when Iris awakened more fully and was able to converse. She'd surmised, from her friend's radiant smile and a few snippets of conversation, that the day had been filled with more than triumph over tragedy. It appeared that Captain Scott McKenna had a lot to do with it. Leigh was glad for her.

She was glad, too, that she'd decided to stop by the ER after leaving the ICU. She'd almost forgotten she'd ordered Sarge Gunther's VA records. How little she'd known about the solemn man who'd worked alongside them. Limping under his heavy burdens. He'd led a lonely and troubled life, crippled by far more than a land mine. The VA included his recently updated contact information. She'd hesitated over her decision. According to the notes, he hadn't seen his only son in nearly a decade. She told herself to stay out of it. That his business was private. Then reminded herself that Sergeant Richard Gunther's photo had made the Pacific Point noon news and then gone national.

Twenty-two-year-old Ricky Gunther had seen it and was grateful she called; he'd been trying to contact his father for several years. He'd returned from Iraq last fall and understood now how tough things got. How wounded a man could be. He'd fly out of

St. Louis on the first flight he could catch. She sincerely hoped the trip would be good for both of them.

Leigh set the curry brush down and stepped to the front of the cross ties. She swept Frisco's dark forelock away from his eyes, then took a deep breath and let it out slowly. "We're going back to San Francisco."

+++

Erin watched Scott as he pointed over the railing to the darkened cityscape below, blond hair and shoulders of his firehouse jacket illuminated by the roof lights. Maybe even by the stars overhead—she'd begun to believe they'd finally aligned. *Thank you, Lord.*

Her breath snagged as he turned, gray eyes glancing at hers. "Pretty great, isn't it? Top of the town hall is the best-kept secret in Pacific Point. Of course, you have to be a fire inspector to get up here." He slid an arm around her waist and drew her closer as he gazed at the skyline again, identifying glittering lights in the distance. "That's the fire station and the lights along the coastline. There's Arlo's, Pacific Mercy, and the freeways. I'll be right there, heading north, first thing tomorrow with Cody."

"I'm glad he finally talked with you about the accident." She leaned against him, feeling a rush of empathy. It had been hard for Scott too.

"He'd been praying so hard for his parents to reconcile. . . ." Scott's voice thickened. "He wanted his family together because he loved them. That can only be a good thing."

"Yes, bless his heart." Erin nodded, grateful Scott and Cody had been so open with each other. "Family . . . it gets complicated, doesn't it?" She shook her head, then chuckled softly. "Especially if they're all crowding into the smallest beach house in Pacific Point.

It's good Elmer's going with Cody. I think my baby niece might be sleeping in his fish tank tonight. Thank goodness Leigh's letting me stay with her this week."

Scott traced his fingers along the side of her face. "You're doing okay with having your dad here for a while?"

"It's important to my mother and to Nana." She took a slow breath and sighed. "To me too. It's going to take time. But I think it could work out this go-round. I want to start trusting in that . . . believing. My parents look happy. Not that there's any room, but I wouldn't be surprised if they danced in that kitchen. I've seen it done before."

"Yeah, dancing. We managed that a few times ourselves, between rounds of CPR and community disasters. We'll have to try it again. After Cody's back from his treatments. Of course, it's not as easy to get away when you have a ten-year-old living with you. Especially if he ends up having surgery. But either way, having him with me—knowing he wants that too—it feels right, you know?"

"I know," she said, her heart warm with growing certainty. That Cody belonged with Scott . . . and so did she. "Very right."

"That means you'll be wearing fishing boots more often than dancing shoes. He's got that El Squid lure, and he's itching to use it. I told him the boat trip's on as soon as he's ready. And—" he traced his thumb along her jaw—"we'll be back in the McKenna pew at church again, starting next Sunday. You can come too. And bring your grandmother. Granddad would love that. And we'll go to your church—trade off. We'll work it out." He grinned. "Am I making your head spin?"

"No," she said, thinking that it was a complete switch: his talking and her comfort with being quiet. So different from that first day when they'd met over the hospital barricade. Funny how it had worked out. She smiled. "But I was wondering when you're going to kiss me."

He laughed. "Fear not, Wonder Woman. You can count on me."

He leaned down and covered her lips with his own. He kissed her gently, then more deeply, wrapping his arms around her and bringing her closer. She kissed him back, breathing in the familiar scent of citrus and smoke, her senses reeling from his amazing combination of tenderness, passion . . . and wonderful, caring heart. When they moved apart at last, her legs were weak.

"I want this, Erin," he said, brushing the back of his hand against her cheek. "All of it. You, Cody . . . God. It all feels so right."

"I think so too," she whispered, having no trouble at all seeing herself on a fishing boat, on a dance floor, and in a church pew beside Scott McKenna. She could easily imagine his voice—that beautiful, rich baritone—singing "Amazing Grace." In fact, she could almost hear it right now. A lump rose in her throat. Those things happened when you knew the source of your strength. And listened with the ear of your heart.

EPILOGUE

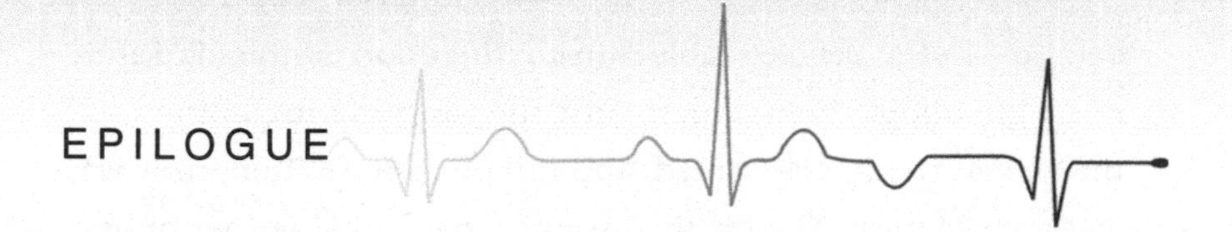

September

Erin peeked into the triage office to find Sandy weighing herself on the standing scales. Four months pregnant and barely beginning to show. "Don't kid yourself. Anything you see there is peanut butter cookies," she teased, thinking of her friend Claire Caldwell, who was due about the same time. "What do we have in the waiting room lineup?"

Sandy stepped off the scale and slid into her white clogs. "Not much. A rule-out appy—his pain's about a four right now. And Mrs. Alton's back with one of her gallbladder flare-ups." She rolled her eyes. "She asked the clerk to switch the TV to *Oprah* while she finishes her chalupa. So, how's our new doc doing?"

"Pretty fair, but . . ." Erin sighed. "He's not Leigh. Actually, that's why I was checking on the waiting room. Since it's not too busy, I might take my coffee outside and give her a call."

"Go for it. It's gorgeous out there. I love Indian summer. I can't wait to get out and enjoy it with Chuck." She patted her tummy. "And Mr. Peanut here. Oh, don't you have that big fishing date tomorrow?"

"Yes." Erin stomach fluttered the way it always did when she thought of Scott, even after six months. "On the *Tuna Helper* out of Monterey. I get to paste a seasick patch behind my ear, pull on the rubber boots, and go a few rounds with a whopper albacore. After getting up at 4 a.m. But this *is* a special day."

She took her coffee—in the San Francisco cup Leigh left behind—to the pebbled table outside the doors of the ER. Sandy was right about the weather; with the morning fog burned off, the air was warm, sea-scented, and full of promise. Tomorrow was going to be great. She hit the assigned speed dial on her phone, praying silently that Leigh's situation had improved. She knew too well how painful family turmoil could be—even without a broken heart. *And a divorce three weeks away.* Erin's shoulders sagged with relief at the sound of Leigh's voice . . . *better.*

"I'm riding," she said, breathless. "Golden Gate National Park. We're finally settling into a routine. Well, sort of." She groaned. "Frisco's determined to put me on a trauma gurney today, and—hey, easy there, big guy. Sorry, Erin."

"No problem. You're moved back into your house?"

"Yes, Caroline's been discharged from rehab and wanted to get back to work, so we're here now. I don't have to commute back and forth to work my shifts in the ER. That's better. And . . ." Erin could hear the pain in her voice. "It will be easier to finish up with those . . . legal things from here. A lot of dividing, packing—you know how that goes."

Legal things. Leigh couldn't even say the word *divorce. This isn't over, friend. Don't kid yourself.* There was a stretch of silence, punctuated by a muffled whinny and the steady clop of hooves. Erin ached to hug her.

"On the brighter side," Leigh said, "I got a thank-you gift from Ana Galvez in the mail yesterday, a crayon drawing. Flowers, the ocean . . . under a sky filled with butterflies. It's good to see such a happy view of Pacific Point. Any more news about Sarge?"

"Not much. The medications and therapy have helped, but that also means he'll be scheduled for trial. I'm going to believe that your character deposition, his son's support, and Cody's sweet letter will have some influence. And I'll have to stop Nana from baking cookies for the judge."

"How is our Iris?"

"I hardly see her! She's taking tai chi, teaching centering prayer at the church, pushing that library cart, and always going on some adventure." Erin chuckled. "With a certain distinguished marine biologist and his yodeling sidekick."

"Good. And you sound wonderful. You sound happy."

"I am. I count my blessings every day, trust me." She rubbed her thumb along the phone. "And I keep thinking that if this can happen for me, then I'm sure that—"

"Don't. Erin, I love you, but please don't. I'm doing what needs to be done. It won't be a happy ending, but it will end . . . and I'll come out alive. If Frisco doesn't leave me in a mangled heap beside this trail. Seriously, I'm a big girl. Don't spend any more precious time worrying about me."

"Not worrying. Praying. I keep telling you that you might want to give it another try."

Leigh sighed. "Just use your heavenly influence to get me back to the stable in one piece, okay? I'd better say good-bye; I think I hear mountain bikes up ahead. Frisco's always sure they'll eat him. I'll need both hands on the reins, and—oh, your deep-sea fishing trip's tomorrow, right?"

"Right." Erin squinted across the parking lot, and her stomach fluttered—big man, small boy. "In fact, I think I see Gilligan and the Skipper right now. I'll let you go. Have a great ride."

"And you . . . you hook a big one, Erin."

"Count on it." She disconnected the call and stood, hands on her hips, watching as Cody and Scott made their way toward her. They passed the corner she'd come to think of as Sarge's spot, where he stood alone on his breaks. Cody broke into a trot. Sun on his curls, face sun-kissed and freckled, and surprisingly steady though his leg was still regaining strength. Infection-free and mending . . . body and soul. Thanks to the hyperbaric treatments, family counseling, and the loving care of his wonderful uncle. She held her arms out to Cody. "Hi, guys."

Erin returned Cody's exuberant hug and then smiled at Scott. He was in uniform, she in scrubs—the same as the day they'd first met. And butted heads. It seemed like a lifetime ago, and the memory never failed to make her smile. "What's up?"

He raised a metal folder. "Your department copies of the fire inspection."

She bit her lip, chuckling. "Aren't they usually mailed? Isn't that by-the-book policy, Captain McKenna?"

"Yes, but—"

"We wanted to see you," Cody blurted. "And make sure you're packed for the trip tomorrow." His blue eyes lit. "We might see whales; did you know that? And I told Uncle Scotty that he should buy you an El Squid lure too. I'm going to talk him into stopping by Arlo's to get one. I'd share mine, but it would probably be better if you had your own. There's a lot of fish out there. I already set my alarm for three thirty, and my clothes are all laid out, and—" He gulped for a breath.

"And we're pretty excited, obviously," Scott said, ruffling his nephew's hair. "I'm driving Cody over to my folks' after I leave here. They're taking him to the movies. So I thought you and I should go out to dinner." He took hold of her hand. "I made reservations. Someplace people can't show up in scrubs or . . . smelling like a house fire. We'll eat, listen to jazz, dance. . . . What do you think?"

"You're saving me. Nana and Hugh are playing Scrabble again tonight. Your grandfather and Jonah against Nana and Elmer. But if I'm there, then—"

"Hold it. Elmer? Scrabble?"

"Iris says it's the only fair way, because Great-grandpa always uses scientific words. So, Elmer gets to use—" Cody shrugged—"goldfish language."

Scott shook his head. "Which is balanced out by . . . Chihuahua?"

"See?" Erin laughed. "You're saving me. Dinner out sounds way better than Scrabble. And your fire inspection report."

He tapped the folder. "Which does note a few things that aren't quite . . ."

She rolled her eyes. "I'm sure of it, Captain. But you have to promise we won't talk about it at dinner."

The look in his eyes melted her heart. "You can count on that."

Erin squeezed Scott's fingers. *And on you, Lord. On you always.*

+++

Scott watched Erin kick off her sandals and walk barefoot toward the waterline, lifting the hem of her long, gauzy skirt. The sunset, orange and pink and washed with purple, seemed to set her upswept hair on fire, loose strands trailing down onto the lacy sweater, bright as embers. As if she were lit inside and out. Exactly as she'd been that first night they'd walked this beach together.

When she'd given him that spontaneous grateful hug and her warmth stirred his lonely soul. The beginning of so much, that led him to . . . He glanced toward the rock at the base of the sea cliff. *To you, God.* And to Cody, new peace with Colleen's death, more happiness than he'd ever thought possible, and to this night.

He exhaled slowly, feeling his heartbeat quicken. Then walked toward her, his tie fluttering in the breeze like the wind chimes on Arlo's porch above. She turned, raised her arms skyward, smiling at him. He told himself to breathe.

"Isn't it the most beautiful thing you've ever seen?" she asked, closing her eyes. "And the sound . . . I always thought it sounded restless, anxious. But that's not true. If you listen, really listen . . ." She opened her eyes as he stepped close. Then her brows drew together as she studied his face. "What? You look so serious."

"I have something for you," he said, fumbling with the paper sack in the pocket of his sport coat. His heart was pounding as hard as the first time he'd faced a fire. "Here."

"Oh." She scanned Arlo's logo, Get Hooked on Our Coffee, and glanced back at him with a confused expression. "Cute. The bow is made from fishing line, strung with . . . Are those little bits of sea glass?"

"Annie's idea," he explained, his mouth going dry. "And Cody thought it should be wrapped."

"Oh, right. The lure. He talked you into buying me the El Squid?"

Scott started to laugh, but it was impossible with his heart jammed in his throat. "We just thought you should have this before tomorrow. Go ahead, open it up. Before it gets too dark to see."

"I'm not going to get stuck, am I?"

He chuckled at the irony. "I think you'll be okay."

Erin untied the fishing line and tucked the sea glass into the pocket of her skirt. Then she lifted the small velvet box from the paper bag and gasped.

And then—because he wanted to do it by the book—he sank onto one knee in the sand.

She looked down at him, one hand on her chest. "Scott . . ." She opened the lid and her eyes widened before filling with tears. "Oh . . . Scott."

"I love you, Erin. Will you marry me?"

"I . . . oh yes. Yes!"

He stood, and she flung her arms around him. "I love you too. With all my heart and soul."

Scott held her against him, his heart thudding against hers, his eyes blurring with tears. "I wanted to do this here. Because it's where I finally figured things out. And a big part of that is you, Erin. I need you. With me, with Cody, and—uh-oh." He leaned back, shaking his head. "Cody. I did this all wrong. Oh, boy."

"Too late, Captain. I'm keeping the ring."

He laughed and pressed his lips to her forehead. "No. I meant I promised Cody I'd say, 'Will you marry *us*?' He said it was important."

She grinned. "It is. And I will."

"Good." He kissed her lips lightly. Then kissed her again. Much more thoroughly.

"Want to see if it fits?" Scott whispered, finally moving away. He lifted the diamond and platinum ring from the box, smiled at her murmur of delight, and slid it onto her finger.

Erin raised her hand, letting the sunset glitter on its trio of faceted stones. "It's beautiful. It's perfect. . . . I'm so happy."

He pulled her close again, wrapping his arms around her as

they watched the sun sink toward the sea. He listened, loving her excitement as she talked about showing the ring to their families, to friends at church and at Pacific Mercy and the fire department. About calling Leigh and Claire. Then he kissed her again, and they were quiet for a long while. Listening. To the sound of the waves, the soft call of gulls, and Annie's wind chimes from the porch on the cliff above.

Sea Dog black, Starfish Latte extra cinnamon. Who would have ever have imagined it? Scott glanced toward the rock rising from the ocean, smiling as the comfort swirled again. An eddy of soul-deep warmth on the beach where he'd struggled against cold and loneliness. Who would have imagined—*planned*—these beautiful miracles? He tightened his arms around his soul mate and closed his eyes.

You, Lord. Only you.

ABOUT THE AUTHOR

Candace Calvert is a former ER nurse who believes love, laughter, and faith are the best medicines. A multipublished author of humorous mysteries, she invites readers to "scrub in" on the dramatic, pulse-pounding world of emergency medicine via her new Mercy Hospital series. A mother of two and native Californian, she now lives with her husband in the beautiful hill country of Texas. Visit her Web site at www.candacecalvert.com.

BOOK DISCUSSION GUIDE

Use these questions for individual reflection or for discussion within your book club or small group.

Note: Book clubs that choose to read *Disaster Status,* please e-mail me at Candace@candacecalvert.com. I'll try to arrange a speakerphone conversation to join your discussion.

1. As *Disaster Status* opens, nurse Erin Quinn smacks her red boxing gloves against a speed bag. Her most frequent prayer is "Keep me strong"—physically, professionally, and emotionally. Why is staying strong so important to her? How did her past shape that need? How did it influence her relationships with men? her relationship with her grandmother? Discuss.

2. Fire captain Scott McKenna has lived his life in the shadow of his heroic father. Why is this particularly difficult for him now? Have you ever felt driven to "measure up" to someone else?

3. Personal reactions to stressful events (like the Pacific Point pesticide disaster) often bring old emotional wounds to the surface (Erin). Or reopen wounds that are barely healing (Scott, Cody, Leigh Stathos). The character of Sarge Gunther gives a dramatic face to the devastating effects of post-traumatic stress. Why did saving Cody Sorenson become so important to him? As

a reader, did the character of Sarge evoke fear or sympathy? a mixture? Discuss.

4. What role do you think Arlo and Annie Popp play in *Disaster Status*? Annie's driftwood and sea glass mobiles are "worn smooth by the sea," like people are by time and tests of faith. Compare and contrast Annie's mobiles with Erin's stained-glass window hanging (how they were shaped, what inspired them, what feelings they evoked).

5. Iris Quinn spends time each day with centering prayer, by sitting still and "listening with the ear of her heart." Do you make quiet time with God a regular part of your day? How does that help you?

6. There are several symbols used throughout *Disaster Status*.

   a.) Erin's fight against the beach house's shower mold continues until an epiphany moment when she pulls down the stained-glass window hanging and lets the sun shine in. What do you think the shower mold represented?

   b.) Scott McKenna (to quote Annie Popp) "battles that cold ocean like a tortured soul" as he trains for Ocean Rescue. Early in the book, he is swept against a large rock and injured. Near the book's end, he climbs up on that same rock and prays for help in becoming the man God wants him to be. In the epilogue, he proposes to Erin on that beach. What significance do you see in Scott's collision with the rock and the peace and happiness that he finally finds there?

7. Iris intends to gift Erin with a copy of the poem "A Strong Woman vs. A Woman of Strength." What impact did the words of this poem have on you? Are you a person of strength?

8. Erin conducts a Faith QD hospital ministry, inviting hospital staff to gather before their shift and ask God to be present during their workday. If it were possible, how helpful would you find that in your workplace? In what specific way?
9. *Disaster Status* offers glimpses into the fast-paced world of emergency medicine and attempts to "put the readers in the trauma room." The book differs from popular TV medical shows because of its faith elements. It could even be described as "*Grey's Anatomy* finds its soul." Did you feel that? Discuss.
10. Forgiveness plays an important role in this book—forgiving others and oneself as well. Scott wrestles with guilt regarding his sister's death and Cody's injury. Erin refuses to forgive her father. Sarge struggles with his role in the death of Gulf War civilians. Leigh Stathos is only beginning to deal with her husband's betrayal. Iris Quinn's quiet strength—and ultimately her forgiveness of the man who assaults her—is a result of her own experience with God's grace and touches the lives of all around her. Do you know people who, like Erin, pull on a pair of boxing gloves against past hurts? or, like Scott, drag themselves through cold seas of self-punishment? How tough is forgiveness for you?
11. Snippets of humor temper the story's more serious moments. Like Jonah the yodeling Chihuahua, the scene at the senior citizens' karaoke night, and the verbal sparring between Erin and Scott. What was your favorite chuckle?
12. The Mercy Hospital series intends to offer both entertainment and an encouraging message of hope. How hopeful did you find the ending of *Disaster Status*? for Erin and Scott? Iris? Cody? Sarge? Leigh? Discuss.

Please visit my Web site at www.candacecalvert.com for more information on upcoming books in this series.

Thank you for reading *Disaster Status*.

Warmly,
Candace Calvert